Y028547

D1141453

THE LOST DIARY OF VENICE

THE
LOST
DIARY

OF
VENICE

A NOVEL

Margaux DeRoux

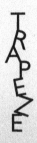

First published in Great Britain in 2020 by Trapeze
an imprint of The Orion Publishing Group Ltd
Carmelite House, 50 Victoria Embankment
London EC4Y 0DZ

An Hachette UK Company

1 3 5 7 9 10 8 6 4 2

ISBN (Hardback) 978 1 4091 8820 9
ISBN (Trade Paperback) 978 1 4091 8821 6
ISBN (eBook) 978 1 4091 8823 0

Typeset by Born Group
Printed and bound in Great Britain by Clays Ltd, Elcograf S.p.A.

MIX
Paper from
responsible sources
FSC® C104740

www.orionbooks.co.uk

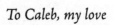

To Caleb, my love

THE LOST DIARY OF VENICE

Prologue

SHE COULD SMELL HIM, STANDING THIS CLOSE. A FRESH-wet scent brought in from outside, where it'd just begun to rain. Warm earth cut by an edge of ozone: the tentative odor of spring. Rose concentrated on keeping her hands steady. *Christ.* Whoever tied these knots had really outdone themselves. Digging with her blunt nails, she finally pried the strings free. As she unwrapped the linen that swaddled the stack of papers, another scent blossomed—the familiar dry aroma of disintegrating vellum. She slid her fingers down the loops of stiff thread that held the stack together. The top page was blank, patinated by a layer of grime. She lifted one corner, felt the threads putting pressure on the already cracking parchment. He leaned in closer.

"Tried to open it, but that paper looks ready to tear." The remnants of a southern accent hung at the margins of his voice; she imagined woodsmoke and stars. "But I thought I saw a few drawings inside . . ."

"Well, I think we should cut these pages loose. Do you mind?"

She looked up. His eyes were dark, iris nearly indistinguishable from pupil.

He shook his head. "Go on."

With small scissors retrieved from the top left desk drawer, Rose snipped the binding. A glint of silver, and the threads lay sprawled and severed on the tabletop. She removed the cover sheet and surveyed the title page. Italian calligraphy swirled across the parchment, ornate designs inked into each corner.

"*Trattato dell'arte della pittura, scultura, ed architettura. Di Giovanni Paolo Lomazzo.*" She read the title out loud. "My Italian isn't very good, but I think '*pittura*' is 'painting,' so . . . treatise on the art of painting, sculpture, and architecture."

"It's a book about art?" He glanced back down at the page.

"That's what the title says . . ."

"Oh—but that's what I do. I mean, I'm an artist." He scraped his fingers through his hair, then crossed his arms tightly, as if he didn't know what to do next with his hands.

I

TIME HAD BEGUN TO LOOP IN ON ITSELF. ROSE NEWLIN realized this one day, on her bike ride to work, when she looked up and noted with some surprise that the red maple trees had budded. Her routine had become so fixed, so circular, that only the seasons seemed to change. First, always, came a bike ride. The wind pinked her cheeks and tugged a few curls loose from under her helmet as she wound her way through the university campus to her bookshop. Then, a quick walk to the café on the corner, with its familiar scent of roasting coffee beans. The barista there wore button-up shirts and had small tattoos on each of his fingers: an arrow, a compass, the figure eight of eternity. Slender tips of more ink peeked out from under his cuffs.

"Good morning, Rose."

"Good morning, Joel. Latte for me, thanks." She always gave her order, even though they both knew what it'd be.

Afterward, strolling back to the shop, she watched fragments of herself slip past in store windows: auburn hair twisted up in a knot, rangy frame she could never seem to add any muscle to. Faded jeans and her favorite knit sweater, a lightweight parka thrown on top. She reminded herself to work on her posture. Her eyes flashed back at her from the glare of glass, green flecked with gold. In certain lights their color seemed to change, tilting blue or nearly gray. Her father had called them "labradorite eyes," after the gemstone.

Rose focused on the cracks in the sidewalk. She didn't need to think about him today.

She reached the shop then and unlocked the door, flipped the sign to OPEN. Though she'd owned the place for two years, each time she stepped inside she still felt a swell of contentment, like a farmer taking in his crops at dusk. *This parcel of life, this here, is mine and mine alone.* She'd decorated the space carefully, filling each nook with well-padded reading chairs and antique lamps. A few months after she'd opened, a stray tomcat had arrived on the doorstep to complete the picture. Black and stocky with one eye gone, he'd claimed the burgundy chair by the front window as his own.

"Wake up, Odin!"

At his name, the cat jumped from his perch and padded over to rub a cheek against her calf. His empty socket was a tight-screwed slash of puckered fur, and when he closed his eyes it was hard to say which was missing. Rose bent to give him his morning scratches. She filled his food and water bowls, then took her seat at the register. Odin leapt to join her, circling several times in her lap before settling down, paws tucked under his chest. The hours passed in a sorting of bills and a shuffle of patrons, an occasional shift of position. Outside, it began to mist, draping a delicate silver beading over the windows, the cars parked outside. A hush settled through the shop. Rose's bun slid loose; even the sturdiest elastic proved futile against her hair, thick and coarse as a horse's mane.

Then the clank of the heater, the creak of the door.

Later, she'd research what had happened to her. She'd learn about the scientific intricacies of attraction, the complex chain of chemicals that flood the prefrontal cortex. She'd underline with blue ink a scholarly article on the way synapses and neurons fire-work the brain, inundating the mind with dopamine. How norepinephrine, a neurotransmitter, dries the mouth, shakes the hands, pumps the heart. How the body experiences obsessional thought patterns and cravings.

None of that could help her in the moment, though, as she floundered: half-standing then sitting again, frantically twisting her bun back in place as the man at the door made his way toward her. He wore a red flannel shirt with the sleeves rolled up and a black quilted vest, droplets of water hovering in constellations across its surface. His dark hair was wet, threaded through at the temples with early gray, and a canvas bag hung from his shoulder. Rose noticed his left thumb was bandaged; when he opened that hand, she saw her name written across his palm in blue ink, a small drop of blood penetrating the gauze.

He said her name out loud, then tucked his hand away in the pocket of his vest.

"Do you know where I can find her?"

"I'm Rose." At her feet, Odin ventured around the corner of the desk to sniff at the stranger's shoes.

"My name's William." He put his other hand to his chest. "I called up to the university library about restoring a book and they said to swing by here. Told me you're exceptional, as a matter of fact." He paused politely for her to say something.

Nothing came to mind.

He cleared his throat. "Do you still do restorations?"

She nodded, rubbing her suddenly damp palms on her thighs under the table, trying not to make any visible movements. It didn't matter: he was too busy wrestling a stack of papers out of his bag to notice.

"Great. I was hoping you might be able to take a look at this." He set the stack down on the desk in front of her. It was wrapped in gray and white striped linen, and tied with twine. She'd known what to do then, at least. As she picked at the knots, he bent to scratch the cat. His disembodied voice floated up from behind the counter.

"So, the story is that my great-grandmother passed away—"

"I'm sorry." A reflexive response. She could hear Odin's guttural purr start up, a small motor.

"Don't be. She was ready to go—beyond ready: a hundred years old. I never really knew her. All the family's moved away, and she was in a care facility with her stuff in storage. Anyway, it turned out I was the only one willing to fly over and go through her things. It was fascinating though, what she had." He stood back up, cheeks flushed. "This seemed like it might be important. It was at the bottom of a trunk with family portraits, her wedding dress, things like that . . . Oh, sorry if I tied it up too tight."

"It's okay." Just as she said it, the twine yielded. After asking to use scissors, Rose carefully angled the blades between the brittle pages; he bent close to watch.

She read the title out loud.

"A book about art," he repeated, gazing down at the calligraphy. "I can't believe it. By Giovanni Lomazzo . . . That's my last name, Lomazzo."

"Then this certainly belonged to your family." Rose set the cover sheet to one side; beneath it was a full page of text.

"Shouldn't you be wearing gloves?" He was staring at her hands again.

"No, that's a misconception."

"Why?" He tilted his head, and she noticed he was a few days past needing a shave.

"Well, a lot of glove fibers—like cotton, for example—have fats and alkanes in them."

His eyes widened, which she took as a sign to continue.

"They insulate your hands, which can stimulate the sweat

glands. Then, as you produce moisture, they'll wick and transfer it to the vellum. So, it's actually better to just handle the paper directly."

"Guess it makes you crazy to see people wearing gloves on TV shows, then."

"Mmm." She squinted down at the second page, which looked like an author's introduction. The ink had faded, but she was able to make out a notation at the bottom: *Venezia 1571.* She lifted the pages to see if the writing continued through to the end of the stack. It did.

"It's dated 1571 Venice. Where did your great-grandmother live?"

"A town called Padua. Wow, is it really that old?"

"I'd say so, judging by the vellum. I don't think Padua is that far from Venice." She bent to examine the writing. He leaned in too. She could smell his breath, tea tree and mint, like the flavored toothpicks sold at health food stores. "Oh! This is a palimpsest!"

"A what-sest?"

She couldn't help but smile. "A *palimp*sest. It means there are actually two documents here." She pointed down at the page, tracing her index finger along the lines for him to see. "The author wrote one text, scraped it away, turned the page, and wrote over the top again crosswise. It might not be the same author who wrote both, but based on the calligraphy I'd bet that it is. What's interesting is how visible the undertext still is." And it was, ghosting beneath the top layer of ink like a weak perpendicular shadow.

"Is it possible to find out what they both say? Both the writings?" He glanced up from the page, eyebrows raised.

"I think so, yes. It might've been an issue if the undertext had been completely scraped away . . . but in this condition? I should be able to render both."

"How does that work?"

"Well, I'll clean up the pages, then scan them. I use a software program to isolate the layers, so they're legible enough to translate." He was watching her lips as she spoke. "If it's an original document and the content is meaningful, it could be valuable. But a full restoration will take time, and some cost." She straightened her shoulders.

He nodded, assessing the pages spread out between them. "Well, you obviously know what you're doing." He leaned in, putting the weight of his bandaged hand on the desk, as if he were sharing a secret. "It doesn't matter to me if it's worth anything, or what it costs to restore. I want to know what it says. I'd like to know—" He stopped, though there seemed to be more to his sentence.

"I'd like to know too. I'll give you an estimate."

"Time and cost?"

"Yes. Time and cost."

His hand disappeared into the back pocket of his jeans and emerged holding a brown leather wallet worn pale at the corners. He flipped it open, took out a thick white business card, and handed it to her. *William Lomazzo.* Website and email, all done in letterpress, with a streak of indigo printed across the top. He shoved the wallet back into his pocket and offered his hand; she extended her own. For a single moment, her radial artery pushed flush to his. Pulse against pulse, between forefinger and thumb, heartbeats separated by paper-thin flesh.

Walking back to where his black Ford truck sat lonesome in the drugstore parking lot, William was oblivious to the rain. He fumbled to unlock the door. Inside, his heat coaxed a thin layer of fog out along the edges of the windows. Tilting his hips up toward the steering wheel, he rummaged around in the back pocket of his jeans with one hand. Rain was coming down in earnest now, playing a heavy staccato on the rooftop.

He found it, fished it out.

The silver band he wasn't supposed to, shouldn't have, taken off. He'd looked through the window of the shop, seen her sitting behind the desk, and suddenly it was in his pocket and he was opening the door. And now he couldn't point to *why* in a way he'd feel comfortable saying out loud. He measured the weight of the ring in his palm, watched how it shone in the flat gray light. Swallowed. The metallic taste of blood; he must have bitten his cheek somewhere along the way. Sitting alone in the truck, William buried his face in his wide hands and spoke simple words to a God he'd long ago abandoned.

2

GIOVANNI STARED DOWN AT THE DRAWING HE WAS working on—a study of dried roses he'd arranged on the table in front of him: crisp petals, wrinkled and withered but still red. He squinted to sharpen the lines. Spirals of shadow and, just below, points of thorn peeking out from under clusters of brittle leaves. He thought of them, not so long ago, blooming supple beneath a summer sun. What was it Petrarch called time? *Our delight and our prison.*

Through the open studio window, the San Zanipolo tower rang, three bells in a major chord. Time to leave. Standing and shaking out his robes, Gio glanced around his studio at the scattered stools and velvet chaises, the delicate screen in one corner embroidered with birds in flight. He noted that the oiled paper tacked across the windows to diffuse the light needed changing. That morning, however, he'd been busy grinding pigment: madder and malachite, orpiment and ultramarine. Lapis lazuli from Far East traders and the unassuming yet crucial coal. Preparations for the work to come.

The bells sounded again, jostling the weighty quiet of the room.

"I hear you, I hear you." With a sigh, Gio untied his glasses, which were fastened to his face with two loops of black ribbon. They pinched his nose, but their thick lenses worked well as magnifiers—certainly better than the bowl of water Seneca would have used. Even though his central vision was still adequate, nothing a squint here or there couldn't fix, he wore the glasses daily. His hope had been they might hold at bay the blackness that hemmed in his field of vision and steadily gnawed away at it. Increasingly, that hope was fading. It'd been just over a year since he'd first noticed the signs, and already a permanent vignette had arrived to frame the world in a disheartening, advancing darkness. Using the lenses felt a bit like trying to clean up spilled wine while the whole house was flooding, but it was all he knew to do.

Gio shook his head, as if that motion could dislodge his thoughts from the rutted path they tended down. Tucking the frames into the pouch that hung at his waist, he rubbed his eyes, then hitched his satchel of supplies up on one shoulder. As he stepped out into the street, the last bell toll sounded.

Under bridges, canal waters reflected hot sun glare and snatches of blue sky, bright streaks of color from painted tenement walls. The smell of stew and a muffled clamor of domesticity wandered through the alleyways, while overhead, lines of laundry swayed in mild breezes. From rooftop nooks, birds murmured and cooed. A cobblestone struck Gio's foot, and he stumbled; righting himself, he caught sight of his own reflection in a pool of dirty street water. Deep-set hazel eyes, straight nose, well-molded mouth. Beard trimmed close to the jaw, cropped chestnut hair that curled at the tips. An unremarkable face, but one that had grown more dignified with the arrival of a few wrinkles, a dusting of gray at his temples.

He pressed onward. From open doorways and windows, dark-eyed children watched him pass.

Before long, he arrived at a great house set back some distance from the avenue. Columns and arches sent shadows curving in the sharp light; from a corner of the garden came the cool sounds of a fountain. Gio approached the front door and peered at the elaborate knocker: a bronze snake eating its own tail. Grasping its head, he pounded. Within moments, a solemn-faced girl in a white apron swung the door open. She stared at him, expressionless, with large brown eyes set slightly too far apart. He fumbled in his pouch for the scrap of parchment.

"Sebastiano Venier is expecting me." He thrust the scrap in her direction.

The servant took the paper, unfolded it, and began to read the summons—signed with her master's distinctive scrawl. The note mentioned in two separate places that Gio should come to Venier's city palazzo and not his family estate in the country. Reading between the lines, Gio guessed he'd be tasked with painting a portrait of Venier's latest courtesan; as he aged, the man seemed to take increasing pride in the beauty of his young escorts. With rumors circulating that Venier—currently a statesman—would soon be nominated "next doge of Venice," nubile companions weren't difficult to come by.

The servant nodded when she'd finished, the center part in her hair drawing a perfect pale arc over the crown of her head. She turned, gesturing for him to follow. She led them left, down a corridor, and up a narrow spiral staircase: the servants' route, more direct than the wide marble stairs in the center of the courtyard. He took care to remember the way. At the top, the stairway let out into a great hall, brilliant sun streaming in through tall windows at the far end. As they crossed the polished terrazzo floors, their reflections shivered up, glassy and distorted. Rows of columns flanked several pairs of doors on either wall, and between them hung drab paintings in gilded frames: women holding lapdogs, or anemic men in naval uniforms. Lesser-known members of the Venier clan, no doubt. Gio squinted at the portraits as he passed. Even with his middling vision, he could tell they were unexceptional: the palettes dull, the proportions uneven—

Abruptly, the servant girl halted. Gio pulled up short just behind her, narrowly avoiding a collision. Pressing her shoulder against the nearest door, she pushed it open.

Inside, the walls of the grand room were hung in rose silk, tinting the light. Heavy drapes had been drawn halfway shut, and on a far hearth, embers from a recent fire smoldered. Gio stepped into the glow. For a moment he lost all focus as his eyes adjusted from the glare of the hall. Gradually, three women came into view, floating before him on plush divans. Their skin was powdered to a satin finish, imperfectly concealed by folds of silk and velvet that dripped and pooled onto the floor. Jewels at their throats and fingers shimmered. Their lips and cheeks were stained the same fever shade, and their hair—yellow, chestnut, red—was piled high, growing upward like strange glossy botanicals. At his entrance, they turned to him in unison. From the ceiling, sharp-eyed Gospel figures peered down in judgment, trapped in the landscape of an elaborate allegorical frieze. The women's powdered breasts rose and fell under the apostles' watchful eyes. The choking scent of perfume mingled with the tang of wine; Gio suddenly felt dizzy. The women's faces tilted toward him as the ceiling shifted closer.

At his right, two men sat on walnut chairs. One's beard and hair were a close-cropped silver, the other's a black so dark it shone indigo. The dark one turned to watch as Gio pressed a palm to the wall. Then the older man stood and with wide, intoxicated steps, veered toward him. Gio blinked against the blur. Suddenly, the weight of Sebastiano Venier's hand clamped down on his shoulder; Venier's pale eyes swung in front of him, cold and brisk as seawater. Gio breathed in the strong odor of wine and tobacco and, beneath that, salt.

"Giovanni! You look faint! Don't tell me you've never seen a pretty girl before!" Venier's voice boomed as if he were still speaking out over a sea. His narrow face, usually so stern—steely gaze, thin-lipped scowl—was now soft with good humor, cheeks ruddy from wine. The women tittered: round, glad tones that drifted up and broke open across the apostles' faces.

"Sebastiano, don't be cruel." The yellow-haired woman at the center of the room spoke, bending to pour more wine into an empty glass at her feet. Her voice was soft, with a scratch inside it like a fingertip curling: *come closer.*

"Here, have a drink." She held out the full goblet.

As he neared to take it, Gio saw at once why Venier had chosen her. She was dazzling in a way only something that won't last can be. In a few years' time, he knew her face would be hardened, her posture settled into the architecture of a body accustomed to use. But gazing at her now, Gio felt the same way he did watching sunrise over the lagoon: a near-painful awe at the excessive grace of nature, its beauty offered up without fanfare or expectation, as if it were ordinary.

The girl's skin was nearly translucent and flush with young blood, a shade richer than the ivory silk of her dress or the ropes of pearls at her neck. Long lashes cast shadows on her cheeks. When she raised her eyes, he noticed their remarkable hue: hovering between blue and purple, violaceous and hypnotic. A sapphire pendant dangling at her clavicle reflected their color; the drape of the stone inviting the gaze to travel downward, to the firm curves of her breasts, as yet unmarred by age or childbirth. Her tinted hair had been oiled and braided in a delicate pattern at her crown, laced through with gold thread, so that all of her seemed to glisten in the afternoon haze. It was for women such as this that men wrote sonnets, wept, or went to war. With a quick squint, Gio understood he was merely the first of many who would be summoned to paint her portrait. As he reached to take the glass from her, she tipped her face and smiled.

All went hush.

In that single lavender beam, she shone a terrible, lovely vulnerability up at him—and without words or logic he understood: it was he and only ever he who could keep her safe.

Then she blinked, and the warm bright light was gone.

"Her name's Chiara." Venier whispered loudly at Gio's side. Turning, Gio saw the man—a former soldier, whose hands had famously killed other soldiers on the rain-soaked decks of ships—reduced to an idolater. The girl shifted her gaze to Venier, small dimples suggesting themselves near the corners of her mouth. Someone had trained her well. Without warning, Gio felt the stare of the dark-haired man on his back.

It was like a shadow, passing.

"I want a portrait to put the others to shame, Giovanni." Venier moved closer, dank breath cloying with wine. "I want you to make Tintoretto's eyes bleed. You know he promised me a picture and reneged to paint for that miserable confraternity." The confraternity Scuola Grande di San Rocco, on whose walls Tintoretto was painting the life of Christ.

Venier grasped Gio's forearm, squeezing it tightly. "I want him to see Chiara's portrait and hate himself." He edged in, thin lips nearly touching Gio's ear. "She's sat for none of them yet, you see—you're the first. Virgin territory." The old man leaned back. "Artistically speaking, of course." He let out a dry laugh that fractured into a fit of coughs.

At the sound, the other man in the room stood.

"You know Corvino." Venier gave a wave of his hand, before turning to hack into his elbow.

Gio did know Corvino, who was handsome in a way that other men noticed: black hair trimmed to skim his shoulders, a prominent brow that cast his dark eyes even deeper in shadow. Muscles moved beneath his robes like horse flank stirs and flexes under hide. He'd arrived in Venice the same way Gio's blindness had appeared: not noticed at all until suddenly he was everywhere. Seated at every important dinner, kneeling in the front pews, walking out from Mass with this senator or that councilman, head bowed. Listening. He dressed in fabric as fine as that of any nobleman, with a heavy gold cross dangling conspicuously. More than once, Gio had overheard him allude obliquely to Spanish connections, to a fortune made in brokering exports with colonists en route to the New World. Yet from the first, Gio had believed Corvino's history about as much as he trusted the street vendors hawking their wares along the Rialto Bridge.

Still, he had to give the man credit for how quickly he'd established himself among Venice's elite. Likely, it had much to do with his looks. It wasn't just that Corvino gave the impression of being a statue brought to life; there was a grace to his gestures, a lilt to his phrases that Gio guessed must have taken years of study. He appeared and behaved the way a nobleman should—but so rarely did—appear and behave: elegant, cultivated, reminiscent of a demigod. For this, he was rewarded with a regular chair at the best dining tables in the city. Yet looking the part is far different than being cast in the role. For all his charm and fancy robes, Corvino still lacked a proper lineage—and without a title, he'd never be allowed any position of real power. Gio sometimes wondered if the senators and councilmen who opened their homes to Corvino ever noticed the hungry way he eyed their fleets of servants, their sumptuous, gilded halls. Likely not—or if they did, they took a perverse pleasure in it. For many of them, envy had become the only measurement of importance. Gio, however, found it unnerving to sit by as Corvino watched others live out a version of life he so clearly felt he was owed.

It came as no surprise, then, when Corvino attached himself to Venier: the statesman had a reputation for being mercurial, as erratic with generosity as with punishment. It was well known he'd arranged an advantageous marriage for the daughter of one of his favorite merchants, pairing her with a noble family that'd suffered recent losses. They'd gained her dowry, she'd gained a title and coat of arms. Yet by the same token, Venier had banished from Venice permanently a former adviser whose counsel had displeased him. No doubt Corvino was hoping to one day be on the receiving end of a warmer mood. Meanwhile, the statesman had likely taken shrewd measure of Corvino and estimated him willing to do nearly anything to earn influence. With a campaign for the role of doge looming on the horizon, Venier would surely put his acolyte to good use. Until then, he let the man chase at his heels like an underfed lapdog.

For his part, Gio simply did his best to avoid Corvino. In his experience, jealousy had a bad habit of fermenting into rage.

"Well, let's get on with it, then." Venier's voice came again, still at a shocking volume. With his coughing fit over, the statesman returned to his chair. Behind him, Corvino remained standing—seeming, as always, to be attending to a deeper and more important dialogue occurring in his own mind. As the room watched, Gio began unpacking his supplies. From his satchel, he withdrew a portable drawing board and a roll of parchment. Next, he undid the pouch that held his boxes of chalks and charcoals. Today he'd propose a composition; once Venier approved, the real work could be done back in the studio.

Stepping into the role of artist like a seasoned actor assuming the stage, Gio once again approached the girl. He brought two fingers to her chin. At his slightest pressure, she swung her head: first left, then right. Squinting, he assessed her bone structure and profile, quickly memorizing her features while close enough to see them in detail. Her face was perhaps the most symmetrical he'd encountered—though he knew enough of womanly arts to spot that she'd intervened with nature on the matters of her brow shape and hair color. As she watched him appraise her, a pang of doubt flared in her eyes. With his back to the others, Gio gave her a grin, a secret reassurance. *You're safe with me, don't worry.* He thought he caught her lips start to curl, then she flushed and wrenched her chin away. As he walked back to his station, Gio made a silent promise to no one in particular that he'd capture the cleverness he'd seen in her, before she trained it completely into hiding.

"We must prepare you for immortality, my dear!" Venier reached out a hand. The first signs of a mangling arthritis could be spotted in the subtle bend of his fingers. The girl leapt up like a marionette at his summons. She was shorter than Gio would've guessed, but as she danced toward Venier even the embers seemed to flare, watching. Following along to a tune only she could hear, the girl glided across the floor, swinging her silks out—first in one hand, then the other. She was teasing them. She dipped and swayed and leapt, bending like a swan to raise the hem of her dress, revealing the length of her leg, her shapely, slipper-clad foot. Then she dropped the fabric and spun, arms arching into the air. Curls fell loose at her neck and temples, the hem of her dress swirling and billowing around her like white-gold petals. Gio squinted. The jewel at her chest fractured light, her slender arms fluttered. The room began to melt away at the edges until it was only her, center stage, delicate and pale.

Then she collapsed in a fit of giggles and ran the few short steps to stand in front of Venier. He leaned forward eagerly, plucking at the laces of her gown. The other women gathered close, laughing and clapping with calculated amusement. As Venier's hands stumbled, the brunette and redhead both reached to help, pulling loose Chiara's stays, tugging down her *camicia*.

Gio knew a woman's body—knew it well, in all its iterations. The rough pink spots some could get at the elbows or below the knees. How flesh tended to fold around the bones, how it would fold around itself if there were more fat on the muscle. *We artists aren't so different than butchers, we've seen it all,* he'd say to his models, especially the new ones, to reassure them. *No need to be nervous.*

But now here he was, watching Venier undress the girl, his veins pulsing as if she were the first.

Her silks had ended in a pile of ripples at her feet, so that her body rose from them like a stamen, her long necklaces of pearls and gold chain sliding into the hollow between her breasts. Lean muscles expressed themselves under curves of flesh; Gio caught a pink flush of areola as she turned, then a shock of downy dark. He willed himself to focus on her bone structure, to measure her proportions. Lazily, she extended both arms toward the ceiling again, arching her back, smiling up at the apostles with both eyes closed. Venus as coquette, drunk on wine and youth. In his mind's eye, Gio saw portraits and sculptures—her form echoing for eternity in paint, in marble, in bronze.

Venier broke the spell with a crude grasp.

Spinning her around, he slapped her buttocks and pushed her toward the center of the room, the evidence of his palm still rosy on her skin. The girls squealed agreeably. Corvino glared out the window. Sashaying toward a divan, Chiara settled into place in one fluid movement—aiming her body away from Gio to reveal the long curve of her spine, the suggestive depressions at the base of her back. Then she turned, glancing coyly over her shoulder.

"Chiara, the breasts!" Venier demanded.

"No." Gio's voice burst out, surprising even himself. He held one hand up to keep her still. "This is better—it'll allow for some imagination. The girl knows what she's doing."

Chiara failed at hiding her smile. Venier pursed his lips a moment, considering the pose, then conceded. "You're the artist." As though unable to stay after being contradicted, he stood. The servant girl emerged from the corner to push the heavy doors open, while Corvino darted to pluck Venier's cape from the chair back. He shook it out with a flourish, then held it open for the statesman.

"I'll look forward to seeing how it comes along." Venier shot a meaningful look at Gio, then busied himself arranging his robes. "Chiara, Corvino will escort you to your appointments."

"I can escort her." Again, Gio surprised himself. Corvino narrowed his eyes. Still in position, Chiara tilted her head. Gio stumbled on, "I'm certain Corvino has more important duties to attend to. And my humors would benefit from leaving the studio more often." A plausible excuse, but only just.

Venier hesitated. Gio held his breath. Then, it was decided. "Very well. See that you do." With a small flick of his robe, Venier strode out the door, Corvino trailing three paces behind. Gio listened to the staccato of their boots retreat into echoes as the two men descended the main stairs and continued out into the courtyard.

He remained alone with the women.

Hundreds of miles away, sun glared brilliant on the Bosporus strait. From the decks of their boats, the janissaries could still hear the bells of the Hagia Sophia beckoning the city to prayer. The whole of Istanbul lay behind them, as if it were floating on the waterway: domes catching the sun, minarets stretching to pierce the sky. Masts of trading ships crowded the harbor, their holds heavy with spices, silks, and slaves. On the other side of the fleet, the horizon stretched out flat and endless.

Then the wind caught their sails, and a mighty gust propelled them west, toward war.

3

ROSE SAT AT THE TABLE IN THE BRIGHTLY LIT DINING room. Joan had put out her seasonal centerpiece: three mason jars, lace doilies tied around their circumferences with raffia, stalks of cheery yellow daffodils crowded inside. That meant it was spring. In the corner, a red-headed five-year-old was happily removing his clothing—holding out at arm's length first his sweater, then his undershirt, before letting them drop to the floor. One foot was clad in a neon blue sock, the other needed washing. From the living room came the strains of Bizet's *Carmen*.

L'amour est un oiseau rebelle / que nul ne peut apprivoiser . . .

"Henry!" Joan strode in from the kitchen just as the boy was considering how best to tackle the issue of his pants. She crossed her arms and glared disapprovingly first at Henry, then at Rose. Rose shrugged.

"He seemed so happy."

The boy beamed his best smile up at his mother, revealing a

missing front tooth. Unconvinced, Joan rolled her eyes and shook her short red bob back from her face.

"Dinner should be done soon," she said, bending for the clothes pile.

Normally, when Rose came across a particularly interesting document, she'd have rushed home to tell her father all about it. She'd have found him in his favorite chair by the fireplace, orange and blue checked wool blanket draped across his knees. Perching on the leather ottoman beside him, Rose would've described the palimpsest, speaking over the raspy white noise of his oxygen machine. They'd nicknamed the squat beige device "Asclepius," after the Greek god of medicine. Her father had been a professor of classics, and even through the drowse of morphine he'd have asked all the right questions: how degraded were the pages, how legible was the undertext. Together they'd have speculated about the author's milieu, her father no doubt recommending some obscure manuscript detailing late Renaissance Venice.

Instead she'd come home to an empty chair, the setting sun touching light to the far edge of the checked blanket, now folded neatly on the seat cushion. Rose had stood in her own entryway, feeling the weight of that silence—then before she knew it, she was knocking at Joan's door, stepping into the swaddling comfort of a lived-in home, with Henry's toys scattered across the carpet and a stack of dishes in the sink. The smell of pot roast and carrots and a rustling from the office down the hall, where Joan's husband, Mark, was sorting papers, sending out one last email before dinner. Joan calling to Rose from the kitchen, excited to hear about her day, even if she had no clue what a palimpsest was.

Rose used to hate Joan. The first time they'd met, they'd both been on break from college, summoned home to Connecticut to have Thanksgiving dinner with their parents' "new friends." Rose had spent the whole meal staring at Joan. At the white barrettes in her hair, little bows molded into the plastic. At the collegiate sweater from her West Coast school and her iridescent pink nails. In the middle of dinner Joan had paused to put on lip gloss, using the wand from a pale tube with the word WINK printed in glitter along one side. The scent had wafted over to Rose, a sticky-sweet intrusion.

"Look, you both have red hair! Sort of like family already." Rose's father had smiled hopefully at them over the carved turkey, steam from bowls of potatoes and stuffing and green beans nearly fogging his glasses. Rose had glared at him, only too aware of the vast difference between her own unwieldy, blond-streaked curls and Joan's glossy, fire-hydrant waves, meant for a shampoo commercial.

Joan's mother, Aileen, had been easier: thick-waisted and gentle, always baking cookies and freezing leftovers and wondering if everyone was warm enough. Her very presence was somewhat miraculous—Rose couldn't remember her father, already old to have a daughter her age, ever going on a single date. Rose's own mother had died the summer before Rose started high school after a brief, brave fight against an unfair cancer. Grief had seared Rose and her father into a team of two then, no new members allowed. Together they'd encouraged each other's introversion—four years had passed in a blur of takeout containers and books strewn across the dining room table, punctuated only by tedious classes and noisy bus rides with a backpack that'd seemed illegally heavy.

The autumn Rose had left for college, her father took an early retirement from the university. She'd encouraged him to join a book club with all his new free time. *You need to do something with me gone. You'll forget how to talk to people like a normal human being.* She'd even found a group, one whose reading list she knew he could tolerate. By chance, Joan's mother had also just joined; five months later and there they were "one big happy family."

After that Christmas, Rose had stayed in school for as long as she could: undergraduate degree, apprenticeship in conservation.

All completed in New York, just a train ride away. Whenever she needed to escape the dazzling chaos of the city, she'd spend the weekend studying in the lull of her father's library, discussing her courses over dinner. Then Aileen died—abruptly, a stroke. Rose had tried to come back more often, but by the time she'd finished her master's, her father's health had faltered past repair. Two wives buried proved more than he was willing to endure. *I'm enduring!* Rose had sometimes wanted to shout, shaking his bird-boned shoulders. *And you're leaving me alone.* She didn't think twice about giving up her small apartment in the city to move back in and take care of him. They became a team of two, again: takeout dinners and books. Public radio programs and medication demarcating their days.

By then Joan had come home too, with an engineer husband and a toddler in tow. She'd cut her hair and exchanged the giggly, lip-glossed version of herself for one with greater girth and calm. Every Monday night the doorbell would ring and Rose knew it'd be her—standing on the doorstep with dinner (casseroles, lasagnas, wide glass pans wrapped in tinfoil and filled with recipes from *Taste of Home* magazine), asking if Rose was getting enough sleep. It was Joan who'd come up with the idea for the bookshop, a way for Rose to establish her restoration business, plus get a small profit from book sales. They lived in a university town, after all; it'd be a perfect fit. Rose had agreed, and in what seemed like the blink of an eye had found herself putting a down payment on a storefront. Sometimes she felt like a movie character in a dream sequence: like she'd just woken up one day and was there, here, back home, a bookshop and cat owner. In the end, she was left with no real awareness of how it'd all happened—just a sense that it was inevitable, her life quietly arranging itself around a particular gravitational pull.

Now, six months after her father's marble headstone had been lowered into the damp cemetery grass, with the empty house hers alone, Rose wound up at Joan's at least one night a week. More, if Mark was traveling for work.

Joan straightened up, the clothes in a tight wad at her hip. She stole a peek at Rose from the corner of her eye.

"Joan. I know it's something when you look at me like that."

"Rosebud, I think you should see the computer. I left the page up." She shifted her attention to Henry, who, deprived of his shirt and hungry, appeared to be debating whether to cry.

Rose's body stood of its own accord.

In the living room, the music swelled. *L'amour est enfant de Bohème, il n'a jamais jamais connu de loi . . .* The glowing square of the computer beckoned her from the far end of the room. As she padded across the carpet, a photo on the screen came into focus. William. Clean-shaven, suited, a more polished sort of handsome than he'd been at the shop. At his side, a woman with Scandinavian good looks posed for the camera. She wore an immaculate white shift dress, hair falling in straight blond curtains from a perfect center part. They'd been photographed at a gallery—behind them hung colorful paintings, blurring into the background. Together they looked impossibly chic, the sort of couple you'd watch stepping into the backseat of a car parked outside an expensive restaurant and imagine what that life must feel like. A short paragraph of text ran down the right margin of the page: his training, a summary of projects with links to each exhibition. Then the last line:

"Lomazzo lives in Connecticut with his wife and their two daughters."

Rose squinted at the screen, trying to interpret his expression. Had she just imagined it then—the surge of warmth when he'd clasped her hand? She didn't remember seeing a wedding ring. Maybe they were separated? A small hope fluttered in the pit of her stomach, immediately squelched by reproach. No, she shouldn't wish for misfortune like that. She must have just imagined it. Staring at the photo, Rose realized with some surprise how far she'd allowed her thoughts to wander: she'd already pictured him coming back into the shop and casually asking her to lunch, as if the idea had just occurred to him. She'd seen them strolling, side by side, beneath the cherry blossoms that would unfurl their origami petals all through town within a month. They'd already gone to dinner together in her mind, even—there'd been candles. Two years of caregiving and here she was, raw with loneliness, spinning up fantasies about the first handsome man to touch her. Rose rubbed her face in her hands until her cheeks tingled with heat.

From the kitchen came the crash of a pan, the quick braying of Henry's sobs. Rose leaned to turn the volume up. Maria Callas's voice bloomed to fill the room, her powerful aria drowning out all else.

Tout autour de toi, vite vite , il vient, s'en va, puis il revient. . . . Tu crois le tenir, il t'évite. Tu crois l'éviter, il te tient . . .

The next day even the sky couldn't seem to hold a cheerful mood, erasing any patch of blue with smudgy gray cloud cover. Rose sat at her desk, watching the passersby out on the street. First the morning crowd, coffee cups in hand. Then a lunch rush of students from the university halls a few blocks away, chattering in pairs, scuttling back to class clutching crumpled to-go bags. Already, she'd casually shuffled through the stack of papers William had left; now she couldn't help but put together a quick assessment of what a repair might cost. The number was high—she brought it down to a more reasonable sum.

No, Rose. He's a client like any other. If it's too expensive you negotiate, the same way you would with anyone else. She brought the figure back up and turned to her email in-box.

William /

The cursor blinked expectantly on the screen. Curled up in his chair by the window, Odin tucked a paw over his good eye.

"Fine, I'll just cut and paste something." Rose announced her decision to the empty shop. She found an old client letter, highlighted the text, and dropped it into the blank message field.

Mr. Lomazzo,

Thank you for the opportunity to work on this project. Attached for review is a detailed summary of my estimate, as well as a draft contract. Please don't hesitate to reach out with any questions.

R.

It seemed formal, cold, but she didn't know what else to write. She fished his business card out from the antique silver tray by her pen jar. william@williamlomazzo.com. Character by character, she typed it in. Hit Send.

She exhaled a breath she didn't know she'd been holding.

The emails to her contacts were easier. These were fellow experts, collectors, and academics she'd met at conferences or online. She asked each if they'd come across mentions of Lomazzo in any other texts, or seen different versions of the treatise. Her own research had left her empty-handed, and she was curious: the title of the document suggested it'd been meant for publication, and Venice had been a publishing mecca. The odds it had gone to print were relatively high.

By the time she'd biked home, one reply was waiting.

It was from Yuri, who lived in New York. They'd struck up an online friendship years ago in a collectors' chat forum. Rose had gathered through conversation that Yuri was older, maybe in his late seventies, with a curious mind and a dry sense of humor. They'd immediately taken a liking to each other and begun a lasting, if sporadic, correspondence. Theirs was a meeting of minds: just like her, Yuri had a fondness for research and what seemed to be a near-photographic memory. His rare-book shop was on the Lower East Side, close enough for Rose to pay a visit, but for some reason seeing each other in person felt like it might alter their friendship. She'd conjured an image of him that she didn't want to disturb: an elderly man with round glasses balanced on the tip of his nose and an erudite glint in his eyes, manning the desk at a dusty, treasure-filled hole in the wall.

Rosie—

I have not personally seen a version of this treatise, but I do remember the name Lomazzo. Years ago, I came across a version of Borghini's Il Riposo with previously unpublished notes included. Have you read Il Riposo? It's a treatise also, published in 1584, after Vasari's Lives of the Artists. It's interesting, but gives enough detail of the Counter-Reformation to bore a priest!

Point is, in going through the notes I recall mention of a treatise by Lomazzo that circulated through Italy in the late 1500s. The impression I got was that Borghini had been influenced by Lomazzo—particularly by his beliefs that writing about art can be an art form, and that art should be accessible to those who are not artists themselves.

You know how ideas were stolen so easily back then (and now, for that matter). My hunch is that this Lomazzo's treatise was appropriated by Borghini to some degree. As for the treatise itself, I've never seen it or heard mention of existing versions. If you have a copy, you should tell your client to publish it. Can you imagine the academics? They'd piss themselves! May get a substantial sum at auction too, if he's hard up for cash.

I hope you are well otherwise, my dear. Keep me updated on how the restoration goes. Life here is good, although I wish spring would hurry up. You know me, Rosie—these old bones can't handle the cold like they used to.

Yuri

Rose had been eating dinner—canned tomato soup and a thick, flaky roll from the bakery she passed on her ride home—when the second email arrived. Her laptop was open on the table next to her, and when she looked up there it was, at the top of her in-box, the only one marked "unread."

R,

Please, call me William. Thanks for sending the estimate so fast, I appreciate it. You're very professional. I've signed the contract and attached a scan here, but I can bring in a printed copy, if that's the way you usually do it (?)

I'm interested in learning more about the restoration process. Do you mind if I stop in from time to time to see how it's coming along?

Thanks,
W

He'd copied the way she signed off, with a single letter. Or did he just happen to do that also? And what did that mean, "You're very professional"? Had she been too formal? Joan was always telling her to loosen up, that her shyness made her seem cold. *It wouldn't kill you to try to smile more, Rose.* But it was his last sentence she lingered on. He wanted to come back to the shop. That meant she'd see him again—maybe soon. She felt her pulse quicken before her mind could interject: *Lomazzo lives in Connecticut with his wife and their two daughters.*

Still, she couldn't help but read the note over three, four more times, leaning forward on an elbow as if getting closer to the screen would help her find some hidden meaning in his words. Her fingers hovered over the keyboard . . .

No.

She should send a reply tomorrow—tomorrow afternoon. Let an appropriate interval pass. She turned back to her dinner. The hunk of bread she'd dipped in the soup had gone to mush, leaving just a sad hard edge of crust poking out from the middle of the bowl. Months later she'd remember that scene: the disintegrating bread, the soup skinning over. She'd wonder if any of her actions could have altered the way events unfolded, or if it all would've turned out the same no matter what she'd done.

4

THE AIR IN THE ROOM GREW PALPABLY LIGHTER AFTER Corvino and Venier departed. The redhead and the brunette shifted into more comfortable positions, loosening the laces of their bodices with the same unburdening sigh Gio made when taking off his shoes at night. Chiara held her pose, gazing at him expectantly.

He rummaged among his things for a stick of chalk, then quickly began to sketch. Holding the board in one hand and chalk in the other, he methodically captured all the small measurements that would help him re-create the composition later. The angle of her knee to the corners of the room, the placement of her arm, the spot where her jawline touched her shoulder. A dozen minute points of connection, intersection, and calibration that would guide him later, through sitting after sitting. Once he'd mapped her body on the parchment he paused, leaning to take a first sip of wine.

"This is the finest home I've seen a courtesan installed in. You must be pleased," he said to the room at large.

"One advantage of knowing a statesman," the redhead observed, before yawning. She had an aquiline nose and the habit of lolling her head back as she spoke, which lent her a snobbish air. Gio had already found her weakness, however: despite the careful application of powders and rouge, he could spot that she was older than the others.

"Venier appreciates having a place in the city to host his dinners." Chiara's tone was formal, a deflection of Gio's actual meaning: *Isn't this cage a lovely one?*

"Yes, they're such fun, you must come to the next." The brunette spoke now, in the sort of high, childlike voice certain women make their currency. She'd wandered to one of the side tables and stood, eyeing a bowl of grapes and twisting a strand of hair between two fingers. "Do you have a girl, Giovanni?" She looked up, her face as blank and perfect as a doll's. He couldn't see Chiara, sitting outside his field of view, but he felt her watching.

"Should we begin with introductions first? Then questions?" He flashed what he hoped was a friendly grin.

"Oh!" Her hands flew up to her chest. "Margherita. And that's Veronica." The redhead waggled her long fingers at him.

"So, do you have a girl or not?" Margherita popped a grape into her mouth, chewing slowly while she stared at him.

Gio cleared his throat. "I had a wife once, yes, if that's what you mean." He kept his eyes trained on the sketch, squinting to bring into focus the lines that were beginning to form the muscles of Chiara's back.

"You had? Did she leave you for spending all your time with courtesans?" Veronica raised a hand to examine her nails.

"No, we were quite happy. She died several years ago."

The women's faces melted into the kind of expression reserved for the tragedies of strangers.

"It was a long time ago; there's no need to be sad for me," Gio reassured them with an equally well-rehearsed smile.

"Haven't you found anyone since?" Margherita sucked another grape into her mouth.

"I haven't."

"Why not?" The girl spoke while chewing.

He paused to consider. How long had it been since he'd thought of her? An image flitted to life in the back of his mind, as though it'd been waiting for the slightest gesture of invitation: her silhouette against the window. Morning sun. The profile of her face, turning to look at him. The curve of her cheek as she smiled—in memories, she was always smiling. He could see the margins of her so sharply. His vision had still been perfect.

"I . . . I don't know. She had my heart. She took it with her, I suppose." He stared up at the ceiling; the apostles were a blur.

"As well she should have. And Giovanni doesn't need us meddling in his affairs, does he? Surely we can speak of lighter things." Chiara stared pointedly at Margherita, an edge cutting through her tone like vinegar in honey.

The brunette flushed, exchanging looks with Veronica. Gio thought he saw the redhead nod. Soon, the girls were filling the air with charming, empty words. He let them chatter on as the tightness in his chest resolved. Their sunny voices chased one another around the room as they recounted the more amusing habits of their lovers and tallied up the trinkets they'd recently received—the sounds drifted into the background as he began to focus on his work. Chiara seemed to have the stamina of an athlete, remaining still even as the light billowed and the girls grew restless, wandering in and out of the great rose-colored room. With the outline of her body finished, he began to layer in the shadows. He leaned closer to the page.

"I need to rest." Her voice broke the protracted silence. With a start, he looked up. Judging by the angle of the sun stretching across the floor, they must have been alone for some time.

"Of course."

She stood, twisting her back. Politely, he kept himself occupied adjusting the final lines of the sketch. Then she strode to refill her glass of wine, and he tracked the way the light attached itself to her body as she moved.

"Why do you think they call him 'the Crow'?" She filled the cup to the brim.

"You mean Corvino?"

She nodded. Gio paused, reminding himself that anything he said might find its way back to Venier or to Corvino himself.

"Well, he is certainly dark-headed—"

"I heard he collects the heads of crows." She interrupted him, spinning to lean one hip against the sideboard. He kept his eyes trained on her face. With a quick squint, he took note of her brows, drawn together; the downward arc of her mouth. Again, he was struck by the perfect symmetry of her features.

"I've heard the same."

"Is it true?"

"I think so, yes."

"It isn't normal." Her voice had hardened, shedding the round, dulcet tones she'd cultivated for clients. "And the servants tell me it's known he'll pay for information about their masters."

"What sort of information?"

"Anything, really. Bastard children, private meetings, their comings and goings. Whose chambers they're visiting and when."

Their eyes met.

"Stay away from him as much as possible. That's my wisdom for you." Immediately, Gio regretted his words. If this had been a test, he'd failed miserably. Silence intruded on the space between them until she spoke again, quietly this time.

"Thank you. It's nice to talk to someone from outside this house."

"I am but your humble servant." Gio bowed in jest, was pleased to see her smile when he straightened.

"Does everyone blabber to you when you visit? Do *you* know

more secrets than Corvino by now?" Her tone was playful, but her stare was calculating as she took another sip of wine, surveying him over the edge of her cup.

"I don't mind listening, and I don't repeat what I hear, if that's what you're asking." She made a small grunt at this that he couldn't interpret. He took another look at the sketch. "Well, I think we've made enough progress for today."

Returning the chalks and charcoals to their boxes, he began to pack his station in earnest. The light had matured into a comfortable peach hue, and his stomach was rumbling impatiently. As he worked, he felt her eyes on him. Finally, he raised his head. She was studying him with a detached air—the same look he must use when assessing his models. Suddenly, he felt exposed and defensive.

"You're not ugly." She stated it like any other fact. *The sky is blue.* He laughed at her bluntness.

"No, truly," she pressed on. "In fact, you're quite handsome, at the right angle. A bit of gray creeping in . . . but other than that, you'd do nicely. Why *haven't* you got a girl—may I ask that? Between us?" She crossed her arms beneath her breasts as comfortably as if she were clothed, the small pearls in her ears sheening as she cocked her head to one side.

"You may." He focused on lining the chalks up neatly in their box, carefully fitting the lid down over them. Memories threatened again at the margins, eager and bright. "The truth is that I've tried. But my wife was . . . different. She read everything, she challenged me. She was smart and curious, and—"

"And that's hard to find again," she finished for him.

He nodded.

"She could read? She had a tutor?"

"No tutor; she wasn't wealthy. Her father enjoyed reading and he taught her. That's all."

"I can read." Chiara lifted her chin.

He smiled at her pride. "And so can your servant girl, I noticed."

"Cecilia? I'm teaching her myself."

"Really. And who taught *you*, may I ask?"

The tendons in her neck tightened, flicking the skin. Her gaze drifted down to her wine. "I—I come from a higher station than the one I now find myself in, let me assure you." Her voice faltered and she gave a half smile, just enough for one dimple to surface momentarily. "You can understand . . . a series of poor business calculations on the part of my father in Rome, and, well . . ." She raised a delicate hand in the air, communicating with a single twist of her wrist the arcing history of a fortune ruined. "I'd prefer not to speak of it, if you don't mind." The eyes she lifted to stare out the window were glossy, capturing the waning light in velvet pools.

"And that story worked on Venier, I take it?" Gio only partially tried to bury his smirk.

The girl blinked at him, hard.

"Oh, Chiara, come now." He continued before she could interject. "I'm an artist—I make my living from men like Venier just as much as you do. Do you think in all my years of painting I've never had a courtesan tell me the best tricks? Conjuring a respectable family line to improve clientele is not a new idea, my dear. However, I must say, few are as successful at it as you seem to be." He leaned to grab his cup, raising it in her direction for a mock cheer before draining the last of the wine.

"My aunt taught me how to read. Domenico taught me *what* to read." She answered his original question abruptly, cutting off any further discussion of her past. Gio took the cue.

"Ah, so you've been to his salons, then." There was only one Domenico she could be referring to. A former senator, the man was most known for hosting gatherings that connected the brightest lights in Venice, from courtesans to foreign dignitaries. *You create art, I create conversations!* he liked to exclaim to Gio whenever he saw him.

"Domenico liked my looks. He's been . . . very kind to me."

"I'm sure he has."

"I owe everything to him." She said it sharply, as though he'd contradicted her. "He gave me all the right books; he even encouraged my study of music. Though now I'm the one who's overlearned and bored in conversations." She brushed a wisp of blond back from her face and took another sip of wine.

"Well, there are worse problems to have than an abundance of education." Gio began to unfasten the sketch from his drawing board. "Perhaps the next time I visit, we can have a lively debate. I promise I'll try not to bore you—or ask too many questions." He shot a look at her while he fussed with the parchment, trying to gauge whether she was still upset that he'd ruined her charade.

"Perhaps." She set her glass down on the cupboard and in three strides was at his side, putting one hand over his own to halt him. Her skin was warm and dry. Taking the board away, she inspected the sketch.

He held his breath, waiting.

"It's true. You have a gift." She handed the board back. At such close range, her violet eyes were arresting. She leveled her stare at him, any last pretense of the coquette abandoned. "I'm so sorry it's leaving you."

Heat tore across his skin.

She raised herself up onto her toes then, draping one arm over his shoulder, placing the other palm flat to his chest. As she leaned to whisper, her mouth nearly touched his ear—a strange, feminine echo of Venier's earlier gesture. His heart quickened. Could she feel it under her hand? "It can be our secret. Just don't squint so much when Corvino's nearby." He closed his eyes when she pressed her lips to the hollow just below his jaw. Then she turned and walked barefoot out the half-open door.

He found himself alone in the room, her dress a bundle of brassed gold on the floor beside him.

In the dove tones of early dusk, the sound of Gio's heels striking cobblestone rang out through the empty avenues. He was headed for the alchemist's house; Aurelio could always lift his spirits. Soon he reached the address: a nondescript door midway down an alley, with red paint peeling off the wood and no knocker. Knowing it'd be unbolted, he pushed the door open and slipped inside, pausing at the threshold to let his eyes adjust to the dim.

Aurelio's studio was a disorienting mix of the mystic and mundane. Drying plants hung from the rafters in clumps of fading, fragrant green, and shelves ran the length of every wall—crammed with clay jugs, books in foreign languages, boxes, and tools that Gio knew no use for. Large worktables occupied the room's central space. These were covered entirely by rock shards, minerals, mortar and pestle, charts of stars, and scraps of parchment lined with Aurelio's indecipherable scribbling. To keep out the prying eyes of neighbors, the alchemist had the habit of leaving his shutters closed at all hours of the day. For light, he set out candles and kept a low fire burning on the hearth. The haphazard glow cast weird shadows that sparred with any sun creeping through the cracks in the shutters.

Gio knew he'd find Aurelio in his usual position: standing before a large pot suspended over the fire, absentmindedly stirring with one hand while reading from a book held open in the other. The glow from the flames made his plump face seem even rounder than it was, illuminating the white curls that ringed his bald crown, so that he looked like an aging cherub. Over the years, Gio had learned that what cooked in the burnished pots was just as likely to be alcoholic in nature as some alchemical experiment. Though he wasn't a betting man, Gio would wager that Aurelio was operating a full distillery in his back chamber. He couldn't be completely certain, however, as the alchemist had never confirmed his suspicions, and Gio knew better than to ask: between the two men hung an unspoken agreement that privacy was an essential condition of friendship.

To the public, Aurelio presented himself as a merrymaker—an affable mystic always ready for an easy laugh and a second helping of what tasted good. For his patrons, he'd accentuate his esoteric pursuits: stroking his long white beard, he'd remind them that the *rubedo*, the miracle that turns all metal to gold, would be well worth the wait. But in practice, he was as shrewd and pragmatic as any businessman. Through his door flowed all manner of trade: tinctures, ointments, potions, and salves. And, of course, his liquors, without which no salon was considered a success. In addition to commerce, Aurelio's talents extended to a prescient knowledge of political plotlines—though how he came by his information Gio didn't want to know. More than once, he'd caught his friend staring into the fire after a long night at the taverns. The expression he found on the alchemist's face then was less jolly trickster than weary magi: the sage behind the jester's mask.

That evening, Gio avoided the usual niceties and immediately turned to the shelves, rummaging through and pulling stoppers, sniffing for the telltale sting of alcohol.

"Not that one," Aurelio instructed sharply, watching as Gio lifted a large jug. "Try the next."

As he set the jug back in its place, Gio gazed into the syrupy liquid. Through the glass, he could see the dark matter was flecked with gold, like so many cat eyes winking in the night. Saying nothing, he picked up the sanctioned vessel and took a long hard pull. The warm burn of liquor slid into his gut.

"An affair of the heart, I presume?" Aurelio asked with a hint of amusement.

"You might say that. Venier's new spoil, in every sense of the word." Gio coughed into his elbow.

"And he wants you to paint her as Diana, I suppose?"

By way of response, Gio took another long pull.

"Well, if rumors are to be believed, soon enough Venier won't be around to trouble you." Aurelio turned back to the fire. Gio waited for more, but the alchemist seemed content to stir what filled the pot.

"Out with it, Aurelio!"

"What's that?" The alchemist glanced over his shoulder with feigned confusion but couldn't keep his mouth from spreading into a grin. Like a child, he delighted in adding a measure of drama to all his conversations.

"Why am I not to see Venier?"

"Ah, yes, well . . ." Turning from the fire, Aurelio rubbed his hands together excitedly. "It would appear Venier may soon become quite preoccupied with a certain Selim the Second."

The candles seemed to dim at the name. Selim II, the sultan of the Ottoman Empire. It was no secret the sultan was plotting, as his father had before him, to gain control of Venice—and, in doing so, to take command of both Eastern and Western trade routes.

Leaning across the worktable with a sudden somber countenance, Aurelio lowered his voice. "You understand that Selim sees Cyprus as a stepping-stone to winning Venice?"

"Yes, of course I do." Cyprus was a source of bitter irritation for the Ottomans: though the island was located just off the coast of their empire, it remained under Venetian rule. As such, it'd long been a haven for Western pirates, who enjoyed nothing more than to intercept trade ships returning home from the sultan's territories in Egypt. If Selim wished to consolidate his power, capturing Cyprus was a critical first move. As a consequence, the islanders feared an invasion the way certain valley-dwelling villagers might fear a flood: knowing it was a matter of not *if* but *when*, and *at what cost*.

"Do you recall when the Ottoman fleet docked near Nicosia?" Aurelio raised his brows; their wispy arches caught the light and turned translucent.

"Yes, yes, of course I do," Gio repeated. All of Venice had heard of the incident months ago, when Ottoman ships had descended upon the small Cyprus town—unannounced and in great number. Imagining the worst, the Cypriots had readied for a siege. Yet only a single man had disembarked: Joseph Nassi, adviser to the sultan. After formally greeting the governor, Nassi had taken a careful tour of Nicosia's fortresses. Then, offering no explanation, he'd simply reboarded his ship and sailed away, the Ottoman vessels trailing behind.

Nassi's face had not been a welcome one. Years earlier, the man had lived in Venice, until officials charged him with dissembling: posing as a Christian while secretly practicing the Jewish faith. True or not, the charge was clearly a ruse for the Venetians to seize control of Nassi's sizable family fortune. Sensing his plight, Nassi had fled to Istanbul. Since that time, he had harbored a well-known resentment against the Republic. After his visit to Cyprus, whispers of an invasion began circulating in earnest. If the island were won, the path would be clear for the sultan to make a play for Venice at last—and for Nassi to see the city that had betrayed him brought to her knees.

Aurelio carried on, the fire sparking behind him. "A reliable source tells me that, very recently, Selim promised to make Nassi the king of Cyprus if the island is taken." The alchemist's face broke open in mirth. "And the fool is so greedy he's already gone and designed himself a coat of arms!" Aurelio let loose a roar of laughter at the absurdity of it, his head rolling back, round belly heaving. Gio couldn't find the humor. Nassi's influence over the sultan was widely known, and organizing an anti-Ottoman league would be no easy task, given the fractured state of Christendom.

Abruptly, Aurelio stopped laughing, his eyes turning sharp. "Venier wants to secure a victory for Venice—he's aiming to be appointed admiral should we go to war. A win over the Ottomans will land him in the doge's seat, without a doubt." Aurelio wagged a finger in Gio's face. "My prediction? Selim's ambassador will be arrested soon. Mark my words."

"His ambassador?"

Aurelio shook his head at Gio's blank expression. "Selim's ambassador to the king of France. He's here in Venice at the moment. Really, Gio, with all the time you spend traipsing about the homes of the rich and powerful, it's a wonder you're not better informed." To this, Gio shrugged and took another drink.

Aurelio reached a hand out for the jug. "Well, if we do go to war, the armory will ensure our fleet is well fortified."

"If Venier sails to fight the Ottomans, what becomes of the girl?" Gio passed the liquor over.

"Corvino will undoubtedly watch after her—whether asked to or not." The two men exchanged a glance. Aurelio cleared his throat. "He won't do anything, Gio. Not while she's in favor."

"Let's pray then that she doesn't fall from grace."

"I'll pray and drink to that, good friend." Aurelio filled two empty glasses that sat on the table.

Outside, the smell of salt rolled in on a courier wind, carrying the threat of rain.

The Ottoman ships cast long shadows across the water. Sailing quietly in the dim, they slid along the coast of Cyprus, toward the village of Nicosia. Well after sundown they skulked ashore, waves cracking open across their sturdy hulls. Under cover of night, the inky shapes of ten thousand bodies crept out onto the beach, streaming upward in dark rivers of clambering limbs, disappearing into the forest. At first light, the men would lay siege to the village that now lay slumbering, unawares. First Nicosia, then Famagusta— the island's two strongholds. Without them, Cyprus could not stand.

From a nearby hilltop, General Lala Mustafa Pasha observed

the progress of his men. At his side, an olive tree shuddered in the wind. *You are right to tremble,* he thought. Soon, he would make the whole island shake under his force. He—Mustafa—who only a few years ago had been nothing but a tutor: Selim's favorite instructor. Now look at him, commanding campaigns! He took a great gulp of chill night air, smoothing his mustache with a press of forefinger and thumb. How many nights had he and Nassi stayed awake, scheming? Nassi yearned to watch Venice burn, Mustafa was eager to prove his worth in battle, they both had the sultan's ear—together they'd made the perfect team. Charting their course into the late hours, weaving a story that would at last convince Selim . . .

Now it was all unfurling according to plan. Best of all was that Mustafa's eldest son would fight alongside him. The general peered out at the clusters of men disintegrating into shadow. His boy must be among them now: healthy and strong, buoyed by the courage of youth. If he performed well in battle, if the strongholds were captured, handsome rewards could await them both. Glory herself lay before them, ripe and open-legged. Mustafa gazed up at the stars, immune to his ambition, hypnotized by their own watery reflections.

The muffled clamor of steel and armor drifted up from the beach below.

5

THE WIND CHILLED ROSE'S FACE AS SHE BIKED, BUT SHE could feel a flush of sun unfurling over her shoulders, and the air smelled of green beginnings. She pictured the book waiting for her in the darkened back room and began to pedal faster, wheels whirring along the white line edging the road. At the café, Joel noticed the change.

"You're here earlier than normal, aren't you?" He glanced up at the clock—a tacky thing that hung above the bathroom door, a lopsided cup of coffee painted in its center.

"Wanted to get a head start on a few things, I guess."

"Guess so." The milk burbled and frothed under the steamer.

She was two hours ahead of schedule to be exact. Thermos in hand, she hurried back to the shop but kept the sign turned to CLOSED. As she set her coffee down on the desk, Odin roused himself. Stretching both front paws out, claws scratching the air, he made a valiant effort to open his one good eye. As soon as he heard the dry rustle of his food bag, however, he sprang to life with a demanding *mew*. After feeding duties, Rose slid open a drawer under the register and fished out an old-fashioned key, cast in an intricate design. She headed down the hall toward the back of the shop, where she used the key to unlock a second room.

If the front was meant to project a cozy, inviting atmosphere, then this chamber was its shadow self: white walled, shocked awake by sterile light. Her true sanctuary. A long table took up the center of the room, glass top reflecting a cold glare from rows of LEDs overhead. A dark-screened computer sat on a desk in the corner, flanked by ceramic speakers. Nearby, an expensive-looking camera mounted on a stand hovered over a drafting table, which was lacquered white and framed by lamps. Open steel cabinets ran the length of one full wall, housing an assortment of tools, brushes, and papers. Concrete-colored linoleum gleamed.

"The operating room" Joan liked to call it.

The manuscript was waiting for her in a neat pile on the center table. Like an athlete before a race, Rose ran through the same routine each time she began work. First, music. Today it would be Beethoven, beginning with the violin sonatas. At the computer, she pulled up a favorite playlist. As the opening strains swelled from the speakers, she briefly considered Beethoven's deafness. What would it have been like to hear the notes fade away? Her thoughts danced in time with the violins. She remembered reading a letter Beethoven had written to his brothers, confessing that he'd considered but rejected suicide. *How could I possibly quit the world before bringing forth all that I felt it was my vocation to produce?*

She also remembered reading that evidence of cirrhosis had been found in his body.

The bulbs overhead shuddered, a fault of the old building's wiring. She turned the volume up and shifted her attention to her tools. Scissors, tweezers, Japanese paper. Knives, magnifiers, small handheld UV lights, scalpels, brushes, mats, pastes—one by one, she took them from their proper places and laid them in order on the worktable. Next, the book. The strings she'd clipped on the first day had left the manuscript a loose stack of stiff sheets. By their relative flatness and the puncture marks along their edges, it was clear they'd been properly bound at some point. She began imagining options for a new binding; it would need to be beautiful—something for William to remember her by. Supple, good-quality leather. Oxblood, perhaps.

Along the perimeters of the pages ran the evidence of time: black smudge at the outer edges, where the fiber was most damaged, torn and faded to near transparency. Then a gradual burnt umber color moving toward center. Only the very middle of the vellum was still pale, yellowed with age. The effect made the book look as if it'd been lightly singed all along the outside.

She removed the cover page and read the title again. *Trattato dell'arte della pittura, scultura, ed architettura.* By Giovanni Paolo Lomazzo. She ran a fingertip over the name, felt the faint ridges pressed into the vellum so many years ago. The very fact that the treatise had been written on vellum was interesting: by the 1570s, paper would have been readily available. Yet it was only the quality of the skin that had let Giovanni erase the first document and rewrite his treatise over top. He must have taken a blade to it, scraping away until the original ink had lightened enough that he could rotate the book sideways and begin to write again. But why? He'd not completely eradicated the undertext, and the result was that the two layers of calligraphy formed a neat grid on every sheet, darker top and faded bottom each vying for attention.

Rose lifted the first several pages, stiff and brittle in her hands, arranging them on the table. She scanned the sentences, tripping over the intersecting lines inked so long ago. Was the lower writing a first draft? She tried to see if she could parse a repeating pattern in the words that ran across and down the pages. The two layers didn't seem to be the same, though she couldn't be sure: her Italian was limited to art terms and useful phrases for travelers, *dov'è il bagno?*

She imagined Giovanni, an artist living in Venice. She could picture that city: canals crowded with gondolas, arching bridges linking neighborhoods together. She'd been there once, during undergrad, when she'd signed up for a summer course on textile repairs. The exchange school was in Milan, but the class had spent a long weekend in Venice. The city had been overrun with tourists even then, an astounding number of groups trailing like ducklings after their guides, who invariably held poles aloft, affixed with brightly colored flags flapping in the breeze. Rose had eaten gelato every single day of that blazing, sun-flooded summer, always the *bacio* flavor, a decadent blend of chocolate and hazelnut she'd been devastated to leave behind.

Rose tried to envision a Venice without tourists—without gelato, even. When Veronese and Titian were still alive and painting, when William's ancestor must have paced the avenues of that glimmering city on the water ... She sighed. The only real way to figure out what Giovanni had written was to get to work. Settling into the task at hand, she began by carefully placing the first pages on stronger backing paper. On a legal pad, she made notes to herself in tidy print, indicating where extra fiber would be needed to stabilize the most damaged areas. With a soft brush, she whisked away any dirt from the sheets, pausing to assess the wax stains left where Giovanni had undoubtedly written by candlelight. As the music surged and ebbed, she focused her attention on the top layer of text. The writing was indeed about art. Over and over, she saw words even she could recognize: *composizione, proporzione, ombra, luminosa.*

Composition, proportion, shadow, light.

After the introduction concluded, images began to appear: elegant portraits of male and female forms, lines demarcating their various parts. Charts and graphs offered a key, demonstrating how a body might achieve proper balance and proportion. The drawings reminded Rose of da Vinci's "Vitruvian Man." If what Yuri had said was true, Giovanni was trying to provide a way for even a layperson to evaluate the quality of a painting. The execution of the sketches was masterful—though they were only diagrams, Giovanni had taken care to develop the musculature of each figure with delicate shading. She tried to imagine what his paintings might have looked like.

What did William's paintings look like?

She'd asked that question of herself every day since he'd first come in the shop, but after what Joan had showed her, she'd decided not to look at his website again. She didn't need to see his paintings to do the work. And the fact was, she'd become surprised by how often she thought of him, vaguely nervous at the number of times a day her mind drifted back to the moment of his handshake, his rough-tender skin—no matter how often she told herself to stop.

Keep it professional, Rose. No Internet searches. No wandering mind.

Pages now occupied the whole of the long central table. They filled the room with a distinct scent: dust and musk, conjuring images of Italian summers, slanting sunlight and bougainvillea on the vine. The smell seemed to creep into her clothes and hair, fogging her thoughts. By the thirtieth page, it was as though she'd absorbed some aspect of the book—or perhaps it'd absorbed her, Giovanni gradually coaxing her to join him in his world of script and sketches. Her sensitive fingers registered each texture on the page. She found herself treating the vellum tenderly, as if it were living flesh.

Obsession was approaching, the way it often did. She could sense it coming on, soothing and hypnotic. Sometimes she wondered if this was how an alcoholic felt raising the glass after a dry spell. Knowing there'd be no going back. If a project excited her, she had the tendency to skip meals, to forget to open the shop or go outside. To stop brushing her hair. She'd been told such behavior was unhealthy—by teachers, by Joan. Even by Joan's mother, Aileen, in her tender, fretting way. *Everyone needs some fresh air, honey.* But her father had always said it was a special person who could focus their attention so absolutely. By the grace of his blessing, she'd never tried to fight it, though her tendencies made a lonesome companion. She didn't care to consider, however, how much her current focus might be related to the fact that the treatise was her one link to William.

After the two hours she'd designated were up, Rose forced herself to unlock the bookshop door and sit behind the desk. To smile politely and recite the right lines—*Would you like a receipt with that?*—her mind still fixated on what lay waiting in the back. When the last visitor left, she flipped the sign again. CLOSED. She stayed well into the night, cleaning, repairing, stacking. The playlist, set on repeat, cycled through in search of its own beginning. A quarter of the way into the book, she lifted another page.

A woman stared directly up at her.

Rose's heart contracted like a fist. In middle school, just after puberty struck, she'd devoured countless romance novels—secreting herself away in corners of the public library to read, too embarrassed to bring the books up to the desk and check them out. In those paperbacks, the female protagonist was usually described as "hauntingly beautiful." Rose had always wondered what that meant, exactly.

This, she decided, gazing down at the drawing. *It meant this.*

The woman's face consumed the page, minutely detailed down to her neck, which descended in quick lines indicating the slope of her shoulders. A single strand of pearls rolled across her clavicle, a jeweled pendant dangling at her breastbone. Her skin seemed luminous, the high planes of her face offset by shadows lingering in the bends and curves of her flesh, chalk and ink transforming the pendant into a glittering gemstone. The woman's features were a study in symmetry and proportion, yet it was her expression that overtook Rose. There was something half-hidden in it, a quality that grasped at the viewer like an undertow. Subtle shading at the corners of her mouth and eyes suggested melancholy, a magnetic vulnerability.

Rose leaned in, trying to dissect the composition. The rich tones of violins billowed out to fill the room, the bulbs overhead flickered. Rose stared at the woman and the woman stared back, and for a moment Rose saw life in those pupils, so deep and dark on the page. For a moment it felt as if the woman were trying to share something very, very important, if only Rose could understand—

She leaned back, blinking. Her heart beat hard against her sternum, her cheeks burned. Barely conscious of her actions, Rose carried the page to the drafting table and flicked on the lamps that were fastened to the edges. The tabletop shot into brightness. Centering the sketch, she pulled the camera forward to take a scan. Across the room, the image appeared on the computer screen. Even pixelated, the drawing still held its power. The skill of the artist was extraordinary—Rose had to assume it was Giovanni's, though there wasn't a signature. She also noticed an absence of perforations along the side of this sheet; the drawing must have been tucked inside the book after it was bound. As she waited for the scan to finish, Rose realized with a jolt she'd never responded to William's email. He'd want to see this.

She clicked Reply to his message and attached the image, then drumrolled her fingertips on the tabletop. Couldn't cut and paste this time.

W.
Thanks so much for returning the contract. I've actually already started work on the book. ~~You'll be glad to know~~ *The pages are in excellent condition, considering their age.*

~~I wanted to tell you~~ To keep you updated, I did reach out to a few ~~friends~~ contacts and have some interesting details about a mention of Giovanni in another text. ~~It's in a version of a treatise~~ It might be easiest to explain this in person when you stop by (which you're welcome to do at any time).

I found the attached portrait in going through the pages and thought you might like to see it. ~~It seems Giovanni was very talented—though I'm sure you're not surprised. :)~~ Giovanni was evidently very talented.

R.

She read it over again. Deleted the last line. Clicked Send.

William was up late. He walked through the muted house into the kitchen and poured himself a whiskey. Ice hit the glass, clattering into the silence. He didn't *want* to sleep was the truth of it. He wanted this time to himself.

Don't get enough time to yourself as is? He could hear Sarah's voice in his mind, sweet and sharp-edged, as he walked back to the dining room. It was true, though, he did get time to himself. After Jane and Lucy were dropped off at school, he had the whole day to himself. But days weren't the same, filled with light and the lists Sarah left on the counter: groceries to pick up, errands to run. Broken bits to fix around the house. *Or call a handyman,* she'd say, and he resented her for that every time. As if he couldn't fix his own home. Well . . .

No, nights were different. He could think at night, read his magazine articles, read his books. Click pointless links on the computer. Get angry at the news. Stare at his own reflection lit up in the windows, sitting at an empty dinner table. A forty-one-year-old. A dad. A man who used to be handsome, was still well known, but now whose hair was going gray—and worse, thinning on top.

Now heads didn't turn so quickly when he walked into a room, and he was forced to admit how much he needed them to, how much he'd relied on that small surge of confidence.

It's all part of the process, William. Not Sarah's voice this time, but their therapist back in New York. Lois. Lois with her carefully modulated expressions and thick gray hair that tucked just under her ears like a cap. She'd always worn the same shade of lipstick—a dark, matte red—and a variation of the same outfit for every meeting: slacks, sensible shoes, a chunky necklace in a bold color over a cream or taupe sweater. "Statement necklaces," Sarah had told him they were called. In the narrow office bathroom, framed inspirational messages hung on the walls—*Start where you are; What you do today can improve all your tomorrows*—and on more than one occasion William had wanted to punch through the glass and tear them right down the middle of their smug, Thomas Kinkade–style sunsets.

It wasn't that he didn't want the relationship to get better. It was just that from the start, Lois had so obviously thrown in with Sarah, so easily understood her side of things. *William, have you been listening, or just hearing?*

But I didn't do anything wrong!

It became his only fallback. Because it hadn't been him—it'd been her. It'd been Sarah he'd seen on the street when he came to surprise her for lunch, Sarah who'd been leaning against the wall outside her office, smoking. Since when had she started smoking again? Obeying instinct, William had ducked under the awning of a bodega across the street to watch, elbowing in between crates of oranges and bananas, browning limes. She was with a male coworker: tall, lanky, floppy brown hair—the sort William could imagine wearing boat shoes with no boat, pressed khakis on the weekends. They were laughing; the man had leaned in to whisper something and Sarah had laughed again, covering her mouth, collapsing one shoulder into his chest. Then they'd finished, thrown their butts on the ground, strolled back toward the glass doors.

That's when he'd seen it: the giveaway. The man held the door open, and as Sarah walked in, he'd pressed his hand to the small of her back, let it slide down over the curve of her pencil skirt. She'd turned her face up and smiled. A split-second exchange—too quick to catch without watching for it.

William was watching. She'd *smiled*.

Then the aftermath, so unremarkable it was painful—so like every other couple they'd known who'd suffered an affair. No, it didn't mean anything, it wasn't about the sex. No, she wasn't in love. Yes, she wanted to try. Yes, for the kids, they should try. No, not just for the kids. For all of them, they should try. And just like that they wilted, deflated, became yet another pedestrian pairing. A couple in the most practical sense of the word. William couldn't tell which hurt most: the act itself, or the way it made him feel so ... ordinary. A man in a marriage that suddenly needed work.

You're a mother! You're my wife! We weren't even fighting! He'd yelled at her quietly so as not to wake the girls—hissing through clenched teeth, awkward and unsatisfying.

I'm a woman, Will! She'd started sobbing, muffling the sound with the sleeve of her terry-cloth robe, which had loose threads at the cuffs, and which he hated.

I felt neglected.

He hadn't wanted to admit that part of him was angry she'd been the one to do it first, instead of him.

What was it Lois always liked to say? *Let's address the core wound.* The core wound, Lois, was blindness. They were two planets orbiting, he and Sarah, and there were whole faces of each other they couldn't see. He'd always understood that. He'd known it from the first gallery show he'd taken her to, when she'd gotten bored and begun imitating the expressions in the portraits, then bit his ear

and suggested cocktails. He'd known she'd only ever be able to judge
his art by how many paintings he sold, that there were vast territories inside him she'd never set foot in—the same way he'd never be
able to appreciate what she did as an attorney, the grace with which
she navigated intellectual property law. She'd tried to describe her
job once, on one of their first dates; he'd made a bad joke about
public domain and ordered another bottle of red. He hadn't thought
it mattered when there were so many other pieces that *did* fit together: likes and dislikes, a stupid sense of humor. And then, so
unexpectedly soon, their girls. Nothing could knit two people together more than that, more than biology. Could it? He thought
she'd understood the arrangement—that they both knew what
they were signing up for, together. What they'd get and not get.

That they were agreeing to say it was enough.

How could Sarah decide to change the rules now, so far in? All
this time, he'd thought their marriage was his one safety net, a thing
to be relied upon: that no matter how far they drifted they'd always
circle back, the way migratory birds find and refind their route.

*How have I neglected you? Aren't I a good father, haven't I always
been there?* She'd started crying again then, in those awkward arm-
chairs Lois had, that looked good from far away but once you sat
down you realized the seat was too hard and the arms oddly narrow. Anytime he'd tried to lean an elbow he'd ended up slipping off
the upholstery, which meant he sat with his hands folded in his lap
because crossing his arms would have made Lois ask why he was
feeling defensive. Sarah had plucked a fistful of tissues from the
box kept on the desk between them, listed a dozen offenses as she
wiped at her eyes: he'd stopped asking about her day, he wasn't interested in her cases, he didn't even notice the last time she'd cut her
hair.

Have I ever noticed your haircuts? To which Sarah had thrown
up her hands and shaken her head at Lois, as if to say, *See what I
mean?*

When it came down to it, though, he did understand Sarah, often better than she did herself. He'd spent years decoding every facial tic, each change in inflection. He might not notice haircuts, but he could tell she'd had a bad day just by the way she touched a hand to her throat. But if he was being honest—and if he couldn't be honest with himself, drinking alone at night, then what was the point?—he *had* stopped asking about her day, about the life going on inside her. They'd both stopped asking. Shifted into autopilot, let habit and routine rule. The same perfunctory kiss in the morning, reading on opposite sides of the bed at night. A single, efficient position for sex. They hadn't been fighting, but they hadn't been connecting either, by any stretch of the imagination.

What you focus on grows. That was another one of Lois's favorite expressions. William had pursed his lips and nodded each time she used it, looking pensive to hide the fact that he found her aphorisms condescending and reductive. But what really annoyed him was that after months of overthinking, he'd discovered the saying was actually apt. Consumed by her own dissatisfaction, Sarah had only focused on his blind spots, his shortcomings. She'd decided not to tally all the ways he had her memorized, all the ways he'd shown up.

She'd decided not to consider whether she ever asked about his art, his ideas, his day.

He didn't bring that up, of course. He could already hear how it'd be thrown back at him: *I'm always interested, you never open up.* In retrospect, he saw that she'd wanted to be found out—she'd wanted to force the issue. Her phone left unlocked on the table, excuses for running late that he should have seen through like wax paper held up to the light, had he thought to question her at all. Had he not completely trusted his own wife. It was only afterward that she regretted it, crying into her pillow loud enough for him to hear, as he slept on the living room couch.

So, blindsided. So, therapy. Then a break from therapy, at William's request, and a move north, at Sarah's request—to the town she grew up in, even though none of her family lived there anymore. *It's a wonderful place to raise kids.* It was also a wonderful solution to William's only real demand: that she no longer be in proximity to that man. Mr. Boat Shoes. At the time, a fresh start seemed the only option, and it all fell into place so easily. A house for rent with separate rooms for the girls. A legal firm looking for a new hire. But now he was realizing how much he missed the roar of the city at night, the ability to turn anonymous just by getting out at a different subway stop. This new place was too pretty, too clean, too quiet. He could hear himself think here.

William walked back to the kitchen. Two more fingers of whiskey, another rattle of ice. He took a sip from the glass; his reflection drank along with him. He wandered to the den. And what would Lois say about what he'd done at the bookshop? Taking his ring off like that. Even he didn't understand it, and he'd replayed the scene dozens of times: peering through the window, seeing her sitting there with a halo of auburn hair, looking for all the world like that Waterhouse painting, *The Lady of Shalott.* Then without stopping himself he was tugging his ring off, pocketing it, opening the door. Feeling something he hadn't felt since his early New York days, when he'd had nothing to lose, burn it all down. When even trash piles had seemed inspiring. He'd been so clear then. Present. Before he'd sold a single large canvas. Before Sarah.

Well, it just goes to show you—

"Oh, shut up, Lois." Out of habit, William sat down at his desk and opened his email.

6

GIO SAT AT THE STURDY WALNUT TABLE IN THE MIDDLE of his room. His drawing board stared back at him, expectant, with a blank sheet of parchment attached. He shut his eyes. An image of Chiara swam forward. He let it compose itself in his mind: form and shadow. The curved planes of her face. He opened his eyes and started to sketch, peering through his lenses. Coaxing the shapes out from the page with smooth, methodical strokes, he stopped every so often to step back and make a correction. After he'd arrived at an outline, he began to layer in shadows with rapid crosshatches. There was a science to this—to the darkness that arranged itself beneath her eyes, in the hollows of her cheeks, and above the cupid's bow of her mouth. He even knew the word for it: *sciographia*. The science of shadows.

As he sketched, he couldn't help but think of Venier, gray-haired and rasping. Breathing his wine-breath over her. He wondered how they'd met. Had Domenico arranged it all? And where had *he* been the exact moment of the brokerage—what insignificant occupation had fixed his attention while Chiara's company was bargained away? Gio cursed himself for missing so many of Domenico's salons, for the way he'd retreated from the world at large once he'd realized he was losing his sight.

As if in response to his mood, angry shouts erupted in the street. Outside the shutters, two young men were grappling on the stones like Grecian wrestlers. Neighbors rushed to pry the boys apart, one already bleeding from a gash across his cheek. This was the third fight in as many days—and just the night before, on his walk home, Gio had inadvertently disturbed a pair of lovers coupling, frantic as dogs, in the shadows between buildings. A strange mood had descended over the city, in no small part due to Aurelio's prediction.

Just as the alchemist had warned, Selim's ambassador to France had been arrested. He was being held on charges even the washerwomen recognized as flimsy excuses to detain a spy. Rumors had begun circulating that Nassi was conspiring with the Jews who, after being expelled from Spain and Portugal, had taken up residence in Venice's Ghetto. The yellow badges all Jews were required to wear had begun attracting increased suspicion—already, Gio had watched a Semite he knew to be an accomplished physician sprint down the avenues, chased by a band of restless drunks. Seemingly overnight, the reality of war had set in. While younger men brawled and boasted, those old enough to remember Venice's last skirmish with the Ottomans looked on grimly and muttered into their wine.

Gio turned away from the shutters and sat back down at his sketch. As the ruckus outside faded, he focused on molding the features of Chiara's face. Her high cheekbones, her clever eyes. Line by line, she began to take form. While drawing, he could let his gaze linger on her in a way he knew he'd never be able to in real life. He took care to capture the lift of her chin, the arch of her right eyebrow. How she held her mouth just short of a smile. As the light outside ripened and warmed, she came to life on the page.

A loud knock interrupted him for a second time. With a start, Gio realized he'd worked through the morning: his stomach was tight and empty. Hastily, he tucked the sketch into a stack of papers on the table and hid his glasses in their pouch. Opening the door, he caught a young page on the stoop preparing to knock again, a clenched fist suspended in the air between them. Behind him crouched Lucio, the neighbor's child, leaning in to eavesdrop. The boy had an abundance of brown curls and a round, expressive face; Gio often used him as a model when he needed to draw cherubs.

"Is this the residence of Giovanni Lomazzo?" The page's posture was stiff, and he kept his eyes trained on a spot just above Gio's head. He wore Venier's livery: navy doublet and hose, topped by a floppy cap embroidered with gold thread. Gio guessed him to be at the nascence of his career. Resisting the urge to grin, he gave a nod.

"Your presence is requested by Sebastiano Venier on Sunday next." The page whipped his left arm up, presenting a rolled parchment. A fat round of crimson wax, branded with Venier's insignia, held the roll together. Lucio's eyes widened. He stepped forward to tug on the man's cloak. "I know who that is!" The boy was afflicted with a lisp.

"Aren't you fortunate." The page straightened up, pulling the fabric from Lucio's grasp. Undeterred, Lucio snatched at the hem again.

"My mother says he's going to be the next doge!"

"God willing, your mother is correct. Now, good day!" The courier yanked his cloak back and, with a curt nod to Gio, spun on one heel and strode off down the avenue. Gio ventured out onto the stoop to watch his retreat, just in time to catch a neighbor's low-hanging line of laundry nearly sweep the lad's cap off. Stumbling and clutching at his head, the courier still managed to fling his robes out importantly before disappearing around the corner. Chuckling, Gio turned back inside, only to find that Lucio had already clambered up onto a chair.

"Where's your mother, Lucio?"

"At the well." The child kicked his feet under the table.

"Ah, I see." Lucio's father had passed away some years earlier, forcing his mother, Francesca, to join her sister's already overfilled household. Though she had the bones of a pretty face, twin lines now marked the space between Francesca's brows, and her hair was shot with streaks of silver—as if some fiend had reached in and sucked her youth away with a single, mighty gasp.

"Well, let's practice your reading then." After scanning the message, Gio set the parchment on the table in front of Lucio. The boy's soft face trembled with concentration as he tried to parse the words.

"Gio, I can't read it. The writing's too fancy."

Gio leaned over to look. "Ah yes, I suppose the scribe did overdo himself, didn't he?" Ruffling Lucio's curls, he sat down beside the boy. Tracing the letters with an index finger, he slowly read the note out loud. It was an invitation to a formal dinner.

"Are you going to go?" Lucio whispered loudly in excitement.

"I think so, yes," Gio whispered loudly back. "I've never been one to say no to a free meal."

"What will happen when you go?" Lucio rested one cheek on a plump fist.

"Well, usually there's plenty of food and wine. Sometimes some of the people drink too much of the wine."

"My uncle does that," Lucio confided.

"Yes, I know." Lucio's uncle was fond of singing at full volume in the avenue on such occasions. "Often, there's music and dancing. There may even be news from Rome."

"You must promise to tell me everything."

Gio smiled at the child's earnestness. "Of course. Now, here, go find your mother." He snatched a seeded roll from a basket on the table and set it down at the boy's elbow. "If you come back later, perhaps we can practice more reading."

Grasping the roll with both hands, Lucio slid off the chair and ran from the room in typical headlong fashion, the door banging shut behind him. Gio surveyed the invitation again, trying to imagine what the evening might hold. Chatter and smells and a blur of faces. He tried and failed to imagine a reality in which Chiara might be interested in him too—the city's most beautiful courtesan and an artist going blind. He smiled without bitterness.

Tossing the parchment aside, he hunted through the stack of papers until he found her portrait again.

On the night of the dinner, a sliver of new moon cast only a dim glow. Gondoliers glided through the canals, the wet push of their oars lapping under the click of footsteps on cobblestone. Murmuring voices echoed in the streets as shadowy figures made their way across avenues and over bridges to the great house on the corner. This was an evening for courtesans. Gio watched as woman after woman carefully navigated the stone streets toward waiting gondoliers, their *chopines*—the high clogs that were so in fashion—forcing them to clutch at the arms of their attendants. In the backs of passing boats, pale faces flickered by.

He entered the front hall unseen, slipping between bodies adorned in vivid silks, jewels, capes lined with fur. Following the crush of the crowd into the courtyard, he mounted the wide formal stairs to the *portego*. Before, the great hall had seemed gapingly empty. Now, tables extended the length of the passage, set with candles and the first course from the sideboard—fresh grapes and marzipan, dense spiced cakes, prosciutto cooked in wine with capers, sliced pork tongues and sweet mustards. His senses swam in the heavy odors wafting from the food, from the perfumed skin of every woman. The room was already clotted with guests, and more were entering in a steady surge. Servants dashed through the jostling crowd, balancing trays of wine.

Gio slid into an empty chair a comfortable distance from the head of the table, where Venier sat, with Corvino to his right. At his left, Chiara looked luminous in the torchlight—and with a heavy hand clasped over hers on the table, Venier blatantly claimed her. Corvino, meanwhile, was already deep in conversation with a stern-looking fellow Gio recognized as Francesco Bressan: Venice's master shipbuilder. Bressan was said to be turning old transport galleys into mighty instruments of war, with forecastles strong enough to mount batteries of guns, culverins, and cannons. The Crow leaned forward to listen to the man, his muscled forearms crossed on the table, sleek hair tucked behind his ears. From time to time he peered up, noting the new arrivals. Gio couldn't be sure but thought he caught a nod in his direction. To be safe, he dipped his head in exchange.

Gazing around, Gio took stock of the attendees himself. He spotted members of the Council of Ten and the Signoria, two Medicis, and a handful of others he knew he should be able to place but couldn't quite. The weight of their dark-robed presence was offset by a profusion of women—all dressed in brilliant hues, breasts propped high, their rouged and powdered faces creasing as they laughed.

"Well, this is quite an evening."

Gio directed his words to the old man who'd slid into the seat beside him. The man's back was curved with age, and wisps of hair swayed at the top of his head, as though they'd been affixed as an afterthought. At the sound of Gio's voice he turned, revealing a pair of eyes gone milky with blindness.

Gio choked on his wine, sending an acrid burn shooting down his throat.

"Mmmm, yes." The old man smiled, unoffended. "I imagine so." His voice was raspy, friable as aged parchment. When his thin lips stretched into a grin, Gio noticed spittle glistening in the corners. "Let's hope it's not a last meal."

"A last meal?"

"Venier's last. If he's appointed admiral, he'll soon be off to fight the Ottomans."

"Do you think he will be?"

The old man sucked his lips in, his useless eyes squinting. "The worse my sight becomes, the better I hear the whispers." He tapped the side of his nose with a forefinger, knowingly. His nail was long, the tip yellow and brittle-looking. Age spots spattered the crepey skin of his hand. "There are a few dissenting voices, but Venier will overcome them." He tipped his head in the statesman's direction. "He'll do well. I stood beside him in many a battle. Years ago, of course. But he's a fighter, through and through." Gio glanced up at their host, already red-faced and laughing. Beside him, Chiara poured more wine into his glass.

Just then, a pair of doors opened midway down the hall. The room filled with the sizzling smell of meat as servants brought out first sweetbreads and liver, then partridge in sauce and spit-roasted rabbit and quail. Exclamations rippled through the crowd at an encore of whole calves' heads and roasted geese. The chefs had masked the geese back into life, meticulously returning each feather to its original place on the cooked carcasses. Soon, every mouth was sheened with grease, the guests glossed in torchlight as they chattered. The conversation swelled to a heady roar, punctuated by shrill female laughter.

"Do you believe we'll win the war?" Gio resumed their conversation.

"I'd put my faith in Venier, that's for certain. He's sharp, with an instinct for survival. I don't see why he keeps that infernal Crow around, but otherwise he's a logical mind. A sound tactician." The old man took a bite and chewed contemplatively, staring out into a personal void.

"You mean Corvino." Gio lowered his voice as though they could be heard above the din and clatter.

"Yes, yes, of course." Swallowing, the old man waved a dismissive hand, unconcerned by who might be listening. "He's a shrewd one, I'll give him that. Pecks his way into knowing just what you want to hide." He leaned in close. With fascination, Gio observed the lack of pupil, the mucous film.

"I've been watching him, you know." The old man shot Gio another thin-lipped grin—then abruptly, his face went somber, loose flesh sagging on either side of a frown. "What Venier wants with him is Venier's business. As I said, he's a sound tactician." Finished with both the conversation and his meal, the man pushed himself back from the table and set to work cleaning his teeth with the nail of his left littlest finger. Gio looked away.

Soon, servants entered to clear the remains of the dinner. Gio spotted Cecilia, with her parted hair and solemn expression, rushing in and out of the room alongside the others. As the main course was removed, delicacies were brought out in quick succession: quince pastries and pear tarts, cheeses and roasted chestnuts, rings of sweet cakes with blood-red jams and spiced preserves. A burnt sugar smell drifted in as the doors swung open and closed. The voices in the room buzzed thickly.

Finally, the eating drew to an end, and Venier stood, swaying. Chiara reached out to steady him; he grasped her hand tightly. *Did she wince?* Gio couldn't be certain.

"Ladies and gentlemen!" The statesman beamed out at the crowd with glazed eyes. "I invite you to join me in the next room for our evening's entertainment." He tugged Chiara to stand and, elbows interlocked, they turned and walked away—down the hall and through a set of doors at the far end. Her pale dress trailed along the polished floor, then slipped out of view like a wisp of smoke.

Instantly, the guests stood and thronged forward, jostling to follow the pair. In the drunken crowd, Gio lost sight of the old man. Then he caught the curve of his shrunken frame, descending the stairs, gripping the arm of his page. Gio watched as the two retreated, step by step, out of the candlelight and into the night's darkness.

When he turned back, most of the crowd had already gone in. Striding down the hall, he navigated around lingering clusters of guests, past the dull portraits, then eased through the door of the far chamber. Inside, the audience had packed itself tightly into the corners of the room—center stage, a troupe of musicians waited, instruments in hand. Sidling along a back wall, Gio peered at the troupe through a sea of heads. The powdered hair of the women rose up around him like miniature geological formations.

Abruptly, the musicians launched into a dancing tune. Just as quickly, a handful of women swirled into arrangement in the center of the floor. Gio pressed his back against the wall. It was peaceful there, watching. Figures swept in and out of his reduced field of vision: swatches of color and slightly blurred forms. Slowly, he moved his head first left then right, scanning the scene. Just as the music ebbed, a flare of gold streaked into view. It was Chiara, standing breathless and flushed in front of him.

"Dance with me."

Without waiting for an answer, she grabbed his hand and pulled him onto the floor. They joined the line of dancers that had already formed, men facing women. With a swell, the music began again, pipe and tabor. He stood still as she circled him with precise steps, the fabric of her skirt held out with one hand like a low white wing. Her cheeks were the same color as the pink embroidery on her stiff bodice. For once, Gio was glad he'd taken care to dress properly. Though his doublet and hose were a subdued burgundy, they were still of fine quality—fine enough for him to be seen dancing with her.

When she returned to position, they bowed to each other.

The men took their turn next. Leaping in short tight bounds, Gio landed along her right side, then her left. A brief surprise crossed her face, and he couldn't help but feel a surge of pride. Blindness be damned, at least he could still dance a galliard. Drawing his fingertips and thumb to his mouth, he gave the symbolic kiss before reaching out. She mirrored the gesture, her hand warm in his. He glided them around the room, her training evident in the way she responded to the slightest pressure from his palm. His heart quickened to match the pace of the drums, the high melody of the pipe rising above the murmur of the crowd.

Though he couldn't spot Venier, Gio knew he must be watching. He tried to keep their motions prescribed, a careful choreography. But as they twirled her eyes shone, her teeth flashed in a reckless smile, and the room dropped away around them. No more staring spectators—no more music, even. All he could see was her face, bordered in shadow, dazzling and mesmeric. All he could hear was her breath in his ear as he pulled her close for *la volta*.

As if they'd done it a hundred times before, she slid her arms around his shoulders when he grasped the base of her bodice. In one sure move, he lifted her up against his hip; her body softened into his. She pressed her cheek to his neck as they whirled, the bones of her rib cage hard under his hand, and suddenly it was only the two of them, outside time, marionettes in the spotlight on an empty stage.

And then it was done. Without any awareness of parting, he saw her standing across from him, taking the final bow, smiling. Dimpling her cheeks, at *him*. He stared, dazed, and she grinned wider, winked one eye in a quick, secret gesture. Then other hands were reaching out, grabbing for her, elbows in his sides as the cast of dancers rearranged themselves on the floor. Someone pushed him backward, harder than they'd probably meant to. He staggered. She laughed at all the attention, a hollow, artificial sound. The walls of the room suddenly felt close.

Forcing his way through the crowd, Gio cut a path toward the entry and slipped outside. Bending, he gripped his knees, fighting to calm his breath. A tangle of music and voices spilled from the seams of the closed door, into the emptied hall, where servants were cleaning the carnage from the tables: spilled glasses and stained linens. Bones and gristle and the uneaten hearts of stone fruits. No one noticed as he made his way to the open door leading to the servants' stairs.

As he descended, a gradual layering of voices grew audible. In the empty lower passageway, torch flames threw wavering shadows across the walls, interrupted halfway down by a brassy yellow beam shooting out from a door left ajar—severe as the bolt from a lighthouse lantern. Silently, he edged toward it.

"And what does Bressan say?" Venier's voice. Gio would know it anywhere.

"The galleasses are ready. Field tests are needed, but Bressan is confident the side cannons will perform."

"Selim has arrested all our diplomats in the empire." Gio didn't recognize the others speaking.

"Yes, but one of Selim's ministers has a physician, a Jew: Solomon Ashkenazi. He's a sworn enemy of Nassi." Venier's voice again. "He's pledged to help us maintain communication—and he tells us what we already know: Nicosia will fall, and, soon after, Famagusta. Cyprus will not stand without her strongholds."

"We cannot wait any longer—"

"We must have the support of Rome." An old voice then, dry and familiar. Gio couldn't quite place it.

"*Yours?*" The words were spoken close, so soft he barely heard. He started.

It was Cecilia, standing beside him with his cloak in her hands.

He took it without thinking. Then, with more force than he'd imagined her capable of, she clasped his arm and ushered him down the hall to the front entrance. Too surprised to protest, he let himself be thrust outside, back into the garden.

"Trust me, sir, you do not wish to be thought a spy," she whispered sharply, her pale face peering out from the shadowy doorframe. Overhead, the trees rustled and shushed at them.

"Thank you." It was all he could manage before the door latched shut and he found himself in the avenues, walking home alone, the stars singeing tight white pinpricks in the sky.

Miles away from Nicosia, the port of Famagusta hovered near the sea. Together, the two cities served as Cyprus's strongholds—though only Famagusta could boast newly restored fortifications, bastions and towers. Snaking in from the countryside, a dirt road wound its way toward the city gates; in the heat of the midday sun it lay vacant and parched. If anyone had been watching, they would have seen a black speck emerge in the distance, growing as it neared, eventually taking the form of a dark-headed boy on a horse. Dust kicked up behind the mare's heels, and with each stride the head of the boy bobbed listlessly: both horse and rider were in desperate need of water. A wooden box was strapped to the front of the saddle, and the boy clung to it as he rode, reins gripped tight in one fist. Tucked away in his pouch was a stiff scroll of parchment with the name of MarcAntonio Bragadin scrawled across it.

Bragadin: Captain of the Kingdom of Cyprus.

The box changed hands four times before it landed in Bragadin's chambers. Another quarter of an hour passed before the captain himself entered the room. He was a tall man, composed of lean lines: limbs roped with muscle, a drooping mustache that lost itself in the whorls of a chest-length beard. When he'd heard a package had arrived for him, he hadn't wondered at its origins. His scouts had already informed him that Ottoman forces had landed, led by Mustafa Pasha.

Yet no one had thought to warn him of the smell.

As soon as he opened his chamber door, the odor thrust him back into the hallway—sulfurous and searing, as if flesh and waste had mingled, then fermented for weeks under the full weight of a summer sun. Bragadin gagged, retreating, stumbling to a narrow window along the passageway to regain his breath. He'd had just enough time to catch sight of a parchment in the room, next to the box; steeling himself, he clasped an elbow over his face and darted inside once again to grab at the scroll. Back in the passageway he gasped, nearly retching, clawing the smell from his beard, grateful no attendants were nearby to witness the display.

Letting a breeze drift over his face, Bragadin turned his attention to the parchment. Slowly, he unwound the document. Written in imperfect Italian, the message contained what he knew it must.

Terms of a surrender.

Dropping his hands, Bragadin gazed out at the sky—a tranquil, cloudless cerulean. As the comforting babel of an unsuspecting marketplace wafted up from the square below, he contemplated the sturdy stone walls that ringed his citadel. He did not know how skilled a commander Mustafa might be, but he knew what mattered most: his men were grossly outnumbered.

How long could they possibly hold?

7

THE LIGHT SAID IT WAS LATER THAN EXPECTED—SHE must have slept through her alarm. Lace curtains in the window stenciled a hot white pattern across the bedspread. All night long she'd dreamt of the woman from the sketch, those hypnotic eyes staring out at her no matter where she turned. The heater clicked on. She'd forgotten to shut it off before falling asleep, and now she was coated in a thin film of sweat. Throwing back the covers, Rose sat up and rubbed her eyes. What time had she gotten home?

The email! Her computer was perched on the bedside table; her fingers were frantic and barely operable as she typed in the password. Wrong. She typed it again. The log-in bar shook its head. Wrong. Finally, her in-box appeared. What she'd hoped to see was there: his response, sent at two in the morning. Had he really been up that late?

R—

Thanks so much for sending this scan. The sketch is amazing!
Would you mind if I swing by the shop, maybe in the afternoon?
I'd love to see it in person.

W.

Rose pushed the keys impulsively.

W—please do. R.

Sent. Sent too quickly—she should have said something else: scheduled a time at the very least. Made an appointment. Written something that conveyed some semblance of professionalism. She stood naked, sticky from sweat and dazed, her words staring back at her from the screen, irretrievable.

The only thing she could do now was get ready. After a quick shower, she stood in front of the bathroom mirror, wiped the fog away with a forearm, and examined its version of her. The heft of her breasts, the slant of her hips. Her collarbone. The mole on her left rib cage. The small birthmark on her neck, like a tea stain. She stroked the wet hair back from her face, watching light attach itself to her cheeks.

Under the sink, she slid open a rarely used cabinet drawer. Inside were two shiny tubes, one long, one short: mascara and lipstick. She unscrewed the mascara and dipped the wand back and forth in the tarry pigment. Leaning forward, lids half-closed, she dragged the brush over her lashes. Their length was always a surprise. The lipstick had been a gift from Joan, from the Chanel counter at the mall. It had a powdery, velvet fragrance. What was it Joan had said? *Rose, if only you'd try.* So, here she was, trying. For someone as unavailable as they came: married, with children. And trying why, because he'd made eye contact? Because their hands had touched, and it'd melted the floor out from underneath her?

Well, couldn't she at least enjoy this feeling—a silver tingle of anticipation, trilling up the length of her skin like fingertips—even knowing nothing would come of it? There wasn't any harm in that. How long had it been, anyway? Rose thought of her last boyfriend, Seth, a fellow grad student who'd worn cardigans with elbow patches and believed in the spirit of socialism, though when it came to dinner and drinks, he'd had decidedly bourgeois tastes. They'd drifted together through shared classes, the way it always seemed to happen. Now that she thought about it, all her relationships— all three of them—had been dictated by the steadying structure of school: study dates, weekend movies, road trips over the holidays. Subdued breakups during the long summers, once because Rose had realized she was so bored that she'd rather study alone, twice because of school transfers. None of them ever getting too serious, the specter of the "real world" always hovering on the horizon, with its implications of tremendous change.

Now she was officially in that real world, where daily opportunities to meet like-minded scholars weren't conveniently provided, her life no longer organized into neat quarters and semesters. That must be why she felt so light-headed, in fact. It was just the thrill of knowing she was going to see someone, on purpose, and discuss topics she cared about. The promise of a meaningful conversation about history and restoration. That was all.

Rose sighed with relief.

"Just enjoy the feeling. It doesn't hurt anyone. And it's good for you to feel something again." She did her best impression of Joan, talking back to the mirror. She leaned closer to her own face. Carefully, she pressed the color along the arc of her lips, then wet them with her tongue, crushed them together to blend the red.

Looking at her reflection, she almost didn't recognize herself.

Back at the shop, Rose left her coffee on the desk and retreated to the operating room. At the drafting table, she arranged the portrait of the woman so that it was perfectly centered. Before leaving, she chose a classical album and put it on repeat; she liked the idea of music playing from the speakers when they came in.

Settling in out front, she went through the motions of work: shuffling papers on her desk, tucking wayward pens tidily into their jar. Odin leapt from his roost on a chair, circling three times in the middle of a sunbeam before flopping down on one side to begin a bath. Dust motes swirled aimlessly in the air above him. Rose scrolled through her already read emails. On the bike ride in, she'd vowed not to just sit and stare at the sidewalk. Yet for the first few hours, she couldn't help but raise her head at even the smallest movement. Finally, after lunch—turkey on rye from the corner deli, bought hurriedly, with furtive peeks out the window just in case he showed up—she forced herself to focus on a single task: tracking down the version of Borghini's *Il Riposo* Yuri had mentioned. She wanted to see the author's notes and imagined William would too. Time slipped by as she burrowed down spiraling tunnels of Internet research. Eventually, she emerged with the names of four promising leads. As the only customers made their way out—a pair of older women with salon-set hair, who'd loudly debated options for their next book club meeting before deciding, definitively, on *Lady Chatterley's Lover*—Rose began to formulate her first letter of inquiry to a collector. She was eight lines in when the door creaked open.

He was wearing the same black vest as before, but had on a navy button-up shirt now, sleeves rolled to his elbows, and a gray wool cap that somehow made his eyes seem darker. As he stepped inside, William palmed the cap off and tucked it into the back pocket of his jeans.

"Hello."

"Hello." She stood, weightless.

"Thanks for letting me come by."

"Of course. Want to turn that around while we're in back?" She gestured to the door.

He looked to see the sign hanging in the window and flipped it over. CLOSED. "Hey, I didn't mean for you to close up. I can come back—"

"No, no, it's absolutely fine. It's a slow day. The portrait's all set up, I can show you . . ." She stepped out from behind the desk and started toward the workroom, beckoning him to follow. She'd worn a skirt instead of jeans for once, and her favorite pair of black mary jane pumps. The heels made a cold clicking on the wood floor. Halfway down the hall, she paused to look back. He wasn't behind her. Retracing her steps, she caught sight of Odin's hind paws, peeking out from behind a bookcase. A few more paces and the whole scene came into view: Odin, shamelessly sprawled on his back, legs splayed in all four directions. William crouching down over the cat, silver ring flashing as his hand moved back and forth across Odin's belly. Both of them framed in a beam of late-day sun.

"Friendly creature you've got here." He looked up and smiled, a dimple digging into his left cheek. She noticed he'd shaved.

"That's Odin. He's completely spoiled." Rose glared at the cat, who purred louder, shooting her a smug upside-down grin. His one green eye nodded shut. "Do you have any pets?"

William gave the cat a final scratch, then stood with a sigh. "No, but we've thought about a puppy." *We.*

"Oh. That's nice." What else could she say? At their feet, Odin gave a disgruntled *mew*, then feigned distraction by rolling over and licking at a paw. "Well, let's take a look?"

"Sure."

This time he followed close behind, waiting politely as she slid the old-fashioned key into the lock. The bolt shot back with a smooth metallic *clang*, like the cocking of a gun. Rose swung open the door.

"So, *this* is your studio . . ." He strode past her, boyishly fascinated.

Trying to keep the pride from her voice, she began to explain the fundamentals of her tools as he paced the long central table, looking at the pages laid out on backing sheets. Her brushes, blades, and fibers—

"Oh! Chopin!" he interrupted, pointing a finger upward, as if the music came from the ceiling. The song had just changed.

"Opus nine, number two." Rose smiled, stepping to turn the speakers up.

"Impressive." He grinned back. "Okay, so, what's the exact process of the restoration—how do you do it?" He bent to peer at Giovanni's writing, hands clasped behind him like he was at a museum exhibition.

"Well, first I do an initial cleanup of any dirt or residue. I'll need to remove a bit of wax here, for example, where he wrote by candlelight." She pointed to a drop of yellowed tallow. He reached out a fingertip to touch it.

"Some of the pages are very fragile. That's why I've set them on backing sheets while I work. If I'm doing a full restoration, I'll repair the tears with a special fiber and match the ink to make the faded words more legible. With a palimpsest I have to be careful not to disrupt the undertext . . ." She trailed off—he'd caught sight of the portrait. A second later and he was hovering over it, palms resting on either edge of the drafting table. As she neared to stand next to him, he shifted to one side, shoving his hands in his vest pockets.

"Extraordinary, isn't it?" Rose whispered, as if the woman could hear. He nodded, then glanced at the lamps mounted to the table.

"Do you mind?"

"Of course not." Rising onto her toes, she flicked each switch.

The gleam drew the details of the image into sudden focus. For a long minute they stood side by side in silence, staring at the sketch. From the page, the woman gazed back at them with her intelligent eyes, her half smile. Erstwhile sunlight fractured in her irises, in the facets of the pendant dangling at her chest.

"And this is just done with ink and chalk. Imagine what his paintings must have been like." William shook his head. "Look at the way he handled that gemstone—that's not easy, to get those reflections."

"Sapphire would be my guess." Rose clasped her elbows in her palms.

"Excuse me?"

"I'd guess the stone is a sapphire. It was a common gem to give women during the Renaissance—it represented wisdom and fidelity. Shows up in a lot of portraits."

"Wisdom and fidelity . . ." William repeated the words. Rose noticed his hand moving in his vest pocket, like he was flipping a coin. "I wonder who she was." He directed his question at the drawing.

"It's hard to say, really. She could have been anyone . . . a model, his lover. His muse. Maybe all three?" In her peripheral vision, she caught him turn to look at her. "It's nice not knowing, in a way. It frees up the imagination. Lets you see her without the assumptions you'd make if you knew who she was."

"I like that. No assumptions."

Standing so close, she couldn't help but think that he was exactly tall enough for her to rest her cheek on his chest, if she just leaned forward slightly . . . The back of her neck suddenly went warm.

Rose turned to the center of the room.

"The book is definitely a treatise on art. Here—look." She gestured at the charts where Giovanni had outlined the proportions of human anatomy. William gave a last lingering glance at the portrait, then trailed after her, moving to stand on the opposite side of the table.

"It almost looks like a reference book." He bent, scanning the writing. "Oh! That's interesting—I see the word *chiara* repeated in the undertext. That's 'light,' right? Chiaroscuro?"

"Yes, exactly. In the top layer there are lots of art terms that I recognize: 'shadow,' 'proportion,' 'composition' . . . Also, I wanted to let you know I reached out to a few experts, and one of them said he'd seen a reference to Lomazzo in a piece by Raffaello Borghini." At his blank expression, she clarified: "Borghini was kind of like an early art critic. He wrote a document, all about religious paintings. It's pretty historically significant. Anyway, my friend said he'd seen a version with the name Lomazzo in the author's notes. If that's referring to your Lomazzo, to this treatise, then you might want to think about publishing when we're done. It could be very important, especially to art historians."

William rubbed the back of his head. "Well, that's great, but— I'll be honest, it isn't really the academic stuff that matters to me. I mean, sure, I'll share it if you think people will want to read it, but . . ." He leaned his hips forward as he looked down at the pages, his belt buckle clacking against the steel of the table. "I'm just mostly amazed to find out that my ancestor was an artist too, you know? What are the odds . . ."

"Well, some people think creativity can be inherited. Is your family artistic?"

"No, not at all. My father's a preacher. My mom—" He scratched a forearm, thinking. His nails were wide and flat. "Well, my mom's a fantastic quilter, actually. That was sort of an 'approved' art form for women in her generation. I'm from the South." He scrunched his face up at her as if that both explained everything and offered some form of apology.

"And your grandparents?"

"My father's father was a tailor, so I guess that's creative. He was an Italian immigrant. I really don't know much about my mother's side except that they were Italian too." As he spoke, he walked around the perimeter of the table, scanning the diagrams, until he ended up next to her.

"Well, quilting and tailoring sound pretty artistic to me." Rose tried to imagine William's grandfather sketching suit designs.

"How about you? Were your family all, um . . . into books?" He grinned at how the question sounded.

She shot a smile back at him. "I should know a lot more about my family tree than I do, unfortunately. I think some of them were Quakers originally; we've been on the East Coast awhile. But my dad was a professor of classics at the university, so—yes, he was into books. Very much so. He passed a few months ago." *Why did she tell him that?*

"Oh God, I'm sorry." He grasped his chin in his hand, like a ball in a mitt. "Is your mom still around?"

"No, she died of cancer when I was a teenager. Official orphan." Rose gave a stiff shrug of her shoulders.

"I'm so sorry," he repeated.

"It's okay. Happens to us all eventually, right?" Her skin felt stretched and hot; she pressed the heels of both palms to her cheeks, then linked her fingers behind her neck.

"It does." He reached out to touch her back.

His hand was so broad it covered the full expanse of her shoulder blade, the tips of his fingers lining up along her spine. It was meant as a sympathetic gesture, she knew that, yet heat still shivered down through her. Her body was disintegrating—all she could feel was the place where his palm spread over her. She was barely able to register that he was still talking:

"Listen, I can get out of here now. I really appreciate you letting me take a look at the sketch though." He drew his hand away, but the sensation of it lingered like a brand.

"Oh! You're welcome, anytime." The words spilled out automatically, a routine phrase her mind was fortunately able to summon, while the rest of her body shook itself out of its stupor.

Still feeling his handprint on her shoulder, Rose opened the workroom door. As she led them through the shop, a new sound emerged to layer over the click of her heels. While they'd been in the back, storm clouds had blown in: now rain streaked down sideways, spattering the windows. Broad puddles were already forming on the concrete outside, the light darkened like a dimmer switch had been lowered.

William stepped forward to peer up at the sky. "Wow, really coming down. Guess we couldn't hear it with the music."

Rose joined him at the window, gazing out at her bike locked to a post on the sidewalk. It had a wicker basket attached to its front; water was now pitifully leaking through the gaps in the weave. More rain pooled on the seat, snaking off in thin streamers. "Why do I always forget to check the forecast?"

He followed her stare. "Did you bike here? I can give you a ride home if you want. It's no problem."

"Really?" Rose took another look at her bike. "Actually, that would be amazing."

He held the door open as she ran to undo the bike lock, her trench coat clutched over her head. At least the canvas was somewhat waterproof. While he waited, she wheeled the bike to her workroom, where it began dripping onto the linoleum. Coming back out front, she wiped the wet from her hands, then picked up her bag from behind the register.

"Okay, ready."

"I'm just around the corner." The wool cap reappeared from his pocket, was tugged on.

They made a run for it, leaping around and over puddles. As they neared the truck, Rose aimed wrong: her foot landed squarely in the center of a pool, water splashing up over the top of her pump.

She squealed and hopped, shaking her leg. William spun around and laughed at her, head thrown back in the rain. It didn't matter, they were both drenched. He pulled a key from his vest pocket and unlocked her side before jogging around to the driver's seat. They slammed their doors shut.

"God, it's pouring." Her bun had come loose; she tossed her head over her knees to gather the hair together, twisting it up into a damp knot. "Nice truck."

"Yeah, it works for hauling lumber; I make my own frames. Okay, where am I heading?" He pulled out into the street, flicking on the windshield wipers.

"Oh, right." She gave him her address, fastening her seatbelt. "Just past the dog park."

"That's fine, I'm out in the burbs." The car picked up speed. For a few moments they drove in silence, save for the pummel of rain on the windows, the soft *swish* of cars passing in the opposite direction, tires churning puddles.

"Want some chocolate?" He pointed to an unopened bar that sat tucked in the center console. Rose leaned to slide it out. Dark cacao and sea salt.

"Okay, but only because it has sea salt on it. . . . Do you want a piece?" She flipped the bar over, tugged apart the stiff adhesive on the back.

"Sure." He held out a hand. Rose cracked the chocolate along its molded demarcations, deposited a section into his waiting palm, the same one he'd touched her back with. She saw lines etched into his flesh, clear and deep, like a tree. The car fell silent again as they both sucked on their squares, grains of tangy salt rubbing the roofs of their mouths. Their heat had started fogging the windows; William turned the defroster on. Lukewarm air began blowing up over the dash.

"So, Rose." He cleared his throat, shifting in his seat. "How'd you get into the restoration business?"

"Well, hmm." She considered, watching rain burst and streak across the glass on all sides. "I've always liked books a lot. Like I said, my father taught classics, so I was in the archives even as a kid. I eventually figured out that I liked books as material objects as much as I liked reading them, so I ended up getting a degree in restoration. That was in New York." She pulled a strand of hair loose at her temple, started twisting it around a finger. "Then my dad got sick, and I needed to come home to take care of him, but I still wanted to work with books so . . . I guess it all just sort of fell into place . . ."

"Well, it seems to be working out so far; the store's charming."

"Thank you. It definitely helps to be by an Ivy League school—most of those students have pretty healthy book-buying allowances."

William chuckled. "I can only imagine. You know, I used to live in New York also."

She glanced at him out of the corner of her eye, his silhouette slipping past houses and lawns, a sudden surge of dark green as they reached the park. "Really? What made you move?"

He cleared his throat again. "Ahh. Well, my wife grew up here, and she thought it'd be a better spot for our kids. I have two girls. Six and nine." There. He'd said it: *Wife. Kids.* Everything out in the open now. The back of his skull prickled; he readjusted his grip on the wheel. Another bout of rain slapped the windshield.

"It's calmer here than in New York, that's for sure." Rose turned to stare again at the water veining down her window. Her seatbelt suddenly felt too tight; she tugged at it, pulling it away from her ribs.

"You grew up here too, right? Maybe you know her—my wife? Her name would have been Sarah Larsen. She was a cheerleader, I'm not sure which school." As soon as he said it, he regretted it: Rose had to be years younger than Sarah, they wouldn't have overlapped. *What was he thinking?*

"No, I can't say that I do. Though I didn't really spend much time with the cheerleaders." She let go of the seatbelt, let it snap back across her chest.

"No, no, of course not." William flushed, staring straight ahead at the road. Rose put a finger up to the glass and drew a sad, lopsided star in the remaining fog, which clung to one corner. Then the wheels slowed, and she saw they'd reached her block. He put the truck in park and turned off the headlights. Overhead, hemlocks shed needles onto the roof, battered by the deluge.

"So, what happens next?" He pulled his cap off again, shoved it into the console next to the chocolate bar. His hair stuck up at odd angles until he smoothed it with a swipe of a palm. The streetlights hadn't come on yet; they were cast in clinging shadow.

"Next?"

"With the book?" He'd shifted in his seat so he was facing her. The outline of his body etched itself against the dim.

"Oh! I'm about halfway through cleaning the pages. I'll scan the top text as soon as I can, then let you know when it's translated. After that I'll start on the undertext."

"Will you tell me if you find other portraits? Or any other drawings? I'd like to see them . . ."

"Of course. And you can always stop by if you're interested in how it's coming along." She said the last bit before she could think better of it.

"Yeah, I just might." The streetlights flicked on then, dousing them in a brassy glow.

"Good. Well. Thanks for the ride, I really appreciate it. And the chocolate." She stuck her hand out, awkwardly. He gave a sideways smile and shook it. The feel of his skin, the same as the first time, rough and warm.

"Anytime."

She leapt out then, swung the door shut, and ran up the walkway to her door.

Twenty minutes later, William eased into his driveway. The rain had slowed to a halfhearted drizzle. He got out, walked around the hood to the passenger's side, and opened the door. It still smelled like her hair here: shampoo, maybe—a clean, floral fragrance. It'd drifted over at him when they first sat down, as she unwound and rewound her bun. He'd wanted to lean into it.

Instead he leaned toward the window and breathed on the glass. The star she'd drawn there reappeared, a faint design. He tugged the cuff of his shirt up over his palm.

Rubbed the star away.

Inside, the house was thick with the scent of roast pork and the hot, starchy steam of potatoes. Jane and Lucy were setting the table, forks and plates, folded napkins. This was Sarah's new habit, to make dinner. When they'd lived in New York, they'd always just ordered in, but here she'd started cooking. Simple meals at first, pastas and rice, then gradually risottos, stews. Sauces for the meat. William had understood what she was doing, that it was her way of trying. *See the lengths I'll go to? Taste my effort.*

He appreciated the meals, he did, but for some reason the image of her in the kitchen with an apron on made him think of the Stepford Wives—as if she wasn't the one who'd been at an office all day—and only drifted him further away from the idea of them together that he still carried. A set of memories of who they'd been, once, years ago. A couple who'd laughed, went out to eat, had sex in the laundry room while the girls were down for their naps. A couple who'd known each other. He wasn't sure now how much he could trust those memories—had part of her always been standing by, dissatisfied?—but he wasn't ready to trade them all in just yet.

Half the time he made dinner before she got home just so she wouldn't have the chance.

He watched Sarah from across the table that night, as the girls chirped about their day, squirming in their chairs. The precise way she cut into her meat, how even her hair was orderly, parted in a perfect line. He thought of Rose's hair, unruly as vines, seemingly one firm headshake from tumbling down completely.

He'd been excited to see her again. There wasn't any sense denying that. He'd stood in front of his closet, wondering what to wear, then tried on three different shirts until he found one that wasn't too badly wrinkled. He'd used hair gel, for Christ's sakes—couldn't remember the last time he'd done that. Sarah took a bite; he heard the small metallic *tink* of the fork against her teeth. Had she felt that giddy getting dressed for work?

He thought of the messages she'd shown him, from Mr. Boat Shoes. He'd demanded to see it all: every text, every email. The only thing he'd asked not to know was his address. He'd started running by that point, miles at night, and didn't want the opportunity. He could imagine himself on some doorstep too easily, sweating through his T-shirt, gripping a bat like an overdressed caveman. *That was mine. My wife.*

You killed it in that meeting. One of the first texts.

Hey, I'd love to get your take on this case. Smoke break?

I just heard about a great new tiki bar. Wanna try it? Sarah loved tropical drinks. William hated anything that could be served with an umbrella. Hated people who used "wanna" in texts.

I finally watched that movie you recommended—you were right. Amazing! William had asked which movie; Sarah had named an old sci-fi film. *But you don't even like that movie,* he'd said, getting angry. *You just know other people think it's good!* It'd felt like a different sort of betrayal somehow. A betrayal of taste.

Then, the clincher. *Did you get a haircut?*

That was the sort of attention she'd wanted: the kind people pay when they're trying to impress each other. Before the curtain's lifted on every flaw and bad habit, when the warm glow of potential still softens all the sharp edges. *Admit it, you were taking a vacation from life!* he remembered whisper-yelling at her during one of their early fights. *You fucking tourist.*

Was that why he'd told Rose about Sarah, his girls? Because he'd walked into the bookshop with his ring in his pocket and watched her flush, and felt that same honeyed light—the allure of being mistaken for a better version of himself? In that second, he'd understood the danger was more serious than he could have imagined: it wasn't just that she might take him for someone greater, it was that through her he could convince himself he was.

Talking about Sarah felt like a form of self-preservation; a desperate measure taken against his own instincts, against the part of him that had wanted to pull Rose into his chest the instant he touched her shoulder. He'd had good intentions: he'd seen how flustered she'd gotten talking about her dad, a comforting gesture seemed warranted—he just hadn't expected to feel such an animal impulse, not from something as innocuous as putting a hand to her back. He'd just spent a year crowing from the peak of his moral high ground; there wasn't a way he could follow in Sarah's footsteps now, not after ending so many fights with that one line she had no counter for:

I would never have done this to our family.

He imagined what Lois would have to say. Probably something maddeningly noncommittal.

These are very interesting thoughts, William.

William set his fork down with a clatter, rubbed at his eyes.

"You okay?" Sarah was frowning at him from across the table. Jane and Lucy kept forming small mountains out of their mashed potatoes.

"Yeah, fine." Suddenly, the image of Giovanni's portrait flashed before him, shadows and light. "But I think I'll head to the studio after dinner. There's a new idea I want to explore."

8

THREE DAYS LATER, GIO ONCE AGAIN STOOD BEFORE THE great house, contemplating the heavy snake's-head knocker. He raised a hand to grab it, then impulsively gave the door a push. It swung open with a halfhearted creak. He ducked through, into the front entry, which stretched out cool and empty. From one end came kitchen sounds, a distant clatter and bang. He hurried toward the servants' passage.

The stairwell was unlit and plunged him into a disorienting darkness. Sliding one palm along the curving stone wall for balance, Gio ascended carefully. As he did, he began to hear voices again, drifting down from the floor above. This time he recognized both immediately: Venier and Corvino. Their murmurs sharpened into meaning as he neared.

"She'll make a fool of you." Corvino's voice was urgent, pleading.

"I am old enough to know the ways of this world, Corvino. What she does or does not do is none of your concern."

The door at the top of the stairs was open a quarter of an inch.

Gio peered through the crack at Corvino's profile. The Crow was staring straight ahead as if a disturbing scene were taking place in front of him, his lips pinched together anxiously. All Gio could see of Venier was his broad-shouldered back, his head of close-cropped gray hair thinning at the top.

"She's distracting you." Corvino turned to Venier, dark eyes scouring the statesman's face. He grasped Venier's elbow. "Bressan needs your attention. We must field-test the galleasses, we must—"

"*We* must do nothing of the sort. *I*—"

A door opened down the hall. At the sound, Venier wrenched his elbow away and strode toward the grand staircase. Corvino trailed behind with clenched jaw, scrutinizing the floor. Gio waited, listening to the mismatched tempo of their heels as they retreated. Then the sound of a door again, scraping shut behind the unseen servant. Gio darted out, scurrying toward the rose-colored sitting room. Before he could reach it, the faint strains of Chiara's voice snared him, twirling out from another chamber. When he pressed that door, it swung open just wide enough for him to slip inside.

Near the far end of the room, Chiara sat at an ornately carved desk, brushing her hair. A mirror was mounted on the wall in front of her; other, smaller mirrors were scattered on side tables, so that the afternoon sun multiplied itself in their surfaces, weaving a drowsy gold matrix. Dust motes floated sideways in the faded beams. A low fire crackled and sputtered on the hearth, and between the hearth and the door stood her bed: sturdy four-postered walnut, with brocade drapes embroidered in a repeating pattern of thistle blossoms. Over the bed a canopy drooped, threaded through with gold. Even the sheets were embellished, with small jewels sewn in at the corners, shimmering in the light. Chiara's tinted hair drifted in slow waves under her brush, and when she moved, the outline of her body revealed itself through the fabric of her linen shift. Gio realized she hadn't heard him enter—he froze at the threshold.

Still watching her own reflection, she began the song again. As she sang, her voice dropped smoky and low, then rose clear and crisp as winter morning. Expertly she rippled through the tune. After one refrain she paused, setting the brush on the corner of the desk before picking up a quill pen, scribbling the song notes on a piece of parchment as if racing to capture the melody before it could escape her mind. The feather of the pen bobbed in the air. Reading over what she'd written, she hummed the snatch of song again, then leaned to make a correction. Nodded in approval.

Gio cleared his throat.

"Giovanni!" Chiara jumped, knocking the brush off the table.

"My apologies!" he blurted, extending a hand as if to halt her from standing. "I was coming to escort you to the studio for a sitting. I—I didn't mean to interrupt."

She stared at him a moment, then bent to pick the brush up, saying nothing. He set his bag by the door, then took another tentative step into the room, approaching her the way he would a skittish animal. "It sounded lovely, Chiara. But . . . am I to understand that the most beautiful woman in Venice is also a composer?" He tried a grin, in part to test her response.

To his relief, she smiled back. Raising both hands, she tucked her hair behind her ears. Undone, it fell past her waist, surrounding her like a downy golden aureole. Glancing at the desktop, she reached out to touch the parchment with her fingertips.

"I've always loved to compose. As soon as I learned to read music, I started writing. It's . . . I suppose you could say it's my passion, though I'm only a woman." She looked up, sharply. "You're curious, aren't you?"

He took two more steps into the room. Her face grew intelligible, serious and bare. He shrugged. "I'm certainly more interested in this version of you. I've met the reluctant courtesan with a noble family a few times already." This earned him another grudging smile. "May I hear it again?"

She inhaled, hesitating. Without thinking, he reached into the pouch that hung at his hip and pulled out his spectacles, dangling them by one of the ribbons. The lenses glinted in the light.

"If my secret's safe with you, yours is with me."

She watched curiously as the glasses spun in the air, then nodded. Plucking the parchment up from the table, she held it at arm's length, took a breath, and began the song again. The sun filtering in through the drapes conspired with the hearth fire to cast her in a mellow glow; the delicate features of her face strained with concentration. As she sang, she trilled her fingers in little waves, indicating where accompaniment might be added.

In an instant, the room behind her slid away as Gio's mind summoned a backdrop of musicians, chiming in with pipe and lute, to weave the song together. There was a mathematical precision to the composition: it quickened in complex ripples and allegros, then slowed to the simplest progression of notes. It was brilliant—anyone could recognize that—and with vague surprise Gio felt his chest constrict, his arms prickle, his skin suddenly too tight for his flesh. As Chiara's fingers murmured to a stop, the musicians behind her disintegrated, replaced by the sturdy walls and bedposts. She held the last note for a fraction longer, then clamped her lips shut. Her eyes shot to him expectantly.

"It's magnificent, Chiara—but I think you might know that already." He caught the corner of her mouth twitch. "Have you shown your work to anyone else?"

"Rarely." She sighed as she sat back down on the stool, crossing one leg over the other, leaning to rest an elbow on the table. Two soft dents marked the flesh beneath each kneecap. "Sometimes I'll sing for Margherita and Veronica, though I think they're both too sweet to be critics—or really understand what they're listening to, to be honest. I showed a piece to another musician only once. He offered to publish it under his own name."

"What was your response?"

"I told him I'd rather my work were never heard for being a woman's than stolen by a man." She stared down at the hand that rested in her lap, palm up, as if reading her own fortune.

"That was the right choice. But your work will be heard, I'm sure of it."

She raised her brows at this, then turned back to the mirror and began pinning up her hair. On the table in front of her a small army of makeup pots, brushes, and perfume bottles stood in formation. Gio moved closer, until he was directly behind her.

"Do you know Aurelio, the alchemist?" He posed the question to her reflection.

"I've heard of him—well, I've drunk his liquor, I should say. At Domenico's. Why?" She shifted her gaze to observe him in the glass.

"He has a theory about artists. He claims we're no different than alchemists; that we're both seeking communion with a force greater than ourselves. He says in the work of a *true* artist, you can feel the thumbprint of the divine." He watched her hands slow their movements at this. "You're a true artist, Chiara. I can tell, even just from that." He gestured to the parchment. "There was . . . a pattern in it, a complexity and a balance . . ." He stumbled, went silent. The right words were there—he could sense their edges in his mind, but for some reason he couldn't grasp hold of them. Her hands had stopped completely, so they rested, fingers interlocked, on top of her head.

"I haven't thought it through as much as Aurelio has, I'm sure." She surveyed her own reflection. "All I know is that when I sit down to compose, I'm surprised by what comes out. I start, and it just . . . takes form. A chord, a progression—and there's mystery in it, because I don't know where it comes from. It's a part of myself I'm not in control of."

She dropped her arms, a lock of hair coming undone at the nape of her neck. "I'll have to think more on it, I suppose. I've never actually talked to anyone about it." She turned to look up at him over her shoulder. "Don't we make a pair, though. A woman composer and an artist going blind." She tried a half smile, but it wilted and died.

He didn't expect the tears. They must have been there all along, waiting.

In an instant she'd leapt to stand in front of him—her fingertips cool on his skin, wiping the wet from his cheeks. He thrust his hands into his robes, bumping up against the smooth weight of his lenses in their pouch. Felt the sudden urge to break them, snap their frame in two.

"I'm sorry. I'm so sorry. And after you said such sweet things." Her hands had stopped moving and now held his face, cheek to palm. Without her shoes on, she stood at chest height, arching her neck just to look up at him. He observed her pupils as they dilated and contracted, black pinpricks floating in lavender.

"May I make a confession?" The scent of rosemary on her breath. He nodded; she kept her hands clasped to his face. "I asked to be painted by you. I saw the portrait you did of Livia Colonna; her husband put it on display at Domenico's. Do you know the one?"

He nodded again, screwing his eyes shut tight. He could recall the painting exactly, every minute detail—down to the small half-moons in Livia's nail beds. He'd noticed the blackness just as he finished it.

"You'd captured her, her essence, in a way I didn't think was possible. That same night, I told Venier I wanted you to paint me. I wasn't seeking a tribute; please don't think this is vanity. I just wanted to be *seen*—the way Livia had been seen." She paused. "The way you'd seen her."

Then she raised herself onto her toes and put her mouth to his.

The soft press of her body against him and the taste of salt—a sudden awareness of how much smaller than him she was, how easily he could crush her. Thick heartbeats filled his head, like a panic of bird wings flapping escape. He opened his eyes; hers were closed in front of him. He put a hand to her chest and pushed. Pushed harder than he'd meant to. She stumbled, the backs of her legs knocking into the stool, eyes shooting wide. A pulse of blood darkened the skin of her cheeks.

"I don't want your charity." The words spoke themselves. As he watched, her face hardened and shut in on itself. She took another step backward, away from his hand still suspended in midair.

It was in this pose that the little dog found them, bounding through the door left ajar. They had only a moment to register the rapid *click click* of his claws on the hall tiles before he burst into the room—a lapdog, low to the ground, with a silky chestnut coat and a short tail that shook the whole of his body. A pink tongue flopped out of one side of his mouth, the world too thrilling for him to contain himself. Showing them the whites of his eyes, he scampered through the room, nearly toppling a stack of books as he tried to leap onto the bed.

A breathless Margherita entered in pursuit. "I'm so sorry, but isn't he darling! A present from Matteo. Here, Nicco, *here!*" Holding up her skirts, she chased after the dog, finally clutching him, squirming, to her chest. He began to lick her neck enthusiastically, tail wagging from between her arms.

"Giovanni! I didn't know you were coming today." Margherita addressed the ceiling as she leaned her face out of Nicco's reach.

"He was just leaving," Chiara interjected, before he could respond.

Margherita's face puckered in confusion. Without registering his own actions, Gio was suddenly at the door. Picking up his satchel, he bowed farewell stiffly, then departed, glancing back only once to see the women standing side by side in the yellow afternoon, the restless animal the only point of motion left.

Before he could raise a hand to knock, Aurelio's door swung open. On the other side, Gio was startled to be greeted by a cloaked figure, hood drawn down nearly to the nose, thin lips creased with lines. Without a word she—or was it he?—edged past, smelling of sage, earthy and sharp. Then they vanished into an alleyway so abruptly that Gio began to question whether he'd seen anyone at all.

"You'll have to forgive Anzola." Aurelio filled the doorway now with his comforting girth and round-cheeked smile. "She's not one for pleasantries. She is, however, gifted at much else." He swung his arm wide, beckoning Gio enter, then shut the door swiftly behind them. Inside, an array of flowers and herbs occupied a center table, grouped together in bunches.

"These are rare gifts. Powerful medicine when used together. Anzola is one of the few who knows the right combination and where to find them." Aurelio plucked a verdant sprig and put it to his nose, inhaling deeply. Gio had heard Anzola's name before, though he'd never actually met the woman. It was rumored she knew the language of plants—that when she walked through a forest, she could whisper to all that sprouted green from the soil, and she'd hear whispers back: the secrets coiled in every root and leaf. She was known to disappear from town for weeks at a time; when she returned, she'd wend her way through the neighborhoods at night, offering salves and potions. Somehow, she always knew which doors to knock on.

Now Gio watched as Aurelio held a dusty purple flower head up to a candle, contemplating its filaments like a scryer looking into his magic mirror. "Incredible, isn't it—that a poultice of these blossoms can ease a grown man's pain." The flame's glow threw the upper half of the alchemist's face into shadow. He continued on, transfixed by the light seeping through the petals, translucent as stained glass. "And to think: the Inquisition wants to burn women like that, simply because they can do more with nature's remedies than most physicians can with their leeches and learning . . ." His mouth twisted, words trailing off. Gio didn't know what to say, so said nothing at all. The game the Inquisition played was one in which they'd fashioned all the rules; it reminded him of the cruel sport cats made of shrews and spiders. Instinctively, he shivered. The movement caught Aurelio's eye; at once he tossed the flower down and clapped his palms together loudly, shattering the somber mood.

"But come, something tells me you have other matters to discuss. Here, have a cup, and you won't mind if I continue my work, will you? I do feel I'm nearly there . . ." Without waiting for a reply, Aurelio snatched up a jug and handed it to Gio, then bustled back over to the table near the fire. Several vials were arranged there, each with a different fluid inside. Gio surveyed a row of mugs hanging from a back shelf and found one that looked reasonably clean. Pouring himself a drink, then settling onto a stool, he began to recount the story of Chiara's kiss.

"Yes, yes, go on" or "Ah, I see" was all Aurelio could muster by way of response as he maneuvered among the liquids, combining and recombining their contents. Behind him the fire crackled, the rims of the glass beakers catching the light. Gio rambled, speaking mostly for his own benefit as he waded through what had happened. As he ran out of words, Aurelio poured the last drops into a single, great vial. Then he clasped a hand to his mouth, a look of childish suspense coming over his face.

Rapidly, the colors in the vial began to transform. First, a heavenly blue ("Unification!" the alchemist cried), then a mossy shade of earth. Aurelio bent until his face was only inches from the glass. A paleness entered the liquid, like smoke, the dark matter rising toward the surface.

"The soul . . . separating from the body," Aurelio whispered.

Suddenly, the mixture began to volatilize. Churning up and down in frenetic motion and speckling white, the glass filled with what looked like infinitesimal snowflakes falling upward. As they watched, the liquid tired itself into ash.

"Wait . . . wait . . . wait," Aurelio chanted. A faint reddish tint struggled to emerge through the dust. It flickered like an ember, faded, came again, then died. After several moments of inactivity, the alchemist leaned forward to peer into the container. Without warning, a loud pop burst out and a dense puff of purple smoke shot up into the air, churning over the rim of the vial with volcanic ferocity.

"*Cazzo!*" Aurelio swore as they both rushed to open the door. Gio couldn't help but laugh: the thick smoke had stuck in streamers to Aurelio's beard, transforming the alchemist into a mythological figure—some wayward god come down from violet clouds. Aurelio shook a fist overhead in fury, only adding to the comedic effect. Still laughing, Gio helped throw open the shutters as smoke continued to pour from the vial. Outside, the shouts of riled neighbor women began to form a chorus.

"Well." Aurelio leaned against the doorframe, gasping for fresh air, but continuing the conversation as though nothing at all had happened. "Of course, you must bring her to Domenico's salon tomorrow."

Gio stared at his friend, now busy finger-combing smoke from his beard. All around them, knee-deep violet mists seeped out into the street. "Why?"

"Maddalena Casulana will be there." As usual, Aurelio offered the name without explanation.

"And . . ."

"And she's just published a book of madrigals."

"A woman? Published?"

"Don't act so shocked, Gio. You said yourself that girl of yours is a genius composer." Aurelio threaded his fingers together, resting his hands on his wide belly. He was grinning at Gio like an instructor who'd just provided the answer to a baffling riddle.

"I know, but—"

"But nothing. A woman composer's been published, at long last.

Bring the girl, introduce her. Offer her a connection. Consider it a sign that Maddalena is here, now. Remember—" The alchemist raised his eyebrows and narrowed his pale eyes, directing at Gio the same enigmatic stare he used on his patrons "*When the student is ready, the master will appear.* Now go, make sure she comes." Clasping Gio's shoulders, Aurelio propelled him out the door on a plume of purple smoke.

Alone in the passageway, Bragadin reread the parchment sent from Mustafa. The offer of surrender was a formality, and both men knew it. When Bragadin had accepted the appointment as "captain of Cyprus," he'd known that conflict with the Turks was unavoidable—though now, in this moment, he had to admit he'd harbored a naïve hope that the fragile peace could hold. But the island was too valuable: Selim's territories encircled the entire eastern coast of the Mediterranean, save for the glaring exception of Cyprus. Once the island was captured, the sultan could advance west, perhaps even to Venice herself. Bragadin couldn't estimate how Cyprus's stronghold of Nicosia might fare under an Ottoman attack, but Famagusta was secure enough. Since arriving in the port town two years ago, he'd employed the best Venetian architects to improve the citadel's fortifications—adding vaulted chambers to every bastion so that gunpowder wouldn't fog his men out as they shot, and niches for barrels and cannonballs. His soldiers might be outnumbered, but they could put up a fight. Bragadin knew it, and knew Mustafa did too. Still, their success relied upon reinforcements from the West; he'd already sent word to the Pope.

The only question was if help would come in time.

Neatly and unhurriedly, Bragadin rerolled the parchment. He thought of the box, sitting in his chamber, reeking. Surely something dead lay inside. What could it be—what would Mustafa think could possibly elicit a surrender? Briefly, he considered returning the package unopened. But no; as commander, he knew it was his duty to look inside and gain as much information as he could.

Burying his face in the fabric of his robes, Bragadin ventured back into the chamber. Immediately, his eyes began to sting from the stench; rushing to the windows, he threw the shutters wide and prayed for a brisk wind. Leaning his head out into the day, Bragadin took a gulp of air the way a drowning man might surface, gasping. Then he turned back to the box. Fumbling, he managed to loosen the twine wrapped around its width. Clamping a hand tight over nose and mouth, Bragadin lifted the lid. Inside, two vacant, bloodstained eyes stared out at him from a severed head. Even though it was death gray and decapitated, he still recognized the face.

It'd once belonged to the governor of Nicosia.

9

DAWN CAME IN FITS AND STARTS, HER MIND TRAILING the fading spark of a dream. Rose woke up, opened her eyes. Her limbs felt filled with wet sand. Outside the window, the sky was a relentless gray. She lay motionless in bed until the heater clicked on, churning raspy warm air into the room. She thought of Giovanni waking up so many years ago. How would a morning have cracked open for him? She had the sudden urge to know—and besides, it was Tuesday, the one day a week her shop was closed. With some effort, she sat up, swinging her feet to the floor.

By the time she'd gotten dressed and drunk her coffee, the morning had already pitched into brightness. Spring announced her arrival with an entourage of blue skies and blossoms, and in every yard, birds optimistically announced their plans for the day. Rose steered her bike toward the university library, the air cool and fresh as a line-dried sheet. She pedaled faster, speeding under the reaching limbs of elm trees and ash, sugar maple and oak.

Crossing the threshold into the main library was like walking into church, an effect that was by design: the building had been constructed to resemble a cathedral, with a massive nave that culminated at the circulation desk. Sandstone walls arched overhead, lit by mounted lamps that cast the hall in hues of gold and bronze. Carved knobs ornamented the ceiling, and corbels jutted from every wall; under wrought-iron windows, sculptures reenacted key moments from the university's past. The weight of history pressed down conspicuously on visitors, reminding them that they trod hallowed ground. Still, Rose couldn't help a small triumphant grin each time she—a woman—passed by all those sculpted male faces, frozen forever in stone. *Sorry, boys, we're here to stay.*

At the very back of the nave was a mural from the twenties, depicting a blond goddess holding a sphere of learning and an open book, standing under the tree of knowledge. Rose always liked to give her a little nod before heading to the stacks. The university had provided her with a faculty badge for helping out occasionally with restoration projects; she swiped it and made her way toward the elevators. She'd memorized the library's organizing principles well enough by now to know which floor she needed.

Exiting, she followed a small sign with an arrow that simply said STACKS. Down a brick-lined hallway, through another door, and there she was: in a low-ceilinged room with row upon row of metal bookshelves extending as far as the eye could see. LED bulbs cast a harsh, unflattering glare, and the air was chalky with dust. Striding briskly down the aisles, she reached a narrow staircase that led up to the next level. The stacks were notoriously labyrinthine; more than once, she'd had to help a panicked freshman find the way back to circulation. As she climbed the stairs, she liked to spy out at the students searching through the book spines, crouching to read, sometimes—rarely—kissing. Occasionally she caught glimpses of her own younger self in the shy ones, tucked away in corners, hoping they wouldn't be interrupted.

The section on European art consumed most of the floor. She wandered until she found the rows on the Renaissance, then pulled a few easy choices: historical surveys, collections of essays on society and culture, overviews of Italian artists. Finding an empty reading table nestled between shelves, she began poring through the books, starting with the essays. Gradually, Giovanni's world ventured into view: a strange intersection of imagination and repression, flourishing creativity and religious extremity. She was surprised to realize the Inquisition was present in Venice just as the Renaissance was ceding to Mannerism. She tried to picture dark-robed inquisitors walking the avenues alongside Titian and Veronese. As she flipped through the pages, woodcut images of witches at the stake didn't stun her, but she had to avert her eyes from an illustration depicting a mountain of rare books being burned in a pyre.

She moved on to the art books. Who might Giovanni have met? He would have just missed da Vinci, but may have encountered Michelangelo, and could have competed directly with Tintoretto—or even Titian himself. She tugged her bun loose and rewound it tighter, considering where Giovanni's paintings might have disappeared to. Were they languishing in some attic, waiting to be discovered? Or did they hang on the walls of a discerning art collector's home, on the coast of the Adriatic, fueling speculative cocktail party debates? She hoped for the latter.

Several books had been mentioned repeatedly in the footnotes. She located one of the computers scattered throughout the floor and entered the titles into the library search engine. Several popped up "Available," with copies lodged in Rare Books and Manuscripts—a separate building, just down the street. She submitted a request for each; by the time she reached the archives, they'd be waiting for her in the reading room.

Back out on the sidewalk, the sun was abrupt and glaring.

Shielding her eyes, Rose hurried down the block and into the next library, feeling like a bookish vampire. She always loved the archives best. Populated by trained staff and serious researchers, it was less crowded, more subdued. The architecture too was dramatically different: unapologetically modern, an oversize rectangle of a building with a façade of granite and marble. The marble was intricately veined and translucent enough to let light seep in on sunny days, gilding the entryway. In the center of the building, a grand tower of rare books rose skyward, encased in glass. If the first library felt like a church, this one seemed like a vast art installation.

Rose made her way past circulation to the back of the building, where she hung up her jean jacket, then stashed her bag in one of the many lockers provided for patrons. Only pencils were allowed in the reading room. She descended the stairs to the lower floor, which was done in plush wall-to-wall beige carpet, and always gave her a brief sensation of stepping onto sand. She aimed for the service desk.

"Are you Rose?"

She didn't recognize the lanky man stationed behind the desk—he must have been a recent hire. As he finished reviewing her request on his computer screen, she looked him over furtively. The tag pinned to his navy sweater announced his name was Lucas. He had an enthusiastic smattering of freckles across the bridge of his nose and wore heavy black-rimmed glasses. Judging by the edge of lens extending past the frames, he was seriously nearsighted. His hair, unruly and brown, turned deep copper where the light hit it.

"I've got your books coming if you want to take a seat." He flashed her a smile. His teeth were surprisingly white, straight and even in the way that only comes from braces. Rose nodded at him, then turned toward the reading room—a great glass-walled space that looked onto a courtyard. Abstract sculptures perched in the gravel outside. Their strange shapes were always jarring, and each

time she was there made her feel as if she'd stumbled into some
De Chirico painting—a brooding, surreal landscape, untethered to
time.

A few students already sat at the tables, scrutinizing their finds;
Rose found a spot near the window. Lucas reappeared from a back
room, pushing a black metal cart. Awkwardly, he maneuvered it to
a halt by her chair, then began setting up her reading station. With
precise movements, he arranged several triangles of foam for the
books to rest on. Next, he laid out a pair of long, fabric-covered
paperweights. He smelled like citrus soap, and his gestures reminded her of a career waiter in a suit and tie establishment—each
action performed with a reverence for ritual. Politely he cleared his
throat, then launched into an overview of the correct handling
methods for rare books.

"Now, you'll want to avoid putting any unnecessary pressure on
the spine . . ."

He proceeded to give instructions, the opening ceremony for all
visitors. Rose listened patiently. She found he did a proficient job,
though he could have stressed the extra attention gold leaf decora-
tion required. Maybe someday she would tell him so, as a compli-
ment. Tucking away the possibility, she began to examine her finds.
The books she'd selected were ornately illustrated, offering a more
complete glimpse of Renaissance Venice than the essays could provide. A city of bridges, at once sumptuous and squalid, intersected
by canals and narrow cobblestone streets where artists, prostitutes,
priests, and merchants circulated with rare liberty. An hour slipped
past without notice.

"Is this for a project?"

Startled, Rose looked up to find Lucas standing near the edge of
her table. His face was strained under competing expressions of
curiosity and embarrassment. With a nervous tug to his ear, he
continued.

"It's just—I haven't seen you here, and by the end of the year I usually recognize most of the grad students. I just was thinking, maybe you were writing an article or something? Or maybe you *are* a student and just haven't been in yet ... ?" He petered out, faltering magnificently over his words.

"It's okay. You're right: I'm not a student, and yes, I am working on a project." She blinked up at him. He raised his eyebrows hopefully and shuffled his weight from one foot to the other.

Rose sighed. "Well, since you're curious, I'm studying a treatise written by an artist—a Venetian artist—in the 1570s. I just ... I wanted to know more about what his world would have been like." She gestured at the books spread open across the table. "Right now, when I think of Renaissance Venice, I just picture stereotypes. You know, masks and canals. I wanted to get a more accurate understanding, if that makes sense."

"Hmm, it does." Lucas frowned, bringing a forefinger to his mouth so seriously she had to stifle a grin. "Let me see what I can find."

Abruptly, he turned and retreated to his computer, where he began typing busily. Rose waited a minute, then bent back to her book. She'd been reading an account of a woman about to be burned alive for witchcraft. Just as she reached the moment the town was gathering for the sacrificial flames, she heard Lucas's voice again.

"I think this might be useful." He was beaming down at her, holding a large box. He set it on the desk, then unsnapped the lid. Inside was a thick black book, worn gray at the corners. "It's just pictures for the most part, but I think it's along the lines of what you're looking for." He lifted a few pages to flash ink drawings, then without further comment withdrew to his desk.

He was right. Inside, gorgeous illustrations revealed Venetian life in the late 1500s. The opulent attire of courtesans that prompted laws against excess, the elaborate robes of the doge. The yellow badges forced upon the Jews to identify them as "other"—hundreds of years before the Holocaust. Detailed sketches depicted the exotic visitors brought in by trade agreements with Istanbul and North Africa.

As she read, the light aged, and the shadows of the sculptures bent and swung across the courtyard in an afternoon procession. Finally, Rose looked up, blinking like a mole emerging from its burrow, to discover with some disappointment that there'd been a shift change. Instead of Lucas, a kindly older woman with heavily rouged cheeks and a floral blouse wished her a very good evening as she left.

The house was quiet when she got home. It was always quiet. Rose went to the kitchen and put the kettle on for tea. As the water heated, she unwound her scarf and tossed it on the counter. From the corner of the living room, her father's chair observed her emptily.

"If you were still here, I could tell you what I did today." Rose stared back at the chair. It remained impassive, leathered wingback, blanket folded neatly on its seat. "Guess I'll just talk to myself."

The kettle whistled at her; she tore open a sachet of peppermint tea and filled her mug with hot water. There was a chill to the air that night. Normally, she would have lit a fire in the fireplace—her father had loved to sit by the hearth, listening to the crackle and hiss of the wood as it flamed. Instead, she flicked the thermostat on and took a seat at the dining room table by the vent. She'd lived in that house since elementary school; she could remember barreling down the stairs on winter weekends clutching a book in one hand, a blanket in the other. Turning up the heat, then positioning her chair so that the hot air blew directly into her blanket. The morning would pass with her huddled over the vent, inflated with warmth, inhabiting fantastic new worlds courtesy of C. S. Lewis, Tolkien, L'Engle.

There's my bookworm. Her mother, blissfully unaware of the hostile cells that would begin dividing relentlessly in her body, making pancakes in the kitchen. Concerto music trembling out from her father's study.

Rose sometimes wondered how Joan's mother, Aileen, had felt, moving through a home she knew had belonged to another woman. Evidence of a previous identity wherever the eye landed: in the Spanish tiles of the kitchen counters, the pendant lights dangling above the dining room table, the table itself. She'd traced the same routines of daily life as her predecessor: kitchen to living room, up the twelve wooden stairs ribboned by carpet. Tugged on the same cupboard door in the second-floor hallway with its stubborn, squeaky hinge. Aileen had been respectful—a framed photograph of Rose's mother had remained on the mantel. Still, she'd added her own signature, updating all the pots and pans, introducing an absurd number of pillows to the couch, all hand-embroidered with flowers and leaves.

In fact, Rose was the only one who hadn't altered anything, unless she counted swapping out her high school bed for a new one sold by an Internet start-up. Even though she owned the home now, she couldn't bring herself to sleep in the master bedroom. Joan had gently suggested selling, but the reality was that the property was a treasure: situated in the best neighborhood, with a charming bay window and a leafy maple in the lawn out front, a façade of limestone and brick. Rose said she'd just needed time. But over six months had gone by and she still hadn't changed rooms. She was adrift, and she was smart enough to know why: because until now, she'd never not had a clear and present goal. For years, it'd been school, earning one degree, then the next, and the next. After that it'd been her father: working to ensure each day was marked by as little pain as possible, reaching the inevitable end as slowly as they could, together.

Now . . . what was she doing? Didn't milestones arrive on the horizon for most people, like road signs indicating how to proceed? Earn the degree, land the job, get the promotion. Marriage, children. What do you do when no next step is offered? No partner in sight, no promotion to be had. She had only herself now, and Rose wasn't sure she knew who that was anymore. Joan advised her to reach out to university friends, but what would she say? *My movie got put on pause while yours kept running. Yes, your children are adorable, aren't they? Yes, it's wonderful that you work for the Smithsonian.*

Now she felt the gaze of both her mother and Aileen from the mantel, Aileen having gained her own spot at the opposite end. She imagined that they were watching her with some concern, Rose's mother in her feathered Princess Diana haircut, Aileen sporting a practical bob that was very similar to Joan's current style, though Rose would never say so out loud. Both of them observing as Rose stayed in every night, chatting idly with an empty chair.

She finished the last few sips of tea, trying to remember how her father had acted with each wife. Her mother had been a researcher; together they'd made a cozy family, reading quietly every evening, separate but together. Aileen, on the other hand, couldn't make it through the grocery store without stopping and talking to at least five people. She'd coaxed Rose's father out to lectures, to movies. She'd even gotten him to stomp his feet at bluegrass concerts. Both versions had been him—each partner just brought out different patterns in his woodwork. Rose liked to think that he'd loved her mother the most, but she knew he'd loved Aileen also; he'd have done anything to make her happy, including listening to bluegrass. She knew exactly what her father would have said on the matter too, quoting Heraclitus: "No man steps in the same river twice." To which Rose would have replied, obligingly, "For it's not the same river, and he's not the same man." After Aileen had died, Rose and Joan had gone through her things while her father sequestered himself in his study, with Brahms furious on piano.

They'd found small slips of paper in her coat pockets: one-sentence love notes he'd tucked away for her to find.

Rose set her mug in the sink, then climbed the stairs. That past Christmas had been the first time in memory that the banister hadn't been strung with a spruce garland. Would she have it in her to hang one next year? How long would she stay in the house, truly? She tried to imagine raising a child in the same rooms she'd played in as a girl. After she'd crossed the threshold of thirty, those sorts of thoughts had begun bobbing to the surface. She could picture a little redhead diving into a pile of raked maple leaves in the lawn. Learning to run the cash register at the bookshop. Then, like a new frame spliced into the film, a sudden image of William—his silhouette in the truck when he drove her home, the outside world flashing greenly past behind him. The weight of his hand on her back. Unconsciously, Rose pressed her own hand to her stomach: flat and firm, hips as sharp as a teenager's.

"Don't get carried away." Tired eyes looked back at her from the bathroom mirror. She ran the tap until the water turned warm, then bent to submerge her face.

William's studio crouched in the shadows near the back fence, dwarfed by white poplar and magnolia trees. A single red oak stood sentry in the middle of the yard, thick-trunked and venerable; he'd hung a swing for the girls from one of its branches when they moved in. Now the rope stirred slightly in the dark air, the leaves making a gentle shushing sound high overhead. He stepped down the three deck stairs and into the yard, met up with the narrow stone path that licked out through the grass. The clouds had retreated enough for him to see star spatter in the blackness above, a sharp crescent moon.

Inside the studio, he turned the lights on and stood, squinting, until his eyes adjusted. Then he went to the window, raising the blinds just enough to crank open the glass, a cool breeze whispering in to shift the still air. Within seconds, moths arrived to flutter at the screen, chafing their bodies against the mesh, struggling toward the light. William tugged the blinds back down.

Shelves lined the far wall, custom made to store his paintings. Methodically, he began pulling out each frame, lining them up in sequence. These were the ones he'd refused to sell. A few landscapes where he could spot the beginnings of the style he'd become known for. Two painstaking self-portraits that made his stomach drop: a younger version of himself sitting at the kitchen table in his New York apartment. Him in the desert on that first solo trip. He'd wanted to go somewhere, see something new, and someone had said *Mojave*. So, he'd sold a painting and bought a ticket—just like that. He could still recall the vast patience of the desert: great rock formations, a bone-deep stillness in the stone and dirt and heat that had settled something down inside him. At night, searing red skies doming over the darkening Martian terrain. He'd done a self-portrait to remember what it'd felt like there, what it'd been to just *go*—because he'd wanted to. Because he could. Less than two years later, Sarah would be pregnant. He stared at his own face in the painting, through a distance of more than a decade now. The full measure of his naïveté reflected back in his open expression, the gleam in his eyes.

The newest sketch sat on a drawing table to his left. Only the earliest suggestions were edging to life, but already it was so different from the others. The curves of a face, the tumble of hair. Elongated proportions in a late Renaissance style. He'd begun blocking out a palette with pastels, choosing deeper hues: the rich tones of a Venetian painter.

The outline of Rose's eyes central on the page.

He'd discovered himself incapable of not thinking of her, no matter how he tried—in fact, the harder he tried, the more she flooded his attention, as if someone had spilled coffee on the cir-cuitry of his mind. A cruel joke of the psyche. After a week when each day ended with a headache that responded to neither pills nor whiskey, he'd decided to direct his energies into art. He'd already been experimenting with elements of Giovanni's style, filling pages with loose figure studies. It was a simple trick to use Rose as a model, to focus on a portrait. Plenty of painters had muses, why should he be any different? Now, the image emerging was an unex-pected blend of mannerist technique and his own impressionist style. It excited him with its difference, but it scared him too: he sensed the path curving ahead in a new direction but couldn't quite see what lay beyond.

Yet what would he do, in the end, with a portrait of a local bookshop owner—especially one painted without her knowledge? Perhaps he'd finish the piece, then keep it hidden, the way Andrew Wyeth had concealed all the paintings he'd done of his neighbor's wife. It could be a quiet inspiration meant for his spirit alone. Wil-liam thought of Wyeth's portraits, the wife's hair always parted in braids, her face pale and impassive. How many hours they must have spent together in secret. And there was the rub: working on the sketches sharpened, not dulled, his desire to see Rose again. He wanted more time to observe her face, the folds of her eyelids, the point of her chin. Was one nostril higher than the other? Did her eyebrows really arch the way he remembered, and at what angle exactly did her clavicle slope? He thought he'd captured the curve of her lip, but now he was second-guessing his own lines.

He wanted answers, he needed to know, with an insistence that felt like compulsion.

Three hours later, William turned off the lights and waded back out into the shadows, pastel chalk buried under his nails. Upstairs, he paused to peek through the crack of Jane's door, then Lucy's. Their bodies made soft shapes in the weak glow of night-lights—one owl, one mermaid—the sound of their breathing labored in the way only sleeping children's breath can be. He turned, heading down the hall toward his own room, the wood floor cold and smooth under his bare feet. Inside, Sarah lay still on her side of the bed.

He undressed in the dark and slipped in under the covers. Pale moonlight threaded through a gap in the curtains, illuminating the outline of her back, the rise and fall of her shoulders. Uninvited, a memory surfaced: an afternoon outside, in the park by their old apartment. It'd been summer; they'd been drinking. Grass prickled and crushed under the weight of his thighs, his back. He remembered watching her hair sway in the light, how the sun sifted through that blond curtain. There'd been nothing more he'd wanted then, but to lie in the heat, half-drunk, with her at his side. He remembered how that'd felt.

Then he thought of the portraits, Rose's face sketched over and over. The urgency with which he wanted to see her again. The way he'd started singing out loud to teenage pop songs on the radio.

Had it been like this for you, Sarah? He wanted to ask her. *Or is this worse?*

Sarah turned to lie on her back.

William traced the outline of her face in the imperfect darkness. Her strong jawline, curved upper lip—features she'd gifted their children. The profile of the woman he'd fallen in love with, once, that afternoon outside when they'd both been drinking. Her blond hair swaying in the light. He moved his hand beneath the sheet, up onto her hip, recalled feeling the gradual shift of her body making space for the bones of their children. Still asleep, she twisted away at his touch, shifting his hand aside.

William turned to face the darkness.

10

HE WAS IN THE CLEARING. AGAIN.

The long march toward it, snow crust breaking open beneath his feet. He walked out in front, ahead of his father. Before them, a copse of trees. A shadow twitched behind the boughs. His knees burned frigid in the snow. His blood swept wide around the expanse of his station, flecks and swaths and founts. So very red against the very white. So very elegant in its arcs, in the measured time it took to mark the snow after every leaden-handed hit.

"You are nothing." His father's voice, suspended in the icy air. "You are nothing."

The shadow hopped. It was a crow, watching him. Tilting and retilting its head with cruel patience. Double-checking each angle with a liquid stare.

Waiting.

Corvino opened his eyes and lay still as the dream receded like fog and his clenched fists released. He turned to face the window. A sparrow perched on the sill, feathers twitching in a mild breeze, claws gripping the stone. Corvino eased himself to standing, then lunged at it. With a jolt and *chirp*, the creature winged away, became a dun blot receding in an otherwise empty sky. Corvino rubbed his eyes with the heels of his hands; his head throbbed, as if he'd been struck. Using his fingertips, he traced small circles at his temples.

The clearing had been his father's favorite place for punishment. Any excuse had been enough. A chore completed too slowly, a spilled mug of milk, a forgotten line of prayer and Corvino would hear that sound he dreaded most: the scrape of his father's chair as he pushed back from the table, turning to the wall where the whip hung waiting. He could still see the instrument, curving limply, waiting to take on vicious life. Its knotted cords and leather-bound handle, caked over with Corvino's own blood, dried black. If he wanted, he could reach a hand behind him even now, feel the uneven map of his skin. His father's enduring signature.

Were the dreams coming because he was approaching the same age his father had been when he fled? Corvino had often imagined that scene: the man arising to discover his only son gone, along with all the silver. Leaving him alone and wretched, with his rages and whip, the rest of the family reduced to markers in the weeds out back. Before he left, Corvino had wanted to confront those women at church who'd doted on his father, to tear his robes away and force them to look at what their soft-spoken widower did to his son. To behold what sort of Christian he truly was.

Corvino knew it was the Devil, not the Lord, that had worked through his father—just as surely as he knew his *real* Father, his shepherd and redeemer, would always provide for him. It had been deep in prayer that Corvino had been shown the gift of his abuses. There was a lesson hiding in the pain of the clearing: that every man has a shadow self, every man has secrets. After poaching and thieving from Mantua to Rome, Corvino began to put his gift to

use. He'd learned which bribes worked best on servants, how to follow someone without being noticed, what price a nobleman might
pay to keep his reputation intact. Soon, he was wearing the velvets
and furs he'd only dreamt of as a boy. And why shouldn't he? The
scriptures gave fair warning: *For nothing is hidden that will not be
disclosed, nor is anything secret that will not become known and come
to light.* The sins of others were not his doing, nor his fault; why
shouldn't he benefit from them? He was devout, he was clever, and
handsome. Yet still society kept him from any real power, simply
because his blood lacked the proper lineage, his name lacked any
title. He deserved prestige as much as—no, *more than*—the plod-
ding, dim-witted noblemen who hosted him for dinners. They
wouldn't have survived a week alone in Mantua without recourse,
yet he had thrived. All without ever missing Mass.

His one true Father would see to it that he was rewarded. Of
this Corvino was certain.

Now he opened the shutters wider to look out over the city as
morning rose in shades of blush and coral. In the distance lay the
harbor, where the masts of Bressan's new boats cleanly intersected
the horizon. Corvino leaned toward them, taking in a great lungful
of sea air. This was the opportunity he'd been waiting for, the chance
to carve a new destiny for himself. Soon, he'd be pacing one of those
decks, as the fleet thrust east. He could picture it now: the stinging
wind, ocean spray misting his face while the sturdy hull cut through
waves. He would make his name at sea—he knew it, he could taste
it, sharp as salt on the tongue. If only Venier would confide in him
more he could even help strategize the attack.

Of course, Venier would invite him to sail with the fleet. It was
only a matter of time; likely he was simply waiting to be appointed
admiral. Once the decision was made public, he might even find a
formal role for Corvino—nothing so grand as captain, but perhaps
a commander of some sort. With the chance to prove his worth in

battle, Corvino could secure a whole new position for himself. War hero, courageous defender of Venice, La Serenissima. Corvino the brave . . .

A gust of wind blew the hair from his shoulders. He raised his chin proudly. In the avenue below, he caught a burst of yellow: a turban, worn by a Levantine Jew walking briskly, no doubt late for an appointment. The Jews were always conducting business of some sort. Corvino grimaced involuntarily. He could never understand why Venice harbored the vermin in such numbers, allowing them to lend money, or trade in clothing and furniture, to become prosperous. To circulate the streets, rubbing shoulders with good and pure Christians. Corvino knew there must be spies in the Ghetto feeding information to the Ottomans. He'd hired three men himself to listen and watch, sniffing out any hint of treachery. He could only imagine how Venier might reward him if he were to discover a traitor in their midst. Until then, he knew another way to make it impossible for the statesman to ignore his usefulness.

A way to ensure that Venier would be named admiral.

At exactly the same moment on the other edge of town, Gio sat up in bed. He was wide awake though he'd drawn well into the night, his nerves crackling and sparking like a strand of hair in a candle flame. He hadn't been able to get to sleep, scenes from the afternoon churning in a useless cycle in his mind—the kiss, his push, her face. Extricating himself from the tangle of bedclothes, he stood and, after dressing, opened the shutters. Cheerful light flooded the room.

Peering at the house next door, he spotted Francesca, sitting with her back to him, busy mending some scrap of fabric. Finally, Lucio appeared. As was his habit, he clambered up onto the sill, tip of pink tongue peeking from the corner of his mouth in concentration. In one hand he held a slice of thick-crusted bread, a scrape of butter across the top.

"Lucio!"

The boy shot to attention at the sound of his name. Gio beckoned him with a wave.

"I'm going to Gio's!" Lucio bellowed in the general direction of his mother. Francesca, now distracted by a cousin who'd managed to get a ribbon snarled in her hair, nodded without looking up. Lucio slid off the sill and vanished from sight. At his own door, Gio waited to greet the boy, who arrived flushed and breathless, still clutching his bread.

"Lucio, I have something very important I must do—and you are the only one who can help. Will you assist me?" Gio lowered his voice in mock seriousness, trying not to smile as the child straightened to his full height and nodded, round-eyed at the promise of an adventure.

"Then it's settled. Off we go." Gio shut the door behind him and led Lucio out into the waking streets. The sketch he'd finished the evening before was a stiff roll in his hand; inside, he'd hidden an invitation to Domenico's salon.

"Where are we going?" Lucio talked around a bite of bread, skipping every third step to keep pace.

"We're going to deliver a very important message." They rounded a corner, Gio steering them over a bridge and toward the Grand Canal.

"A message? For who?" Lucio wiped a smear of butter from his cheek, then licked it off his hand.

"To a nice young lady. I'm afraid I've upset her, but I'm hoping she'll listen to you."

"How did you upset her?"

"I said something foolish."

"Ah." The boy nodded, as if understanding completely. They

continued on in silence as they traced the great waterway—Lucio distracted by the scenes flashing past through open shop doors: the apothecary's shelves of labeled jars, the tailor's lads already bent over needle and cloth. The butcher with his cuts of raw meat, pierced and glistening on hooks. The knife grinder pedaling his whetstone, the baker stacking rounds of nut brown loaves that warmed the air with the smell of wheat. Farm women lined the footpath, crouching behind woven baskets filled to overflowing with ripe fruits carted in from the countryside.

Finally, they arrived at the house. The glass windows reflected the view, as if bits of sky and garden had found their way into the mortar.

"Is she rich, Gio?" Lucio gaped up at the building.

"That doesn't matter. Just take this and knock on the door. When the servant girl answers, tell her it's for Chiara. Can you remember that? 'Kya-rrra.'" He thrust the rolled-up sketch into Lucio's small hands. "Here—here's her name if you forget. You can read it." With his index finger, he underlined the calligraphy across the front.

"Where are you going to be?" Lucio asked anxiously, wide eyes darting up at Gio.

"I'll be . . ." Gio realized he hadn't thought that far. He squinted around, then pointed to a corner of the building partially obscured by cypress trees. "There—right there. No one will see me, but I'll be close by. There's nothing to worry about. Just remember, it's for *Chiara*." He pushed the boy up to the door and pounded the heavy snake's head, then picked up his robes and scuttled around the house. Kneeling in the dirt, he found a view of the entrance through a gap in the boughs. The minty scent of tree resin flooded his nostrils.

He'd only just hidden himself when the door opened and Cecilia's profile emerged. She stared stonily down at the child in front of her. Lucio said something Gio couldn't discern, gesturing to the name on the scroll. Without responding, Cecilia shut the door. Lucio stood waiting, shooting nervous glances toward the patch of trees. Just as the boy was turning to walk away, the door reopened and Chiara stepped out into the light. She was wearing a pale blue *gamurra*, her blond hair gathered loosely at the nape of her neck. At the sight of her, Gio ducked away, pressing his back against the cool stone of the house. When he leaned forward to look again, the boy was gone.

He could only wait. A quarter of an hour passed, then a half, then a full. He counted the ringing of the bells throughout the city: San Basso, San Fantin, San Felice . . . the churches formed a refrain. With each gong, a new bubble of anxiety. He hadn't thought this through enough—what if Venier arrived? What excuse could he possibly give the statesman for sending a child into his home, uninvited, with an uncommissioned sketch of Chiara and an invitation to a salon? Gio envisioned different versions of the same uncomfortable scene, until Lucio finally emerged. He had a triumphant grin on his face and was carrying a woven basket nearly the size of his body.

"Giovanni!" The boy struggled to cross the garden with his load.

"*Shhh!*" Gio held a finger to his mouth as he trotted out, just in time to see a drape yank shut in an upstairs window. Quickly, he opened the gate and shepherded the boy back out to the street.

"She knows you're here . . . I'm sorry." A dusting of crumbs around the extremity of Lucio's mouth caught the light with a powdery finish.

"You told her I brought you?" Taking the basket from the boy, Gio peeked inside. A fine embroidered linen was tucked over lumps of all sizes. Tugging one corner free, he saw bread and cheeses, preserves and marzipan. Francesca was going to be pleased.

"I didn't want to lie to a lady, Gio." Lucio wiped his face with both hands.

"Don't worry—she would have guessed even if you hadn't told her. Did you show her the parchment? What did she say?"

"She liked it—it was a wonderful picture, Gio. It looked just like her!" Lucio's voice was animated: Chiara must have fed him sugar. "She's very beautiful," the boy added.

"I know. Did she read the other piece of paper with the sketch?"

"Yes, it fell out when she opened the picture. What did it say?"

"Did she burn it afterward? Did you see her put it in the fire?"

"Yes, yes, but what did it *say*, Gio?" The boy skipped a step to keep up.

"Never mind that, what did you two talk about?"

"Well, I told her how you make drawings for me, and how you're teaching me to read. And then the servant girl . . ."

"That was probably Cecilia."

"Yes, she brought out a little book, and I showed them how I could read, and then we played with Nicco, but then Nicco peed on the floor and had to go away, and that's when I came out. Can I go back to visit again soon, Gio?" Lucio offered up his most imploring face.

"Perhaps." Already they were nearing home: crossing over the last footbridge, passing through the small square with its familiar cluster of aproned women at the well. Before they separated, Gio handed the basket back to the boy. As he shut his door, he could hear Francesca's exclamations through the still-cracked shutters.

She'd seen the invitation; that meant she might come to Domenico's. As he readied to walk to his studio, Gio couldn't help but feel the thrill of excitement, a thread of nervousness woven through it.

The city of Famagusta could not stand much longer—and once she fell, the whole of Cyprus would be claimed by the Ottoman Empire. The fate of the island balanced on a saber's edge. Bragadin's fortifications were impressive, there was no doubt of that: miles of reinforced walls, towers, and earthworks topped with cavaliers. All of it ringed by moat. An architectural feat, one that any captain could take pride in. Yet it didn't alter the fact that this was the only remaining stronghold on Cyprus, and that Cyprus was surrounded by sea—there could be no influx of men across the border, there was no nearby king to beseech for aid. Their only salvation relied upon relief from the west, and Bragadin had sent word weeks ago. If Cyprus were won, the victory would only propel Selim onward, spurring him to conquer more territories. Surely the threat of a Muslim invasion would be enough to unite the bickering Christian nations?

Surely it wouldn't take so long to organize a league?

Bragadin had rejected Mustafa's offer of surrender based on the belief that support would come, but each morning he prayed for the sight of friendly sails, and each morning he was refused. And no matter how many well-planned attacks his soldiers executed—burrowing out like vermin under cover of night to slaughter unsuspecting Ottomans, collapsing their tunnels behind them—his troops were still outnumbered, their supplies dwindling. Meanwhile, the Ottomans had enough men to last for months, all of them ready and willing to die for Islam.

Once more, Bragadin looked to the horizon, scanning for sails.

11

IT WAS A SLOW DAY. THE UNIVERSITY HAD BEGUN ITS READing period: the week or so of intense study before final exams. The whole town turned subdued, as students retreated to their halls, emerging only for takeout food or to indulge in a brief constitutional. The stress was palpable, seeping out from campus like a gas leak.

Rose sat at her desk, spinning a pen around her thumb. All her emails had been answered, all her orders were complete. She'd finished lunch, but it was too early for an afternoon snack ...

What did William's paintings look like? In the lull of an empty shop, with the sky neither gray nor blue but an ambivalent inbetween shade, she couldn't convince herself not to look. As she typed in the URL, Joan's voice chirruped in her head: *Too curious for your own good, Rosie.*

An abstract composition filled the home page. A forest landscape. Loose brushstrokes, a departure from the detailed work of the masters she'd been looking at lately. Still, his skill was evident:

plots of perfectly rendered leaves and berries created contrast with an otherwise impressionist style. A subtle and nuanced palette. Rose clicked GALLERY, and rows of thumbnails filed onto the page. She started at the beginning. It was interesting, scrolling through this way—following along with his changing interests and attentions. The subject matter was mostly naturalistic: roils of sky over windswept fields. A river thrusting and churning through a reaching stand of pines.

His face.

The self-portrait was sudden and unexpected after so much nature. In the painting he stood in front of an old green truck, a weathered-looking Ford F-100 with its door cracked open. It was a desert scene: dust and scrub and a splintering wooden fence behind him, the sky a placid, burning blue. His face and the front half of the truck were rendered so realistically they could have been a photograph, down to the crumpled corner of a pack of cigarettes on the driver's seat, the sheen of cellophane. The rest of the scene swept into suggestion, broad strokes of pigment and gesture. She leaned in. The expression on his face wasn't one she'd seen before: open and grinning, an edge of recklessness in the set of his features. A glint in his eye. She wanted to clamber in through the open truck door and sit herself down, feel the backs of her thighs stick to the hot leather seat. He'd slide in beside her, pedal the gas. Together, they'd watch dust clouds spin up in the rearview mirror . . .

A loud knock on the door. Rose looked up and it was him—William—bending to peek through the glass. For a split second she wasn't able to process the shift in context and felt like she was looking at another painting. Then her mind skidded into the present, and she quickly closed the search tab, as if he could see the screen. Heat seared across her face.

"Hi! Hey!" He poked his head through the open door, then stepped inside. He looked different today, wearing a dark V-neck sweater with the crisp white collar of a buttoned shirt poking out, sleeves pushed up. She could picture him in New York dressed like that. A wave of regret washed over her for choosing such a plain outfit that morning: jeans and an oversize gray sweater that was gently pilling under the arms. On her feet, a pair of trusty, battered Converse. Why couldn't style come naturally for her the way it did for some women, like being left-handed? She plucked at her sweater, trying to straighten the shoulders.

"You'll never guess what the exhibit is at the university!" William interrupted her train of thought, walking toward the desk with his phone held up, waving the screen at her.

Rose already knew what it was but feigned ignorance, leaning in to read the title: "Muse: Inspiration in Renaissance Italy." The university gallery was only a few blocks from her shop, and she often stopped in on her way home. Four months ago, when the show opened, she'd taken a quick sprint through the rooms. She should have thought to mention it to him . . .

William tapped an index finger on the screen. "It's all about Italian Renaissance paintings! Perfect timing, right? The only thing is that it ends today—"

"Oh, that is perfect timing! Are you going to go?"

He raised his eyebrows at her, then bent studiously over the phone, scrolling through the page. "Oh, yeah, well. I was going to go, definitely. I just wasn't sure . . . Would you want to see it too?" Was she only imagining it, or was color rising to his cheeks, the sides of his throat? "I mean, it's pretty close, right? But I guess it's still business hours here, huh?" He scratched the back of his head and glanced around the deserted store.

"Technically yes, but it's reading period—one of my slowest weeks. I can absolutely go, that'd be fun." Already she was shutting her computer down. Odin didn't even bother to wake up from his nap on the chair when she flipped the sign and locked the door, stepped out with William into the mellow afternoon light.

They walked side by side down the street, lined with old brick buildings and oak and hemlock trees, the occasional elm. Rose tried to peek in to see if Joel was working at the café, but the glare from the window only threw their own reflections back at her: wind gusting her curls loose, William's hands buried in the front pockets of his jeans. Once again she cursed herself for dressing so plainly, as she double-stepped to match his stride. They passed the flower shop, an Oscar Wilde quote chalked in cursive on a sandwich board out front—*A flower blossoms for its own joy*—the pizza parlor, the theater building advertising its last performances of Shakespeare's *Twelfth Night*. Then the gallery came into view around the corner, an unassuming entrance tucked in among so much neo-Gothic architecture, all arches and pillars chiseled from limestone.

Inside, they made their way to the elevator, its doors gliding shut behind them. The sudden shift of gravity as they slid upward. Their reflections shone back at them here too, warped in the slick metal. Alone together in a close gray box.

Ding! Fourth floor, special exhibitions.

They stepped out into bright white light. Down the nearest wall ran the curator's introduction in large-font text, explaining that each hall explored a different aspect of the muse. Rose read through quickly; as she waited for William to finish, she peered around. They were the only ones there, save for an elderly attendant in a far room, wearing the gallery's uniform of dark sweater and slacks, a bulky walkie-talkie clipped to his belt. Rose watched him look up and notice them, then straighten his posture, folding his hands over a portly belly. The man had downturned eyes and drooping jowls, and Rose couldn't help but think of a sleepy Saint Bernard.

Then William finished and they pivoted in unison, drifting toward the first hall. Rose had never seen the gallery so empty; even the scuffling of their shoes seemed impolite in the dense silence. Abruptly, William halted at the entrance to the room.

"Are those studies for *Primavera?*" He cocked his head, the way he might look at someone he wasn't sure he recognized.

"Yes, I think so . . ." Rose trailed after him as he strode to stand in front of a pair of sketches. Each was several feet tall, done in charcoal on heavy paper. One showed a group of women dancing in a grove, diaphanous gowns fluttering, slender toes pale in the dark grass. Branches arched overhead, weighed down by pendulous oranges. The second study was of a woman with an embroidered robe draped over one shoulder, her face angled to stare out at the viewer with a serene, inscrutable expression. Above her a portly, blindfolded Cupid hovered. The sketches were hung side by side, so that Cupid's bow seemed to be aimed at the women in the orange grove. Nearby, a large-scale print of the completed painting—housed in the Uffizi Gallery in Florence—was mounted for comparison.

Rose bent to read the description of the painting out loud. "It's supposedly an allegory of spring, with Venus as the central figure, since she ruled the month of April." Gazing back up at the robed woman, she briefly wondered what it must have been like to live when gods and goddesses governed the months. It was the end of April now; she imagined Venus smiling benevolently down on them as they wandered the empty gallery. And poor blindfolded Cupid drifting above. Rose squinted at the Three Graces dancing in the grove. Which of them would his arrow pierce?

"William! Look—there! On her neck!" Without thinking, Rose grasped at his forearm. Warm, sturdy muscle, the bristle of hair under her palm. "Oh! Sorry!" She clutched her hand back, gaping up at him wide-eyed. Her cheeks were burning, undoubtedly fuchsia, nothing to fix it.

He was grinning down at her like she'd told a joke. "It's okay. What am I looking at?"

"Oh—the necklace, there. On that one." She pointed up at the Grace in question, still pressing the hand that had touched him to her chest. "It's just like the one in Giovanni's portrait. I didn't see it—" She almost said "last time," but caught herself. William didn't seem to notice but stepped closer to examine the sketch.

"It *is* like Giovanni's, isn't it . . ."

"And it's a sapphire!" She was already pulling up search results on her phone. "Here, listen to this: 'The dancing Grace in Botticelli's *Primavera* is seen with a sapphire pendant. At a time when bodies were believed to be governed by four temperaments, the sapphire worked to cool fiery passions, and the gem was thereby associated with wisdom and fidelity.'"

"Wisdom and fidelity. Guess that confirms it." He scratched his jaw, dissecting the image. "And is the model for this Venus the same as in *The Birth of Venus?*"

"Well, let's see." Rose located the small placard explaining that room's theme. The first time she'd visited the exhibition she'd just breezed through, mostly curious to see what the university had been able to get on loan; now she wished she'd been more thorough.

"Okay, so this room is about the myth of the muse." She began to paraphrase the curator's notes. "Botticelli is usually linked to a specific model, Simonetta Vespucci, who was the great beauty of her time. People identify the Venus in *Primavera* and *The Birth of Venus*, as well as several other portraits, as her." Rose glanced up to see one of the paintings in question hanging on the next wall. A woman's profile, brassy blond hair braided and knotted, decorated with pearls. "But I guess there aren't many facts to prove that these women are actually Simonetta. The paintings could just as easily be ideals of beauty." She quoted the last line of the notes directly: "Yet the notion that Botticelli fell so in love with Simonetta that he repeatedly painted her likeness, even a decade after her death, persists to this day."

"What do you think of that?" William was examining another painting now, hung in an overwrought gold frame. A satyr, kneeling over a nymph.

Rose shrugged. "We all love a good love story." She paused, considering. "But the way we tend to think about muses seems so patriarchal to me."

"What do you mean?"

"Well, I don't mind how the Greeks understood the muse, which was as sort of a divine spirit—separate from the artist—who would come visit him or her and inspire the work. But this interpretation . . ." Rose gestured loosely at the women in the room, with their swan-like necks, their fair hair falling in uniform waves. "It just seems like 'muse' is a nice word for a woman the artist is sleeping with, or wants to sleep with, right?"

William gave a sharp cough, then tugged at the corner of his collar. Rose continued, oblivious. "I'm sure I'd feel differently if we saw as many male muses, but it's always a woman who has these ideals of beauty, or chastity, or *whatever* projected onto her. I mean, women weren't even really allowed to be artists themselves until relatively recently."

A twinge in William's gut. He could envision his studio now, page after page filled with sketches of Rose's face littering his desk. He'd been sneaking looks at her all afternoon, trying to catch the way light hit her bones, every quirk in her features: the slight asymmetry of her eyebrows, the bump in her nose. Reminding himself it was all for his art. Had he been projecting his own ideals onto her? Suddenly feeling claustrophobic in his own mind, he shoved his hands into his pockets.

"So, should men not make portraits of women at all then, or . . . ?"

"Oh no, I think it's natural to want to paint the object of your affection, right?" She turned to him, her eyes gray against the stark white walls. "And I know women have inspired lots of great art, and that's wonderful, it really is. I just wish there was more equal representation, that's all."

William bobbed his head as if he'd been chastised, bending to examine another piece. Had she offended him? Frantically, Rose tried to recall if there'd been paintings of women on his website. She hadn't seen any . . . then suddenly, thankfully, she remembered what was in the next hall.

"But actually, speaking of equal, I think there are some sketches of men coming up." She made a show of peeking through the doorway into the next room, as if she didn't already know what was there.

"Well, let's see?" William swung a hand out, inviting her to lead the way.

The next room *was* filled with images of men, although, upon closer inspection, they all turned out to be the same person. Sketched by Michelangelo, in the distinct red chalk the artist favored, most of the drawings—like the studies for *Primavera*—were practice for later paintings or sculptures. Quick, gestural renderings of torsos, profiles of faces, the shapes of thumbs and feet. Some were clearly unfinished, with whole sections that seemed more like absentminded doodles. Rose half-expected to see a Renaissance grocery list scrawled in one of the corners. *Loaf of bread, jug of wine.* After they entered the room, their Saint Bernard attendant meandered out into the previous hall, offering them the illusion of privacy.

"Okay, my turn." William stood in front of the curator's sign. "So, you'll be happy to know this is about the male muse." He shot a grin at her. "All the art is dedicated to Tommaso de' Cavalieri. He was a nobleman from Rome, and apparently Michelangelo was completely in love with him. Hmm." He crossed his arms, frowning at the text. "I definitely don't remember that from art school."

"I think they used to sweep those sorts of details under the rug..."

"Well, truth be told, I wasn't the best student. I barely remember anything about the Renaissance. Time to buy some books, I guess." He sighed and rubbed his cheek.

Rose's ears perked—*should she get him an art book?* Books were her specialty, after all, so it would make sense ... Immediately, her mind began rifling through the possibilities. She stepped closer to read the notes over his shoulder.

"Was it unrequited? Hmm, doesn't say . . ." She was near enough to smell him: earthy tang of skin and some warm spice, like dry grass in summer. Vetiver maybe. Had he put on cologne? When he sidestepped to look outward she did the same, watching him assess the walls crowded with letters, poems, and sketches.

He gave a low whistle. "That's a lot of art for it not to be requited."

"I'm pretty sure no matter what, Tommaso would have had to marry if he was a nobleman." She began tracing the perimeter of the room, hands clasped behind her back. "Poor Michelangelo. But at least some great art came out of it?"

"That it did." Again William thought of the sketches he'd done, the magnetic pull his studio had been exerting on him lately, with a force he hadn't felt in . . . how long? In years? "But if they couldn't be together, or if it was unrequited, then is making all this with one person in mind . . . is that weird? Is it sad?" He wished it was just an idle question.

"Well, it's not like he could help how he felt, right?" Rose stared at a drawing of a brawny Zeus, considering. "I think making art is the highest form of expressing that longing then. What are his other options, getting depressed? Drinking too much wine? At least this way something beautiful comes out of it . . ."

"At least there's art," William repeated. Rose nodded, and they both went quiet then, walking in a slow choreography through the room, squinting at the work. Tommaso with an eagle. Poems written for Tommaso. Sketches of Tommaso's knees and profile. Silently, they ambled into the next hall, walking in slow motion past the last few portraits of Greek muses, neither of them ready to be done quite yet. Then William ducked his head, and she noticed a pair of double doors just past him.

"Want to see the sculpture garden?"

He spun around, following her outstretched finger. "Sure!"

The garden was really just a balcony with one set of sculptures on either end. They rambled to the edge to look at the city stretching away below: rooftops and neat green rows of trees domed by cloud-swirled sky.

"I still can't wrap my mind around how old the book is." He leaned to rest his forearms on the ledge.

"I know. Giovanni could have even met Michelangelo if he had gone to Rome. And Titian would have been alive in Venice when he was writing the treatise. Think about that!"

William gave a scoffing laugh. "And here I am, painting second-rate landscapes."

"Don't say that." Should she tell him she'd looked at his website? No, better not. "I'm sure your paintings are wonderful."

He stared ahead, as if trying to spot something on the horizon line. "They sell well, but that doesn't really mean anything. I've been wanting to change my style for a long time now."

"Are you going to?"

He looked back at her over one shoulder. "I think so, yeah." A quick grin, like he had a secret, then he turned to gaze out at the city again.

They fell silent; a breeze picked up and stung Rose's eyes, drawing water. She wiped at them with a knuckle, then wrapped her arms tightly around her waist. Another question surfaced, was out of her mouth before she had time to second-guess it:

"Are you glad you moved here?"

William shifted off the ledge, began rolling his sleeves down. He gave a sigh that was heavier than she would have expected. "I'm still getting used to it, to be honest. I miss the city more than I thought I would. Even the sounds at night. I *miss* that." They both observed the grid of streets stretching out below, clean and orderly. "How about you—you were there for school. Do you miss it?"

Normally she would have said yes, named reasons that were similar to his. "No. I like the quiet here. I find it calming."

"I can understand that."

Another wave of silence, then he looked down at her and nodded as if she'd asked another question. Wordlessly, they made their
way back to the elevator. Rose gave a small wave as they passed
their attendant; he closed his eyes at her and dipped his chin into
his jowls. At the elevator, William held the door open, then pushed
the lobby button with his thumb. She tilted her face up toward
him.

"Hey, thanks for getting me out of the shop. This was really
nice."

"It was, wasn't it?" The elevator felt warm and close after the ter-
race.

Out on the sidewalk, he studiously kicked at a nonexistent pebble. "Do you want a ride, or ...?"

"Oh! No, that's fine, I brought my bike, and it's a nice day." She
peered up at the white whorls overhead. "Nice-ish, anyway."

"Okay, well ... see you around? Maybe I'll come by again, if you
find another sketch or something?" His expression was hopeful.

"Absolutely. I'll count on it." He smiled at that. After a beat, they
both turned and walked away in opposite directions.

On the drive home, William replayed the afternoon. Looking at art
with her, taking turns reading the curator's notes out loud. Sharing
a single interest. How long had it been since he'd wandered a gallery
like that, actually talking about the pieces? Long enough for him
not to remember the last time.

There was something else to it, though—the pleasure of being
around a woman who didn't regard him with pity, head leaning to
one side, asking how he was, *really*. William, the cuckolded husband. The man who couldn't keep his wife loyal. They'd told only a
few friends back in New York what had happened, but inevitably
everyone found out. *Pigs in mud*, he thought, getting to enjoy drama
like that without any risk to their own marriages. In particular, he

remembered running into the wife of an old art school friend on the way to the same subway turnstile. She'd always been flirtatious with him, shooting little glances out of the corner of her eye during dinner parties. That afternoon, though, she'd looked at him like he was a child whose toy had been taken by the class bully, then forcefully tugged him into a hug that taught him even hugs could be humiliating—a cloying, maternal embrace. He'd lied about which train he was catching just to get away.

With Rose, though, he could suspend history, at least for a little while. He could be himself again—William the successful artist. William the Man Who Has It All. He hated to admit how much he'd loved watching her blush after she grabbed his arm, how it'd fanned to life a dormant virility, prowling in some lower recess. Was that how Sarah had felt with Mr. Boat Shoes? Had there been something in her life she'd wanted to suspend, leave behind, even for an afternoon? Why hadn't she ever talked to him about it?

"Goddammit, Sarah." William smacked the steering wheel with the heel of his hand. How did she always manage to get him to start seeing her side, no matter how angry he was at her? He glanced at the clock on the dash. He could still stop for food before she got home. He couldn't handle her cooking, not tonight.

The grocery store doors slid open to harsh glare and shining linoleum, an inexplicably loud nineties boy band song blaring over the speakers. William swung his cart aimlessly through the maze of canned and dried goods, the outer ring of produce clinging greenly to life. A package on a bottom shelf caught his eye. Drink umbrellas, bright cerulean and pink. A flash of tropical cheer tucked in between plastic forks and sacks of paper napkins. He picked a box up, tossed it in his cart.

As he kept roaming the aisles, he began to wonder when he'd see Rose again.

12

DOMENICO CRIVELLI WAS A PROFOUNDLY BALD MAN with a compensatorily thick beard that reached nearly down to his breastbone, lustrous and gray. Similarly, what he lacked in height he made up for in girth, with a round belly and perennially red nose betraying a lusty appreciation for life. Although he was a nobleman—and a former senator—by evening Domenico was more likely to be carousing with poets than dining with politicians. Tonight found him flitting around the entrance hall of his home like a portly moth, greeting each visitor with ebullient kisses and exclamations before darting off to the next new arrival.

"Giovanni! Welcome, welcome! Word tells me you're painting a portrait of Venier's girl?" Domenico's eyes were glassy: he'd gotten a head start on his own refreshments.

"I am—in fact, she may be here tonight."

"Superb!" Already, Domenico was glancing past Gio, eyeing the next group of visitors walking in the door. He gave Gio's shoulder a friendly slap, then glided away toward a matron bedecked in pearls and feathers. "Madam, you look as beautiful as the day I first met you!" Domenico's voice melted into the chatter of the guests.

Gio squinted around, finding a nook near the entrance to station himself in. The main room was choked with an assortment of characters—some clutching small pieces of art or books, others instruments. One woman struck his eye: she'd piled her auburn hair into a crown of curls that framed her face, which was dominated by an aquiline nose. The curls, paired with her stiff posture, reminded him of the proud lion sculpture that guarded the Piazza San Marco. As she crossed the floor, Domenico bustled to meet her.

Aurelio, meanwhile, made his presence known well before he actually appeared, the unmistakable boom of his laughter bouncing in from the street. When he arrived, Domenico clasped both hands to the alchemist's cheeks, pressing their foreheads together. They exchanged quick words, and Aurelio gave several pats to the leather satchel slung over his shoulder. Arm in arm, the two wandered from sight, heads bowed together conspiratorially. Shortly after, servants began distributing trays of ruby-red cordials in long-stemmed glasses. Gio took his, wincing slightly at the powerful combination of berry and liquor. By the third sip, however, he tasted only sweetness.

Soon Aurelio reemerged and made his way to Gio. "I see you've found some libation?" He nodded at Gio's glass, eyes twinkling.

"And I see you've been sampling your own wares." Gio reached out to pinch a ruddy cheek. Aurelio cheerfully batted the hand away but did not disagree.

"A new recipe using juniper berries! I'm working on it with an alchemist up north, it's our secret project." Aurelio waggled his eyebrows at Gio. "Come, let's greet Maddalena." With that, he launched his body into the crowd, guests turning to raise their drinks in cheer at every step. Aurelio happily greeted each one, somehow never breaking stride. Gio followed in his wake, blinking hard against the glare of crystal, the glint of silk and gems in the light.

As they approached, Gio recognized the woman he'd been watching earlier. The lioness with the regal bearing—of course it would be her. She was deep in conversation with a frail-looking man he recognized as a member of the Orsini family, no doubt explaining in tedious detail the features of his father's famous garden. Aurelio thrust himself into their circle.

"Maddalena, my dove! Meet Giovanni Lomazzo." Leaning as close as his belly would allow, Aurelio continued in a mock whisper, "He's a genius painter; you really ought to sit for him."

"Oh, don't believe a word this man says." Gio took her extended hand in his. Her skin was cool and damp. She wore a row of gold-banded rings—pearl, emerald, ruby—and when he bent to kiss her knuckles, a pleased smile stretched across her face.

Then a murmur passed through the crowd, and without seeing her, he knew she'd arrived. In the gaps between bodies she glimmered into view, wearing her signature ivory and gold. The men in the room turned to her like plants toward sunlight—jealously, Gio shot forward, weaving through the throng to offer his elbow.

"Come, let me introduce you." With a half nod, Chiara draped a hand over his forearm. The whole room seemed to stare as he ushered her back to where Maddalena and Aurelio stood chatting. "Chiara, may I present to you Mistress Maddalena Casulana. She's recently published a book of madrigals." Gio couldn't help but beam as he watched her digest the words.

"You . . . you've published?" For a moment, Chiara lost all decorum. Blankly she stared at Maddalena—who seemed uncertain what to make of the girl before her, who looked so very much like a courtesan.

"Chiara is a talented composer in her own right." Gio rushed to salvage the introduction. "I must confess, it was my hope you might encourage her to continue her pursuits." He felt Chiara squeeze his arm.

"I see." Maddalena smiled knowingly, nodding and narrowing her eyes, newly assessing the girl. "You know, Isabella de' Medici was my champion. I never would have succeeded without her. We women must help one another." Her voice was polished as a pebble in a riverbed. "And, of course, there are men, like Domenico, like Giovanni here, who support us. A rare few who understand how much we have to offer and are not threatened by our gifts."

She lifted her eyes to scan the room. "There are still more who'd prefer we stay as subjects, of course. But an ocean can turn its tide." Maddalena straightened her shoulders, staring down sharply into Chiara's face. Even with her *chopines* on, Chiara stood a full head shorter. "We simply must have faith and continue our work. Now come, tell me of your music." She took Chiara's elbow and led them for a slow turn around the room.

Gio watched them walk away, tracking the melody of Chiara's voice until it was lost in the dense hum of conversation. Then— before he could register what was happening—Aurelio had dragged him into a back corner where Domenico stood waiting. Slinging an arm over each man's shoulder, the alchemist leaned in dramatically.

"Gentlemen, it is official. Venice will sail to fight the Ottomans."

The news came as little surprise. Domenico pursed his lips and plucked at the end of his beard. "Has a league been formed? Surely Venice cannot sail alone."

Aurelio leveled his gaze at Gio. "Gio, the dinner party you recently attended was in fact an excuse for Venier to impress upon the doge the importance of defending Cyprus." The dry, familiar voice he'd heard—suddenly, Gio remembered where he knew it from. Aurelio lowered his voice further. "Nicosia has fallen, and Famagusta cannot hold much longer. Christian forces have been organized, though the worry now is that we'll be too late."

"I confess, I overheard some of their talk." Gio confided. "They spoke of the new ships Bressan has designed. But the doge said he required the support of Rome—"

"And we have it." The alchemist cut in. "The Pope has given his approval now that the Spanish have agreed to fund the mission. Venier is eager to leave at once; he's a hairsbreadth away from being named admiral—there's just one pesky dissenter in the Senate. Claims some statesman, a relation, of course, has more experience." The Senate determined matters of Venetian policy, including military operations; as in all political bodies in Venice, only noblemen were allowed to participate. Aurelio pulled them in closer. "And, it would seem that Don Juan of Austria's just been appointed—"

A flurry of movement in the center of the room interrupted their discussion. Servants carrying low-backed chairs had arranged makeshift theater seating, and now Maddalena and three plain-faced women were taking their places center stage. With a start, Domenico scampered to stand before them, waving his arms at the crowd like a misplaced conductor. As guests began to take their seats, he cleared his throat and raised a glass, waiting for the room to settle. Gio and Aurelio stayed in their corner, tucked away stage left of the singers.

"My friends, I am honored to introduce Mistress Maddalena Casulana, who visits us all the way from Milan. This evening she will be performing from her recent book of madrigals, *Il primo libro di madrigali*. These are the first compositions ever to be published by a woman." Domenico held one finger in the air as if to impress upon his audience the singularity of the achievement.

"Tonight, we witness history. Please enjoy as Mistress Casulana performs 'Morir non può il mio cuore.'" Bowing deeply, Domenico backed offstage with a sweep of his arm, returning to stand by Gio and Aurelio. The audience applauded raucously, plied with liquor and ready to be entertained.

Maddalena and her singers stood in silence, exchanging glances. Then in perfect unison, they launched into the madrigal—a tightly composed piece built on a rigid traditional structure. Playing on a contrast of pitch and language, Maddalena's voice undulated sensuously as the lyrics recounted a forbidden love affair.

"*Morir non può il mio cuore . . . Ma trar no si può fuore del petto. Vostr'ove gran tempo giace . . .*" The women's voices rang like chimes, alternating tones weaving together. From his vantage behind the singers, Gio could easily observe Chiara, seated in the first row. Hands clasped together in her lap, she leaned forward, mesmerized. He wondered if she recognized that for all the polish and professionalism of Maddalena's composition, it lacked the emotional charge of her own work. Likely not—her face was turned up like an acolyte. For once, he wanted to look away.

Trying not to squint too noticeably, Gio scanned the room. Overall, the crowd appeared engrossed, though Gio caught a few older men clearly working to keep their eyes open. One or two women shot glances in Chiara's direction, not bothering to conceal their jealousy. Toward the back, far figures became unfocused impressions of personality and color.

Corvino.

Gio was never prepared to see the Crow, even when he should be. And each time it was the same: heart quickening and a sudden sense of being thrown off-balance—like walking into a room where every painting was tilted an inch to the right. Leaning against the doorframe, the Crow was nearly completely obscured by a wall of floating faces and hillocks of hair. Yet even behind the swaying crowd, he formed an unmistakable dark blot, his constant gold cross floating on his chest like an insignia. Gio squinted harder, realizing Corvino's stare was locked on the back of Chiara's head.

"The Crow will get a taste of his own medicine soon." Aurelio's voice in his ear. The alchemist leaned to whisper, his belly a comforting heft against Gio's arm. "Venier left him with the girl while he met with the doge, and he'll leave him again when they go to war." Aurelio said the words like a warning.

"Corvino *wants* to sail with the fleet?" The Crow had turned his head; Gio stared at the fuzzed line of his profile, the contrast of his pale skin against his dark hair.

"Corvino wants war more than anything else." The alchemist shifted, breath hitting Gio's neck in warm bursts as he spoke. "I believe his dream is to sail alongside Venier and make a name for himself. Soon he'll see how far outside the circle he really stands."

The madrigal ended just then, and they parted to clap along with the crowd. When Gio glanced back, Corvino was gone, an empty space remaining where he'd stood, as if no one else wished to occupy it.

Hours after the performance, Gio set out walking toward home, alone. Chiara had been sequestered in a corner with Maddalena and several noblemen for the better part of an hour. Rather than stay, staring like a fool, he'd thanked Domenico and slipped out—obscured by a group of guests departing in a flurry of waves and bows and rounds of farewells. Now, following the bends and curves of the canals, he pulled his robes close against the chill air. Overhead, stars whirled peacefully in the inky void, their doubles twinkling in the water below. Even the moon seemed content to drowse in her own effulgence. It was hard to imagine that not so very far away men were filling one another's bellies with lead shot and blades. Gio buried his hands in the folds of his cloak, watching the tips of his boots pace the stones.

A gondola slid up beside him.

"Gio."

It was Chiara's voice, unmistakable, though her face was hidden beneath the fringe of the gondola's canopy. Gio halted. Glancing up and down the avenue, he saw only empty cobblestone and shadow. From a bridge up ahead came the displaced echo of a woman's laugh. Quickly, he maneuvered into the boat, exchanging a look with the gondolier, a wide-faced lad who nodded with the kind of solemn understanding that can only pass between men.

"We shouldn't be seen together so often, Chiara." His weight rocked the gondola as he navigated to the back bench. The hood of her robe tumbled down, tugging a few blond strands loose from the mound of braids she'd pinned at her crown. As he settled in beside her, she laid her head on his shoulder. He breathed in the sweet musk of her perfume: flower water and cloves.

"It doesn't matter. Venier will be off to Cyprus soon."

"Yes, leaving the Crow behind to watch your every step."

"Don't say that." She groaned, bringing a hand up to cover her face. He changed the subject, keeping his voice low.

"I'm glad you came. I was afraid you wouldn't."

She sat up to look at him. "Gio, she told me her work was going to be performed for the Duke of Bavaria this winter. A woman—a woman from Siena, no different than any other—performing her compositions for nobles and dukes!" Moonlight filtered in through the fringe of the curtains, illuminating her clavicle while her face remained in shadow; he thought of Titian's *Danaë*. Her eyes shone at him through the gloom, then she bent to rummage for something in her cloak.

"She gave me a copy of her book; let me read to you the inscription." Her hand emerged holding the thin volume of madrigals, bound in red leather. She cleared her throat.

"Here it is: 'I want to show the world, as much as I can in this profession of music, the vain error of men that they alone possess the gifts of intellect and artistry, and that such gifts are never given to women.'" She snapped the book shut—the slap of paper cutting through the thick calm of the night. "The vain error of men." She repeated the line from memory, thumping on his chest with her fist. He grasped his breastbone where she'd hit him, laughing at her excitement.

"Are you mocking me?" Her eyes narrowed.

"No, no, no. In fact, Chiara, it's my turn to be serious." He brought a hand to her shoulder, felt the fibers of her robe crush a little. "Maddalena is very brave, and of course it's wonderful that she's been published. But . . ." He hunted after the right words. "The truth is that her compositions are just like all the others. There's nothing unique about her music; nothing challenging. Perhaps that's why she was able to be published, in fact. Because her work is so safe."

A look of confusion crossed Chiara's face, and he resisted the urge to shake her. "What I'm trying to say is that *your* work is brilliant. That song you shared with me was beautiful, but it was also unusual. Different. And so, it's even more important that it's heard." She'd gone silent, her head downturned, staring at the book in her lap. He reached to clasp her hand in his. "I only ask that you don't idolize Maddalena. Please. Just think of her as . . . as an older sister, clearing your path, making the world ready to hear your voice too."

She said nothing, her eyes still fixed on the book. With his thumb, he rubbed the ridgeline of her knuckles, listening to the sleepy noises the water made against the boat as they rocked. Finally, she spoke.

"The picture you sent was beautiful."

"You're beautiful."

She smiled. "You *saw* me."

"I hope I did." He reached to tuck a pale wisp of hair behind her ear. "I hope I do."

She looked up at him. "It was never charity, Gio." For the second time she leaned to put her mouth to his. He felt the slip of wet skin, a warm, lingering taste of liquor on her tongue; he didn't try to push her away.

In the shadows, trailing far behind them, Corvino cursed the gondola's cabin. He was certain—well, nearly certain—that he'd followed Chiara's vessel as it emerged from the cluster outside Domenico's salon. And now, here was that artist, stepping into the boat.

He'd have to keep a closer watch on them both.

Shouts erupted from the market square in Famagusta. One of Captain Bragadin's soldiers was loudly proclaiming to all who'd listen that he'd killed Mustafa's son—Mustafa, commander of the Ottoman forces that were even now laying siege to the citadel. He'd seen that face before, he swore it on his mother's grave. At a feast in Damascus during peace times. He swore it on his mother's grave. Now he'd killed the boy and taken his saber for bounty.

Bragadin heard the shouts as he paced the length of the defense wall—in an instant, he was rushing down the stone stairs, the crowd parting before him. As he approached the center of the square—forearm raised against the blazing midday sun—the soldier who'd been shouting pivoted toward him. Balanced on his upturned palms, as if in supplication, lay a saber. Bragadin's mind reeled backward in time: a slingshot in reverse. What was it the beggar woman had said to him so many years ago? Snatching at his arm in the crowded bazaar, peering up at him with that wizened face, that silver stare? "You'll be killed by the whip, but you'll die by the saber." He reached for the hilt of the weapon, saw a streak of dark along the blade's edge.

The blood of Mustafa's heir.

13

ROSE STOOD IN JOAN'S KITCHEN, AMID THE WHITE-AND-blue tile countertops. Floral wallpaper spread cockscomb and peonies up to the ceiling. The window behind the sink was open, faint birdsong drifting in from the backyard. At a round Formica table, Henry sat staring at a bowl of half-eaten spaghetti—in his efforts to wrangle the strands of pasta, he'd ended up covering much of his face and some of his hair with sauce. Chewing the tip of her thumb, Rose watched him maneuver the fork again.

"Oh, for heaven's sake, Rose, stop biting your thumb. Here, can you help?" Joan handed her a wet rag, gesturing with a jerk of her head toward Henry. She turned back to the counter, where she was slicing rhubarb. It was in season surprisingly early, stacked up at the local grocers in neat pink and green stripes. On the spot, the two had determined to make a pie. While they'd fashioned the crust, which now sat cooling in the fridge, Rose had rambled on about the book, Lomazzo, William. Their visit to the university gallery. Joan had let her speak without interruption, listening patiently as she unraveled her tangled thoughts.

"I wonder what Giovanni would say if he could see William's paintings." Rose swiped the rag now between Henry's fingers while he watched, placid as a calf. The marinara in his bangs clashed sharply with his red hair.

"Rosie." Joan moved to put a hand on her hip, realized it was wet with rhubarb juice, and shifted to lean her weight against the counter instead. She was wearing a faded gingham apron with ruffles along the edges that had been her mother's. "Are you sure you're not spending too much time with this guy? I mean, he's married. With kids." Instinctively, she glanced at Henry. A quick snatch of melody burst in from the finches darting outside.

"Joan, he's just a client."

"Do you normally go to galleries with your clients?" Joan raised her eyebrows, skeptical.

"Come on, it's not like that." Rose thought of the way she'd caught him looking at her as they wandered the exhibition, and her conviction faltered. She bent to focus on wiping the sauce from Henry's hair.

Joan reached for a dish towel, began drying her hands. "Now, I'm not saying what it's like or not, all I'm saying is there are plenty of fish in the sea. Available fish." She tossed the towel on the counter, then picked up a slice of rhubarb from the cutting board, swirled it around in the dish of sugar she'd set out. "I still don't understand why you don't just try the apps." She popped the rhubarb in her mouth, began crunching loudly.

"Ugh, not this again." Rose went to the sink to rinse the rag out. She *had* tried the apps. At least, she'd gotten as far as attempting a photo of herself, a humiliating exercise of wandering around the house with her phone raised in front of her, searching for the most flattering lighting. What was the best angle for her chin; should she leave her hair up or style it? How? She'd taken twenty photos, then scanned through them, each one worse than the last, her face pulling awkwardly. She'd turned to the computer, searching online for "profile photo tips for women," then compared herself to the artful examples that'd lined up on the screen.

She'd decided against the apps.

"I'd just rather meet someone the normal way, that's all." Rose took both ends of the rag in her hands and twisted, watching the red wring out into the streaming water.

"Sweetie, apps *are* the new normal." Joan spoke in between more bites of rhubarb. "But if you're set on just 'bumping into someone,' then you actually have to get out there. Make yourself bump-into-able." She licked the leftover sugar granules off her fingers loudly, the sound like punctuation. "I think the problem is that you've just been isolated for too long. Working so hard to get the business up, looking after your dad for what, almost two years? Taking care of him like that? You know I always told you that you'd be better off—"

"Enough! That's enough, Joan." Rose didn't mean to sound so harsh. Outside, the birds lulled; for a moment the only sound in the kitchen was the slap of water against the steel sink basin. Rose turned the faucet off.

A sudden crash and clatter—Henry had knocked his plate to the floor. He shot a panicked expression up at his mother. Instantly, both women turned to the mess, Rose bending to right the bowl, Joan snatching a roll of paper towels off the counter. As Henry watched from his chair, they scooped the slippery pasta up with their hands. By the time the ruined noodles were down the garbage disposal and the floor had been wiped clean, a careful and unspoken agreement had arrived to hold the evening together.

An hour later the oven door opened, blasting dry heat. The pie emerged, flaky and golden, filled with bittersweet juice.

Rose gave up trying to keep the shop open through the university's study and final exam weeks. She put a sign on the window, KNOCK LOUDLY, and propped the door to the back room ajar. Steadily, the number of completed pages grew: neat piles, all dusted, wiped, daubed, and mended. Fixated, she tracked Giovanni through his charts and diagrams, page after page of mostly indecipherable musings. From what she could gather based on her poor Italian, the text focused on a range of topics: proportion, color, perspective—*proporzione, colore, prospettiva*. A slim chapter seemed to address the planets; constellations scattered the margins. Andromeda, Ursa Minor. Lyra and Pegasus. Rose made a note to research what Giovanni might have known about astronomy. She lifted the next page.

Sciographia. The word was written in calligraphy at the top of the parchment. Rose knew what it meant from the one psychology course she'd taken. *Sciographia*: the science of shadows. Her mind flickered to that second year of college; she could picture the carved-up wooden desk she'd sat in, nearly smell the tobacco-and-aftershave scent wafting from her professor as he paced the aisles, reading aloud from the textbook in a historical baritone. What was it Jung had said? That the shadow contains all the pieces of ourselves we reject and hide—and that the shadow must be confronted.

"Easier said than done, Jung." Rose reminded herself to maybe stop talking out loud so much when she was alone.

Giovanni's approach to *sciographia* was decidedly more practical. The chapter began with a list of colors, matching each with its complementary hue to be used when depicting shadows. Indigo for yellow, a touch of red in the shade cast by a green object. *Indaco, rosso, verde.* By the sketches that ran down the margins of the next sheets, Rose could guess that he was summarizing the different kinds of shadows: the darkness that lingers in the creases of eyes, the shapes cast by a body; how they bend and lengthen in the light. She turned the page.

A man she knew stared up at her.

A wave of recognition, swiftly replaced by disorienting confusion—like spotting her doctor in the grocery store squeezing avocados. Those eyes, inked hundreds of years ago, she knew those eyes. But from where? The figure regarded her with an expression so familiar it was as if they'd just seen each other.

Then she realized: they *had* just seen each other. It was William.

It was him, undeniably, yet not him. Over the course of two pages, Giovanni had drawn a series of small sketches with a ribbon of text running down the centerline, like the illustrated poems of Blake or a children's book. And in every scene was an almost-William. The figure had a close-cropped beard, but unmistakably the same features, the same attitudes of expression. The only conclusion was that these were self-portraits—of Giovanni. How else could a looking-glass-world William be peering out at her from a treatise written in 1571?

Rose took a steadying breath, then began to examine the images in order. *Logical, methodical.* Her grad school mantra, resurfacing like muscle memory.

In the first sketch, Giovanni had drawn a woman who was half tree: branches forked from her shoulders, her arms reaching up among them, slender fingers sprouting leaves. Her hips barked into trunk. Where her feet would have been, she was planted in soil, a wayward root dangling off the edge of the page. Pale hair coiled over her breasts, and her face was downturned. Rose bent until her nose was nearly touching the page, scrutinizing the lines.

It was the same woman as in the portrait. It had to be.

From the upper edge of the page, an egg-shaped object was shown descending from turbulent clouds. Delicate ink strokes gave it depth, the impression of carrying weight. In the next scene, the egg had crash-landed at the base of the tree-woman, shell shards scattered among her roots. A single hand, splayed, poked out from a gaping crack. The tree-woman reached to grasp it, and in the following image, a winged Giovanni emerged from the wreckage of the egg—the tips of his feathers extending off the vellum, a whip of fabric modestly covering his lower torso.

Down the margins of the second page, Giovanni and the woman appeared to be having a serious discussion, their heads bowed together. Then he spread his arms around her waist and dislodged her, roots whipping loose in a wild patterning. In the final scene, the tree-woman was depicted tall and blossoming, a pastoral landscape hazily filled in behind. The winged Giovanni crouched in her branches, holding her cheek in his palm, whispering in her ear; shadows suggested the warm light of afternoon. An overwhelming sense of intimacy pervaded the sketches. The text running down the center of the page pulled at Rose the way hieroglyphics did, promising a narrative.

Barely aware of her actions, Rose carried the pages to the computer. Over the next hour, she wrestled with three different online translators until a passable English version emerged:

Long before you or I may remember lived a being of [marvelous? miraculous?] composition. Half woman, half tree, she was planted in a barren field — (here Rose hadn't been able to parse the calligraphy) the ends of the earth. She was beautiful and fair, yet her face was often sad. She was [declining? diminishing?] in that desolate place. One day she looked up and to her surprise saw a white egg — from the heavens. It fell and fell and fell, and, upon landing, the [creature?] inside pleaded for escape. The tree, being very good and kind, helped to free this one from its — Out came a man with the wings of an angel. So sweet are the — of fate that instantly the [knot?] of love was tied between them. The man prayed her tell him how he might

repay her kindness. She begged for him to save her from that
— place.

As everyone knows, true love [bonds?] the will of the lover
to the beloved. He wrapped his wings about her and — up into
the sky. From far above, she spied a hilltop — in flower and
stream. It was there he planted her, and in that fertile land she
grew ever more beautiful. Forever after, the man would fly
both far and wide, then return to rest in her branches to tell her
of all — She would show him her blossoms and feed him her
[harvest?] and together they were very happy.

It reminded Rose of a parable, but without the moral lesson.
What would William think? She'd send him a scan but knew he'd
come in person to see it. Her heart quickened at the thought, and
immediately she pictured Joan, her raised-brow, skeptical expression in the kitchen earlier that week.

"He's just a client." It seemed less convincing stated out loud to
an empty room. She *had* to break that habit . . .

At the drafting table, Rose flicked on the lights to take a scan of
each page. She noticed that, like the first portrait of the woman,
these pages didn't have any perforations to indicate that the sheets
had been part of the original binding. Likely they'd been inserted
into the book at a later date—

Ding! The computer chirruped, interrupting her thoughts. The
final scan had been rendered. This time, she wrote the first thing
that came to mind:

W—
I just came across these sketches in the book (!!)
     Let me know if you'd like to see them for yourself?
                                                    —R

Sent.

She rubbed her eyes. It was late; she didn't want to think anymore. When she looked back at her screen, she saw a new message—not from William, but from Lucas, using his university email address. He must have tracked her down through the library system.

Rose—
A few books recently came across my desk that seemed potentially useful to your project. I've attached the details below.

All my best,
Lucas

Synopses and citations ran in a list at the end of his message. They did seem useful. But how likely was it that so many books had just "come across his desk"? More likely he'd been bored and gotten interested in her project. Rose pictured the gangly librarian with his thick glasses and smiled despite herself, mentally scheduling another visit to the university. She stood, feeling slightly off-balance.

After the glaring light in the back, the darkened bookshop felt like a child's bedroom: slumbering shapes glazed in the amber glow of streetlights. She gathered her bag and helmet from under her desk and tiptoed over to Odin's chair, ran one thumb across his whiskered cheek. Disturbed from dreaming, he gave a drowsy *mew* and stretched both front paws out. The fur of his belly was warm from sleep. When she took her hand away, he curled up again, burrowing his nose back under a paw.

She biked home alone, with the stars white-hot and burning overhead.

"I know, but your claws might rip my dress." The next day, Rose had decided to wear a dusty-pink work dress someone had once told her brought out the color in her cheeks. For his part, Odin had decided that he very much needed to sit in her lap. He yowled indignantly at the rejection. As recompense, Rose reached to scratch behind one ear, which he begrudgingly allowed.

Then William was there, rapping the glass with his knuckles, pushing open the door. This time, instead of a cap or phone in his hands he carried a small Tupperware container, fitted with a red lid, which he held out as he walked toward her.

"Figured since I was taking up your lunch hour, I might as well bring you something to eat. . . . It's a quiche, hope that's all right."

"Oh! Thank you." She reached to take the container from him; the bottom was still warm. "That's so thoughtful, William." The shape of his name felt good in her mouth. "Here, let me show you the sketches, I've got them all ready." She set the Tupperware on her desk and headed back toward the workroom. He followed close behind. She was suddenly acutely aware of the air passing over the tops of her shoulder blades, where the dip of her dress left the skin exposed.

"Oh!" Her hand slipped on the doorknob. She looked up and he was smiling down at her, standing close in the dim-lit hall. She grasped the knob again, swung the door open.

"The pages are on the drafting table, just there." She gestured inside.

At once, he strode to the sketches. Looking over the images, he blew his breath out through his teeth in a not-quite whistle. She moved to stand beside him. He reached to even the edge of one sheet, and she caught the same scent as before, soil and warm grass.

"This is almost surrealist. Look at the detailing in the feathers." He bent closer. "Wait, is this the woman from the portrait?"

"I think so. I compared little elements, like her mouth. Her jaw. Her chin, here." Rose pointed to the most look-alike image. "And . . . you do realize that the man looks *just* like you, don't you?"

"Like me? Really?" William frowned at the figures.

"Well, there's a beard and, you know, *wings*, but—your eyebrows, your nose, your eyes. It's you."

He straightened up, drawing a hand to a cheek as if measuring his own jaw against the one on the page. "You're right. I'll be damned." He thought for a moment. "You think it's Giovanni?"

"I do. And I did a translation of the text too. It's rough, I just used online translators, but you get the idea." She picked up the printed-out page from the counter and thrust it at him. "I was just too curious not to know."

He didn't respond, already reading. Rose fell silent. She watched his eyes dart across the lines, glancing down between sentences to follow along with the sketches, then looping back to reread the words. Finally, he looked up.

"Well, it's strange, but beautiful. And romantic: they rescue each other." He reached to scratch the back of his head. "I think the ending is supposed to be happy, but it seems kind of sad to me. It doesn't feel like they get to *be* together—not really."

"I had the same impression. And the way he drew their expressions, the shading . . . it all feels a little melancholy. Bittersweet."

"I suppose that's how a lot of love stories go, though, isn't it." A statement, not a question.

Rose nodded. "Orpheus and Eurydice."

"Lancelot and Guinevere."

Silence pressed down on the room. William broke it with a polite cough. "I wonder if they ended up together. Giovanni and the woman." He was looking at the final scene.

"I hope so."

"So do I."

"Even if they didn't, at least they did here. That's what I've always loved about art . . . it creates other realities."

"What do you mean?" He'd shifted so that he was facing her, one hip leaning against the table.

"Oh, it's like what we talked about at the gallery, with those Michelangelo sketches. No matter what their actual situation was, Giovanni could still create this world for them." She gestured at the pages. "The art makes it real in its own way, doesn't it? It keeps them alive, it keeps their experience—or the idea of that experience—alive."

"That's a nice way to look at it." He grinned, dimple threatening to show.

Receiving his approval felt like stepping into a warm spotlight; when he smiled at her she couldn't help but do the same. She didn't know what to say next, though, so she turned instead to stare at the center table. The rest of the treatise sat in tidy piles, waiting to be scanned.

"Do you think there'll be more drawings?" His voice was oddly loud.

"Actually, I'm almost finished cleaning all the pages well enough for the first layer of text to be translated. So, I don't think so."

He raised his eyebrows. "Already?"

"I've put some extra hours in." She could hear Joan's voice in her head: *That's the understatement of the year.* "For the undertext, I'll need to do more work restoring the ink so it's legible enough to render." Anxiously, she clasped her hands together, tracing circles inside her palm with one thumb. "There's something else, though, I should mention."

"What's that?"

"Well, the writing deteriorates as the book goes on. Pretty quickly."

"Deteriorates? Like it's harder to see?"

"More like it seems it was harder for him to write. The lines start to wobble. The letters get a little illegible." She looked at him leaning against the table, at his open, quizzical expression. "I think he may have been losing his sight, William."

Pity and helplessness in equal measures darted across his face. "Seriously?" He rubbed a hand over his head the wrong way, causing the hair on top to stick up, like it'd done in the car when he'd driven her home. "Well, I hope it was old age. For an artist to lose his sight . . . Is there any way to know how old he was when he wrote this?"

"Not unless we can get some definitive dates on his life, so . . . no. Not really. I'm sorry."

"Nothing for you to be sorry about." He reached to touch the corner of one page. "Do you suppose that's why he wrote the treatise? Kind of a final big project?"

"It definitely could have been. As the book goes on, the writing gets shakier, but it also seems like he was writing faster. He forgets to cross t's, for example. It took me a while to figure out what was happening on the page, but I think he was rushing to finish."

"Ugh." William squinted up at the glaring lights overhead. "I can't even imagine what that must have been like. Well, that makes me understand *why* a treatise, at least. He probably wanted to record what he knew, what he thought. For posterity." He crossed his arms, surveying the stacks of paper on the center table. "I get it, even if I still can't believe it: a treatise on art, written by my . . . whatever he would have been."

"Before he died, my father worked on a book too. A survey of the classics. I think it's natural to want to leave your ideas behind." Rose felt a small tightening in the back of her throat.

"I'm glad he got the chance to do that." William's voice had gone tender.

"Me too."

Overhead, the lights shuddered and flared; without words, they left the room and made their way back through the shop. Rose paused at the door stoop. The day had gone chill: wind threaded around her body, passing through the thin fabric of her dress, coaxing out the curls at her temples. William stepped out onto the sidewalk, then hesitated, glancing down at her.

"You'll let me know as soon as the translation comes in?"

"Of course." A wisp of hair blew in front of her eyes. Carelessly, he reached out to tuck it back again.

The sudden, rough softness of his fingertips against her ear. A gentle weight. So natural she didn't startle, just shut her eyes at the touch, dissolving into the feeling.

Then he pulled his hand back, turned, and walked away.

From the doorway, she watched him go: both hands shoved deep into his pockets now, the curve of his shoulders receding down the sidewalk until he disappeared around the corner. He didn't look back.

Rose closed the door, her whole face tingling as if she'd been slapped. She flipped the sign again and went to the front desk. The Tupperware container sat waiting for her, small beads of condensation pockmarking the plastic. When she opened the lid, the pressure inside released with a soft sigh. She picked the quiche up and took a bite. It was well herbed and flavorful, with still-warm cherry tomatoes dotting the top. They broke open sweetly under pressure. When she was done, she wet the tip of her index finger, dragged it around the edges of the container. Held the taste in her mouth for as long as she could.

14

THE OFFICIAL ANNOUNCEMENT OF WAR COINCIDED WITH Carnival season and sent an electric charge coursing through the festivities. Puppeteers scrambled to create Ottoman effigies, and street performers hastily revised their villains into evil Turks. By nightfall, the avenues howled and shook.

The celebrations were set to culminate in the Piazza San Marco. Several days before, Aurelio had taken Gio to visit his favorite mask maker: an old man by the name of Jacopo. His shop was tucked behind a bend in a narrow alleyway, completely hidden from view of the street. A sign swung overhead, but the letters had long since faded into unintelligible patches of peeling blue paint; as they entered, the door hinges creaked.

Inside, Gio didn't know where to look. Everywhere were masks: displayed on a wide table in the middle of the room, stacked atop one another on shelves that extended, floor to ceiling, across the walls—masks of every shape, size, and color, with vacant eyes all waiting to be filled. They seemed to be staring at him expectantly;

no matter where he turned, Gio felt watched by gaping, empty sockets. As soon as he stepped inside, he had the urge to flee.

Movement in a far corner halted him. It was Jacopo, glancing up to nod at the visitors from his work desk. He was older than Gio had anticipated: his back made a nearly perfect bow, and his impish face was held upright by a neck that seemed all tendon—yet his eyes were clear and sharp as a sparrow's. With a gnarled hand, he beckoned them in.

After introductions were made, Gio retreated to wander the store while Aurelio and Jacopo settled into the easy conversation that comes between friends who've watched each other age. Inspecting the masks more closely, Gio couldn't help but admire Jacopo's craftsmanship. The faces were all well formed, reflecting various attitudes and emotions. Gio found himself most intrigued by the grotesque ones: those with hooked noses and contorted folds of flesh, frozen expressions of horror and rage.

As he scanned the center table, he caught sight of an unusual texture. A row of feathers, coated in thick black paint, like a bird caught in tar. Leaning forward, he tugged at the tip of one. As he pulled, the mask balanced on top slid to one side—revealing a crow's head underneath. Made from leather, wood, and wing, the mask had an aggressive brow and an intricate pattern tooled along the sides. A cruel beak extended outward, meant to hide the wearer's mouth. Slitted eyes glared up ominously, as if eager to take hold of Gio's own.

"Ah yes, that." Jacopo had been watching. "A special request from Corvino. He was quite specific with his instructions. Horrifying, isn't it?" Crossing his arms, he gave the mask a sidelong glance. "I almost prefer not to acknowledge I made the thing."

"Well, it makes my skin crawl," Gio conceded. "Which means you did a masterful job." Carefully, he balanced a plain white mask over the head, which only partially hid it, black feathers stubbornly creeping out at the edges.

Jacopo shrugged, then turned to Aurelio. "He mentioned it would be his last celebration before the fleet left. Do you know which ship he plans to sail with?"

"I think the better question is if he'll be allowed to sail at all. It's my belief Corvino is counting on promises yet to be made." Aurelio raised his eyebrows meaningfully at Jacopo, who gave a low whistle. Before Jacopo could ask any more questions, Aurelio swept to Gio's side, his hand a warm weight on Gio's shoulder. "Come, friend, help me pick one."

Eventually, they decided on a flamboyant purple affair for the alchemist, with a puff of dyed feathers unfurling from each side. For himself, Gio chose a simple mask, painted blue.

The next day found Gio, Chiara, and Cecilia in a gondola, heading to their first sitting at his studio in the *castello*. As they glided through the canals, Chiara let one hand graze the surface of the water, ripples arrowing out from her fingertips. Overhead, the shadows of bridges swept across them in the blunt midmorning light. Whenever she spotted someone she knew on the avenues—which was often— Chiara would bend over the bow, waving and loudly announcing that she was to have her portrait done, making mock coquettish poses for their amusement. In the back of the boat, Gio and Cecilia were obliged to lean against her sudden movements: without counterbalance, they'd all be sent tumbling into the canal. Behind them, Gio could hear the gondolier swearing under his breath, wrestling with his oar. When they arrived at the studio, Gio scrambled out first, turning to help Chiara step ashore in her high *chopines*.

Inside the workshop, Chiara swept into the center of the room and took a slow spin, surveying the space. On a large easel, Gio had prepared the canvas—coated in gesso, dried and ready—while on the hearth, embers from a morning fire sparked and faded with the regularity of breath.

"And who are *these* women?" Chiara had spotted the few nude sketches he'd done, among all the landscape paintings that lay stacked against the wall. She strode to stand in front of them, hands on her hips.

"Just models." Gio kept his voice light. "None as beautiful as you, don't worry."

"All your lovers, of course." Her tone was playful, but as she turned back to the center of the room, he saw her lift her chin.

"No, of course not!"

"You don't keep an assistant?" She continued on as though she hadn't heard. She'd tied her hair up in wide braids that day, woven through with white silk ribbon. The finer strands at her temples had come loose, and they floated around her face when she moved her head.

"I work better alone. Besides, assistants are known for telling secrets." At this, she looked at him sharply—she was still thinking of the models. He squinted his eyes in an exaggerated gesture only she could see, and her expression warmed. She spun on one heel, sauntering to the stool placed in front of the easel; as she sat, she flicked her skirts so that they whirled out in perfect pleats. Folding her hands in her lap like two pale dove wings, she turned to face Cecilia.

"Well, fortunately for you, Cecilia is very good at keeping secrets. Aren't you, Cecilia?" Cecilia nodded obediently from her post in the corner, where she'd stationed herself to be out of the way. Gio observed once again the clean white part that divided the girl's brown hair and her serious, plain features. She made a solemn counterpart to Chiara's dazzling beauty—like Clymene, the ox-eyed handmaiden to Helen of Troy.

"Giovanni is worried you'll tell Venier that his sight is weak and he prefers to wear spectacles when he works. But you won't tell, will you, Cecilia?"

Gio started, felt heat rush to his face. Cecilia's eyes went wide; she shook her head.

"See? She's very loyal. And now your secret's shared, so there's no sense in pretending and squinting the entire time you're trying to paint. Isn't that better?" Chiara smiled and recrossed her legs, clearly pleased with herself.

"I suppose." Gio had to admit she was right. It'd be much easier to just use his lenses—and besides, it wouldn't be long before his sight was claimed altogether. Little to lose at this point. He shot a glance at Cecilia, who was looking at him with a combination of fascination and pity, and cleared his throat. "Well, now that you know all my secrets, shall we begin? You can change just there." He pointed to the embroidered screen in the corner.

While Cecilia set about removing Chiara's gown—not without some audible effort—Gio tied his lenses on. Rummaging in a cabinet for a swatch of silk, he selected a fine measure of azure blue, which he laid by the stool. After some time, Chiara emerged from behind the screen like a nude Venus come to life. Two paces after came Cecilia, red in the face, arms heaped with fabric that she began draping over a chaise. Neither made any comment on his spectacles. Chiara had kept her jewelry on—sapphire pendant, long strands of pearls, delicate gold chains—but she'd unbraided her hair. It tumbled down the length of her back, still faintly crimped, and as she walked toward the hearth Gio watched it waft behind her in a haze of translucent blond, following the roll of her hips. He turned and caught Cecilia watching too.

"Just as before?" Standing in front of the embers, Chiara held her palms out behind her back to warm them. Cecilia retreated to her spot in the corner.

"If that's comfortable enough for you, yes. I think it's a strong composition." He gestured to the stool with the bolt of silk draped on the floor beside it.

She sat with her body angled away from him, her face peering back over one shoulder, in the same pose they'd settled on in Venier's salon. Gio had retrieved the original sketch he'd made; glancing at his notes, he approached her to make a series of small adjustments: "the knee a bit toward me," "the right shoulder back . . . more . . . yes, there, that's good." She fixed him with her gaze as he guided her, his fingertips grazing her skin. He bent for the swatch of silk that lay on the floor and caught her crushed-flower scent. With the fabric in one hand, he leaned to drape it, reaching both arms around her. The soft exhalation of her breath skimmed his forearm—

He stopped abruptly, sitting back on his heels. *Careful, Gio.*

"Cecilia, would you mind assisting me?" The girl darted forward eagerly, as if she'd been waiting to be asked. Working together, they tucked the silk in place around the base of Chiara's torso, styling it to fall in a careful pattern of ripples and shadows. Gio rose to his feet and stepped back, assessing the composition. "Perfect."

He'd prepared his palette earlier that morning, mixing and testing colors until he'd arrived at each precise combination. Dipping his brush in a pale yellow ocher, he began forming the outline of her body. As always, she held herself impressively still. Cecilia likewise kept so quiet in the corner behind him that Gio had to remind himself she was there at all. Gradually, the first layer of the composition revealed itself in form and negative space. The stiff bristles of the brush moving over the canvas made a comforting rhythm, like waves lapping onshore. When Chiara spoke, it startled them all.

"Venier will be appointed admiral soon and leave with the fleet to Cyprus."

Gio thought of the old man at the dinner party, what he'd said of Venier: *A sound tactician.* "That doesn't surprise me. But I heard there was some dispute in the Senate over his election?"

"Oh! Just some nobleman who thinks his own cousin is more experienced and is trying to sway opinion. Venier isn't concerned." Chiara swept a hand through the air, as if she were flicking away a pesky insect. "It'll be resolved. Venier told me a victory over the Ottomans would let him die a happy man." The muscles in her jaw pulsed.

"Why does that seem to trouble you?"

She thought for a moment, staring into space. Then she met Gio's gaze. "Is there anything that would let you die a truly happy man? One goal you want to achieve?" *Before you go completely blind.* He finished the sentence for her in his mind.

"Yes, there is; I'd like to write down my perspectives on art. There are surveys of architecture, medicine, politics. There's even been a treatise on human anatomy, based on Leonardo's sketches. But . . . what I want to write is different."

"How would it be different?"

He stepped back, brush in hand, assessing his progress as he spoke. "I want to write a treatise on art: as a philosophy and a discipline. Because it *is* a discipline, with rules and techniques and theories. But unless you've trained with a master or been educated, all of that is hidden—and so paintings remain mysterious, in a way. There's a distance that's kept between the art and the viewer." He swirled his brush once on the palette, picking up a hint of burnt umber.

"I want to explain the fundamentals so people can recognize what goes into a strong composition and start to make judgments of their own. Art should be for everyone, not just the wealthy or the trained." He peeked around the canvas at her. "In a selfish way, I also want to know I'm leaving something of myself behind—how I view the world."

He could tell she wanted to ask another question but was holding back. "What is it?"

"Why did your wife die?"

He hadn't anticipated that. His face must have broadcast distress: Chiara dropped her pose and turned to him, bundling the silk up in her lap. Her chest and neck had gone splotched with red.

"I'm sorry, I just—"

He held up a hand to halt her. "She died giving birth to my son. He died as well. Why do you ask?" He could hear the words, but they seemed detached from his body, as if he were listening to the voice of a stranger. She was looking at him with the expression people give someone just after they've stood up from a hard fall. *Are you sure you're not hurt?*

"Oh ... The way you spoke about your treatise, as if you wanted it to be your legacy—"

"Because I don't have children. I see." The tightness in his chest began to unwind. He stared at the easel as he spoke so that he didn't have to see her watching him. "I suppose you could look at it that way. But I think I'd want to write it even if my son had lived. I'd still want to share my thoughts and everything I've learned. I'd still want to have an influence, to ... to feel like I've added my voice to the conversation."

"I understand." Chiara paused. "I'm sorry."

"I just wasn't expecting the question ... All of that happened years ago." He set his brush and palette on the stool and picked up a linen rag.

"Have you started writing yet?"

"No, but I will." He caught her arching her brow. "*I will*—that's a promise to you. And now it's your turn." He wiped a streak of paint from his hands with the cloth. "What is it for you? What would let you rest in peace?"

"I'm not sure. I know it's music, but ... I think it's also something more than that." She frowned, then looked up. Her smile was unexpected, a stray shaft of light. "I do feel I have more options now." He couldn't help but smile back.

"I want to travel!" From the corner, Cecilia said the words with such force, and looked so completely shocked by herself afterward, that they both burst into laughter. Blushing furiously, the girl threw her arms tight about herself.

"Well, my dears, I say let's raise a glass to all our hopes and dreams!" With that, Gio went to the cupboard to retrieve a wine jug and hunt for mugs.

The air stayed warm well after sundown the evening of the final festivities, and revelers choked the streets. Sounds of celebration ricocheted off the walls of Gio's chamber as he dressed, fastening a black velvet cape at his neck and securing the mask he'd bought from Jacopo over his face. Earlier in the week, Aurelio had invited him to join his party in the Piazza San Marco, but Gio had declined—the combination of a crowd, darkness, and his eyesight only promised disaster. Instead, he'd scouted his own location: the second floor of the partially completed San Geminiano church. Though far from finished, the structure was stable enough, and its position guaranteed an unadulterated view of the square. Now, all he needed was to get there.

He stepped into the street. At once, the thick snake of bodies winding their way toward the center square swept him up in its current. Pangs of warning fluttered in his chest. The light was already dimming and torches had been lit, sending shadows skittering across his field of view. On all sides, masked faces surged forward. Hidden behind his own blue disguise, Gio scanned the crowd anxiously. From every angle, low-cut gowns exposed breasts of all sorts—bare nipples, goose-pricked flesh—while closer inspection of the more modestly attired women proved them to be men masquerading. A beggar he recognized from the taverns passed by, dressed in a nobleman's costume. Someone's version of a jest. Laughter and chatter from the crowd tangled with the melodies of street performers, until he felt hemmed in on all sides by a buzzing wall of sound.

Gio kept close to the rails as the rabble crossed over bridges, peering down at the splendid, fantastical boats sailing past in the canals—strung with garlands and banners, the vessels left a disarray of flowers and ribbons floating in their wake. At their helms, common servants posed, heads encircled with crowns. The night throbbed with a primal pulse. Gio slid his mask up onto his forehead to wipe the sweat from his eyes, squinting to keep focus amid the confusion of flesh and costume, torches and crashing drums.

He let the momentum of others carry him forward. As the throng spilled out into the piazza, he traced his way along the edges of buildings until he could slip off into the narrow passageway by the church. Days earlier, he'd scouted a gap in the wall here, hidden behind a wooden plank. The plank was lighter than he thought it'd be—he shifted it to one side easily, then stepped into the church, pulling the board back again to disguise his entry.

Immediately, the sounds of the crowd were muted by degrees. Through the round, glass-less second-story window, torchlight poured in from the street—garish yellow against the starlit sky, so clear and cold and far away. A fresco covered the back wall of the great chamber. The face of Mary Magdalene peered out at him from the gloom, with heavy-lidded eyes and a gilded halo. A piece by Vivarini; Gio would recognize his work anywhere. Breathing in, he caught the scent of wood shavings and fresh plaster. He crossed the floor and began to climb the skeletal stairs that hugged the front wall, leading to a narrow platform beneath the window.

Midway up, a scraping sound—nearer than the buzz and howl of the crowd in the square: the sound of the board being pushed aside again. Crouching in the shadows against the wall, Gio watched as a white-masked figure stepped inside the room. Slender and draped in a burgundy cloak, the man peered about the chamber. Spotting Gio, he tossed his cape over one shoulder and bounded toward the stairs.

Hastily Gio stood, on instinct brandishing the knife he kept strapped to his thigh. The short blade glimmered in the light from the street, halting the stranger on the fourth stair. Looking up at

Gio, the man smiled beneath his white demi-mask and slowly withdrew his own sword. It extended fine and silver and sharp.

Suddenly, Gio's blade seemed childishly inadequate.

"Who are you—what are you doing here?" Gio grimaced at the tremor even he could hear in his voice. The man said nothing, but cocked his head. Gio stepped down a stair, repeating his question—louder this time, with the knife raised in front of him. He'd played spectator at enough fights to know the value of aggression. One more step and the man broke into laughter.

Lovely, girlish laughter.

"Chiara?"

She sheathed her sword and slid the mask up over her face. Her hair was slicked back into a tight coil, and as she climbed the remaining stairs between them, Gio saw she'd inked a thin mustache along her upper lip. Her robes were richer than any he owned, no doubt on loan from Venier.

"I'm sorry I scared you. But who else would know you're here?" Leaping up the final stair, she placed a kiss on his cheek.

"I wasn't scared." Gio realized he'd forgotten he told her his plans for the festivities while they drank wine in the studio.

"Of course you weren't." She smiled, flashing her dimples, and tucked her arm into his. Together, they continued up the remaining stairs to the platform. Stepping carefully across the loose beams, they made their way to the window. Gio settled down onto the ledge, leaning his back against the curving stone. Nestled in front of him, Chiara swung one leg out over the spectators swarming below. Her cheek rested in the hollow just beneath his shoulder; he wrapped his arms around her as they watched the flow of movement in the square. From far away, it seemed like a dance: wild swirls of costume, moonlight and torchlight reflecting off the painted masks.

Suddenly, the sky lit up with a thunderous clap and bang.

Fireworks! Sparking founts of bronze light streaked across the night, dazzling the stars into silence. The crowd roared in approval. Gio looked up at the display, squinting to sharpen what he knew were crisp patterns to anyone else's eye. Chiara pulled his arms tighter around her, threading her fingers through his.

"I suppose we've received a few gifts from the East," she whispered into his neck.

He squeezed her hands. Safe in their roost, he began to relax. Colors and forms arranged and rearranged themselves in the composition below with pleasing regularity. Her body against him felt like an extension of his own; he pressed his mouth to the crown of her head. As the fireworks continued, he glanced down the avenue that fed into the square.

He must have stiffened—she sat up with alarm. She followed his stare into the street, and they watched together as a figure darker than all the rest strode toward the piazza, his face consumed by the head of a crow. *Corvino.*

"I see him," she whispered.

"Get back," Gio urged. "Now!"

They scrambled off the ledge, crouching like children to peer out; Gio tossed his cloak across her shoulders to hide them both from view. As the sky cracked and strobed, they tracked Corvino's movements through the square. With so many bright costumes, his dark figure seemed at times little more than a shadow, slithering around revelers like a muddy eel in clear water.

"Where is he going?" Chiara's breath drifted over, laced with wine.

"If I know Corvino, he has some aim." Gio grasped her shoulder, pulling her closer. "Just watch."

Through the slits in his mask, Corvino scanned the crowd. Overhead, fireworks singed the sky, illuminating faces in powdery white flashes. He was searching for someone—a man he'd been told would be dressed as Bacchus, cloaked in blue with a golden sash. At every step,

Corvino was pushed and jostled, the shouts and laughter only worsening his headache. He couldn't hear his own thoughts. He grasped the wineskin slung over one shoulder, reassured himself it was with him still . . .

Where was the man? He was supposed to be near the San Geminiano church, but Corvino couldn't spot him. He felt his heartbeat quicken, pounding his eardrums like fists. He'd thought it through so carefully. Every detail, every nuance accounted for—yet he hadn't thought through what would happen if he couldn't find his prey. Where was he?

There.

As if the Lord Himself were intervening, the throng parted and Corvino glimpsed the face he was after: a white porcelain half mask, upper lip frozen in a frolicsome grin, crowned by a garland of imitation grapes and leaves. Blue robe. Gold sash. Just as he'd been told.

Corvino shouldered through the crowd, careful not to push anyone so roughly that they'd turn and remember his presence. Instead he ducked and wove, maneuvering closer. Blending into the shadows with his black mask, his dark robes. The night smelled of sweat and gunpowder, sickly sweet fragrance. Shapes took on a burnished tinge as the crowd roiled and swayed, lit up by the blazing sky.

The face of Bacchus floated closer, closer still.

Corvino steeled himself. Think of Venier. He tried to imagine the statesman upon hearing the news, how he might repay Corvino for his loyalty, his ingenuity. Corvino could picture it: Venier's brow furrowing as he contemplated what role to reward his talented companion with when the fleet departed . . .

Now. The moment was upon him, and it required grace. Corvino began to rock, moving with the gyrations of the crowd, the roar of their conversation, with the rhythm that blared from the nearest cluster of musicians. He stumbled, feigning drunkenness. As he did, he hoisted the wineskin higher. Bacchus stood directly before him, howling at the sky. A boom and a flare, artificial light sprinkling a metallic fountain over the square. Bacchus arched his back, pounding a fist on his chest in approval.

Think of setting sail with the fleet. Think of the possibilities.

"Drink!" Corvino bounced his wineskin at the man, opening the spout. Face frozen in mirth, the cheerful god drained what was left in his goblet, then raised his glass toward Corvino. Carefully, Corvino filled the cup nearly to the brim with claret-colored liquid.

"Drink! Drink!" he shouted again, grasping the base of the goblet as Bacchus guzzled, pressing the rim into the man's mouth, protruding below his demi-mask.

"I'll have a taste of that!" A nearby reveler jutted forward, his own cup at the ready. Corvino feigned another stumble, wine spilling out over the stones as he whirled away, sealing the spout with a resin stopper in one swift motion. He continued to stagger, playing the drunkard, ignoring the hiss of the jilted bystander, who quickly forgot his upset as the sky once again burst with light. Corvino snaked and bobbed through the crowd, until he'd achieved some distance. Then he straightened his back and hastened his pace.

Away. He had to get away.

Gio and Chiara watched the dark figure disappear back down the alley.

"I don't understand . . . he just came to pour that man a drink?" Chiara had brought one hand to her mouth, was nibbling the nails of her first two fingers.

"Do you know who he is?" Gio squinted, trying to identify the man's companions, but with so many costumes the task was impossible.

"Gio—look! He's choking!" Chiara grasped his shoulder. "He's choking!" she repeated, and indeed the man was: clutching at his chest and neck, silver goblet upended on the stones. The man tore off his mask; in the next burst of light Gio could see a beard trimmed in a tidy square, gray hair fuzzing down over the man's ears. His face contorted like one of Jacopo's awful creations, mouth agape, as he dropped to his knees. On all fours now, he began vomiting violently, a churning gush of turbid bile. Those around him sidestepped backward, disgusted by the mess.

"He's . . . Gio, *what's happening to him?*" Chiara clutched Gio's thigh. By the next strobe of light, the man had collapsed into a puddle of his own sick—a mound of blue and crumpled gold, motionless on the cobblestones. Gio thought of Chiara's dress: how she'd left it in a gilded heap on the floor of the salon that first day.

"He needs help!" Chiara rose, was nearly to her feet before Gio could grasp her waist and tug her down, clutching her body to his.

"No, Chiara—look—it's done." He whispered in her ear, holding tight to her from behind, her ribs pressing against his forearms as she panted. But it *was* done: from below, screams filtered up over the noise of the crowd as horrified spectators began to understand that the man was not drunk but dead. Carousers at the opposite end of the square, misinterpreting the sound, erupted at the call with a terrible glad mimic.

Chiara made a low moan and began to crawl toward the wall; Gio unlatched his grip on her waist and shifted to sit beside her. All color had drained from her cheeks. With their backs pressed against the stones, they listened to the tumult outside.

"Haven't you seen a man die before?" He investigated her face. Her breath was coming in shallow gasps. She shook her head, and he noticed her pupils had dilated into wide black rings, violet-rimmed. "It happened so fast."

"Some poisons work quickly. Corvino may have crafted it himself to do just that."

Before he could halt her, she'd taken his hand and brought it in under her robe, pressing his palm flat to her chest. Her heart was thundering—rapid pulse of muscle behind bone.

"Can you feel that?"

Gio nodded.

"*We're* still alive." She wet her lips with a quick dart of tongue. He nodded again. She leaned closer then, sliding his fingers in under the neckline of her tunic, pressing her mouth to the soft of his neck. As Mary Magdalene gazed over them with her calm eyes and demi-smile, Chiara used the weight of her body to pull him to the unfinished floor. The white-hot crackle of fireworks lit her up from above, searing her image into memory: the curve of her mouth, the dip in her throat. Hips and knees, knocking and sliding as they fumbled to fit themselves together. Hard muscle below her ribs. Slick tongue, skin gone taut. Salt taste and the bite of adrenaline, the smell of crushed flowers tilting in on waves.

It was true: the man in the square was dead, but they were alive—and they reminded themselves of it with breath and grasp and thrust; with that pleasure which lives along the slender edge of pain. When Gio finally lifted his eyes, they rested on Mary's halo, glinting at him in the night.

At last, Captain Bragadin did see sails on the horizon—but they came from the wrong direction, and the banners they flew carried no crosses. Legions of more Ottoman fighters swarming onshore to join Mustafa's army.

Meanwhile, his men were nearly out of powder.

When a neatly turbaned messenger arrived, bearing the promise of safe passage to those who wished to leave the city, the captain could not refuse. He was not a cruel man. All useless mouths were allowed to flee: the old, the very young. As thousands flooded through the city gates, the enemy offered them warm meals, fragrant with spices.

"It's a trick to break your spirit," Bragadin told his men, but still he watched them sniff the air like dogs, tracing the scent of meat.

15

HIS THUMB HAD HEALED. WILLIAM STOOD AT THE BATH-room sink, inspecting the still-pink seam that ran nearly to his palm. He'd cut himself weeks ago, assembling a telescope for Jane and Lucy so that they could see the stars. To help them keep track, he'd attached a poster of the night sky on the fridge, using a magnet of the moon from Georges Méliès's movie *Le Voyage dans la lune.*

The nice thing about stars was that you could rely on them. They wouldn't just wander off from their constellations if you happened to look away.

He ran the water, then rubbed the soap bar under the stream, watching lather build. He shouldn't have touched Rose like that. It was far too intimate a gesture—not like putting a hand to someone's shoulder. Yet in the moment, it'd come too naturally to second-guess. But how would she interpret it? How did he *want* her to interpret it?

DON'T OVERTHINK IT was a sign he'd taped up in his studio in the city.

He dried his hands.

Out in the living room, Sarah was kneeling on the carpet, queuing up the girls' thirty minutes of after-dinner TV time. William retreated to the kitchen and finished cleaning up. He opened a cupboard and found the box of umbrellas where he'd stashed it, behind a sack of flour. He pulled it out, then arranged the rest of the ingredients he'd purchased on the counter. Coconut cream. Frozen pineapple. Limes. Dark and white rum, both. He began combining them, eyeballing measurements, going heavy with the rum.

Feeling guilty, William? Lois's predictable voice in his ear, red lips pursed in a tight button, the face she always made when asking rhetorical questions. *Beginning to understand how Sarah felt, why sh—*

He flicked the switch on the blender, then turned it to high, drowning out the chatter in his mind with the sound of chipping ice. He remembered they had a pair of hurricane glasses somewhere, an old wedding gift. Rummaging through cabinets, he finally found them. The piña colada poured out custard yellow and frothy. Then, the final touch: two bright cerulean umbrellas with origami-thin paper, flimsy wooden stakes. He carried the drinks out, proud as a golden retriever with a tennis ball, and offered one to Sarah. He watched her smile and frown at the same time, bemused.

"What's this?" She shifted position on the couch to take the glass.

"Just a little surprise, thought you might like it." A generous warmth spread in his chest.

"Aw, Will. You haven't made me a fancy drink in . . ." Her eyes met his, and he caught her try to swallow back the sentence. *In forever.*

He was saved from response by the girls, closing in like hyenas, demanding to know what they were drinking and why they couldn't have any, until finally William was forced back into the kitchen to blend a kid-friendly batch, to much squealing adulation. Afterward, Sarah watched the news while Jane and Lucy played on the floor. Coloring books and plastic princesses, sparkly unicorns prancing across the carpet. *A dozen new troops on the ground.* He ran a bath, then Sarah marched them upstairs; an hour later and the tub was drained—bubbles still clinging to the sides, both girls tucked into bed, with their night-lights and stuffed animals for company.

"I'm going to read for a while, okay?" Sarah poked her head into the living room from the hallway. Her hair looked untouched from the morning, still twisted back in a smooth spiral.

"Sure. I'll be out back."

"Thanks again for the drink, that was really sweet of you."

William nodded. "Well, I saw the umbrellas, thought why not." He watched her stare, half-smiling, as if waiting for him to keep talking. When he didn't, she gave a quick nod, then ducked away, disappearing down the hall.

So, it'd come to this: he was socially awkward with his own wife.

He grabbed a bottle of whiskey, then slid the back door open one-handed. The air was warmer than it'd been the last time. Summer would be here in the blink of an eye. High overhead, the leaves of the old oak rustled in the wind, whispering quiet secrets he used to know by heart.

In the studio, the images of Rose that he'd sketched lay stacked in a pile. He hadn't been able to keep working on a portrait, not after what she'd said in the museum about muses—when he looked at the pages now, an uneasy mixture of shame and embarrassment churned his gut. Instead, he unfolded the large printouts he'd made earlier that day of the scans she'd sent, the story of the egg and the tree. Before printing, he'd cropped and enlarged the pictures, so that now he had a nearly full-page version of each of Giovanni's sketches. He pinned them to the wall in sequence. In a corner sat an old six-disc CD player, a sentimental relic from his past; he pushed Shuffle, watched the machine diligently skip through the tracks. The synth opener to "Once in a Lifetime" came burbling through the speakers. Perfect. Turning up the volume, he clutched the neck of the bottle and went back to stand in the middle of the room. Took a long sip.

Swirling liquor around in his mouth, he stared at the sketches. *Why did they make him sad?* It was a beautiful sadness, but sad nonetheless—a strange and lovely longing. He examined the yearning in Giovanni's expression, how he put his hand to the woman's cheek in the final scene. Had he just put his own hand to Rose's face that same way? Had he looked so piteous?

He had to make sense of it. He had to understand the sadness, get inside it and live there awhile. Maybe if he did that, he could find his own way through.

William began to mix paint.

Rose woke up to find that the morning sun had already sent the clouds into retreat, leaving only a pastel gauze straggling at the edges of the sky. On her way to the door, she picked a gauzy blue scarf to wrap around her neck, then stepped out into the brisk and brightening day.

At the archives, the comforting soft-sand carpet and dry book smell welcomed her home. She'd replied to Lucas's email and within minutes he'd written back, assuring her the books would be ready. It was good timing; she needed a distraction. All she'd been able to think of for days was the weight of William's fingertips on her ear, the warm graze of his skin, the memory turning tender as a bruise when he didn't write or stop by the shop again. And just like a bruise, she couldn't stop touching it, revisiting the moment. She wanted to tell Joan, tell anyone, get confirmation: *That wasn't a nor-*

mal gesture, was it? What could it mean? Instead, she'd tried to pass the hours working on the undertext, but even Beethoven at high volume couldn't halt the scene from replaying in a maddening loop. A change in routine, a visit to the library, was just what she needed.

As she entered the reading room, Lucas smiled broadly. "Ready and waiting," He gestured to a cart behind the service desk, already stacked high with books.

"Thank you so much." Rose glanced around. The room was more crowded than usual with students rushing to footnote final papers, but a seat by the window was still open. She pointed and Lucas nodded; together they made their way to the table.

"I hope these will be useful." He began his usual choreography, arranging paperweights, setting out the foam bookstands.

"Oh, I'm sure they'll be great. So . . . all these books just 'came across' your desk?" She couldn't help but smirk up at him. He raised both hands, guilty.

"Okay, okay, I maybe did some digging. After you left, I realized I didn't really know much about that time period either, not beyond the broad strokes. So, I poked around a little. Out of curiosity." He selected an oversize book, laid it out in front of her.

"It's incredibly fascinating. The artist you're studying was Venetian, right? Fifteen seventies?" She nodded, watching as he turned the pages until he reached an elaborate woodcut display of ships in battle. "So, Venice had just gone to war with the Ottoman empire. Which was really significant. If the Ottomans had won, they could have taken all of Italy—the same way they'd taken Constantinople! It would've changed the whole face of European history. Anyway, that particular war ended in the Battle of Lepanto." He frowned, looking down at the picture. "The Venetians had just invented a new kind of boat . . . here—see here." He pointed at one ship in particular, cannon muzzles poking out of it portside. "Essentially, they took old merchant boats and transformed them into warships, with way more firepower than a normal galley. The Ottomans never anticipated that."

"I recognize this ship from a sketch in the book!" Rose couldn't keep the excitement from her voice.

"That doesn't surprise me. I'd imagine everyone in Venice was pretty focused on the war—and I think the boats were a big deal in terms of new technology. But you'll never guess who was in that battle!" Lucas straightened up and raised one finger, eyes sparkling as he paused for dramatic effect. "Don Juan of Austria!" A student at a far table glowered at them; Lucas gave a curt nod in response, then leaned down to continue in a whisper. "Can you imagine? Don Juan fighting against the son of Süleyman the Magnificent on the Mediterranean?" She noticed his eyes were actually hazel: kaleido-scopic brown and green with pinpricks of pupil at their centers.

"Is all of that in this book?"

He turned the pages back to the beginning of the chapter. "It all starts here." He tapped a fingertip on the first phrase of a para-graph. She bent forward to read.

> Upon the death of Süleyman I, his son, Selim II, assumed the throne.
> Such a dramatic change in power left Venice concerned for the safety
> of Cyprus. This concern turned to fear after an unexpected visit by
> Joseph Nassi to the harbor of Famagusta, on the eastern shore of the
> island . . .

For the rest of the morning, Rose was lost in the rich history of the Battle of Lepanto. The Ottomans and Venetians had main-tained a truce for a surprising number of years, based on mutual trading interests. But in 1571, under the rule of Selim II, the Turks had decided to make a gamble for the Venetian-claimed island of Cyprus. First, they'd targeted the town of Nicosia, before continu-ing on to Famagusta. In response, Venice had pleaded for help from the Pope, who was eventually able to cobble together a Holy League, after much cajoling. Port towns along the Mediterranean began bustling with activity as the Christians banded together against a common threat.

With a jolt, Rose recognized a familiar name in the chapter— one she'd often seen repeated in the undertext of Giovanni's book: Sebastiano Venier, admiral of the Venetian fleet. She sat up with surprise, darting her eyes to Lucas, who'd gone back to his station at the service desk. He noticed her startle and looked over, cocking his head; she beckoned him with an excited flap of a hand.

"Look! This name is in the book too!" She stabbed a finger at the paragraph. He bent to read along.

"Do you think the author was documenting current events?"

"I don't know what to think. I've seen the name in the under- text: it's a palimpsest." She didn't need to explain the word to him; he nodded, knowingly. "The top layer is definitely about art, but maybe he wrote something completely different first? I think it was in fashion to write histories, political commentary, things like that . . . I have to wait for the translations to find out for sure."

"Translations?" Another tilt of Lucas's head.

"Yes, I'm actually repairing the treatise. I'm a book restorer, I guess I didn't mention that." Rose smiled, only slightly guiltily. "I use a translation agency for any foreign-language manuscripts."

"Oh, *you're* the restorer!" Lucas grabbed the back of a nearby chair and spun it around to sit beside her. "I've heard about you," he whispered. "The staff said you're amazing." A year ago she'd assisted with the restoration of several documents from early-modern Japan, part of a bestowal. Rose could feel the blood rushing to her cheeks. She shrugged.

"I can't believe you let me lecture you on how to handle books last time." He rolled his head back to look at the ceiling, in exagger- ated exasperation.

"No, no, no, you did a great job!" she insisted, to which he threw a hand up in mock protest. "I should have said something, I know. I was just so focused on figuring out more." She surveyed the books spread open across the wide tabletop. "But I think I'm done reading for the day. This room is making me sleepy." Outside, the sun had intensified, turning the glass-walled reading room into a greenhouse. Like wilting orchids, most of the students had already abandoned their efforts.

"Well, great timing. Looks like my shift change just got here." Lucas nodded toward the front desk, where the bloused and powdered woman had taken up her station and was already sorting through paperwork. "Let me get my things and I'll walk with you?"

"Sure."

A shimmering heat welcomed them outside. It was one of those summer days that had lost its place and turned up in spring, foreshadowing the coming season and confusing all the plants. Immediately, Rose tugged the scarf from her neck, as if it were strangling her.

"This is ice cream weather." Lucas squinted up at the blazing blue.

"Let's do it!" Rose's voice was partially muffled as she unwound the last loop of silk.

"Get ice cream?" Lucas hitched up the straps of his backpack, as if she'd suggested a ten-mile hike.

"Yeah, there's a good spot just through campus." She couldn't say exactly what had come over her other than the bright expansiveness of a warm spring day: sunlight filtering green through the leaves and the contagious enthusiasm of the birds. It was a day that begged to be basked in—going straight home felt like an unconscionable act.

"All right, I'm game. Is that yours?" He was pointing to her bike now, chained up on the rack next to only one other one: an army green cruiser, which he began unlocking. Rose nodded, then keyed open her own lock, threw it into the wicker basket along with her chains. She swung up onto the seat and wheeled a lazy loop in the street in front of him, smiling.

"Onward, Captain!" He gave a laugh and kicked off, following as she led them down a narrow, stone walkway and into the streets, past tree-lined courtyards and the historic freshman dormitories that wouldn't have seemed out of place at Hogwarts. Rose let the lightness inside fill her to the brim. She lifted her feet off the pedals, hovering them in the air as they cruised down the white line. Lucas darted forward to bike beside her every so often, teeth bared in an openmouthed grin, shadows of branches and bursts of sun flashing across their faces.

They arrived at the ice cream shop windswept and warm. There wasn't a line at the register, and only a few students slouched at the tables.

"What's your favorite flavor?" Rose asked as they stood side by side at the counter, reading the menu posted on the wall behind the cashier—an undergrad girl with hoop earrings and acne scars, a pair of distracting false eyelashes glued to her lids.

"Will you judge me if I say sweet cream? It's, like, even more boring than vanilla . . ." Lucas cringed and pushed his glasses up.

"Ha! No judgment. Mine's mint. What even qualifies as an exciting ice cream flavor anyway?"

He tugged on his ear, considering the question seriously. "Oh, maybe something really artisan, like caramel balsamic swirl, or—"

"So, one sweet cream, one mint? Cone or cup?" Line or no line, the cashier didn't have time for their debate. They both got two scoops, in waffle cones, Lucas deriding the inferior quality of sugar cones in the process, with Rose's full support.

Back out on the sidewalk, they entered into a competition with the sun for who could reduce their scoops faster. Without discussing a destination, they began ambling side by side down the street, past shops and restaurants.

"Now honestly, when is the last time you've tried sweet cream?" Lucas turned to walk backward in front of her for a few steps.

"I—I don't know that I've ever had it." Rose contemplated her ice cream history.

"Try! I haven't even taken a bite from that side." He offered his cone toward her. She accepted, grasping the paper napkin wrapped around the base, taking as delicate a sample as could be managed.

"It tastes like . . . well, like sweet cream! That's really nice, actually."

"I know! Thank you." He said it as if she'd just settled some long-standing dispute. "It's the most comforting flavor there is."

She laughed, and they kept strolling. Conversation came easily: each of them had a background in archival studies, though she'd focused on restoration while he'd taken the librarian route. She discovered he was a closet medievalist, while he got her to admit a secret passion for miniature books from the Victorian era. They both bemoaned the shifting status of print in the digital age, Lucas offering up anecdotes from his time assisting students. "I swear, I've never felt older than when explaining how card catalogs used to work." Rose squinted at him furtively, trying to guess his age. By the beginnings of crow's-feet near his eyes, she felt safe saying midthirties. A few years older than she was, maybe.

Before she knew it, they'd made a wide, meandering circle and wound up back at their bikes, loitering awkwardly next to the rack. To her surprise, Rose realized she wasn't quite ready for the conversation to end. She hadn't felt nervous once or had to remind herself to just be herself.

"I guess . . . let me know if you 'come across' any more books?" She made air quotes with her fingers, grinning.

He laughed. "Absolutely, I will." Still smiling, he pushed his bike out onto the sidewalk. "So . . . see you around?"

"Sure."

He took off down the street, then turned to try to wave goodbye at her, front wheel wobbling. She laughed and waved back. She was halfway home before she began thinking of the treatise again.

William's fingertips brushing her ear.

16

MORNING RAISED HERSELF IN CLEAN BLUE NOTES. With sunlight dappling the canal and birdsong in the air, the day broke fresh and bright and pure over a city still swathed in the haze of its own debauchery. Gio roused himself to sit at the table and write in his journal. The vellum he used had been a gift from Domenico, who'd pressed it into his hands late one night. It was of particular quality; the scratch of his quill on its pumiced skin was one of the few things that made waking up bearable. In the comfort of his morning routine, the memory of Bacchus seemed no more than a fragmentary nightmare. But as he wrote, the outline of events sharpened themselves—the way the man had fallen to all fours in the square. It'd been no dream.

Gio recorded the details of what had happened, as he did so many other mornings, fueled by the fear that when his eyes finally failed, they might take all his memories with them. It was irrational, he knew that, but still he was compelled. His pen hovered over the page. Should he write what he'd done with Chiara, what she'd done with him? It was what he wanted to remember most, in vivid, singular detail. But what if someone were to read it? Gio considered what Venier might do if he found out—then considered the mood the city was in. What might change once the fleet departed, with most of Venice's young men in her hulls?

What might Corvino do if he were left behind?

Drawings, then. Sketches were safe. Sketches were more accurate than words. He could capture the moments he wanted to hold on to, tightly: the arch of her back, her jawline. The tender curves of her inner thighs. How her hair had spilled out onto the floor after she'd tugged it loose. He made small drawings with her face tilted away, always, or in shadow. The press of her hip bone against her skin as she lay on her side. This was what he wanted to record, knowing he'd be forced to give it all away. *Let me keep this one moment, just this one.*

When his eyes tired, he dressed and stepped outside. The avenues were empty, save for scavenging fowl and rats scurrying along the walls, nosing about in the remnants of the night before. Beneath the chill, a thread of warmth knit itself through the air in a suggestion of spring. Without thinking, Gio found himself walking toward the great house.

Chiara had left the church first the night before. He'd waited alone in the empty building for a full half hour after she'd gone, lying on his back, hands folded under his head. Tracking her movements in his mind. He'd pictured her returning home, changing out of her costume, Cecilia helping her into her four-poster bed with its clean linens. The brocade curtains drawn over her sleeping face, as peaceful as the moon.

He held the images close, knowing full well she'd rejoined Venier's party—entering with some amusing tale of getting lost in the crowd, laughing and smiling and tossing her cape. Performing. Kissing Venier before he could see how smeared her makeup had become. In his mind, the two Chiaras had traveled in tandem, tracing divergent paths. He'd comforted himself by imagining that the ghost Chiara, the returning-home-safe-and-alone Chiara, was the one they both wished for.

Arriving at the house now, he paused to lean against a linden tree across the street. He looked up at the windows for signs of life. Nothing. A lone thrush winged across the pale sky. The broad leaves overhead rustled, then went still. It was too early. Perhaps he'd continue on to the harbor.

Suddenly, the door of the palazzo was flung open. Gio ducked behind the tree, pulling his robes in tight. The backs of two men came into view, walking away from him down the avenue. It was Venier, head drooping, with Corvino behind. Straight-backed, the Crow reached to clasp one hand on the statesman's shoulder, but Venier shook him off. Corvino dropped a pace, chastened; in single file, they disappeared around the corner. Gio counted to fifty, then dashed across the avenue.

Inside, the house smelled stale. The scent of alcohol mingled with that new devil, tobacco, to create a particularly rank odor. The muted figure of a servant shuffled across the courtyard, arms clasping a bundle of soiled linens. In the shadows of a far corner, a peacock pecked at grain spilled over the stones, flashes of cerulean as its head bobbed. Before anyone could notice him, Gio hastened up the spiral staircase to the grand hall, nearly skating across the freshly polished terrazzo.

Chiara's door swung open at his touch. She was sprawled on her belly in the bed, sheets tangled at her ankles. Her hair was loose, tumbling in uncombed swirls across the pillows. The red and gold brocade curtains had gotten twisted around their posts, and her costume from the night before lay in a forgotten heap on the floor next to a pair of overturned goblets. Squinting at him, she groaned in greeting. Gio bolted the door behind him, then strode to throw open the shutters. Unforgiving shafts of light streamed into the room, prompting more groans and a pale arm to be thrown over a paler face.

"Why are you so cruel?"

"I see your night continued on past me." Gio tried and failed to keep the jealousy from his voice.

"Venier was obliged to celebrate Don Juan's arrival in Venice, and I was obliged to join them." She eyed him from under the crook of her elbow. A tendon flexed in her leg as she rolled onto her hip to face him; Gio marked the contrast between the dark mound at the base of her stomach and the tinted gold hair that snaked over her shoulders, her chest, the pillow. His throat tightened.

"Venier could barely stand, he'd had so much wine. Asleep like a babe as soon as he lay down." She smiled at him, all dimples, the remnants of her inked-on mustache smeared across one cheek.

"Was Corvino with them?"

"No. I think he came this morning, but I didn't see him—I don't know that I could have managed it. I told Venier what happened..." At Gio's face, she rushed to clarify. "Don't worry, I didn't tell him I was with you."

"What was his response?"

"He asked me to describe the man; I did as best I could. He thinks it was his challenger from the Senate—the one who wanted his cousin appointed admiral. He was quite angry with Corvino. He said he would've been named admiral regardless, and to have his opponents killed is likely to do more harm than good to his reputation." She stretched her legs, kicking herself free from the sheets. Gio watched her ribs expose themselves for a moment under her skin.

"Well..." He scratched his beard. "There isn't any way to *prove* the man was killed..."

"No, but he was still troubled by it—I think he's off now to see what can be done about declaring it the result of some condition.

He was really quite angry," she repeated, before completing her turn and falling onto her back, continuing to speak primarily into her elbow. "He said Corvino's too ambitious for his own good—he said he's overreaching his station."

"I would agree with that. And now we know what he's capable of." Gio grasped the back of his neck, thinking.

"Yes, but still—we cannot live our lives afraid of those who confuse brutality with power. If we do, we only prove them right." She rubbed her face with both hands. "So, I refuse to be scared of him. I *refuse*. He doesn't deserve my fear."

"Well . . . can you at least refuse quietly, for my sake?" Gio shot her a sideways grin. "Any other news from Venier?"

"Apparently Don Juan came to personally oversee the delivery of extra rowers. He said our fleet is desperately short on manpower, and they're set to leave—"

A loud knock on the chamber door. Chiara bolted upright, eyes wide. Without a word, she gestured frantically to the space beneath the bed. Feeling more like an adolescent inamorato than a respectable artist, Gio knelt and lay flat on his stomach, shimmying in under the bed frame on elbows and knees. From his vantage, Chiara's bare feet dropped into view, a bright pink blister on one heel. She padded over to the door and swung it open. Two more pairs of feet entered the room, clad in servants' shoes and, to judge by their sidestepping shuffle, holding something heavy between them.

"Your bath, my lady." An unfamiliar voice, dry and brusque—certainly not Cecilia.

"Thank you. That will be all."

"You won't be needing assistance, my lady?"

"Not today." A pause as the servant digested this evidently unusual dismissal. Then movement again, the scraping *clang* of the bolt. Chiara's hand reached down past the bed frame, her fingertips waggling at him. Gio squirmed back out and stood, batting the dust from his robes.

"She could hardly believe me bathing myself."

"We'll need to be careful when I leave. I should have just knocked, I don't know what I was thinking."

"Poor things will be occupied with cleaning, I'm sure." As if exhausted by the mere thought of so much work, Chiara yawned. The vinegar scent of old wine drifted off her. She strolled to the basin, stepping in delicately as the steam unwound around her. He watched as she bent to fish out a submerged linen. "I spent this morning wondering why that poor man died. Then I realized I should probably be worrying about whether or not we'll win the war." With both hands she wrung the rag out.

"We can't afford not to." As he spoke, Gio moved to stand behind her, reaching to take hold of the linen. She let him, her eyes drifting shut. He dunked it in the warm water again, then squeezed it over the crown of her head, dispensing a rush of liquid that wet her hair and slid down her back, licking the long ropes of muscle guarding her spine. She turned to speak over her shoulder at him, eyes still shut.

"What would happen if we weren't able to beat the Ottomans back?" Her lashes were as long as a child's.

"I'd take you away, for one. I won't see you become the property of some Ottoman mongrel." He plunged the cloth in the water again. Grasping her wrist between his forefinger and thumb, he raised her arm, tracing the linen along the underside of her biceps and the hollow of her armpit, down the curve of her side.

"Oh, they can't *all* be mongrels. They just believe in their Holy War as much as the Pope believes in his." She stretched her free arm out in front of her, spreading her fingers wide to look at the light seeping through the webs of flesh between them. "And besides, Domenico told me that Selim's mother, Roxelana, was a courtesan once. Süleyman loved her so much he married her—he broke all the rules for her. I'd like to think her son might have a special fondness for women in my profession."

Gio said nothing but bent to soak the linen again, staying crouched low to wash her thighs. The soft down on her legs was dark, like the hair under her arms; briefly, he considered what she'd looked like before she'd tinted her hair so light. She dropped her hands, one landing on his head to absentmindedly pull at his curls. "Roxelana was a smart woman. She rose from a slave girl to the empress of the East."

He glanced up at her. With her face scrubbed clean, her skin had the smooth, cream-top look of the very young. Then she shifted, and the light attached itself to the tender rounds of her breasts, her hips. He reached up to clasp her waist. "Chiara, under Ottoman rule, you would never compose or enjoy any of the freedoms you have now. If we lose the war, I'll make sure you're taken somewhere safe."

"Freedoms?" Her tone made a sudden, hard pivot. She pushed his hand away and turned to glare down at him, water sloshing over the lip of the basin. "Please, enlighten me on the freedoms I may currently enjoy? I'm a courtesan, Gio." She flung her hands out to either side, then slapped them on her thighs, as if the wet sound somehow punctuated her point. "I have only the Four Orders to look forward to—and you know them just as well as I do. Tell me the Four Orders, Gio."

Gio sat back on his heels. He felt her watching him and started using the cloth to mop up the water she'd spilled. He weighed whether or not all the wine she'd had the evening before was entirely worn off.

"Say them, Gio. Tell me the Four Orders. I want to hear you say them." She sharpened her glare, still staring down at him. A stubborn insistence had knuckled into her voice, the threat of something lacking all order trembling just beneath. Dutifully, he began.

"Innkeeper, procuress, washerwoman—"

"Beggar. See, you *do* know them. All I can look forward to with my many freedoms." She tried to smile but fell short, ending in an odd grimace.

"You . . . you could be married—"

"Purity is the only real advantage in the marriage market, and I'm afraid that's no longer one of my offerings." A hollow laugh from the back of her throat. "But yes, I suppose I could be married off for breeding. Perhaps Venier will be kind and pass me on to someone grand?" She laughed again, harder this time, letting the weight of her head drop back, exposing the curve of her throat. "Or I could become a nun—can't you picture me in the robes?" Her laugh began to wobble and unspool, and with a start Gio realized she was crying, naked in the tub. Before he could halt his own actions, he found himself standing in the water beside her, the hem of his robes floating, liquid seeping into his leather boots. He pressed her head to his chest. Wet hair clung to her skull, her spine shuddering under the flat of his hand as she sobbed into his shoulder. Inexplicably, he was reminded of an afternoon from childhood, when he'd wandered into the countryside and come upon a bird who'd tumbled from the nest too soon. Carefully, he'd held its quivering body in his hands, helplessly looking up at the bundle of twigs that perched too far for even his reach.

"Chiara—we'll find a solution." He was grasping her face now, using his thumbs to wipe beneath her eyes. She stared at him blankly, unblinking, lashes clumped together in spikes, irises dulled gray. "You will never be a nun or a beggar. And you'll only marry if that's what *you* desire. And—if we've really no other options— then . . . then we'll dress you as a boy, and I'll convince Aurelio to take you on as an assistant!" He got a crooked grin at this. "You can help him turn lead into gold. Or, at the very least, you'll learn to make a strong drink." Her smile broadened, and she swatted his hands away to wipe at her own face. Then she straightened her shoulders and lifted her chin.

"You're standing in my bathing tub, Gio."

"I suppose I am."

"Then I suppose we ought to get you dry."

Time was his last remaining luxury, and he spent it on her extravagantly then. Inch by inch, he committed to memory all the parts he hadn't been able to see properly in the gloom of the church, until she blushed delightedly at the attention. Afterward, they lay in a tangle of limbs on the bed, the weight of her head against his chest. He combed his fingers through her damp hair, watching the pale strands sift in the light.

"Will you tell me now, Chiara?"

"Will I tell you . . . ?" She tilted her face up toward his.

"I know there weren't any bad business dealings in Rome. How *did* you become a courtesan?"

She groaned and pressed his hand away, lacing her fingers through his. "I thought you men all preferred mystery and intrigue . . ."

"I'm not all men." He grinned down at her.

"No, you're not, are you." She sighed and rolled onto her back, raising both legs in the air to flex her feet. A narrow vein showed itself blue at one ankle. "There isn't much to tell. My aunt was a courtesan also; she did well in Rome until recently. Pius V is particularly harsh toward the profession, as I'm sure you know." Gio nodded—over the past few decades, Rome had grown increasingly difficult for courtesans and prostitutes. "She came to Venice and invited me to live with her. I didn't have a dowry, so it seemed the best decision." She let the weight of her feet drop back down into the sheets, then rolled up onto an elbow. Her eyes caught a sparkle. "She's brilliant, my aunt; she orchestrated everything. She arranged for me to entertain a few foreign dignitaries and tell them my story, knowing they'd boast to the right noblemen. You know how it works: if you repeat a lie enough times it turns to truth. Once my history was in circulation, she had me attend Domenico's salons, where I could make the best connections. Like pouring milk for kittens." She tugged his beard playfully.

"And what of your parents?"

Her hand arrested its motion, and she gave a nearly imperceptible shake of her head; he nodded in understanding. She turned to study the bluing sky through a gap in the drapes. "Can you answer a question for me now?"

"Of course."

"What's it like?" She didn't look at him.

He knew what she was asking. "It's like . . ." He groped for a way to tell her, to explain it. "It's like a fire or a flood. Completely out of my control, and I can't fight it no matter how much I want to." He gazed up at the billows and folds in the canopy that drooped over them. "You feel deceived by your own body, because it takes time to understand what's happening. Your mind tries to compensate for the lack of vision. Then one day you realize you've lost all the edges. They're just gone. Black. After that, you realize the blackness is slowly . . . moving toward center. And what you *can* still see in the middle is blurring. Aurelio gave me lenses, but that's the smallest part of it. It's the blackness that's the trouble." He bit the inside of his cheek to halt the panic in his chest from spreading upward.

"I'm so sorry, Gio. I know you don't want to hear that, I just—"

"I know. You want to say something, but there aren't any words. Not for this." He fell silent a moment. She brought her fingertips to his temple and began to stroke his hair; her touch was repetitive, calming, like the rhythm of waves or breath. He tasted blood in his mouth and realized he'd bit his cheek too hard. "I thought that after I lost my family, I wouldn't feel pain again—that nothing could compare. But this, losing my art . . ." He closed his eyes. "I don't know who will be left after it's gone."

"What do you mean?"

He tongued the cut in his mouth, thinking. "I put all my energy, every thought, into my paintings. It's as if part of me was always standing by, studying the light, planning the next portrait. My wife hated it—she said she only ever got half a husband. I couldn't explain it to her, what it's like to create art. How it doesn't feel like a choice; how it feels like some other force is moving through me when I paint. Now that it's going away, I don't know what I'll be left with, who I'll be. And suddenly I can't help but question if I've ever really lived—now that it's too late to change it. What did I miss, always standing by?" The corners of his mouth tugged down.

"I feel the same way when I'm composing." Chiara caught his curls in her grasp and shook his head gently. "You followed your passion, Gio; don't second-guess that now." He reached up to clutch her hand, pressing it into the pillow, and turned to look at her. Pale hair bent in waves over her shoulders, shading her face; the space between them seemed to dissolve.

"Chiara, do you know that before I met you, I'd asked Aurelio to give me a medicine? A potion to help . . . to help end it. When Venier summoned me, I took it as a sign: it would be my last portrait. And then it was you, and here I am, and I'm not standing by anymore, not even a little. And all I want is to feel it—this—as much as I can." His composure faltered, wet creeping in at the corners of his eyes. She freed her hand and grabbed his shoulder then, tugging stubbornly until he moved to lay over her, his weight pressing them both into the mattress, his face buried in the crook of her neck.

"You are the only man who's ever believed in me," she whispered into his ear. He bent to kiss her neck through her hair, and she smiled—a sweet, sad smile he couldn't see.

The vicious blast of a mine signaled the end. Lodged in a moat beneath the main tower of Famagusta's defense wall, it made a muffled roar, shattering stone from mortar. As Ottoman soldiers advanced over the rubble toward the city, Captain Bragadin ordered a counterexplosion, using the last of his powder. Dense rock lurched skyward—only to return to earth, burying scrambling soldiers with a crushing finality. Undeterred, more Ottomans swarmed through the gaping hole in the wall, stepping on their own dead and dying—ribs and limbs cracking underfoot, blood staining the stones. All around, a panoply of gore that survivors would never be able to explain with words.

"Again!" Bragadin shouted. Dust obscured his vision, his voice splintered from use. The pattern repeated itself: crush and swarm, crush and swarm, until of the thousands, only a few hundred Ottomans remained. Yet a few hundred was too still many: Bragadin's men were out of powder, and the city was without food.

Cyprus was on her knees.

17

DREAMS HAD STARTED TO COME. AS SOON AS WILLIAM closed his eyes they'd flood in, like water seeping under the crack of the door. Rich swathes, swatches of oak hue. Shapes full of movement and mystery. Eyes peering at him through boughs—now green, now gray. The press of shoulder blades against skin, feather, and bone. Powdery eggshell shattered at his feet.

Giovanni's story of the bird and the tree was coming to life in his dreams—and then, later, on canvas. The new paintings emerged quickly, as though they'd already agreed upon their compositions and were just waiting for his brush. A wild energy pulsed through him, all the stuck parts dissolving in a flow of fresh current. He woke up feeling weightless. He'd read about a heroin high once, probably in the *Times*. Over coffee and toast, he'd skimmed a description of the sensations: sensual, nerves sparkling, a warm rush of contentment. This didn't seem so different. Quieter maybe, more constant. Like hearing strains of classical music from a neighbor's open window: an unshakable sweetness dancing beneath the everyday noise.

The new pieces were unlike anything he'd made before. Night after night, he'd slip out the back door and into his sunless kingdom. He'd paint until he grew dazed, until his hands became useless at mixing color. Then he'd creep inside on careful footsteps, satisfied in a way he hadn't felt in years—years that now unraveled behind him, surreal and sepia toned. It was the same rush he'd experienced after moving to New York, when he was just discovering the style he'd become recognized for, when he knew without a doubt that he was onto something, that it was *working*. He began staying in the studio later and later, just him and the moon, newfound companions. He tried to paint in the afternoons but couldn't. The daylight was too cheerful, too garish for the work that needed doing. His creativity was a nocturnal one, emerging in the silence, compelling him to action while the rest of the world fell away.

When he finally did sleep, the dark images would come again, readying him for another round. Moody dreamscapes: a glittering desert, marked by the black and deadened husks of trees. Boughs ending in hands, fingertips reaching toward an impassive sky. He was alone there, a wanderer. Cobalt blazed overhead; his bare feet slid, were buried in sand, hot grit between his toes and sun searing the back of his neck. He was looking for something, searching. Tumbling down dunes, falling onto his knees, then scrambling up the next rise only to be met with a vast and undulating topography, alike in all directions—a heat halo shimmering over a perfect pattern of receding pyramids, dead trees stark columns rising from the sand.

And then, after endless nights spent rambling the same landscape, he saw it: a glimmer at the top of a far peak. A glint of blue, a barely there flush of green. He ran, arms flailing, sliding down the dunes. Faster and faster, like someone had sped up the tape. Everything black, now bright—and after that it was always the same. He'd find himself suddenly kneeling at the base of her trunk, eggshell shards littered all about, iridescent on the inside like abalone. Her chameleon eyes peering down at him through branch and limb, hot wind whipping hair across her face. A sapphire pendant dangling at her neck fractured the light, blinding him. Then she'd reach out. Night after night, Rose would reach out and put a hand on his shoulder, and he'd know it was her.

It was always her.

He had the same dream, exactly the same, for weeks. Then one night, just as he reached her it all changed, a record skipping tracks. The sand beneath him shifted, hardened, became the old oak pews of his father's church, a building he'd last set foot in twenty years ago. Wide shafts of sunlight waded through the dense air. Beads of sweat coiled the hair at the napes of the women's necks, dappled the starched shirt backs of the men. The preacher himself was drenched in his own secretions, voice bent with southern cadence and the weight of brimstone.

His father, the preacher.

Even now, William could hear his father's words echoing: "The sin is in the mind." His voice boomed out, ate into the sticky air, swelled to fill the upper chambers of the hall. The good book was a weight in William's hands, its gilt-edged pages gleaming in the light. He looked to his left. She was there with him too, now dressed in white linen but still wearing the sapphire. Rose sitting on the pew next to him, sunlight on the nape of her neck. *The sin is in the mind.* The book an anchor in his hands.

Rose on the bench beside him, hair tumbling down, tress and curl.

His body moved of its own accord. He felt her stiffen with surprise, then grasp back at him. In the dark, half-asleep, it was Sarah's fingernails between his shoulder blades, Rose's clavicle arching back. William pressed his face into her shoulder, biting skin. Outside, the rustling of trees. In the night, in his mind, the body thrust into the bed was Rose's—hair branching over the pillow, skin pale as eggshell. After, as they lay breathing into the hush, Sarah rested her head on his chest. Quietly, she began to cry.

"I missed you so much, Will."

At the window screen, insects roiled to get out of the night.

The English translation of the top layer of Giovanni's text appeared in her in-box sooner than she'd thought it would. Rose scanned the generic message the agency sent with each project, then clicked the link to download the file:

A TREATISE ON ART
By Giovanni Paolo Lomazzo

She scrolled through the table of contents. Chapters traversed topics she'd already been able to identify: color, shadow, proportion, but also ventured into more esoteric themes—like how a man's character is revealed by his physical body, or the emotional qualities of constellations. Carefully, Giovanni was defining a category for painting among the recognized arts, referencing a string of philosophers and mystics. It was clear he was staking his claim: writing around the perimeter of the discipline, weaving art theory together with practical advice.

Best of all was the chance to hear his voice. After a formal introduction, typical of the time period, his prose ebbed into more conversational language. He was educated and passionate, so enthusiastic that sentences sometimes ran for half a page. It was easy to imagine talking to him, going to the tavern for a pint, debating the nature of art into the early hours. She could only guess what reading the translation would mean to William.

She prepared the package, diligently following the same procedures she used for every client. One simple copy, printed and spiral bound with the binding machine she kept in back, one digital file on a thumb drive. No special touches. She hadn't heard from him in weeks, not since he'd last been in the shop—not since he'd brushed her hair back with his hand. Not hearing from him, not seeing him, made her stomach clench, summoned a frantic static to play in the background. She'd even been avoiding Joan, who'd know right away that something was wrong. Rose couldn't bear to tell her what had happened, could imagine the face she'd make: bit-lip disappointment and I-told-you-so eyes. He wasn't just like any other client, after all.

But now she had a reason to reach out. She'd keep it purely professional. Surveying the neat stack of papers with the drive balanced on top, she agreed with herself it was as it should be. At the computer, her fingers grazed the keys.

William, the translation is wonderful.
William, the translation is ready. I can't wait to show it to you.

William . . .

Best to just copy and paste again. She'd done a translation job last fall . . . searching through her sent mail, she found it. Borrowing the letter in full, she substituted the names, changing a word here or there. At the end, she added a line: *You're welcome to pick the materials up from the shop, or I'm happy to mail them.*

After she sent it, she reread it, everything she wanted to say buried in the white space between the lines. The formality felt like a way of telling him he didn't have to worry, that he could come back to the shop and everything would be the same. *You touched my ear, but I will be a consummate professional. It's all right to come back, just come back, please.*

She printed out another copy of the treatise, which fit into her bag if she rolled it at the edges. After giving Odin an absentminded scratch, she locked the door and started the bike ride home. It was dark outside already, and there was a chance he'd be there tomorrow.

William arrived promptly at the start of her lunch hour. Rose stood up behind the register when he opened the door, smoothing out her emerald green blouse. This time, she'd remembered to bring her lipstick and had spent the morning retreating into the bathroom every hour to reapply it.

"Thanks for the email." At the desk, he slid his bag off his shoulder and dropped it at his feet.

"Of course." Rose smiled and grabbed the translation, which she'd kept at the ready, holding it out with both hands like a sacramental gesture. Blinking rapidly, he took it, then set it down sideways on the desk between them.

"Listen, before I dive into this, I just wanted to apologize." He was talking too quickly. Her expression must have been one of confusion, because he licked his lips nervously and kept explaining: "It's just that last time, I didn't mean to, um . . ." He made a tucking gesture near his ear.

"Oh! Don't worry about that at all." Rose knew her cheeks were burning, they couldn't not be. He was taking the moment back, he hadn't meant it. It hadn't meant anything at all. She felt sweat, prickling and hot, gathering in the folds of her arms.

"It was just an automatic response, I wasn't thinking—"

"I didn't think anything of it, really," she lied. They were both speaking too fast now.

William dragged a hand downward over his mouth. "I just didn't mean to overstep . . ."

"Consider it forgotten." She wiped her palms together in the air, a motion of finality, and forced a cheerful face; her stomach doubled in on itself. He looked at her warily, then warmed, leaning in over the book.

"Thanks." Sideways grin, dimple like a flash of sunlight. Then he was glancing down, opening the spiral binding. "So, you've already looked at this, right?" He turned to the table of contents. She tore her eyes from his face and focused back on the book.

"Yes, it's amazing." She couldn't help but start pointing out the titles. "It's about art, but also so much more. Look—this chapter's all about the nature of planets . . . and there's a bit on the qualities of man I think you'll like . . ."

Both their faces were bent over the book now. The translators had formatted the document so that the original text ran on one side, with the English version on the other for easy comparison. He could feel her breath on his arm as she flipped through the pages. The image of her on the church pew next to him flickered to life, her hair falling down her neck.

"Here, it's right here—I think this is so interesting. He was trying to describe how character and mood affect appearance. Honesty, sadness, envy . . . it's all there." Rose tapped the page with two fingers. "Art theory mixed with a little psychology." She fell silent as he scanned the passages.

> Strength. Strength has lofty, stout, and sturdy actions: so as to look big, always composing his body with a good carriage; not flagging and dilating his limbs as weak and weary bodies do . . .

Their heads were nearly touching over the desk as she leaned in to read along with him. He turned the page.

> Adultery. An adulterous man may be patterned after the body of Mars, who by reason of his heat and dryness is by nature prone to rash actions . . .

William straightened, took a step backward.

"Oh, look—there's also this whole other section, all about war and how to draw battleships." Quickly, Rose flipped to a spot in the middle of the book. "Here—here's a description of a new kind of ship the Venetians designed to fight the Ottomans. They went to war the year this was written."

This captured his attention, and he ventured forward again. "It even discusses the mechanics of the side cannon." She ran an index finger under the detail.

He glanced up, curious. "How do you know all that?"

"Well, I wanted to understand the time period better. Working with the book, I felt like I got to know him a bit and I wanted to learn more. About Giovanni, I mean." Her tongue felt clumsy. "I did a little research into what was happening at that time in Venice . . ."

"What did you find out?"

"Oh, it's fascinating." The words began to tumble out easily then—she hadn't realized how much she'd been wanting to share what she'd discovered with him. "A war between a Holy League and the Ottomans was starting—"

"Christians fighting Muslims? Sounds familiar."

"I know, right? But here's the thing: the leader of the Venetian fleet was a man named Sebastiano Venier. That name—Venier—I see it repeated over and over in the undertext."

"Do you think Giovanni knew him?" His eyes lit up at the possibility.

"I don't know . . . it's impossible to say without a translation. The undertext could be anything; it could easily be a history of Venice, actually, which would explain why Venier's name is in it so much. Those types of texts were pretty popular at the time. Giovanni could have experimented with that first, before the treatise. I've been trying to sort out some of the sentences but between the faded ink and my non-Italian, it's kind of a lost cause." She gave a small shrug.

"At least we'll find out soon enough, right? And I can't wait to go through all of this." As he spoke, he closed the spiral-bound translation on the desk between them, then bent to tuck it into his bag. "I'm glad it seems like this is interesting to you." He straightened up, scraping a hand through his hair.

Was he leaving—so soon? Rose rushed to keep the conversation alive. "Oh, it absolutely is. You can tell that he's figuring out art's place in the world, how to communicate it. At the end of the day, he's an academic, really. But just hearing his voice, and then how amazing the sketches are . . . he's gotten a little under my skin." Without thinking, she tucked a loose curl back behind her ear; realizing the gesture she'd made, she glanced up at him anxiously.

He wasn't looking at her. Instead, he was gazing out the window at the sidewalk, where office workers were strolling to lunch without their coats on, woolly white clouds drifting aimlessly overhead. "I get that. Seeing his art is actually what inspired me to change direction with my painting. I'm working on a completely new series now." He directed his words out to the day at large.

"Really?"

"Yeah, that story of his, the egg and the tree—it sparked something, and now it's like I can't spend enough time in the studio." He turned back to her, a new glint in his eyes.

"You're working with Giovanni's sketches?" Rose tried to imagine the images, so clearly mannerist, translated through William's own style.

"It's definitely different." He gave a short laugh. "But it's just what I needed—I haven't been this excited to paint in I don't know how long."

"That's wonderful—I'd love to see them!" She realized how it sounded and quickly clarified: "I mean, if you have a show or something."

"You'll be the first to know." He gave a spontaneous wink. Outside, the clouds broke apart, and a sudden light flooded in to illu-

minate her face, turning her eyes as green as her blouse. He noticed
the color on her mouth. He considered again how easily she'd fit
against him, how her head was the exact height to rest on his chest.
Then he remembered the weight of Sarah's head on his chest in the
night.

Odin chose that moment to leap off his chair with a loud *mew*.
Distracted, they both watched him pad over to a bookcase, rub his
cheek on the wooden corner, then disappear behind it. As if that
was his signal, William bent for his bag, hoisting the strap up over
one shoulder. As he stood, a book stacked on her desk caught his
eye.

"What's that?" The book had a bright red dust jacket with a
painting by Titian on the cover: a nude model reclining on a chaise,
clutching a fistful of flowers.

She froze. She'd never been able to lie—even a white lie was a
challenge—and now here he was, putting her on the spot. Rose
fumbled in silence for a second, then gave up. "It's . . . ah . . . it's for
you, actually. I remembered in the gallery, you said you needed
some art books, and this one gets good reviews. It's all about Venetian painters." After his apology, after he'd taken back the moment
that she'd spent every day trying to decode, she'd decided in an instant not to give the book to him. If she were a craftier person, she'd
have thought to hide it with papers when he bent down.

He raised his eyebrows, surprised. Quickly, she tried to make it
seem more casual than it was instead of something she'd spent
hours tracking down online. "It's not a big deal, I was just doing a
purchase order, and I get discounts anyway. Here, you can take it
with you." She picked up the heavy book and hoisted it toward him.

Taking the spine in one hand, William flipped the book open.
Inside, the pages gave an illustrated account of the Renaissance in
Venice: how the relationship between Venetian and Dutch painters
introduced to the Italians a new technique called glazing, using oil
paints, while the debate over which mattered more—drawing or

color—grew heated. Vibrant full-page reproductions documented the rivalry among Titian, Tintoretto, and Veronese, which had led to an explosion of work produced for churches and patrons.

"This is fantastic . . ." William thumbed through the pages.

"There are so many weird, fun facts in there too." Rose eyed the paintings as they spun past. "They were even grinding up glass into their pigments so they'd reflect more light."

"I should really know so much more than I do; I was just never much of a student. I always chose painting over reading." He shot a sheepish look up at her, then darted his eyes back to the book.

"Well . . ." Rose didn't know what to say to that: who could choose anything over reading? "You're learning now. We both are."

"It's definitely more fun to learn together, though, isn't it?" He continued flipping through the pages slowly.

"It is." She spoke quietly, not wanting to disturb his train of thought.

"I like these conversations we have. Talking about art, ideas . . . Maybe I can still stop by sometimes, even after the book is done." He didn't look up but kept his head bent, studiously examining a portrait of Veronese.

"You're always welcome here." Her heart beat against her sternum, a caged animal. He nodded, as if they'd made an important agreement.

A breeze rattled the door.

He snapped the book shut abruptly; the sound clapped through the stillness. "I should go." He said it louder than he'd meant to. When he looked up, her face was flushed and confused.

"I'll let you know when the undertext is done." She raised her voice up at the end, as if it were a question.

"Thank you. For everything." He held the book up with one hand and waved it in the air, nearly stumbling over the doorstep on his way out.

Three minutes later and William was sitting in the drugstore parking lot again. It'd begun to rain, and the patter on the roof and windows encased him in sound. He pulled out the transcript from his bag slumped in the passenger's seat, opened it to the first page, and began to read. Eventually, he got to the chapter on character and emotion. After Adultery came Fidelity:

> Fidelity is sincere, fair, and trusty, without the mixture of other motions, and is most commonly found in content and moderate men.

Rivulets of rain shivered down the windshield. What kind of man was he? Could he call himself content? Moderate? A recent afternoon surfaced, when for no clear reason other than the house being empty, he'd thrown a wineglass against the kitchen wall.

Why the hell had he apologized for touching Rose, then turned around and asked if he could keep coming back to her shop? What was he thinking? William bent and pressed his forehead against the cool steering wheel. He was losing control; the borders of his life were splintering out. What was he doing in this town, even? He sat up, caught sight of his own face in the side mirror. A memory materialized suddenly, from childhood. It'd been summer, oppressive southern heat, asphalt softening in the roads. His parents had taken him to a carnival show; he'd gotten lost in the house of mirrors. He'd kept trying different routes, panic rising, running harder and harder into his own reflection until he'd broken down and an attendant had to escort him out.

Where was his attendant now?

Propped up next to his bag on the seat beside him, the nude on the cover of the book gave him a sidelong stare. Should he have accepted the gift? Why didn't Sarah ever give him books like that—

did she not think he'd like them? Maybe she just understood him too well and knew that he'd only ever get a third of the way through before abandoning it. He wanted to be the sort of man who read art books, he did. Rose thought he was that sort of man; couldn't he become that? Couldn't he change?

William peered around the parking lot to be sure it was empty, then let loose a howl in a voice he didn't recognize, silent behind the glass. On the pavement outside his door, a large black crow pecked at a discarded Styrofoam container. The bird raised its head at William, staring curiously, as if he looked familiar.

18

THE CROW WAS A DEEPER BLACK THAN THE NIGHT SKY. It stood at the window, shifting foot to foot, sometimes bending to sharpen its beak on the sill. Corvino sat up in bed. The crow surveyed him with liquid eyes.

Corvino. The word pierced his mind; language without sound.

Have you forgotten, Corvino?

The crow tilted its head, feathers glossing purple in the weak light of the stars. Was it growing? Stretching its wings, it swept into the room—claws extending to land with a *skritch* on the wooden table just beyond the bed. It tucked its wings neatly back then, feathers shuffling into place with a dry rustle.

"Forgotten?" Corvino couldn't be sure if he spoke the word or only thought it.

No man can serve two masters, Corvino. Yes, the bird *was* growing, by imperceptible degrees: it'd somehow become the size of a small dog. Beneath its feathers, muscles twitched.

"I serve only the glory of Christ!" Corvino was certain now that

he spoke aloud; the sound of his voice punctured the heavy stillness of the room.

The crow shook its head as if in disagreement and began to pace
the table, beak pointed downward, claws scratching the wood. *You
desire what you do not have and fix your heart upon your own gain.
And what has come of it? Venier is leaving you behind.*

Corvino felt heat rise, his ears tingling as he remembered the
scene. *I need to trust those around me.* That was the way Venier had
put it, not even looking up from his desk, when he'd announced
that Corvino would not accompany the fleet to battle. Corvino
hadn't consulted him before eliminating the senator, a fatal misstep
that no amount of persuasion could remedy. And when Corvino
suggested he might join the fleet anyway, Venier had laughed at
him—laughed in his face!—and he'd understood at once that such
impetuousness would cost him any remaining respect, or opportunity.

"I'd angered him, that's all. A simple misunderstanding." Corvino tried to rise to his feet but discovered he was unable, frozen
upright in the bed with his sheets a twisted whorl around his waist.
The crow lowered its head, darting beady eyes at Corvino. Downy
feathers shot into view, then disappeared again beneath the sleek
black mantle.

Sin is crouching at your door, Corvino. The crow had grown even
larger as it spoke. Its pupils lacked irises, like orbs fashioned from
wet tar. *You are corrupt and deluded by lusts.*

Suddenly it was his father's voice, scorched with anger, filling
the room. The white clearing emerged; Corvino could nearly feel
the sting of blood in his eyes. His father's words pummeled the silence.

You are nothing.

The bird shifted its weight from side to side, as it paced on
scaled and knuckled claws. The table groaned. The crow stopped
moving; it seemed to be contemplating the shelves on the back wall,

where rows of skulls were neatly lined up, hollow sockets attending, beaks cold and naked in the gloom. Next to them sat Corvino's equipment for mixing potions: mortar and pestle, glass and copper vessels.

With a jerk, the crow turned to face Corvino again, extending its wings to their full breadth, until they skimmed either edge of the table. *Put away your old self, which is corrupt.* His father's voice echoed louder, as the crow's eyes became two dark tunnels, boring into the void.

Leave Venice—for good, Corvino. There is no life for you here.

Then the bird began to shrink. In measured wingbeats, it flew to the window ledge then plummeted out, was caught by an invisible hand of dark air. Far in the distance, Corvino heard the caw and whoop of its murder. His head began to throb.

In the avenues below, Aurelio scuttled homeward. He turned back once to glance up at the chamber window, its shutters still open to the night. As he did, a single black feather drifted down from the folds of his robes. He bent to snatch at it, then ducked his head, melting into the shadows.

By week's end the weather had turned unseasonably cold, an opalescent sky doming the city. As expected, Venier was appointed *capitano generale da mar*, admiral of the Venetian navy. He would report to Don Juan of Austria, who had a new title now: captain of the Holy League, overseeing the entire Christian fleet. The women of Venice began to grimly prepare for life without their men, flooding the churches to pray for mercy and protection.

Little time was wasted after the announcements, and soon Gio found himself accompanying Chiara to the harbor to see the fleet off. They'd met in the courtyard of the great house, Gio arriving to find her dressed as modestly as any respectable matron might be, her hair coiled in a design of glossy plaits. She gripped his arm

tightly as he escorted her out a side door and into the waiting gondola, stepping carefully to preserve the cleanliness of her hem. Gio
noted with approval that she wore her lowest *chopines;* passersby
could easily mistake them for a pair of honorable citizens.

The gondolier took them as near as possible to where the fleet
was docked. Already, onlookers choked the avenues, boats jostling
against one another in the canals. Out in the gulf, just past the harbor, they could spot the mast tips of the fleet—sails raised and
whipping in the breeze. Disembarking, Giovanni raised a forearm,
preparing to press a way inward.

Suddenly, Corvino appeared at their side, silent and immediate
as a specter. Without a word of greeting, the Crow stepped in front
of Gio. Under pressure of his glare, the throng swiftly parted to
make way. *A Devil's Moses,* Gio thought, trailing close behind; as if
hearing, Corvino peered backward. Purplish circles ringed his eyes.

With the Crow as shepherd, they made their way to the front of
the crowd. The great ships hovered on the water, wide hulls towering over onlookers who'd pressed themselves up against makeshift
barriers. The ocean made a greedy sucking sound as it slapped the
bows of the boats, the wooden pillars of the docks. Cheers and calls
of grief rang out, punctuated by the shrieks of gulls. A salty breeze
undid the hair around Chiara's face and filled Gio's lungs. After
what seemed an interminable length of time, each captain appeared
on the deck of his galleass. At their center posed Admiral Venier,
standing beside his barrel-chested deputy. In the boat to their right,
the elegant Don Juan, commissioner of the flagship *Real.* In the
background, the full fleet swayed. Galleys and galleasses, round
ships, frigates, brigantines—all armed with mighty cannons and
mounted with culverins, steel catching the light with a flinty glare.
As the soldiers waved and bowed, their audience clamored. Flowers were thrown into the harbor, women wept into linens. Small
children shook their fists overhead, shouting nonsense.

Gio stole a glance at Corvino. He was staring out at the boats with a hard expression. The wind came again and he squinted into it, hair whipping back. The bite of sea air had brought some color to the man's face, turning his beauty heroic. If this were all a play, without a doubt Corvino would have been cast as captain. Gio could imagine him commanding even the Argonauts, raising the captured fleece in one oversize fist, an army of men cheering him on.

Arms crossed tightly over his chest, the Crow surveyed the waving commanders. A muscle in his jaw pulsed. As if feeling Gio's eyes upon him, Corvino turned and, for a fraction of a moment, a face beneath his face revealed itself. Emotion trembled across the Crow's features. *The man was trying not to cry!* Gio's own expression must have betrayed his surprise: as he watched, anger displaced any sign of grief, until the Crow had him fixed in a look of bald fury—as if he, Gio, were the source of all ill fortune. Gio froze. Then, with a rough shake of his head, Corvino thrust away, elbowing through the crowd, his retreat marked by a wake of lurching bystanders.

At that same moment, the boats heaved themselves into motion. Massive oars swept through the air in synchronized arcs, then plunged violently into the sea. The raised sails caught hold of the wind, snapping like flags.

Amid the confetti of a thousand handkerchiefs, the fleet departed eastward.

Outside Gio's window the next morning, silhouettes of rooftops fuzzed and bled into the still pale sky. The blackness was getting worse. Each day now began with a gut-wrenching inventory of what new territory had been lost to the darkness, that thief in the night. Gio tried to guess how long he had left—probably far less than his hopeful mind could imagine. He rolled over in bed, groping on the floor for spectacles, vellum, quill, and inkpot. Dabbing the ink, he began his morning journaling: scrawl, dip, scrawl and dip again. Soon, the writing gave way to sketches of Chiara. He filled the margins. Chiara standing in the bath. Chiara sleeping beside him in the afternoon, rumpled sheets framing her body. Her face turned, always.

"*Lunatics!*" Aurelio didn't bother to knock but threw the door open with a bang. All the blood in his body seemed to have migrated to his head, turning his face a deep crimson. As the alchemist stood on the stoop, chest heaving, Gio scrambled to tug on his doublet and hose.

"Who do they think they are to do such a thing? Come, Gio, we haven't a moment to lose!" Behind Aurelio, neighbors were rushing past, nearly sprinting down the avenue. Without any other explanation, the alchemist turned and rejoined the fray. Quickly, Gio tugged his spectacles loose and tucked them into his pouch, snatched up his robe, and darted out the door to catch up. As they hurried along with the crowd, Aurelio told him the news.

"It's Anzola. There's been testimony against her—and now these idiots of the Cattaveri are announcing her charges. There's a chance she'll be handed over to the Inquisition."

Gio thought of the cloaked woman, how he'd last seen her slipping off into the shadows outside Aurelio's home. "What is she accused of?" The Cattaveri supervised the Ghetto; normally, they kept their meddling strictly to Jews who'd violated one of their many regulations. Gio knew they'd summon the Inquisition only on suspicion of heresy.

"They're claiming she's a Jewess and a dissembler—posing as a Christian, refusing to live in the Ghetto or wear the badge. They're also charging her with sorcery. She may be a Jewess, I don't know one way or the other, but that second charge is . . ." Aurelio scowled and quickened his pace.

"Who would accuse her of being a sorceress?" As they rushed along, Gio felt a bit like Lucio: struggling to understand, bounding forward every third step to keep up.

"Any apothecary, that's who. They all think she takes business from them—though, of course, half their shelves are stocked with her herbs." Aurelio shook his head. "Or maybe a Church official, if her treatments worked better than his prayers. I don't know, Gio." The alchemist threw his hands in the air. "It could have been anyone. But I won't stand for it! They call men physicians, but *she's* a sorceress! Now they've put her in the stocks, I've been told." Even Aurelio's ears had gone pink.

"The stocks?" Gio had heard of only a handful of well-known criminals getting the stocks—and only ever men. Around them townspeople bustled, animated and chattering. Gio could hear snatches of conversation as they passed: *Jew, witch, the stake.*

"What will happen if she goes before the inquisitors?"

"I don't want to consider that possibility just yet, Gio." Aurelio tugged on his beard anxiously. "But I won't let them make an example of her. Not her."

The two men fell silent then, hurrying toward the square. When they arrived, it was already crammed with spectators—though with some aggressive shoulder thrusts and fist shaking from Aurelio, they managed to squeeze their way to the front, where a small half circle had been established. In the center, a straight-backed magistrate was reading from a scroll, quoting Thomas Aquinas. He was pious-looking and young: narrow face, thin lips, pale from too much time spent cloistered. Beside him, a wooden contraption with two slabs had been set up, out of which poked the head and hands of Anzola.

In the light of day, Gio wondered how many people had actually ever seen the woman properly. He'd only ever heard of her nighttime exchanges, a hand slipped through a crack in the door. Now as he regarded her, she seemed neither male nor female. Her face was bare and etched with lines, her eyes deep-set and hooded: yellowgreen, like a fox. The wiry silver hair she usually hid under a hood was loose now, caught back by the clasp of the stocks. Exposed in the sunlight, she seemed ancient and ageless at once, a crone in every sense of the word. Gio squinted. Her skin shone in spots, where she'd been spat on by the crowd. As the magistrate began to call out her charges, she screwed her eyes shut.

"It has been testified that the woman you see before you, one Anzola Leví, has posed as a Christian while practicing the religious rites of a Jewess." The magistrate's voice was shrill and reedy. "This is a violation of the regulations governing dress and residence to which all Jews are subject, and she kneels before you as a dissembler." At his words, the throng erupted, swaying and shoving forward; Gio widened his stance to keep from being knocked to the stones.

Emboldened by the audience's response, the official thrust out his bony chest and raised the scroll higher. "Furthermore, it is claimed this woman has performed acts of witchcraft in the presence of Christians. The Cattaveri is still uncertain if the accused has lain with a Christian, thus bringing him into religious error and heresy."

More insults surged from the crowd. Someone threw an overripe tomato. Narrowly missing Anzola, it burst against the edge of the stocks, wet pulp and seed splattering her cheek. She winced, then twisted her neck to look back at the official. "You have no proof of my faith!" Her voice was surprising, a full half octave lower than typical female speech—less that of a grandmother than a priestess.

The magistrate shouted to be heard over the clamor. "By the second testimony, it has been claimed this woman gave bewitched powders in drink to children suffering from the falling sickness ..."

"Flower essence and herbs to bring equilibrium," Anzola shouted back.

The crowd swelled again. The edge of the circle knitted tighter. Gio stumbled, grasping Aurelio's shoulder, pushing back against the elbows that poked his sides. He felt his breath begin to shallow, sweat beading his temples as if even the sun overhead had drawn

closer. Another tomato was thrown, then an egg. The tomato fell
short, splitting open on the stones, but the egg hit just left of Anzola's nose. It shattered and cut her; Gio squinted, saw a red tinge
to the jelly that glazed down her chin. His stomach clenched. As
she spat shell shards and bloodied yolk out onto the dirt, the spectators cheered—a tangle of angry, riotous noise. Pinching his
mouth in disapproval, the magistrate glanced down at his robes
and took a prim step backward.

Gio turned to gaze at the sea of snarling faces. He wondered if
any of them understood the reality of the danger Anzola was in, or
if they actually wanted to see a woman they'd known for years burn
at the stake. Just that week, he'd heard a story in the taverns about
another woman, executed for heresy in Amsterdam. They said she'd
cried out to God so loudly her own neighbors had stuffed her
mouth with gunpowder before raising her into the flames. Looking
at Anzola hunched and bound, with the crowd frenzied and baying
for a spectacle, Gio felt a chill pass over him. The magistrate began
to recite the next charge.

"Enough!" An explosion at his side. Before Gio could register
what was happening, Aurelio was pacing in front of the horde,
robes whipping back as if there were a wind. He glowered at the
audience like they were misbehaving children. Next to the alchemist's commanding figure, the magistrate seemed a useless errand
boy.

"You women! To think of it!" Spit flew from Aurelio's mouth
with each consonant, glittering as it arced into the air. "How dare
you show your faces here? How many of you have begged this
crone for herbs to aid your aches and cramps? To ease a babe to
sleep? To prevent another child?" Aurelio's outstretched finger con-
demned each face it crossed. Stunned, the crowd fell silent.

The alchemist bellowed on, the only voice in the square now.
"And you men! Do you fool yourselves into believing I don't know
who among you has sought her help? Has asked her to remedy

your impotent members? Your hairlessness? Your disease?" At this, the magistrate moved to intervene. Aurelio raised a hand and the man halted, ducking his head like a reprimanded hound. He blinked about frantically for reinforcement. The crowd stirred uncomfortably.

"Has she not helped you all?" At the alchemist's side, Anzola began to weep. Her tears mixed with the yolk and pulp on her face, forming a sickly sheen. Aurelio brought his voice to its full capacity. "Perhaps I ought to write a list of all those she has helped and why. Will that make you remember? Shall I post it in the square for all to see? *Shall I?*" For a moment under the glare of the sun, the alchemist seemed to swell in size, every color heightened: beard shocking white, skin violent pink. Along the perimeter of the square, bystanders began to slip off into alleyways, the crowd loosening at first, then openly dispersing. Gio tracked one man in particular as he shuffled away, shoulders clenched up tight near his ears. Watching him go, Gio realized he was witnessing shame expressing itself through the body. A spark lit in a corner of his mind.

Turning back to the stocks, Gio was startled to find the blind man from Venier's dinner party whispering to the magistrate. His shrewish page stood off to one side, peering at the retreating spectators. As the old man spoke into the official's ear, the magistrate began nodding, eyes trained on the ground. He fished a key from his robes and extended it in Aurelio's direction. The alchemist snatched at it, then quickly knelt before Anzola. The few remaining onlookers began protesting, like chickens clucking after their feed.

"You cannot do this! She's been accused a witch!" A shrill voice, coming from a sour-faced woman Gio recognized from Mass. She was watching Aurelio undo the locks, fists balled on her wide hips.

"Oh hush, you old hag!" Aurelio didn't bother looking up. "We both know what she gave your husband, don't we—and aren't you glad she did?" The woman's eyes went wide and her mouth gaped open, then shut again like a fish. Bundling up her skirts, she scurried away, muttering prayers that sounded more like curses.

Finally, Aurelio succeeded, throwing off the top panel of heavy wood that had bound Anzola's wrists and neck. Holding the woman by the crooks of her elbows, he helped her to straighten. Face slick, hair hanging in sweat-soaked ropes, she collapsed into his arms.

I need to trust those around me. Corvino paced the avenues briskly, like an arrow shot toward its target. *I need to trust those around me.* The phrase had stayed at the forefront of his mind, shouting out any other thoughts, Venier's dismissive wave replaying in a loop even as he slept. And worse, before the fleet had departed, Corvino had overheard Venier discussing future plans for his whore; through the cracked door he'd caught mention of an allowance, private lodgings in the city. All for spreading her legs! Well—he would show Venier who was to be trusted. He'd seen the way she'd looked at that artist, dancing *la volta* with him at Venier's feast. Under Venier's own roof, they'd looked at each other that way! Then later, after Domenico's salon, he could have sworn he saw the artist step into her gondola. Corvino was no fool. He'd noticed the ink smudges on the man's fingers—he was writing something. Love letters? Groveling poetry? Whatever it was, Corvino would find it. Any shred of evidence and Corvino would coax it out like a splinter, collect it, display it like art upon Venier's return. *See what you think of your precious whore now.*

Without warning, his mind leapt to the crow's visit in the night, its voiceless command to leave the city. Simply an apparition, nothing more. A waking dream, the raving result of worry and lack of sleep. No, he would not leave—Venice would yield to him yet. If only Venier had let him sail! He would have fought piously on board the fleet, he'd have defended the very soul of Christendom! But no matter. He'd simply need to find other ways to make his name known, to earn his rightful station. His Father would provide for him, he need only stay the course. *We will reap at harvest time if we do not give up.* Corvino quickened his pace, darting down the avenues that lay deserted while the whole town gawked at that hag.

He'd show Venier who was to be trusted.

His journal was gone.

Returning home from the square, Gio had been forced to follow the pace of the dispersing crowd, and now he found his door ajar. Heart dropping, he lunged inside to see at once that his rooms had been ransacked: chairs overturned, cabinets and chests torn open, clothes and papers strewn across the floor. His eyes darted to the tilt of his mattress; the inkpot he kept beside it had been knocked over, was now leaking black onto the floor. He rushed to pull the bedding up, clutching about blindly. The floor was flat and cool—empty.

They'd found it. *Corvino* had found it.

Who else could it be? If the Crow harbored any suspicions about his relationship with Chiara, the distraction in the square had provided an ideal opportunity to search Gio's chamber. *Why hadn't he been more careful?* Gio pictured all his sketches, how he'd filled every margin with Chiara: her feet, her elbows, her mouth. He leaned back onto his heels and let out a howl between clenched teeth.

A second man arrived at the gates of Famagusta—again neatly turbaned, though this time his hand was bandaged, his dark eyes like bloodshot marbles. The parchment he bore offered another promise: that no citizens would be harmed if Captain Bragadin surrendered. With resignation, the captain retreated to his chambers. As he bathed, his cuts and scrapes turned the water pink then crimson, muscles aching with each bend and twist. He oiled his beard until it shone, then called for his royal robes. With stiff joints, he mounted his favorite steed. If he must surrender, he would do so with dignity. In a single line, he and his commanders crossed the bridge that now spanned the moat outside Famagusta, as the citadel smoldered behind them.

Less than two hours later the heads of his commanders were mounted on pikes, their empty eyes staring out, fixed in horror. Slow-draining blood dripped from their cleaved necks onto the floor of Mustafa's tent, wet earth absorbing the viscous red. Bragadin's gaze, however, was fastened not on their faces but on Mustafa's open hands.

In each palm rested one of Bragadin's own severed ears.

"My son, my son. You murdered my son," Mustafa kept repeating in a language Bragadin would never be able to understand. Still, he could guess at the meaning. Once again, Bragadin saw his own soldier turning toward him in the market square, displaying a blood-streaked blade. Proclaiming to all who'd listen that he'd slain Mustafa's heir.

Once again, he heard the beggar woman's voice: *You'll be killed by the whip, but you'll die by the saber.*

19

ROSE WAS MAKING PROGRESS ON THE UNDERTEXT. SHE'D matched the fade of the ink Giovanni had used nearly exactly and could now start filling in the obscured sentences. Since Giovanni had only partially scraped away the original text, large patches of words were left clearly visible in the margins, escaped fragments of thought. She tried to piece them back together, turning the repair into ritual. It was more than she needed to do, but it'd make translating the undertext easier for the agency. It was also a welcome distraction, forcing her mind to focus on something other than William. His last visit had left her disoriented—why had he apologized, then asked her permission to keep coming back to visit? She wanted to sit and pore through books on behavioral science, chart his various probabilities of meaning. As always, she wanted to talk it over with Joan, but she knew that the second she got to the part where he'd brushed her hair back, Joan would stop her, raising one hand in the air and shaking her head emphatically, the same gesture she used on Henry when he was about to do something that was strictly forbidden. *Oh no, that's quite enough.*

He'd apologized for it, though, that was the snag her thoughts kept catching on. He'd taken it back. Was she supposed to trust his words—which told her that he enjoyed her friendship, period—or was she supposed to trust his actions? The way he'd touched her, how she'd caught him looking at her in the gallery more than once. He'd *winked* at her during his last visit. What had that been about? Now she knew there were full articles online, dissecting over twenty different types of winks and the message each might be sending. She was almost starting to resent him for this: that she'd become a woman who looked up articles on websites meant for teenage girls, sitting alone at her dining room table, eating canned soup.

She'd stopped making eye contact with the portraits on the mantel weeks ago.

Yet even if his actions were more real than his words, where did that leave her? He was married . . . at least, he still wore a wedding ring. The mind, she was discovering, was a dangerous place: a dark wood with winding paths that beckoned her into uneasy territory. Not knowing what else to do, Rose turned to the work. Letting the treatise consume her felt like a safe choice, a familiar obsession. *Better the devil you know.* So, she allowed herself to stay up late, huddled over the pages. Patching fibers, tracing ink. Meticulously avoiding the fact that the treatise was her one link to William, the way an ice skater glides around rough patches on a lake.

She began to move deeper into the undertext. As she did, she saw the same names repeated there: *Venier*, of course, but also *Aurelio*. Another word as well, *cortigiana*. Courtesan. Could the woman in the portrait be a courtesan? It seemed likely—a wealthy man's companion as the artist's muse. Rose considered the idea as she worked. After an hour, she went and retrieved the sketch of the woman from the stack, then balanced the portrait upright on the countertop, like a patron saint overseeing her repairs.

Already, a large portion of the text was ready for translation. She couldn't wait any longer. Shuffling through the pages, she found the spot where sketches of the woman began to appear in the margins. Taking a section of about thirty sheets, she scanned them, then imported the images into her software program. After a bit of fiddling, she was able to isolate the bottom layer of writing. Rendered in red, the text was even more legible than she'd hoped for.

With a *ding!* the program produced a file of Giovanni's hidden script, ready to be sent to the agency.

The next morning, Rose woke up exhausted. Between the half-closed drapes, a small bluebird bobbed on a branch outside her window. It flitted its wings and ducked its head, delighting in the morning sunshine.

No. She wouldn't open the shop today. It was a Sunday, and the students were gone anyway—the whole town was asleep for summer. In the kitchen, she made a French press, then retrieved the paper from the stoop, tightly rolled in its dew-pocked plastic sleeve. Two cups of coffee later and midway through the Travel section, a knock sounded at the front door. For no logical reason, she wondered if it was William.

It was Joan, looking as tired as Rose felt, her red hair pinned back haphazardly. Henry stood in front of her, grinning and clutching a plastic fire engine.

"Oh good, you're home. I absolutely need a trim and the salon can fit me in now. You can watch him for a little while, can't you?" As she spoke, Joan touched the back of her head self-consciously with one hand, pushing Henry over the threshold with the other.

"Sure, I was going to close the shop today anyway. I can take him to the farmers' market."

"Oh, that's perfect, thanks so much. I'll just pick you up there?"

Joan threw this last sentence over one shoulder as she retreated toward the family van, which had been left idling in the drive. She slammed the door, then backed out and disappeared around the corner at a questionable speed for a residential neighborhood. Henry remained on the doormat, unbrushed hair still fixed in a ruddy swirl from sleep, beaming up at her.

Rose didn't have a car—driving gave her anxiety, and everywhere she needed to go was within biking distance. When she was with Henry, they took the bus. It was always a tremendous adventure for him: swiping their passes, then pressing his small nose to the glass as they rumbled toward town. *There's the garden! I can see the river! Look at that truck!*

People assumed Henry was her son when they went out together. Rose enjoyed the misperception, the sympathetic smiles she received from other mothers, her temporary admission into their circle. The bus that day wasn't particularly crowded: only locals, now that it was summer. An older woman who'd penciled in her eyebrows using an odd shade of navy, a thin man in a short-sleeve button-down and, inexplicably, a beret. A few students still in town for the summer, their requisite earphones in, white plastic knobbing out.

After three stops a teenage couple got on, the girl in a black crop top and fraying denim shorts, the boy wearing baggy jeans and expensive-looking sneakers. His hair was dyed an impressive shade of platinum, nearly white. Rose watched them slump, giggling, into the seats that ran below the windows. They must have gone to an event the night before: they still had neon-colored wristbands on. The girl was tugging at hers, trying to get it to tear. She made an exaggerated performance of it, knocking into the boy's shoulder, laughing. With a swoop he grabbed her wrist, then brought it to his mouth. Biting the band, he wrenched at it with his fingers, her arm hanging limp in front of his bared teeth. The gesture was sudden, animalistic. The girl abruptly stopped laughing and stared at him intently. The lengths of their thighs were touching, rocking with the motion of the bus.

Then he succeeded, and the band snapped loose. He smiled triumphantly, wiping his mouth with the back of one hand. She was smiling too, rubbing her wrist, but something had altered between them. A change of color in her expression.

Rose thought of William's hand again, grazing her ear . . .

"Auntie Rose, is it time to pull the cord yet? Is it time?" Henry turned toward her then, putting his little palm on her thigh as if she were just another piece of furniture, an extension of the bus seat. A warm wave of comfort rushed in to displace what she'd been feeling. Rose glanced out the window.

"Almost, Henry. We're the next stop."

The market had more stalls than she'd remembered. Families and couples milled leisurely down the aisles, and near the entrance a small band of high schoolers played earnest covers of sixties folk songs. Several stands offered samples speared with toothpicks: melons and figs, cubes of bread for dipping into olive oils or slathering with jam, slices of tangy cheese. Midway through the maze of vendors, Rose had already acquired a bag of salad greens and a tub of honeycomb she probably didn't need but was drawn to for its gooey fractal symmetry. She glanced down at Henry and saw that he'd managed to smear jelly across one side of his face, nearly to his ear.

"Henry, how on earth . . ." Rose rummaged around the bottom of her purse for the packet of wipes she knew to keep.

"Rose!"

She recognized the voice, though at first she couldn't place the lanky man behind the farm stand, with the afternoon sun casting his face in shadow. Then he moved, and she caught a tinge of auburn, a ruddy halo encircling his head.

"Lucas?" She gave a quick swipe to Henry's cheek, then ushered him toward the stand, remnants of berry still clinging to his chin.

Ducking under the tent, she saw that the sun had multiplied Lucas's freckles, lightened his hair to near copper.

"Hey, it's good to see you!" He was wearing a blue apron. The farm stand was one of the largest at the market, tables loaded with cherries and rhubarb, summer squash and greens.

"Is this your farm?"

"My family's, actually." He pointed toward the banner pinned to the tent fabric behind him. RIPE EARTH ORGANICS. "They were a little shorthanded this week, and the library is slow. Summer break and all . . ."

"You have red hair, like me!" Henry was pointing a berry-stained finger at Lucas's head.

Lucas laughed. "Yep, and freckles too. I wouldn't be surprised if you get a few of these when you get older." He tapped the bridge of his nose.

"Really?" Henry widened his eyes, then squinted up suspiciously. "Where do they come from?"

"Well, I have it on good authority that they're fairy kisses. You get them while you're sleeping."

Henry let out a soft "oh," his mind immediately busy sorting out the logistics of fairy visits.

"Your son?" Lucas asked, tilting his head. For a second, she was reminded of the little bird outside her window earlier that morning.

"No, my nephew. Henry, this is Lucas. Lucas, Henry."

"My mom is her sister," Henry stated matter-of-factly. "Aunt Rose doesn't have any babies because she isn't married."

"Henry!" Rose shushed the boy. Henry looked up at her with a confused expression, his jam-stained mouth dropping open.

"It's okay, Henry. There are lots of people who aren't married yet." Lucas waved his bare left hand up in the air. "It takes time to find the right person."

"Who's this, Lucas?" An older woman had materialized at Lucas's elbow. She had wire-frame glasses and a mane of gray hair twisted back in a tortoiseshell clip. Her formidable bosom was covered by an apron with EAT LOCAL printed across the front.

"Rose, meet my mother, Theresa. Mom, this is Rose, she's a book restorer. I helped her with a project."

"Ohhhh, *Rose*. Hellloooo." The woman winked profusely at Lucas while wiping her hands on her apron, then offered one to Rose to shake. "Earl! Earl come over and meet Lucas's friend from school!" She turned and flapped an arm at her husband, a heavyset man with a bristly salt-and-pepper beard that splayed across his chest.

"Mom, it's a *university*, please. We didn't meet on a playground." Lucas shot Rose a look of exasperation, and she noticed with some amusement that he'd gone pink. Earl wandered over, hitching up the back of his jeans although he wore a pair of suspenders. He reached out a callused hand toward Rose; his grip was surprisingly gentle. Standing side by side, he and Theresa reminded Rose ever so slightly of overgrown hobbits: she could imagine them having second breakfasts and afternoon tea, picking berries in fields as idyllic as any in the Shire.

"Nice to meet you, Rose. Can't say I know much about what Lucas gets up to with all those books—" Earl's voice was deep and sandpaper gruff.

"He's a bit of the black sheep of the family," Theresa interrupted, cupping a hand to the side of her mouth in a mock whisper, as if Lucas couldn't hear. Rose smiled politely, not sure how to play along.

"I go to a playground!" Henry announced loudly, catching up to the conversation.

"I bet you do!" Theresa put her hands on her hips, puckering her face at Henry before exclaiming "Oh! Oh my!" A group of women wearing matching purple workout T-shirts had descended upon the stand; Theresa and Earl bustled over to help them weigh their produce.

Rose inched toward the end of the table. "Well, your parents are adorable."

"Pros and cons, pros and cons." Lucas grinned at her. "But I really can't complain. My biggest childhood trauma was probably the outfits my mom decided to dress me in."

"Please tell me there's documentation."

"Oh God, I'm sure." He cringed. "So, how's your summer so far?"

"Good, I've just been wrapped up in that project. I need to get outside more." Rose was suddenly aware of how pale her skin was compared to Lucas's healthy tan.

"I get the exact same way when I'm working. Is it going well? Did you ever figure out the undertext?"

"I sent a portion off to the translators, I'm expecting it back any moment."

"Oh, bated breath!" He rubbed his hands together excitedly.

"What's a bated breath?" Henry chimed in again from below. Rose and Lucas met eyes, both squinting, considering the best answer.

Lucas responded first. "It's when you're so excited, you almost hold your breath."

Rose's pocket started vibrating. It was a text from Joan, waiting for them in the parking lot. "That's his mom . . . we should go. It was really nice to see you again, Lucas. I need to get back up to the archives soon." From the corner of her eye, Rose could see Theresa watching them as she pretended to reorganize cartons of cherries.

"Oh, about that—I'm actually heading to England for a few weeks." He undid and redid the ties of his apron nervously. "I'm working on an exhibit of medieval manuscripts in collaboration with Oxford. So, I'll be heading over there to get it all sorted out, do some sightseeing."

"But, that's perfect for you!" Rose batted at Henry, who was pulling on her purse.

Lucas couldn't keep his face from breaking open with excitement. "I know, I can't believe it's actually happening! Hey, one question." He tugged on his ear. "I have this thing, it's silly really, but I like sending postcards when I travel. Can I send you one?"

"Of course!" She started rummaging through her purse for something to write on. Henry was gazing up at her with basset hound eyes. "Okay, Henry, what is it?"

"Can we get some cherries?"

By the time Rose had retrieved paper and pen and jotted down her address, Lucas had already handed Henry a brown bag full of fruit, on the house, shrugging off her protestations. When she turned to wave goodbye, Earl and Theresa raised their hands also, the three of them standing together in the warm light, framed by their harvest.

Rose gave most of the fruit to Joan, but saved a basket of cherries for herself. The next night, well after the sky had gone star speckled, she retreated to the couch—a striped affair that was more than a decade overdue for an update. Stuffing a pair of pillows into one corner, Rose managed to create a relatively comfortable nest for herself. She was working her way through her father's library; next on the list was Seneca's *Letters from a Stoic*. On the table beside her, a bowl of cherries cozied up to a steaming cup of chamomile. Just as she'd gotten settled, her phone chimed with a notification: an email from the translators.

The pages of undertext that she'd sent were complete.

"Well, that was fast." Out of habit, Rose glanced at her father's empty chair. He would have reminded her that summer was likely the agency's slow season. Her laptop sat on the dining room table, next to the morning paper; in three strides, she was clicking to download the document. The first line blinked up on the screen:

For these past many years, I've relied upon Sebastiano Venier's patronage.

Was it a diary—could it be? Hastily, Rose clicked Print. Nearly tripping on her way down the hall, she stood over the printer, which she'd hidden in the laundry room, resisting an urge to tug at the sheets as they slid out. She couldn't wait for the job to finish— instead, she took the first few pages and slid her back down the washer until she was sitting cross-legged on the tiled floor. She'd put the dryer on to run earlier; now it made a comforting, rhythmic rustle next to her as she read.

Today I was summoned for a portrait of Venier's favorite courtesan. Without a doubt, I feel my life has been changed irrevocably.

Over the next pages, Giovanni's world came into view, like reaching the summit of a mountain to finally see the landscape spreading out below. Characters were introduced: Aurelio, whom Rose took to be a friend, and Venier—here Rose recalled the portraits from the archive of the admiral, white-bearded and stern. A man named Corvino, whom Giovanni described as "cruelly handsome." Though he never gave the name of his new muse, Rose couldn't help but assume it was the woman from the portrait.

What she'd wanted so terribly she now had: a way in. An open door, offering passage to Giovanni's life—into the world of the man who was and was not William. The last page came quickly, leaving too many unanswered questions. Why had Giovanni scraped away his own diary? Why did Rose have such an uneasy feeling about Corvino? After she read the final line, she lay her head against the washer to think it all through.

Already, she knew she'd wake up early the next day, shut the door of the operating room, and work without rest until the full diary could be translated. Until it was finished, completely. Even though finished would mean an end of reasons for William to visit. She imagined the shape of his absence—an empty doorway, no more looking up to find him standing there, broad shoulders block-ing the light. No more of that new smell he'd brought with him last time, linseed oil cut with turpentine. Still, Rose knew that she'd finish the work madly, compulsively. She wouldn't be able to help herself.

William. William would want to read this.

She rose to her feet, muscles stiff from sitting, and left the warm, dryer-sheet-scented room to stand in front of the computer again. Clicking it awake, she created a new message with the transcript attached.

W—

The translated pages are here. It's what I think we'd both secretly hoped it would be.

                                        R

She knew, without a doubt, he'd show up at the shop the next day. She forced herself up the stairs in the dark and stretched out on the bed, still dressed. She fell asleep that way, one palm over her chest, her metronome heart.

20

"YOU KEPT A JOURNAL?" CHIARA'S EXPRESSION WAS DUMB with shock.

"I didn't write your name in it. I just ... drew pictures. And never of your face! I can easily say they're of someone else, a different woman."

Chiara shook her head. She'd gone the same shade as her pearls. "But if Corvino argues that he's seen us together—"

"It could be used to convince Venier, I know. I don't think he *has* seen us, but he could say what he wants and use the journal to make his case. I'm sure he knows exactly how to take advantage of Venier's jealousy. But he won't do anything before Venier returns, not without his consent. That means we have some time to think of a plan."

For a moment they stood in silence. They were in the rose-colored sitting room again, Gio's supplies slumped in a heap near the door. He'd come on the pretense of escorting Chiara to another sitting, but after taking one look at him, she'd dismissed Cecilia.

"Fetch us some wine please, and some of those small cakes from yesterday afternoon if you can find them, take your time." Once they were alone, Gio had told her what happened, trying hard to keep his voice steady. Now she strode to the hearth, observing the remains of that morning's fire, holding one palm out as if the room had gone cold, the other pressed to the bodice of her silk *gamurra*.

"I don't care if he knows. Let's just go somewhere new, Gio— together."

"Chiara, I'll be blind within the year—"

"I don't care, Gio." She turned to him, face still pale, two strokes of pink marking her cheeks as if she'd been struck.

"Chiara, you must understand. I won't be able to paint without my sight. That means no more income from portraits. And if Venier denounces me to my patrons, denounces us . . ."

"I don't care, Gio!" Her voice cracked. "I *hate* him—"

The door burst open then, halting their conversation. Instinctively, Gio stepped two paces backward. It was Cecilia, carrying a tray loaded with wine, glasses, and assorted cakes, trailed by Veronica and Margherita. They'd just heard the news of Anzola and were eager to discuss it—Margherita at once launching into a breathless and dramatically embellished recounting of events as the girls found seats and Cecilia distributed drinks and small plates.

"I heard they'd even begun building a stake when that alchemist stepped in!" As usual, Margherita spoke with her mouth full.

"Oh, Margherita, please—I don't think it went to those extremes." Chiara brought a hand up to finger the necklaces at her chest.

"It could have. The Cattaveri are growing bolder." Gio shot a warning glance at Chiara. She turned away. He took a sip of wine; it was lukewarm, round and tannic in his mouth.

"But what if she really *is* a Jew?" Veronica lounged on a chaise, grooming her hair with a little ivory comb. "She should be punished for what she's done—masquerading as a Christian, living outside the Ghetto. If she's dissembled, she must be taught a lesson."

"Veronica!" Chiara's eyes widened in surprise.

"Chiara, everyone knows the Jews are dangerous; they have spies all over Venice. The sultan's adviser, that Nassi, he's a Jew—he must have informants in the Ghetto. Likely they're feeding him information as we speak, the rats." Veronica held up a fistful of hair, inspecting the ends. "And if they go about pretending to be Christians, dressing as us, trading in our markets . . . how will we ever feel safe? Portugal expelled them, Spain expelled them. I don't see why we don't do the same."

Chiara opened her mouth at this, though no sound came out.

"An excellent suggestion."

Corvino's voice was close and dry, and it sucked the air from Gio's lungs. The room turned to watch as the Crow sidled in from the shadows of the hall, through the door left gaping. With one hand he smoothed his hair, then spotted the wine and empty goblets on the sideboard and strode to pour himself a glass. All Gio could do was stare. He pictured the Crow rifling through the pages of his journal, examining his sketches. It was a deeper humiliation than being caught without clothes on; another man viewing not his body but his mind, his daily thoughts and concerns. Judging his privacies without his permission. Gio imagined leaping up, bolting across the room, knocking Corvino to the ground and pounding his head into the stones until he felt bones crack. But no, the Crow still had powerful connections, and worse—he had the journal. Chiara must be protected at any cost. Gio remained in his chair, watching.

"Well. I'm glad *someone* agrees with me." Veronica gazed down her nose at the Crow, assessing him anew.

Corvino spun his glass once, watching the liquid swirl. He raised the goblet to sniff at the wine, then made a delicate grimace. "At the very least, they ought to be made to convert." He took a long sip, surveying the room.

"Perhaps they don't convert because—in addition to not believing—they're forced to forfeit all their worldly goods upon baptism," Chiara countered from her seat in the middle of the room. She was angry; Gio could tell, by the hard set of her mouth.

"Ill-gotten goods extorted from desperate Christians!" Corvino glared at her, and Gio felt his throat tighten.

"Oh, they can't all be ill gotten. And I wonder if you would find it so easy to convert yourself. Imagine being forced to give up all you owned, all your fine robes and jewels, then banned from practicing your usual trades . . ." Here she looked pointedly at Corvino's fur-trimmed cape, his gleaming gold cross. They all knew what Corvino traded in—did she want to provoke him? Gio stared at her, trying desperately to warn her not to speak so boldly, but she didn't glance in his direction.

The Crow's eyes narrowed. "You have a woman's weakness of mind." Leisurely he strolled across the floor to glance out the window. Then, suddenly, he whirled about so that he was standing directly behind Chiara; in one sure move, he looped a finger under the longest strand of pearls that hung at her neck and began pulling upward, slowly. "You forget that the Jews do not deserve their riches: only the righteous are worthy of reward." Gio stared, horrified, as the pearls slid up, up, up, skidding over her bodice, past her other chains, until they were pressed taut against her throat. Chiara didn't move a muscle, all the color seeping from her face. Corvino's gaze drifted to the ceiling; for a moment he seemed to be addressing the apostles painted overhead. "The Jews know of the existence of the true Lord, and yet they turn their back on Him. The word of the Lord is clear on the matter: *Whoever does not abide in me is cast out like a branch."* With a flick of his wrist, Corvino let loose some slack. He shook the pearls free from her other necklaces, then spun the strand up over Chiara's head.

"Such branches are thrown into the fire and burned." The Crow took four paces, then tossed the pearls into the hearth. They fell in a glimmering coil over the embers, sparks shooting up. The room sat in stunned silence—all except Corvino, who retreated to the sideboard to refill his glass. Gio watched as Chiara stared at her defiled necklace, spots of red flaring across her chest and neck like ink stains. Once more, he tried and failed to catch her eye.

Then, unable to restrain herself, Cecilia darted from her post in the corner. Kneeling before the hearth, she took up the poker and fished the necklace out; the strand clattered onto the floor. Fortunately, the embers hadn't been strong enough to scorch the pearls, though they were too hot to touch. The Crow curled his mouth at the sight of the servant girl, crouched over her mistress's jewels, then took another sip of wine. As Cecilia stood and hastily retreated, head bowed, Veronica cleared her throat in the corner.

"I've heard it said many times: *Any who try to turn you away from the Lord should be put to death."* Gio couldn't tell if she actually agreed with the Crow or was simply trying to break the tension with more conversation, but he thanked her for the distraction.

"Exactly." Corvino raised one hand to his temple, began rubbing a circle with his fingertips.

"Oh, please—you only go to church to find new companions!" Chiara came back to life, turning to glare at Veronica, any remaining polish chipped from her voice.

"That doesn't mean I'm not an honest, baptized citizen!"

"How on earth can you—can any of us—stand as judge? Isn't every courtesan just as sinful in God's eyes?" The splotches on her chest and neck had become small continents, flushing over pale skin.

"Chiara, it's not the same! We aren't common prostitutes ... and besides, what would happen without us? Men would be reduced to *sodomy*. We are saving them from an even worse fate—even the Pope knows it." Veronica leaned forward on the chaise, her expression pinched and disdainful.

"I just ..." Chiara stuttered after the right words. "Well, I know it's said to repay no evil for evil. Shouldn't it be up to God to do His own avenging?" The afternoon light caught a sheen of sweat at her temples.

"Chiara, if the Jews do not repent, they are a threat to all of Christendom. Who's to say how many honest Catholics they've already convinced to abandon the faith?" Corvino raised one finger in the air, reciting: "*If anyone entices you to worship other gods, you shall surely kill them; your own hand shall be the first against them.*" Clutching his cup of wine, the Crow looked like a terrible imitation of a priest—black robed and brooding, with bloodshot eyes.

"Well, I heard a 'sinful' Jewish doctor is living in Selim's court and providing us with valuable information about the sultan's plans." Chiara straightened her shoulders defiantly. She darted another glance at her pearls, cooling in a pitiful heap on the floor. *Careful, careful ...* , Gio shouted at the girl with his mind. Corvino frowned, crossing his arms delicately so as not to spill his wine.

"*Solomon Ashkenazi.*" As he said it, his eyes probed Chiara's face. She blinked, and he had his answer—it was the same name she'd heard. He scoffed and shook his head.

"Venier tells you too much. Who's to say *you're* not a spy?" Before she could protest, he kept on, his voice stealing louder. "And he shouldn't put so much faith in messages from the East. Our victory will be thanks to Bressan's new galleys, nothing more."

Chiara raised her chin. "You seem to have all the answers; it's a wonder Venier didn't bring you along."

She'd gone too far. Corvino blanched beneath his already pale skin, lips pressed tight in an angry trap. In the background, the rustle of Veronica's dress, a nervous cough. Tucked away on a chaise in the corner, Margherita clutched at her cake plate, looking ready to cry. Frantically, Gio scoured his mind for a safe way to intercede.

Nicco did the job for him, bursting into the room with a yap and a whine, charging straight toward Margherita. As she knelt to clutch the wriggling pup, Corvino let his glass drop. It cracked in large shards, the glittering sound causing even Nicco to freeze. Without a word, Corvino swung his cape and left, the door slamming shut behind him.

His spilled wine pooled on the floor, garnet red.

"Why did Veronica say that?" Chiara asked, stroking her hair up over the back of her head, so that it tumbled across his pillow. Through a gap in the shutters, the light was stretching shadows, signaling evening. Gio rolled over onto his side and nestled his face in the crook of her neck where the skin was softest.

The Crow's departure had left everyone shaken; shortly after, Gio had made an excuse to return home. Not two hours had passed when he heard a knock at his back door, which opened onto the canal. It was Chiara, standing on the stone stoop that jutted out into the water, dressed as a gondolier—complete with plumed velvet cap pulled low over her eyes. As he opened the door she leapt inside, brushing past his shoulder to land on the floor with barely a sound from her leather-soled slippers.

Poking his head out, Gio saw a narrow gondola bobbing in the current, tied to one of the iron rings that dotted the building's wall. In the canal, other boats glided past. From open windows all along the waterway, neighbor women were leaning out to string up laundry or dump kitchen pans, calling and waving to one another. Overhead, sparrows whirled from perch to perch among the rooftops. A gondola with a bulky cabin floated by, blocking Gio's view. He turned to shut the door, locking it with a thrust of the bolt.

"Chiara, what are you thinking coming here with so many eyes watching?"

"I'm thinking Cecilia's brother is a gondolier and will agree to say he paid you a visit—he's already lent me a costume, after all." Chiara held her cape out with one hand and tipped her cap at Gio. "Besides, you said yourself that Corvino won't do anything until Venier returns. If we've already been found out, how much can it matter?"

"Corvino could come here to find us and bring witnesses. That's how much it can matter!" Gio glanced at the front door to be sure the bolt was firmly in place.

Chiara followed his gaze, then tossed her cap on the table. As she walked toward him, she shrugged her cape off her shoulders. "They'd still have to get through that door—and by then I can be in the boat and gone! Please, Gio, I don't want to feel alone, not right now." She let the cape drop to the floor. Beneath it, she wore a loose tunic clearly meant for someone larger. She draped her arms across his shoulders, and he felt the hot press of her mouth on his neck. Once again, he considered how little time he had left to see her; when she led him toward the unmade bed, he offered no resistance.

Later, as they lay with legs interlocked and her head a warm weight on his chest, he pondered her question. "You mean, why did Veronica say that about the Jews?" He shifted to sit up, eyeing the mound of clothes on the floor, then leaning to extract his trousers. "Well . . . war makes people afraid. Everyone's searching for some-one to blame for the situation we're in. Selim's adviser is a Jew, so it's easy to say the Jews must be conspiring with him. Here—we should get ourselves arranged . . ." He retrieved the gondolier's hose from the pile.

Chiara took the leggings, sliding off the bed to stand in front of him. Her skin caught gold in the last of the sun that filtered through the cracks in the shutters, tinted hair swaying loose over her breasts. He wished he could paint her as she was in that moment—

barefaced and faultless. Then she frowned and shook out the hose as if they'd done something to offend her.

"Well, it's easy because Jews have already been made into the enemy. After all, they're the ones who killed Christ, as the priests are so quick to remind us." She was standing on one leg now, wobbling as she tugged the hose upward.

"It wasn't always that way, you know." Gio pulled his own trousers on in one easy motion.

"What wasn't?"

"The Jews weren't always blamed for killing Christ—at least, not the way they are now. Did you know that images of the crucifixion used to show Jesus alive on the cross? They were supposed to remind us of his power over death. And they showed Roman soldiers as his executioners, not Jews."

"Why did it change?" Chiara paused, staring at him. She was still naked from the waist up. Gio snatched her tunic from the floor and tossed it at her; she caught it distractedly.

"I don't really know. Just . . . over time, everyone started to focus more on the pain and suffering of his death. His bloody crown of thorns, all that." Gio fumbled with his own doublet. "Maybe it was to stir up emotion, to unite Christians. Nothing helps that more than having a common enemy . . ."

"And we don't have too many Roman soldiers walking around anymore, but plenty of Jews." Her head emerged from the shirt.

"Exactly."

"I guess it isn't so different from how the Ottomans are hated . . . and I know it's not just Christians, it's all of them—each trying to rule over the other." She let out a groan, then twisted her hair up with both hands, bending to find the carved ivory hairpins that had fallen on the floor.

"You want us all to be one happy family, is that it? Angels and bearded prophets singing down from the clouds together?" He grinned at her.

"Yes, I do. And who knows, some of the angels might like the prophets' beards!" She dropped her pins and leapt at him then, pushing them both back onto the bed. He clutched at her, just under the arm. With a squeal and a squirm, she nuzzled her cheek onto his chest. She fit so perfectly there, just below his shoulder. He'd taken to imagining that somewhere in the great beyond, they'd been molded together in the pose, then cut apart, like Plato said. No matter how they began, they always ended up that way: cheek to chest, him stroking her hair back absentmindedly. He bent to kiss her temple.

"Well, it's a lovely thought. And, you know, Jesus had a similar idea—what did He say? 'Love one another as I have loved you.' Unfortunately, this 'Holy War' has very little to do with religion, I'm afraid. It's really just a matter of trade routes and power. You know that. And I don't think the victor—on either side—will be very loving to the loser."

"Do you think we'll win the war?" Her voice was small.

"I do. Anything can happen at sea, but Corvino was right—Bressan's new boats give us an advantage."

"And, I know you hate him, but Venier *is* a brilliant commander." She nestled in closer.

"I don't hate him, I just don't want to talk about him." He grasped at her waist, stroking the valley made between her ribs and her hip.

"Well, say we *do* win the war. What happens then?"

"I don't think much will change. The Jews will stay in the Ghetto, paying their taxes, lending money. The Ottomans, however, will be much less of a threat." He squinted out the shutters to see if he could sharpen the edges of the clouds sailing past overhead. He couldn't. On his chest, a sudden dampness—cupping Chiara's cheek in his palm, he turned her face up toward him. Her eyes were glossy.

"Chiara—"

A loud bang on the door. They both sat upright, a single thought joining their minds. *Corvino!* Gio raised a finger to his lips.

"Giovanni, you beast! Open this door at once!" Aurelio's voice tore through the quiet. Chiara let out a cry of relief that was half laugh, half groan and shook her head, wiping her eyes with the backs of her hands.

"One moment, Aurelio! And a bit of warning next time!" They scrambled to finish dressing, Chiara kneeling to find her pins again, then tucking her hair up into her cap as Gio helped fasten her cape over her shoulders.

The back door opened out into the flat light of early evening. Holding the gondola steady, he helped her step back in and untie the anchoring, water sloshing and slapping the hull. Balanced in the stern, she was taller than he was. As he looked up at her, she pressed two fingers to her mouth, then extended them to his. Behind her, the sky had gone gray. While Aurelio continued to rattle the front door, she dipped her oar; Gio watched as she glided away, feathered cap nodding, the current swinging around the narrow boat to carry it off. His mind flickered, went dim. The image of her receding from him, rippling arrows of water in her wake . . . it was as if he'd seen it before, would see it again—like a single frame from a recurring dream. When she rounded the corner at the far end of the canal, he thought he glimpsed her looking back.

"*Giovanni!*" Aurelio's voice came like a horn blast, enough to vex the neighbors.

Gio rushed back inside, threw the bolt, and opened the front door. On the stoop, the alchemist stood with a large wicker basket under one arm. Behind him loitered two young men.

"My dear Giovanni, don't you know spontaneity lies at the heart of the true artist?" By the twinkle in his eyes and his tight ruddy cheeks, Gio could tell Aurelio was in his cups. "And here we are, to aid in your cause with a spontaneous feast!" The alchemist laughed at his own poor joke, slapped Gio's shoulder, and stepped across

the threshold. As the two men trailed in after, Gio realized he recognized them—a musician and poet respectively, both whispered
to be prodigal talents. By their gait, it was clear that they shared
Aurelio's condition.

"Well, there's little I can do to stop you now."

"Oh, did we interrupt?" Aurelio grinned and wriggled his eyebrows at the tangled bedsheets and the open back door, which
hadn't latched properly and now swung out over the canal. As Gio
went to shut it, the alchemist heaved his basket onto the table.

"May I present to you Torquato and Ippolito? Torquato, Ippolito, Giovanni Lomazzo." Aurelio offered introductions with a
flourish of one hand, then unceremoniously began to unload
breads, sweetmeats and cheeses, several pouches of wine, and a
large flask of liquor.

"We've just convinced old Alvise's wife down at the tavern to sell
us her larder," Ippolito explained, stumbling slightly over his own
words. Before Gio could reply, the young man saw a lute resting
against the wall. He picked it up and, with surprising precision,
began to pluck a pleasant tune. As Gio helped Aurelio unpack, he
leaned to mutter in the alchemist's ear.

"Corvino has taken my journal."

Aurelio's eyes darted to the dark stain on the floor next to the
bed. "How bad is it?"

"Nothing written, just sketches—and I never showed her face.
Still—" Gio felt his cheeks burning. *How could he have been so foolish?* Reprimands had been echoing in his mind since he'd discovered the book missing, a circling pattern of self-shaming.

"It could become his word against yours. I see. Hmm . . ." The
alchemist buried his chin in his beard, thinking as he set pots filled
with salted butter and jams on the table. He dug one hand back
into the basket. "Well. What's done is done. I suggest you don't take
any rash action. In the meantime, let me see what I can do to re-

trieve it." His fist emerged, grasping a crock filled with some type of meat preserved in its own fat. "Have a seat, Gio, put it from your mind." The alchemist dragged a chair out as if Gio were the guest. An empty mug sat conveniently on the table; Aurelio filled it nearly to the brim with wine.

"I suppose you're right, as ever." Carefully, Gio raised the cup.

The hours passed easily in drink and food and conversation. By nightfall, the group sat with their chairs pushed back, bellies full. The air was still warm, heralding summer. They'd propped the shutters open—above the rooftops, stars glittered and winked, the soft lapping of the canal a steady murmur in the background. Their conversation meandered from art and music to war, until a somber mood descended. In a lull of quiet, Ippolito leaned for the lute again. This time he sang along, an old ballata they all knew by heart: "O Rosa Bella." The tune looped around on itself with a comforting repetition, like a lullaby from childhood. As if on cue, Lucio scrambled up onto the windowsill, knocking the shutters wider. Ippolito abruptly stopped playing while the four men watched the boy tumble into the room.

"Wanting to join, I see?" Gio laughed and helped the child up and into a seat of his own, tearing a portion of bread for him. Introductions were made, and Ippolito began the song again. Under the music, Gio could hear the boy lisping along with the chorus.

O rosa bella
O dolce anima mia . . .

When it was done, the group applauded. Ippolito gave a playful bow as Aurelio stood to pour another round of sweet liquor for the table.

"And how is the painting coming along?" The alchemist glanced at his friend curiously.

"It's coming. I can still do it." Gio understood what Aurelio was asking. "And I'm sure that at the very least, Corvino will see to it that I finish, for Venier."

"Corvino?" Lucio perked at the name. "I know who that is! Once, when Marco and I were playing by the well, he yelled at us for being in his way. He said that at night he turns into a big hungry crow, and if we didn't behave, he would come eat us up. Is it true, Gio?" He looked up at Gio with wide eyes, the closeness of night making monsters seem real. "Can he really turn into a crow?"

Before Gio could respond, Aurelio interjected: "No, Lucio, it's not true. Only very, very special people can turn themselves into crows—and Corvino's not one of them." The alchemist leaned to ruffle Lucio's hair.

"Do you want to hear a happier story about a bird? A story for only the sweetest of dreams?" The poet had barely spoken all night, but now he bent forward into the candlelight. He had a wan face, an adolescent-looking mustache wisping outward beneath a long and slender nose. His eyes were owled, with heavy lids that made him appear either perpetually in thought or half-asleep.

Lucio nodded.

"Once, a long time ago in a distant land," the poet began, his voice lilting slow and wistful. "Where the brushes and shrubs trembled in morning breezes, a beautiful and gracious lady lived. But this was no ordinary lady . . ."

The poet continued, weaving the tale of the tree and the bird, the egg and the soil. The spell of the story lured the group into its grasp, the way an ocean tide pulls bits of shell and glass from shore. Gio's mind wandered naturally to Chiara. He pictured her, a wide blooming tree, himself a bird with perfect sight. He would draw the story for her as a gift. An imagined world they could share, a secret place just for the two of them. For always.

On the table, the candles flickered, casting a circle of light against the darkness.

Captain Bragadin's ears were gone, but he could still hear. Sound lurched into his skull devoid of place, ambient and disorienting. He reentered his city of Famagusta, this time as a prisoner, with beard and mustache shorn. Shackled now, he stumbled forward. Loose ropes from his restraints thrashed out behind him like snakes, stirring up dust. In front of him, the heads of his commanders sailed, pierced on tall spears held aloft; their blood streaked down the poles, drying rust colored in the heat. Passing through the empty avenues, Bragadin felt the invisible eyes of his people upon him—all those he had failed. They hid now, behind barricaded doors and in cellars, knowing what was to come. The downward swing of a fist.

The Ottomans led Bragadin to the harbor. Using ship rope, they lashed him to the main yard of a galley, then raised him up. Looking out over the city, he could only watch as fleeing citizens were chased down and slaughtered with less reverence than was given beasts. He hadn't imagined there could be a worse sound than the orchestra of men in battle, but now he heard it—the screams of his own people rising from every corner of the citadel. He saw throats and bowels freely opened, women held down to be raped. From his vantage, he could see it all.

"Can you see Christ?" The soldiers mocked him from below.

Afterward, he was tied to a column in the main square. There, they flayed him alive—carefully and unhurriedly, as if it were an art, peeling his skin back like thin parchment to expose the raw and bloodied flesh. Extra attention was paid to his face, to preserve the dignified shape of his features while, underneath, he was deformed into a spectacle of pain. With savage, unknowable sounds, he begged for death.

He remained alive until they reached the base of his spine.

When it was done, Mustafa ordered his hollow skin to be pickled and stuffed with straw. They dressed him back in the royal crimson robes, which draped weirdly now over his knobby figure, and sat his husk on an ox to be paraded through the town. With straw poking out from his empty eyes, Captain Bragadin stared, unseeing, as his city passed him by.

While what was left of Captain Bragadin marched through the streets of the citadel, the full force of the Ottoman navy sailed, miles and miles west of Cyprus. The coastline had long since vanished behind them; now the boats wound through the islands scattered across the Mediterranean, their course charted for Italy. When they met the Christian league, both fleets would be poised to fight for the fate of Cyprus—and for Europe herself. Although Mustafa and his men had taken Nicosia and Famagusta, Cyprus's two strongholds, their victory was a fragile one. If the Christians defeated the Turkish forces, they could easily regain control of the territory. If, however, the Ottomans dismantled their opponent, the empire was ready to open its maw—conquering more islands, advancing even to Venice herself. The possibility was not inconceivable.

Perched in every crow's nest, soldiers scanned the horizon for the first sight of sails.

Ali Pasha, admiral of the Ottoman fleet, paced from bow to stern. He considered what an Ottoman victory could make possible: the light of Islam spreading across Europe like a sunrise from the East. And he could have a hand in it all if he fought well. Selim had even entrusted him with the Banner of the Caliphs—a massive flag embroidered with text from the Qur'an and the name of Allah in golden letters. It flew from his mast now, snapping and whipping in the wind, prompting him and his men to excellence. Ali shook his head. He could never understand the shortsightedness of the Christians. How could they despise the Jews for not recognizing

Jesus, even as they themselves refused to perceive that the prophet Muhammad (peace be upon Him) was sent to continue His very work? How could they not recognize that this was the advocate Jesus Himself had foretold?

Ali leaned over the railing, breathing in the tang of salt air. Before the fleet had departed from Istanbul, he'd received word that Mustafa's son had been killed during a raid on Cyprus. Now Ali pulled at his beard, watching the soft ripples of the boat's wake echo out into the endless fabric of the water. Silently, he whispered a prayer that Mustafa wouldn't let his anger overrule him.

The breeze took his prayer and sent it flying out across the empty sea.

Without meaning to, Ali pictured his own youngest son sleeping at home, the rolls on his arms and legs soft as dough. He heard the sound of his wife singing to him in the morning, as the early sun slanted in, already warm. Ali thought of his own singing, reciting the *adhan*, the warbling call to prayer he'd never tire of, never not feel was a calling back to his very self . . .

No. He could not think of home now. Now was the time to be Kapudan Pasha, a grand admiral. He gazed at the ocean below, which undulated like some great beast breathing. The surface shifted and rippled, fracturing his reflection—for a split second, Ali saw his own bearded face severed from his shoulders. He started, standing upright. It was only a reflection, nothing more. He repeated the words to himself.

It was only a reflection.

21

"ID YOU READ IT?" HIS VOICE WAS BRIGHT AND ANXIOUS as he entered the shop. "Can you get coffee somewhere? Talk about it?" He was wearing a short-sleeve button-up shirt; Rose tried not to stare at his bare arms. She glanced down at her watch. It was after four o'clock, late enough to close.

She nodded. "There's a place on the corner."

Joel wasn't behind the counter when they walked in. Instead, a heavyset girl with black-framed glasses and blunt Bettie Page bangs took their order. William paid for their drinks—shaking his head when she reached for her wallet—then led them to a corner table. They sat down opposite each other, near the large picture window stenciled with the café's name. The slanting light cast typographical shadows across their faces. The girl carried their drinks to them: milk nearly pillowing over the rims, two hearts marking the froth.

Rose took a sip, watched her espresso-heart stretch and tear, small white bubbles of foam gripping the edge of the cup. For a long beat neither spoke. Rose didn't know where to look, so she stared at his hands, at the dark hair on his wrists and the veins that branched out around his knuckles. In his grasp, the cup seemed comically fragile. She examined her own slender fingers, her bird-boned joints.

"I just . . ." He stopped, then continued on. "I wanted it to be a diary, that was my dream, but I never actually thought it would be."

"I honestly didn't think it was. There weren't any dates, which is usually the telltale sign." She looked through the window at the flower boxes outside, petunia petals flaming violet in the sun. "Can I tell you something?"

"Anything."

"Ever since I saw the first portrait, I couldn't get that woman's face out of my mind. I even started having dreams about her and Giovanni." She glanced back. "Have you had any dreams?"

"Yes." He was staring into the surface of his coffee.

"William." He raised his eyes when she said his name. "Do you think Giovanni had a child with her? Because he doesn't seem to have any children when he's writing, but you look just like him, you obviously have the same genes. I guess he probably had brothers or sisters, but still . . ."

"You like the idea of them being together." A flash of smile before he took a sip, mouth disappearing behind his cup.

"Don't you think they were, though? Those sketches, with the story . . ."

"She was definitely his muse, in the sense of the word you don't like—"

"Ohhh," Rose groaned playfully. "I just meant that I wish we got to see more work from female artists, especially in the Renaissance, that's all . . ."

"I know, I know, I'm only teasing." Another grin. "But if she was the courtesan to an admiral, an affair would be pretty risky business, wouldn't it?" He set his cup back in its saucer carefully.

Rose realized she'd never considered the possibility of an unconsummated relationship. Her face must have betrayed her, because William tucked his chin, shooting her a piteous look. "Hey, I didn't mean to burst your bubble—we just don't know yet one way or the other."

It wasn't like her to gloss over black-and-white facts. It wasn't like her at all. Shame churned her stomach, the same feeling she remembered from childhood when she'd raised her hand in class and given the wrong answer, seen all those watching faces, smirking. How could she have been so foolish—to get invested in a relationship she might have simply made up? Still, something in her resisted. "But, that story of the egg and the tree, all those sketches . . . They're so intimate . . ." She tried for more words but sputtered out.

William thought of his own paintings, the series he was now nearly finished with. Canvas after canvas, marching melancholic images across his studio walls. "Maybe that was the closest he could get, or"—he saw her face fall again and rushed to appease her—"or maybe they *were* together, maybe they do end up together."

Rose had to laugh at his efforts. At herself. "Sorry, I . . . I've just spent so much time with the book, I started imagining too much—"

"No, you could be right about them, we don't know yet. I *do* know you've done an amazing job with the restoration." A half smile, shadows sliding across his face.

"Oh, it's not even finished."

"But it's being translated already, so fast. I'm impressed."

Feeling herself flush, Rose looked down and studied her coffee. William coughed politely, then steered them back to the book. "I still can't sort out why he wrote over his diary, though."

"I know. That's what I don't understand, either. *Something* must have happened for him to scrape it away like that. If he was in Venice, it wouldn't have been hard to find other paper to write on." Rose pondered. "I guess he could have moved somewhere else and had to reuse the vellum, but . . . I don't know. It feels like more of a personal choice. Mostly because he kept the undertext so clear in certain spots—and it isn't like he scraped away any drawings."

"I wouldn't erase my journal unless I was trying to . . . maybe close the chapter on something? Or unless I knew I wouldn't be around to reread it, I guess. I'd scrape it away to protect my privacy."

"Or to protect the people you were writing about. Aurelio could have been a target for the Inquisition—they definitely considered alchemy a kind of sorcery. The diary could've been used as evidence." She thought again of the woodcuts she'd seen in the library, of so-called witches being burned at the stake.

As they drank their coffee they continued to speculate. Who might have turned Aurelio in to the inquisitors? What other reasons could Giovanni have had to write over his journal? They agreed that the unnamed woman was likely the figure from the portrait, and considered when Venier might have left for battle—and what could have happened in his absence. Finally, William asked the question they'd both been wondering all along.

"How do you think it will end?"

"I don't know. For some reason, I feel nervous. I have no idea why, but I'm worried something bad might happen. Might *have* happened."

"What if it did?"

"Then it's a tragedy, I guess. We add them to the list."

"Tristan and Isolde, Giovanni and . . . whatever her name was." He swirled the last of his coffee before drinking it.

"Exactly." She considered the mark her lipstick had made on the rim of her cup.

"Do you think it's worth it? Him finding his muse even if they weren't able to be together?" He was looking down into his coffee dregs, as if he'd find the answer there.

Rose thought about it, flicking her spoon back and forth on the table, light flashing and spinning over the concave silver. "Yes."

"How so?"

She weighed her words a moment. "Well, look at that beautiful portrait, those sketches. They exist because of her—and they let us see through Giovanni's eyes all these years later." She started flipping the spoon faster. "And she could have been part of the reason he pursued his dream and wrote the treatise. She could have helped motivate him to do that, you never know." The spoon flew out of her grasp, clattering onto the floor at his feet. He bent to pick it up. She looked at the back of his neck as he reached down, the arc of dark hair against his skin.

"So what's *your* dream, then?" He straightened up and set the spoon back on the table next to her cup.

"What do you mean?"

"Well, Giovanni had his treatise . . . what would your goal be?"

"A survey," Rose blurted out before thinking. "I want to put together a history of restoration. Something to get people—especially students, I guess—interested in conservation." The idea had been simmering in the back of her mind for a year, slowly taking form. She'd never spoken the wish out loud before, not even to Joan; once the words left her mouth she felt exposed, transparent and breakable as glass.

"Help them appreciate the art form a little bit?"

"Sure—something like that." She took a sip from her cup even though there wasn't any coffee left.

"I like that." Another flash of dimple.

She smiled back at him, then silence. What to say next? "And you—you've found a new style for your paintings . . ."

"I have." He was fingering the faint scar on his thumb.

She forced more polite words into the space between them. "And, now you know your ancestor was a painter too. Remember that first day, when you realized it was a book about art?"

"I do." His hands closed in around his empty cup, knuckles

squeezing white. For a moment, she was afraid he'd crack the ceramic. "Thank you for all of this, Rose."

"But I didn't do—"

"You did, though. Thank you."

She waited to see if he'd say anything more. Finally, he raised his head, and they both glanced around the café. They'd stayed longer than they should have. The barista had begun to count out her register, letting the coins clatter loudly back into the till. Taking the hint, Rose stood to leave. William followed suit, plucking her jean jacket up from where she'd draped it over an empty chair back. Standing behind her, he held it open. First the left arm, then the right. His breath on her neck. The barista watched them from the corner of her eye.

Out on the sidewalk, the sun was slipping behind buildings, turning the sky a lullaby of faded peach and lilac.

"I'm this way." He jerked his head in the direction opposite the bookshop. She nodded, raising one hand in goodbye. Then, in an instant she'd spend hours reliving, dissecting, and interrogating, he grasped her wrist and she was suddenly tucked against him. His right arm had wrapped itself around her back, her cheek pressed into his shirt, just beneath his shoulder. She could feel the heat of his chest through the cotton and hear his heartbeat: a muffled pounding.

She shut her eyes.

She fit him perfectly, just as he'd imagined she would. He was holding her in both arms now; her weight against him, the arch of her back under his hand. The powdered-flower smell of her. She tilted her head up, and he pressed his mouth to her temple. For a long moment they remained there, exempt from anything but sensation, familiar as if they'd been molded together that way. Then her voice in the air outside them, quiet and low.

"William . . ."

He understood her tone, knew what she'd say next. "Don't, just—"

"What are you doing?"

He didn't let go, but shifted so that his cheek was against the side of her head, his mouth hovering just above her ear. When he spoke, warm breath skimmed her skin. "I don't know."

"You're marr—"

"I know. I know that, Rose."

She pulled back then, to look up at him, without stepping away; one of his palms still lay heavy across the small of her back, another in the gap between her shoulder blades. His face was so close she could see the texture of his skin, her own reflection suspended in his dark pupils.

"So, you aren't . . . separating, or . . . ?" The second she said it, Rose realized with a terrible, crystalline certainty that this had been her unspoken wish all along, ever since Joan had shown her his website. This entire time, all these weeks, she'd been holding out space for hope, for a possible path for them both. One in which his every gesture was imbued with meaning, all his commitments resolvable in a way that freed him—and cleared her. And somehow, inexplicably, she'd kept those desires half-hidden from even herself. In an instant she felt dissociated, as if she were standing outside her own body, watching an alternate version of herself stare up at William with a grasping expression.

He dropped his arms and took a step back, then rubbed his face in his hands. When he reemerged, his skin was pinked and he looked profoundly tired. "No. We're . . . we're trying to make it work." His mouth pressed into a straight line.

Rose heard her voice without being conscious of forming words. "Then I don't think this helps."

He didn't say anything but crossed his arms and shook his head. He was staring at the laces in his boots. She kept going. "I think we say 'enough' now, William. Because I can't be—"

"I know, and I would never ask that of you. None of this is fair to you. I'm sorry." He glanced at her and his eyes were wide; he seemed scared and she suddenly realized that he was. "I'm so sorry," he repeated, then turned around abruptly.

She watched him walk away. The broad slope of his shoulders, his hands shoved into his pockets.

"William." He halted at his name and looked back at her, half-turning. She would never have imagined herself capable of doing what she did next, but she did it all the same: took the four steps to meet him and lifted her hands to his cheeks. His stubble pricked a rough pattern into her palms. Rising up on tiptoe, she sailed her face to his, eyes open until they shut. Mouths touching then parting, firm and warm and sleek and no separation then, just a joining, and they fit together perfectly, and it wasn't over, it was still twisting, and a single breath ran through them both.

Then she pulled away, but not too far, close enough that he was able to rest his forehead against hers. Her feet were still on tiptoe; she was clutching the back of his neck.

"*Now* enough, okay?" She barely had to whisper. The hair at the nape of his neck bristled between her fingers. He nodded, the movement rocking her head along with his. His hands had found their way to her hips.

"Okay."

She didn't look at him again, just stepped and spun and started walking back toward the shop, the taste of him burning her tongue. As she passed the café window, she glanced in at the barista clearing their table. She saw the shape of her own mouth on the rim of the cup, a dark red stain on white.

Enough. Rose thought. *That's enough now.*

William drove north not knowing why, trees and houses flashing past. The sun was still fading as he crossed the wide river that snaked through town. Soon, he'd reach the freeway. He could continue on, farther—to other cities and streets and lives. On an empty stretch of road, he made a wide loop to turn around, the yellow centerline running flat in both directions. Slower this time, he slid past the same houses as before, rooms lit up now against the dusk.

He'd turned the ringer on his phone to Silent hours ago.

The gravel of the driveway crumbled softly as he eased the truck in and turned the ignition off. He stayed in the driver's seat. Through the front window he could see pizza boxes on the dining room table, opened and already abandoned. It must have been a hard day at the office if Sarah had ordered pizza. After a long while he finally got out, shutting the door quietly. He pressed the flat of his palm to the hot hood and breathed in a lungful of fertile air. Letting his head fall back, he stared up into the sky. Stars were just beginning to wink awake. What could he ask for, from the great namelessness, to help him now?

Instead of going inside, he traced the length of the house, heading toward the backyard. As he passed by the windows, still-life scenes from his own world slid into view: the dining room table, plates cleared but crumpled white napkins still littering the surface, grease stains seeping through the cheap cardboard of the pizza boxes. Then Sarah's empty office, papers in neat stacks on the desk, light from the hallway spilling in through the half-open door. He knew the girls would be in the living room by now, their faces bathed in the electric blue of a cartoon character's great adventure.

He unlocked the studio door and slipped inside. From the walls his paintings stared back at him: feathers and broken shell, the pattern of tree bark, the texture of sand. Before the book, he never would've imagined making paintings like this, but now they seemed inevitable—the single answer to a formula. He felt a ghost sensation on his palms: the small of Rose's back, the tips of her shoulder blades under his hands again. His throat tightened. What had he done? What would he do next, when the rest of the translation came back?

Suddenly, he remembered his own journal.

As a rule, he didn't keep diaries, but this had been an experiment, a New Year's resolution he'd maintained with perfect discipline, then gradually abandoned once Sarah had come into his life. By pure chance, it'd turned into a record of their first year together. He must still have it somewhere, in the archive of past lives he kept stashed in the cupboards. In seconds, he was kneeling on the floor in front of the open cabinet doors, frantically pulling out boxes. A half hour later and the room was littered with scraps of notes, books, photographs—small treasures only he knew the secrets to, the memories that could unlock them.

Midway through the fourth box, he stopped and leaned back on his heels. A photograph stared up at him from beneath the papers and books. Sarah. Sarah and his own face, unrecognizable with youth and happiness. They were sitting outside at a dinner party, looking at each other, empty platters and half-full glasses on the table in front of them. Without even trying, he remembered the evening in perfect detail—how the host had spilled wine on the white tablecloth, the glowing lights strung from the trees overhead and someone's good-natured bulldog wandering the grass behind their chairs. How they'd walked home hand in hand in the night, passing a teenager with a lit sparkler spraying gold into the darkness. They'd just found out she was pregnant. The camera had caught them sharing that terrible wonderful secret, lost in a small universe of three. He remembered it all.

So much returning without warning or order. The walk-up they'd rented together that was so small they'd called it Château Bateau and laughed and didn't care and set up a crib in the corner. How he used to watch her get ready in the morning in the narrow bathroom next to their bed. She'd leave the door open while she did her hair and put her makeup on in the round mirror they'd kept until it broke in a move. He'd had an old acoustic guitar back then—a beat-up Fender rescued from a yard sale—and every night he'd pluck out melodies while Sarah drowsed beside him, her belly growing, growing, more each day. He didn't know how to read music, so he'd sound out the songs by ear. He learned to play a halfway decent version of "Blackbird" by the Beatles, and he'd always end with it, singing along with himself, wondering if their daughter would recognize his voice when she arrived. As soon as they had the money to spare, they'd said, they'd sign him up for real music lessons—they'd shook on it even, with absolute solemnity—but of course that became just another plan they never got around to doing. One of the many vows they weren't able to keep. The guitar itself left the house on a false pledge, loaned to a guest who'd never brought it back. William hadn't forgotten it over the years, wondering from time to time if Sarah ever thought of those nights, all the promises they'd made to themselves. To each other.

"We're trying to make it work." That's what he'd said to Rose; but how was he trying, really? By buying flimsy umbrellas and bringing Sarah drinks she hadn't asked for? How was she, by cooking elaborate dinners he didn't need? They'd run into marriage without any foresight, and now they'd run away from the mess they'd made. At least, they'd tried to run away. He thought of the awful quote hung in Lois's bathroom: WHEREVER YOU GO, THERE YOU ARE!

He thought of how warm Rose's mouth had been. The animal instinct that had surfaced, howling, inside of him. The way she'd looked at him from the start like he was the only one who could turn the lights on. The same way Sarah had looked at him once, a long time ago. He remembered that now.

At the last parent-teacher conference he'd gone to at Jane's school, the instructor—a soft-faced, goateed man in his fifties who'd worn striped socks with his Birkenstocks—had explained

how he used analogies when teaching. *It helps the students understand relationships.*

Tongue is to taste as nose is to smell.

Rose is to William as Sarah used to be to William. As William
wants Sarah to be again.

He got the lesson, finally. It wasn't just that he could understand
what Sarah had gone through now—the choices she'd made and
why. It was that he could remember what it was he wanted back.
It'd taken Rose for him to get it; he'd had to feel it again as real as
he'd ever felt it. William stared down at the photograph in his
hands. What would "trying to make it work" actually mean at this
point? He had an idea: no more tongue-biting omissions in the
therapy chair. A few more arguments, maybe more than a few. The
chance that he and Sarah might become greater strangers to each
other before they could move toward center.

He'd have to be the one to start this time.

The house was quiet when he crept in through the back. He set
the photo and the journal on the coffee table, then ventured down
the hallway. Yellow light edged out from under the door to Sarah's
study. He rapped lightly on the wood with his knuckles, then
turned the knob. She glanced up at him the same way she might
have if he'd been a job candidate coming in for an interview: peering over glasses that perched at the tip of her nose, pen in hand,
suspended in air.

"Hey, you." His voice fractured.

She frowned, capping her pen. "Where were you tonight, Will?"

"Sarah, I think we need to talk." William stepped into the room
with his wife and closed the door behind him.

22

SLEEP WOULDN'T COME, SO HE ABANDONED TRYING, SLIP-ping out into the vacant avenues, wrapped in his fur-lined cloak. Over the years he'd grown attached to this time: the murky hours between midnight and dawn, when he could wander the city freely. No one staring at him as he passed, no pretense of importance to assume. Corvino only wished the night would be darker—the light from the moon and star-flecked sky outlined each shape with a silver sheen, and after a few moments his eyes would always adjust. He craved a darkness he could disappear into, but he'd settle for this partial gloom.

Before long, he found himself outside Venier's palazzo, as if some memory stored in his muscles had walked him there unwittingly. It was a windless night; no rustle of leaves, no flickering lamplight. Even the gurgle of the fountain out front seemed hushed. Corvino leaned against the trunk of a linden tree. He wondered what mood the admiral would be in when he returned. Would he even care to see the artist's notebook? It'd contained less—far less—than Corvino had hoped for: just pathetic sketches in the margins, none of them even showing a face. Over the past few days, he'd been weighing whether to present it at all. Corvino stared up at the pattern the leaves made against the night sky, shadow overlying shadow. Why was he being punished this way? Hadn't he endured enough?

The scrape of a door opening.

In the quiet of night, the creak of hinges was unmistakable. Pressing close to the tree, Corvino pulled his cloak up to cover his face. It was a side door that had opened—he waited while the mystery person tiptoed across the lawn and unlatched the front gate. She also wore a black cloak, but no cap, and in the moonlight her tinted hair shimmered.

Venier's whore.

She set a bulky woven basket down at her feet, then used both hands to quietly relatch the gate. Tucking the basket into the crook of one arm, she turned and darted off down the street. Corvino let her get some paces ahead before he emerged, following behind with careful steps he'd long ago trained to be silent.

Where could she be going?

She moved faster than he'd imagined she could—no longer clad in tall *chopines*, her slippered feet leapt over the cobblestones. He fought to keep pace without being seen, pressing into the shadows, catching her rounding corners just in time to trace her path. He scuttled over bridges after her, dodging the intermittent glow of streetlamps still smoldering from the night's flames. As she wove through the empty avenues, he tracked the pale flash of her hair. *Where* was she going? He didn't recognize the route: none of Venier's acquaintances lived in this part of the city, and the artist's home and studio were in the opposite direction. After a series of sharp turns, it became clear there was only one place she could be heading toward.

The Ghetto.

Ringed by a tall stone wall, the Ghetto had been constructed to keep its residents safely shut away from the rest of Venice during the night. Crouching low as he mounted the last bridge, Corvino peeked up just in time to watch the wide gate swing slowly shut. Darting forward with both hands outstretched, he caught the edge—barely, but he caught it. As if truly a shadow now, he remained pressed against the oversize door, holding it ajar. Waiting. Normally, he knew the gate should have been guarded; undoubtedly the girl had bribed someone to step away from his post. The city was verging on lawlessness already, and the war had only just begun. Once again, Corvino cursed himself: if he'd been more cautious, he could be sailing with the fleet at that very moment, miles away already. Instead he was here, alone, spying on an insignificant whore.

Still, he *did* want to know what she could be up to. When it seemed enough time had safely passed, he pried the gate open just wide enough to slip through. Inside, looming wooden houses lined the narrow streets: having no more room in their Ghetto, the Jews had been forced to expand upward. Closed shutters in every window made the tall buildings look as if they too were asleep. A maze of alleys threaded away in every direction—achingly empty, haphazard lamps spilling a wavering light across the stones. Corvino leaned his back against the wooden gate, eyes shut, listening for footsteps.

Silence.

It was so still he could hear the babble of the canals that wove invisibly through the neighborhood. Where had she gone? Why was she here? He ran through a list of possible reasons in his mind. Did she have a Jewish lover? She could have met him in the marketplace; he was always warning Venier not to let her circulate among the shops so freely. He tried to picture her slipping away to visit some wealthy moneylender, or even a publisher—stealthy midnight liaisons made more exciting by the specter of heresy. But no, he couldn't see it.

What had been in the basket she'd carried? She'd been bringing something here; she must have had a purpose. Corvino's mind spun back on itself, a fast spindle winding thread, reviewing every detail he could grasp. He thought of her face in the parlor that afternoon, how pale she'd gone when he spoke of the Jews—and the small spark in her eyes as she defended Ashkenazi. At the time, he'd been too pleased with himself for provoking her to question her reaction. Now he weighed the facts.

Could the girl be a Jewess?

The more Corvino considered the idea, the more it firmed into truth, the way a far-off object becomes solidly itself as you approach it. He recalled what the old chambermaid had told him of her habits: *She tints her hair every chance she gets, lord knows how dark it'd be otherwise.* And what was it Venier said of their meeting? *Domenico found her for me—her father was some sort of merchant in Rome, though I can't imagine where a diamond like that has been hiding.*" Corvino didn't need to imagine. With a sick knot in his stomach, he realized exactly where she'd been hiding.

"Where are you hiding now?" He whispered the words out loud in the dark, as if she would emerge from the shadows to tell him.

Jewess.

He felt sure of it with a marrow-deep certainty. But, if it *were* true, that would mean she'd lured Venier into heresy. *Heresy!* If any of Venier's enemies discovered it, the admiral could be brought before the Inquisition. He'd be prevented from becoming doge—and worse, he could be put on trial. Corvino imagined Venier: beard shorn, wrists shackled, cowering before the same men he'd always entertained so generously. Forced to explain how a mere girl had deceived him.

Corvino's heart began to pound, his mouth suddenly gone dry. What would Venier be willing to do to prevent such information from coming to light? What favors would he think to grant? Images began to flash before Corvino's eyes: he could be given a nobleman's daughter, a title, a position on the Great Council. In time, he could even become a senator. He tried to lick his lips, but his tongue felt thick, course as sand; his heart struggled to slow its pace. So his Father had not been punishing him after all by holding him back from sailing with the fleet—it was only that He had better gifts in store for Corvino. How could he ever have doubted?

Still, he would need evidence, he would need proof. He had to learn more. He had to flush her out. *Whoever does not abide in me is cast out as a branch; such branches are thrown into the fire and burned.* He whispered the words as if they were an incantation.

Afterward, he wouldn't be able to recall exactly how it'd started. He'd only remember a cresset lamp to his right, coil of rope still burning in its basket, glints of amber and gold winking at him like an invitation. Then, as if he'd simply willed it all into being, tongues of flame were licking up the sides of the wooden houses—florid, burnished orange. The boards were parched as tinder, and the greedy flames made easy work of them. As the sky began to brighten in the east, smoke from the blaze unfurled in earnest: black and choking, blocking out the stars.

"*The day of the Lord comes; the sun will be dark at its rising and the moon will not shed its light.*" Corvino chanted the words out loud, over the screaming that came from every direction now: shouts and cries and wails that blended into an incoherent mass of sound. Faster than seemed possible, the smoke grew to apocalyptic scale, billowing out in great black gusts. All around, Jews flooded past— panic-stricken and soot streaked, yellow badges flashing like sparks of flame caught in their robes. Beneath the noise of the crowd, a relentless crackle and sputter.

The fire easily outpaced Corvino as he maneuvered toward the heart of the Ghetto, scanning the crowd for that one familiar face. By now the ground was littered with belongings: abandoned trunks that had proven too heavy to carry, their locks broken, contents

scattered. Shattered plates and vases, strewn clothes. Corvino el-
bowed forward as men and women scrambled around him, bags
thrown over their shoulders, clutching armloads of goblets, mounds
of silks, wailing children. They knocked his shoulders, fleeing in
the opposite direction.

"*He will baptize you with the Holy Spirit, and with fire.*" Corvino
was shouting now, head pitching back with abandon. Paintings
sailed past, some with ripped canvas waving from their gilded
frames like tattered sails. Overhead, flames blazed from burnt-out
shutters along the upper stories. Cutting through the cacophony of
the crowd came an irregular, splintering roar as roof beams crashed
down, floors collapsing. Corvino's eyes began to sting. Up ahead, he
saw the narrow bridge that linked the two neighborhoods of the
Ghetto. He moved toward it. The fire had yet to jump the thin ribbon of canal, though smoke blew thickly forward like a ghastly her-
ald. "*Repent and be baptized! He baptizes with Holy Spirit and with
fire!*" he howled wildly as he crossed the bridge. No one paused to
listen. Then—could it be?

A streak of palest gold halfway down an alley.

She was smaller than he expected when he came up from behind, one arm swinging across her chest, the other encircling her
waist. Feather light, easy to lift off the ground. She fought against
him, elbows and kicking heels—useless motions, like a fish flailing
on a hook. She screamed, but what was one girl's scream in the
midst of such a fire?

The wind shifted. A doorway to his left swung open, beckoning
them.

"God provides," he whispered into her neck. Her skin smelled of
crushed flowers and cinder. When he dragged her inside, her heels
scuffed frantic patterns in the dirt. He kicked the door closed,
sending it shuddering into its frame. The house had been
abandoned—chairs upended and a trunk sitting open in the mid-

dle of the room, linen tumbling over its edges like a ransacked hope chest. A coil of rope snaked out of the trunk, frayed from recent cutting. With one thrust of his leg, he swept her ankles from under her—a sharp, shooting pain as her shins hit the floor. Then his knee was between her shoulder blades, her face pressed to the ground. Both arms yanked behind her; the harsh burn of rope at her wrists. When she cried out, dirt got in her mouth, bitter and dank. Craning her neck, she saw that the glass had been shattered from the window above them. She could hear people running through the avenues—so close.

She screamed again.

No one came.

He flipped her over roughly; the back of her head cracked against the floor, and she saw sparks flare, like the fireworks at Carnival. Her vision wobbled, doubling. Then his face was above hers. Time seemed to lag and stutter; she considered that this was the closest they'd ever been. Red veins webbed the whites of his eyes, and her own reflection stared back at her, caught in the black of his pupils.

"I know what you are! Jewess!" He nearly choked on the word, spittle catching in the back of his jaw. His thighs were pressed over hers, heavy muscle pinning her down. He was so close now—his hair fell around her face like a lover's would. His hands gripped her shoulders; something jagged was scraping her back. She watched a vein in his forehead pulse. The hot weight of his body was crushing her, bruising her legs, her ribs. If it were any other man, she'd know what would come next: her dress ripped, held down over her face, her hips battered into the dirt. But there was no gleam in Corvino's eyes to cut the anger—instead they flashed hard, black and depthless as a bird's. She felt the sting of bile creep up her throat.

"You've brought him into heresy!" His breath filled her nose, sickly sweet. "God will watch you burn, Jew-whore!"

A resolve deep inside her fractured. "*I am the whore?*" She was screaming now—it was too late, she couldn't stop. "You killed for him. You sold your soul! You're a greater whore than I'll ever be!" She writhed under his grasp. "And you're nothing to him, Corvino! You're nothing! *Nothing!*"

Suddenly a close, dry rustle, nearly inaudible over the shrieks and tumult of noise outside. It was a crow winging, claws outstretched, to perch on the sill of the broken window. Corvino looked up, and a darkness fell across his eyes, like a hood tugged over the face of a noosed man.

He was in the clearing once again.

White snow and a copse of trees; the copper taste of blood on his tongue.

The sky domed above him, a gray arch ringed by treetops. It was silent now, perfectly still. Heavy snowfall muted even his breath, boughs bent under the weight of ice pack and frost. This time, though, Corvino was the one who was standing. In front of him knelt a boy, his face turned away. The boy's hands were bound behind him with rope, palms pressed together in a downturned prayer. Beneath the hem of his tattered robe, bare feet edged out, pink and chapped. The boy shivered. Corvino looked up at the tree nearest them. The crow was perched there, watching.

Corvino looked down at his own hands. They held a length of rope.

He swung the cord. It whirred through the silence of the clearing and struck the boy's back with a fleshy clap. The boy shuddered, but did not call out. In the distance, the sound of a woman's scream—a faint cry from deep within the wood. Slowly, Corvino stamped in a circle, snow crunching metallic under his feet. He scanned the trees for movement. The forest was frozen, perfectly silent and empty, as if time itself had iced to a halt. Then the crow shifted on its branch, and a dusting of snow sparkled down.

Corvino fastened his grip.

"*Repent.*" It was his father's voice on the vapor of his own breath. "*Repent.*"

Again, the whir, the rope cutting silence. Stroke by stroke, the wool was gnawed from the boy's back. Again, the faraway screams—a ghost sound that trailed each whip of the cord, like smoke from a torch. Again. Again. Again. Corvino's arm began to tire. The boy's skin had split; the rope was soaked in blood. Blood spray on the white snow around him, a familiar, spattering pattern. Blood on the boy's robe, hanging in shreds from his opened back, ragged and wet. The crow nodded. Again, Corvino adjusted the cord in his hands, repositioned his feet in the snow. In the pause, the boy turned.

It was him.

How young he'd been; he'd forgotten that. Wide eyes, lashes matted with tears. Blood caked in the corners of his mouth. Corvino froze, his own self staring back at him. *What had he done?* He gazed at his broken skin, oozing and raw. His scars began to throb.

Then the crow tilted its beak upward for a grating *caw*, chest bobbing with the effort. At the call, others began to appear: summoned from every direction, stiff wings beating the air. They swooped down from the treetops that ringed the clearing—as they did, the trees shimmered and flattened, hardened into the walls of the house. The crows converged in a blotted mass of black, streaming through the open window. In a volley of feather and claw and open beak, they whirled around Corvino, striking him from all sides with their bodies, plucking and tearing at his robes, his face, until he saw only streaking black and flashing eyes. Talons pierced his shoulders, slashing skin, screeching was thick in his ears.

The rope dropped from Corvino's hands, and he ran.

It was a pair of old women who brought her back afterward, wrapped in a blanket like a swaddled child. They said they'd found her in the Ghetto, nearly unconscious, crawling from a doorway on chin and knees. One of them still carried the rope they'd cut from her wrists, as if to say, *This, here, was how it was done.*

Hundreds of miles away, Venier paced the deck of his boat. On all sides, the Holy League rocked, galleasses forming murky clusters on the water. Occasional motion on deck gave the only sign that the fleet was not a figment—some collection of ghost ships adrift among the islands. Sails cracked in the night breeze as the boats adjusted their course. Before even a suggestion of morning, Venier and Don Juan swung their ships into the agreed-upon formation, approaching the coastline of Greece from the west. The sea, flat and complacent, stretched out to meet mountains in the distance— slumbering shapes that thrust their curves against the still-dark sky.

On the eastern shores of Greece, Ali Pasha's fleet floated like ducklings behind his flagship, the *Sultana*. Soon the sky was easing its way from iron to ash, and the great sails were raised, flexing taut in a chill breeze. It was too early even for *fajr*, the dawn prayer. Inky contours of men moved around the deck, crouching and dashing from bow to stern. Sound carried over the water: shouts and orders and snatches of song while the mountains looked on, hunched and silent. Then—

"Karga! Karga!" First one voice, then many. Overhead, the darting arrows of crows, swooping across the sky, their wings blotting out the stars. Their caws were sharp and relentless, as if they had something urgent to tell. To see a crow before battle was an ill omen, and now here flew a countless brood. Ali Pasha watched with a sinking heart as they winged in a circle around his mast, then disappeared into the sky: shadow absorbing shadow until their calls could no longer be heard.

The sun began to rise in earnest then, just as the Holy League emptied out into a gulf. Even Venier's most hardened sailors turned their eyes heavenward, toward a sky awash in a concert of blush burning azure—a miracle of color echoed in the rippling mirror of the sea. Suddenly, calls from the lookouts overhead.

"Sails to the east! Sails to the east!" Venier's men turned as a unified body to watch as Ottoman sails appeared on the horizon, one after another, flying from what seemed to be endless masts.

Hastily, Mass was heard aboard the league's ships, while the Ottomans performed their own rituals—prayers to separate Gods floating up into the same impassive sky. From his position on the opposite side of the gulf, Ali Pasha gave a nod, and the drumming began: a wild booming that smothered the sound of his own heart. The beating roared out with a riotous rhythm as the whole of the Muslim fleet rocked forward into battle. Facing their opponents, Venier's forces stood at attention from bow to stern: archers, gunners, and cannon loaders. At the front of the fleet sailed Don Juan in his flagship. Overhead, the image of a crucified Christ rippled in the breeze. With placid, bleeding eyes, it gazed across the waters at Ali Pasha's mast, where the Banner of the Caliphs—embroidered endlessly with the name of Allah—danced and waved.

A westward wind began to blow.

Ali Pasha nodded again. Cannon blast rocked his boat backward, momentarily drowning out even the drums. A formal invitation to battle. Don Juan, standing at the helm of the *Real*, returned the signal. Cutting through the mild waves, the Ottomans formed a traditional arc. Like a sickle, they swept forward with the wind at their back.

The Holy League approached.

Leading the center division, Venier felt a surge of excitement course through him: the familiar quicksilver that only ever came before a battle. Were the Ottomans confused, he wondered, at the fleet's arrangement? It was a careful choice he and Don Juan had made to place the transport ships on the front lines. How surprised the enemy would be when they realized the galleasses had cannons mounted to them! He squinted, measuring the Ottomans' distance. Nearer, nearer . . . let the lines close in . . .

Now! He gave a sign for the gunners to release their load. Brilliant flash and a blast from the galleasses—the roar of cannon shot, iron balls charging indiscriminately through wood and flesh. The impact lifted one Ottoman vessel clean from the water. With horror, Ali Pasha watched it smash back down on the sea: a shattered, flaming skeleton.

The Ottoman ships swung close then, sprinting over shallow waters to fire their own cannons at point-blank range. A volley of arrows trailed the iron blasts. The dense din of shouts and screams, both sides now speaking a common language. Faster than seemed possible, gun smoke gathered thick as fog on the water—so thick that Don Juan didn't see the *Sultana* approaching. Only the jolt of impact told him he'd been breached, his galley rocking side to side. Peering through the woolly haze, he caught sight of the standard: the name of Allah rippling gold and relentless. Then a swarm of bodies, tumbling on deck with sabers drawn and glinting. On all sides, soldiers began opening one another in a symphony of gore: hacking limbs, halving faces, staining the frothing waves red.

Across the bay, Venier tracked the event: The *Sultana*, clashing with the *Real*! The victor would decide the fate of the battle. Would it be the image of Christ or the name of Allah left mounted in the air for all to see? He must get to Don Juan! Venier whirled, bellowing at his men. *Forward! Forward!* A spray of seawater hit his open mouth.

The taste of blood and salt.

An arrow pierced his leg, its point finding home between tendon and muscle. He cried out and staggered, but did not abandon his post. An Ottoman boat was closing in on his galleass—now, when he most needed to get to Don Juan's aid! With a crossbow, he shot at the approaching vessel. The arrow lodged in a janissary's throat; Venier didn't pause to watch the soldier try to pull it loose, blood gurgling between his fingers. Instead the admiral drew another arrow. Shot again.

23

ROSE WAS GLAD WHEN HER DREAMS TURNED TO BATTLE. After several nights of fitful sleep—visions of William's face, the hot press of his mouth—she'd begun to dream of Venetian battleships. The boats from her library books come to life in epic proportions, sketches mingling with her own memories of ships until the galleasses fighting one another in the night shifted from wood and steel to ink and chalk smudge. Great wooden hulls churned the Adriatic, sails taut in the flexing winds of sleep. Men scampered on deck in her mind's eye, oars pumping in time with her heartbeat. Floating insignia: large crosses swinging in close, burning white. The star and crescent spinning, a universe of its own tilting off its axis. She awoke with lingering sensations of rocking.

The dreams came as a result of overwork. Repairing the under-text was a delicate matter, requiring more patience, more time. Rose surrendered herself to the work, gave her obsessive tendencies full permission to run riot—the way an unhinged gardener might allow his creeper vines to spread, until trembling green leaf obscures even the windows of his home. And unhinged was how she felt: off-balance, precarious, uncertain of what she might or might not do. She was in outright battle with her own thoughts now, willing herself not to imagine him, feel the weight of his palms on her back. Not to check her email compulsively, not to stare out at the street with unfocused eyes.

Under normal circumstances, a client would have reached out after so many weeks—stopping by or sending a note with a casual but curious subject line. *Just checking in!* William's silence only heightened the fact that what had happened between them wasn't normal, they had crossed a boundary, there could be no salvaging or repair. While her conscious mind advised her *forget, forget, forget,* Rose's subconscious wandered like a distraught child, chasing after feelings it'd grown attached to. Unstructured time became dangerous.

In an effort to regain a sense of control, she established a careful order to her days, shortening the bookshop hours so that she could spend more time in the back. The treatise helped distract her, but another motivation compelled her too, kept her moving like a puppet on strings: there could be no closure until it was done. Finished completely. As long as the pages remained spread out on the back table, every time she turned on the lights to the room, she was forced to relive what had happened—her naïve, hopeful questioning of him—and her stomach would clench, a vague swell of nausea surging upward. She couldn't think of being touched by him, not after so long alone, and not want to do something desperate and wild: scream in the street or wander out into the cold water of the sound with all her clothes still on.

And so, work. *Logical and methodical, Rose.*

Finally, she gave up and closed the shop for a week. Summer had arrived in full—cloudless blue skies and shadows pressed flat under the weight of sun, humidity grounding the birds in tree limbs, where they ruffled their feathers for breezes the way dogs pant. Everyone was on vacation; Rose made the sign in the door look like she was taking one herself: CLOSED FOR THE WEEK. HAPPY SUMMER!

In the back, she reconstructed the undertext completely, cleaning and repairing even the most minute offenses. Her spine ached from bending over the pages. Her hands began to cramp unexpectedly during the day. She understood now that certain drawings were illustrations from Giovanni's diary: sketches of clog shoes and a small dog, musical instruments and combs. Trappings of his time with his muse. Then there were the grand ships that sailed across the margins, islands he seemed to have sketched absentmindedly. Rose tracked him as he grew increasingly distracted by the war.

It was late when she finished the last sentence. She surveyed the stack: all repaired, scanned, and sent off for translation, the original pages waiting neatly to be re-bound. Complete. She approached the woman's portrait, still balanced on the countertop. Rose knew it was her own imagination, but she seemed to see a glint in the woman's eyes, a tilt of approval in her half smile. Reluctantly, Rose picked up the page and put it back in its old spot inside the book.

Suddenly, the room seemed unbearably empty.

The next morning, she collected the paper and the mail, tossing the stack of envelopes and magazines onto the kitchen island when she came back inside. Her eyes burned from staying up so late; she shuffled to the counter to pour a coffee. Clutching her mug in one hand, she riffled through the paper with the other. It was a slow news day: record heat for the second summer in a row. Someone's dog had gotten loose and managed to jump into the country club pool.

William was having a show.

She nearly choked on her coffee, quickly setting the mug down to cough until her throat cleared. He was having a show soon to kick off the fall season—there was a full write-up in the Arts and

Leisure section. Alongside the story they'd printed a photo, clearly taken when he'd lived in New York: he was wearing a leather jacket, standing in front of a blurred-out café and gazing not into the camera but off to one side, grinning as if someone just out of view had said something clever. Dimple on full display.

Rose flipped the paper over, slapping the story facedown on the counter. Carefully, she rolled the entire section up and carried it to the recycling bin as if it contained anthrax or the bodies of dead spiders. She shoved the pages down into the plastic bag, let the bin lid flap shut. Blood pulsed in her ears. He was having a show and he hadn't invited her. Of course he hadn't. Thoughts crowded her mind, jostling for attention; she felt dizzy. She should sit down. No, she should have some breakfast first, settle her stomach.

She did both. While finishing a bowl of microwaved oatmeal at the dining room table, she unlocked her phone and began scrolling through the App Store. She didn't care to question it. Instead, she just focused on hunting down the familiar bright logo and hit Install.

The app opened, consuming her home screen. "Edit profile." She was supposed to upload a photo now. Rose remembered the last time she'd tried this exercise and the images that had resulted, each one more uncomfortable than the last. *Just do it, Rose, don't overthink it.* She glanced down; she was still wearing her robe—likely not the right message to send. Abandoning her empty bowl on the table, she bounded upstairs and dug out a clean white T-shirt from the bureau. She didn't have the heart to try to solve her hair, but she did put on mascara and lipstick, blotting and reapplying the way the Internet had told her to do. Hoping the neighbors wouldn't notice, Rose ventured into the backyard. If she positioned herself facing the light, with the green hedge behind . . . She snapped five photos, picked one, and set it as her profile. *Just get it done.*

Back in the kitchen, she continued filling out the prompts. "About Rose." Oh no, a self-description was required. What should she say? *Semi-hermit with obsessive tendencies. Incorrigible helluo librorum* . . . She stared at the blank text field, all cleverness seeping from her fingertips. What would be accurate but also make her sound normal—fun, even? The type of person someone would want to spend time with, share dinner with? She tapped her thumb against the side of her phone case. *Don't overthink it, don't overthink it.* Her mantra was starting to seem more like a plea. Maybe she should begin with her day job—it was likely something a date would want to know:

"Bookshop owner, specializing in rare books and restoration."

What next? Likes and dislikes, probably, to be sure they have the same tastes:

"Likes: reading, libraries, coffee, cats, classical music . . ."

No, maybe not—she could imagine other women posting about skydiving or their exciting European adventures. Books and cats might not fare well in comparison. What, then? Maybe just a quote, people like quotes. Whole books of quotes were published each year, after all. Rose fumbled around in her mind for something appropriate. Seneca sprang forward first to volunteer, a sentence she'd recently underlined as good advice:

"Begin at once to live, and count each separate day as a separate life."

There, that would do. It was an encouraging statement and a good conversation starter. Short and sweet. She clicked Done and returned to the main page. Time to see her matches.

The first candidate appeared, and her heart sank—but not because of what he looked like, which was an older, puffy version of every football player she remembered from high school—because of how many photos he had. There he was on a beach, clutching a bright fuchsia cocktail decorated with a pineapple wedge. There he was standing on the deck of a boat holding up a shimmering silver fish, which was bleeding from the gills. Other photos showed him laughing with friends, and then, for some reason, in the interior of a car wearing sunglasses, sitting in the driver's seat. Telling all who looked that he traveled, was adventurous, not a vegetarian, and had both social and driving skills! Rose realized the only photos she had on hand were of books, close-ups of Odin sleeping in particularly endearing poses—sometimes with the tip of his tongue gently poking out—or candids of Henry.

Still, she'd created a profile. A profile was progress, and progress was good. She could add more photos later, maybe Joan could help. The thrill of her own daring buzzed beneath her skin. She gazed at the new app on her home screen, nestled between podcasts and the weather, bright and promising. This called for another cup of coffee and perhaps one of the sweet almond biscotti she usually reserved for the weekends. As she waited for the kettle to heat, she sorted through the rest of the mail she'd abandoned on the counter, resolutely steering her mind away from the thought of William, wearing a suit at his show. Standing in front of paintings inspired by a text *she'd* repaired, *she'd* made legible for him . . .

A postcard slid out, nearly skidding off the counter, as if purposefully trying to distract her. On the front was a collage of miniature books, arranged for scale around a half-farthing coin, which was stamped with the bust of a young Queen Victoria. Rose picked the postcard up, flipped it over:

Rose,

Greetings from Oxford! I hope this card finds you well. You'd love it here: the library is a treasure. I must confess that I did stumble upon an excellent miniatures store, so you may have a new little book to add to your collection soon.

Looking forward to another visit when I'm back. Bated breath!

Cheers,
Lucas

Rose could picture him there, biking through the green campus, along the river Thames. Visiting Oxford Castle or the botanical garden. Getting lost in that grand old library. She smiled at the thought, then glanced at the calendar hanging next to the fridge. School was set to start in just a handful of weeks.

He'd be back soon.

24

GIO WALKED HOME FROM THE FIRE. ALONG WITH NEARLY all of Venice, he'd stood on the opposite edge of the canal that ran outside the Ghetto, watching until the danger had been contained. The sun had set while they looked on, casting the sky in a resplendent glow, torching the haze clouds coral and gold. The prettiness of it had made a difficult contrast to the scene below. Beyond the open gates of the Ghetto, charred black buildings smoked and steamed. Crumpled bodies lay in the shadows of the guarding wall, waiting to be carted to a makeshift hospital that was hastily being assembled. The odor of wet coals and burnt hair—the uncomfortably familiar scent of roasted flesh—drifted across the crowd. Bystanders thronged the avenues shoulder to shoulder with survivors, barefoot and ash marked, their faces dazed. From all directions, the ambient sound of wailing. As soon as he heard it was safe, Gio had turned to go. When he arrived at home, the smell of smoke was there too.

Then a knock at the back door. It was Cecilia perched in the bow of a gondola. Her mouth made a tight slash in her wide face, and without knowing why, he'd known it was all wrong. No time for questions then—he'd just snatched up his cloak and stepped into the boat. *Faster, faster* was all he could think as the oarsman steered them on. The canals were choked: the entire city had descended into the water it seemed. The gondolier maneuvered them through as best he could, Gio clutching the sides until his knuckles went white to keep from shouting. *Faster, faster.*

Finally, they arrived.

Inside, the sensation of things not as they should be. The light was dimming but no torches had been lit, and the house was oddly mute. No servants running between floors, no clatter from the kitchen, no music from a distant chamber. Gio trailed close behind Cecilia, watching the heels of her slippers dart out from under her skirts as she sped up the spiral staircase and down the hall.

Inside Chiara's chamber, candles cast long shadows. On the far side of the bed, Veronica and Margherita perched on stools. Their *camicias* were rumpled, their undone hair falling over their shoulders like mantles. The drapes had been wound open to reveal Chiara, lying facedown on the bedding, one cheek pressed into a pillow, the sheets pulled up tight over her shoulders.

Gio took two paces into the room, blinking. In the corner was a bathing tub. It must have been recently used: rags slopped over the rim and were dripping onto the floor, making a small pool of wet no one had bothered to mop up. Streaks of red stained the white linen. His stomach knotted.

"She was asking for you." Veronica frowned at him. Without makeup on, she looked years older, tired. Gio stepped closer, and Chiara opened her one visible eye to give him a sidelong glance. Her still-damp hair snaked out darkly, and over her cheek fell what looked like a shadow. As Gio neared, he saw it was a bruise, blossoming in sick greenish shades. Wordlessly, he reached to draw the bedclothes down; as he did, she twisted her head to bury her face in the pillow. Linens had been bound to her torso—shoulder to hip—with thick strips of cloth. Suggestions of pink dappled the white in places where the blood was seeping through.

"She's been lashed. He *lashed* her." Margherita scooted forward on her stool. She was holding back tears, her pretty face crumpling in on itself like a pastry taken out of the heat too soon. Gio didn't need to ask who'd done it.

"I don't understand. She's Venier's favorite. Why would he—"

"We don't know, and she won't tell us." Veronica leaned forward to tug the bedclothes back into place, tucking them over Chiara's shoulders as briskly as a nursemaid.

"Is she . . . will she—"

"She'll heal. The doctor said there may be some scarring, but he stopped before any more damage was done, thank the Lord." Veronica absentmindedly made the sign of the cross, then stood.

"And Virgin Mary," Margherita chimed in, wavering to her feet like Veronica's echo. In silence, the three of them gazed down at Chiara's body, outlined under the bedding. She'd kept her face hidden in the pillow, as if excusing herself from the conversation. Gio observed the slow rise and fall of her back.

"Something must be done," Veronica said sharply, raising one eyebrow at Gio. He tried to think of an answer, but his mind felt stunned and slowed, lagging two paces behind. Chiara shifted then, keeping her face down but reaching a hand out from under the sheet toward Gio. Easing to the edge of the bed, he folded her palm into his own. Her skin was feverish, dry. A rope burn looped her wrist, angry and red. The knot in his stomach cinched tighter.

Taking Chiara's movement as a sign, the girls turned to leave, Margherita casting back sad doll eyes. The door creaked shut behind them. In the heavy quiet of the room, Gio extended his other hand, grazing the back of Chiara's head with his fingertips. She stiffened at his touch, then relaxed, letting him stroke her hair. After a long while she turned, face emerging, eyes still closed. Gio took inventory of the damage. Bruised cheekbone. A cut near her nose, another just above her brow. All of her swollen, and the tender beginnings of more bruising in the inner rim of her eye.

"Why'd he do it, Chiara?"

Her lashes lifted, and he saw that the white of her visible eye was now an unnatural yellow. "I can't tell you." Her voice was scorched from smoke or from screaming.

"Chiara, I won't be upset if—"

"Not that. He didn't want that."

Gio exhaled deeply, feeling a pang of guilt for how relieved he was. "Then why?"

She shut her eye again. He watched a tear form in the corner of her lashes and drop, tracing gravity over the bridge of her nose. A strand of wet hair clung to her temple in a whorl; he caressed it back.

"You won't love me anymore." Her bottom lip had cracked and bled at some point, and now a dark scab was forming, like a seam down the middle.

"Impossible." With the back of one knuckle he gently wiped at the wet under her eye. "Chiara, I need to understand. Please."

"He saw me."

"He saw you . . . Saw you where?"

"In the Ghetto."

"Just now, during the fire? Why were you in the Ghetto?"

"I went to visit my aunt."

"What was your aunt doing in the Ghetto?"

"She lives there, Gio." Chiara said the words slowly, as if he were a child.

"I thought your aunt was a courtesan . . ." His mind struggled to fit the odd-shaped pieces together. "Your aunt is a Jewess?" His eyes darted to the roots of her hair, charcoal beneath the artificial tint. "*You're* a Jewess? You're a Jewess." He repeated the words, repetition turning them into fact.

He wanted her to shake her head to tell him he was wrong. Instead came the crying. She tried to hold it in, shuddering. Her face crumpled into a version of her he didn't recognize: lines pinching her forehead, broken blood vessels like filigree under her pale skin. An image of their first meeting darted into his mind, gilded and glimmering. Her floating on the divan in the great rose-colored room, offering him a glass of wine. Shining up at him with that lavender light. Asking an impossible promise.

He hadn't kept her safe.

Not knowing what else to do, he stroked her hair in silence. As she struggled to slow her breathing, he worked to put the story in logical order—as if knowing the narrative could somehow change its ending.

"Is your aunt . . . did she—"

"She wasn't harmed. She sent word to Cecilia."

"Why hide this, Chiara? I've heard of Jewish courtesans—"

"Who are treated like curiosities, Gio. Do you imagine I ever could've had this?" She tugged her hand from his to gesture feebly at the room. "My aunt was a Jewish courtesan—I saw her life. If she hadn't married when she could . . ." Wet had gathered along the edge of her nose; she rubbed at it with a fingertip. "They make us wear *badges*, Gio. You don't understand."

"I—I certainly don't understand why he'd hurt you so badly just for dissembling."

"Because . . . if Venier had knowingly lain with a Jew . . ." She let the sentence trail off.

"He could be accused of heresy." He finished the thought for her.

"They'd make an example of him." As she wiped her eyes again, he noticed dirt still rimming her cuticles, clinging to the skin under her nails. "I think Corvino wanted me to confess." She tried to turn onto her side, winced, and abandoned the effort. "He tied my hands up, Gio. The things he was saying: Bible verses, over and over. It made no sense, he was someone else. I thought he was going to *kill* me—I thought I might die there, all alone." Her voice rose in pitch, tears slicking the hollows of her eyes.

"How did it end?" He gathered her hand up again, absently stroking the back of it.

"I don't know." She was staring at the wall behind him with a flat expression. "I couldn't take any more—the *pain*, Gio. I was scream-ing and no one came to help me. No one even came. Then, it all just … went black. I don't remember anything. They had to tell me afterward that a pair of old women brought me back; they said they found me crawling out of the house. I must have told them where to take me, but I don't remember—I can't remember."

The sobs came quickly then, too fast to stop. He leaned to stroke her hair, to press his mouth to her cheek, to her temple. Whisper-ing gentle quiet words until the ragged edges of her breathing soft-ened and she slept.

He left before dawn. Overhead, there was a marked absence of stars: the haze from the fire still obscured the sky. After the chaos of the day, the avenues and canals seemed strangely emptied out, the town retreating into itself, mute with shock. When he got to Aurelio's house, a burnished glow leaking through the shutters said the alchemist was still awake. Oddly, the bolt was thrown; Gio pounded a fist on the door. With a minor degree of clatter, the hinges opened an inch. Gio found himself staring into a pair of va-cant, milk-blind eyes. It was the old man he'd sat next to at Venier's feast—the one who'd convinced the magistrate to free Anzola.

"Giovanni!" Aurelio appeared then, reaching to open the door wider. His own eyes were bloodshot; he didn't look at Gio but in-stead leaned out to peer up at the sky before clasping the old man on the shoulder. "Our friend here was just leaving."

The old man nodded absently, with a backward gesture into the room. At the summons, his shrew-faced page materialized. Grasping the old man's elbow, the page escorted him out. Gio stepped aside to let them pass.

"I trust we will speak again soon." Gio caught the smell of arsenic on the old man's breath, mossy and metallic.

Aurelio nodded and waved them off. From the stoop, Gio watched as the two figures waded into the murky predawn streets, until a quick tap on the shoulder from Aurelio beckoned him inside. As the alchemist bolted the door behind them, Gio thought he spied a half wing of dark feathers splayed on the table—then Aurelio passed in front of him, taking up his usual spot near the fire, and when Gio looked again, the feathers were gone.

He rubbed his eyes and leaned a shoulder on the doorframe.

"Here before sunup, hoping Corvino didn't follow you?" Aurelio began fumbling with his beakers, the low embers in the hearth glowing feebly. At his elbow, a cup of liquid sat steaming.

"Do you know what he did to Chiara?" Gio crossed his arms.

"I know what he did to the Ghetto."

"The Ghetto?"

"Yes, it's unfortunate. Our friend was particularly displeased: he had priceless items stored there . . ." Aurelio trailed off, his eyes losing focus as he scanned the jars that sat along the back wall.

"Chiara." Gio struggled for words.

Aurelio's attention veered back sharply. "I know all about Chiara—that never should have happened. Ah, well, such is the nature of free will I suppose." The alchemist took a sip from the cup on the table as calmly as if they were discussing the weather. "Don't fret, Gio, arrangements have been made." He set the cup back down.

"What arrangements?" The heavy, spiced air and flickering lights were beginning to throw Gio off-balance.

"Yes, well. We could return her to family in Padua, of course, but I believe it better to send her to live with Maddalena in Milan."

Aurelio turned to face the fire, warming his hands. At his movement, the flames seemed to liven, crackling and flaring. "She can continue her music studies there, and Maddalena has agreed to provide her with lodging and a position as a tutor."

"How has Maddalena possibly already agreed? I don't understand." Gio heard the plea in his own voice, a nearly childish whine.

The alchemist spun around. "Do you imagine I simply totter about this room all day making liquors and useless magics, Gio?" His tired face went slack with frustration. "No! I know things beyond your comprehension, and I have the foresight to prepare for what is to come!" Behind him, the fire hissed and sputtered like a refrain. "A single glance, one small gesture, a change in the wind . . . you may not notice such trivialities, but I understand them in all their complexity. I know what actions men will take, and I know what is written for us all in the stars!" For a moment, Aurelio seemed to grow larger, his shoulders extending toward the ceiling, robes billowing out like two black wings to send shadows skittering across the wall. Sparks from the fire sprayed red ocher and gold.

Gio blinked hard. *Was he this exhausted?* When he looked again, Aurelio had contracted to normal proportions and was calmly moving between beakers and bowls. "Everything in life, Gio, including us, can be broken down into its basic elements. Those who understand what lies within them can remake themselves according to their own design." With patience now, Aurelio mixed the fluids. "Yet a man who does not acknowledge all aspects of himself will never gain mastery over his fate." A purple smoke began to spiral slowly upward out of the beaker, noiseless as a snake in the grass. "Are you familiar with the myth of Aristeas, Giovanni?"

Gio shook his head.

"Ah, well. No matter." Aurelio squinted curiously at his friend, then bent back to the vials. "Chiara will go to Milan. This is where her path now leads. We'll send her off when the messenger comes to say we've won the war. The distraction will suit our purposes."

"We've won?" Gio glanced down, noticing a stool he hadn't seen before placed at his knee. He sat and put his head in his hands. In the hearth, the embers now crackled cozily.

"We will. News will arrive within the week: during the celebrations, we'll spirit Chiara away." Aurelio pulled on his beard, observing Gio. "You may go along with her if you'd like . . ."

Still staring down at the floor, Gio could only nod.

It was the moment soldiers would recount years after, late at night in taverns: the instant the reserve boats came bearing down. Venier's men reached the *Real* at the same time the Spanish division arrived—gunners releasing volleys of lead, galleasses shaking from cannon thrust. The Ottomans were dismembered. Turkish soldiers began to swim toward shore by the hundreds, like spawning carp, while the Christians impaled them. Then the head of Ali Pasha— brave, honorable Ali Pasha—was raised up on a pike for all to see, his face gone bloodless. Under a shorn straggle of beard, the ragged flesh of his neck was still vivid red.

Through the smoke and blaze, the name of Allah was torn from Ali's flagship and replaced by an image of Christ nailed to the cross.

25

"WHAT DO YOU MEAN, YOU'RE DONE WITH THE APP? Didn't you just get on it?" Joan spun around on the sidewalk and held out a hand. "Henry, keep up with us, sweetie."

The three of them were strolling downtown, on a mission to buy a birthday present for one of the moms at Henry's school, but taking their time window-shopping in the languishing afternoon heat. The students had begun trickling back, and the town felt alive again, humming with new blood. All the shopkeepers had stocked their shelves with fresh fall inventory and arranged new displays in their windows. Overhead, the rustling leaves had reached a pinnacle of green. Soon their color would begin to change—Rose couldn't wait for those explosions of crisp red and yellow, brilliant pink even, scattering through the air and blanketing the sidewalks: the cacophony of nature as she bedded down to rest.

"Joan, on that app, I was asked for—" Rose hesitated, glancing back at Henry, who'd reluctantly torn his gaze from a toy store window and was now catching up to them with a dramatically morose look on his face. She leaned and whispered in Joan's direction "For *inappropriate* photos not once, not twice, but three times." She held up her fingers for effect.

Joan rolled her eyes and hitched her purse strap up higher on her shoulder. "There are always a few of those types in the mix, you can't expect—"

"Joan, I was asked if I'm DTF! Do you even know what that means? I had to look it up online!" Rose's voice was quickly edging away from a whisper. She caught Joan trying to stifle a laugh, spinning her face toward the shops. "Oh my God, you *do* know what it means! How on earth?"

"Sweetie, I watch so much more TV than you. And anyway, I think you're using the wrong app, that one is for millennials." Joan ruffled her hair with one hand, surreptitiously glancing at her own reflection.

"*Was* using," Rose corrected her. "It's deleted, trust me."

"Well, regardless, there are much better ones to be on, more adult ones. I can help you set them up, I bet I'd be great at the profiles!" Joan's eyes sparkled with excitement. "Ohhhh, and a friend of mine just told me about an amazing matchmaker, I guess her specialty is . . ." Her voice thinned out: Rose had halted in front of the furniture store.

Through the window she'd caught a fleeting glimpse of a couch more beautiful than she thought couches could be. Now she stood transfixed. The fabric was a creamy taupe, the best of both brown and gray. Two rows of buttons ran across its back, forming cozy-looking dimples in the woven jacquard. It was a couch that begged to be curled up in, that seemed to call out: *Here I am, come sit and read.* Rose inched closer to the glass.

"You know you can go in, right?" Joan was watching her with a bemused expression. As if in a daze, Rose went to the doors and pushed her way inside. Henry ran in front of them, clambering up onto the couch as soon as Rose took a seat. He bounced on the cushion beside her, legs sticking out in the air.

"What do you think, Henry?" Rose asked, watching for a sign. By way of response, he giggled maniacally and plunged facefirst into an artfully placed throw pillow. Rose glanced up at Joan, who stood nearby with arms crossed, mouth twitching in a hopeful half smile. She raised her eyebrows at Rose, a silent question. Rose nodded, feeling the same tingling buzz of excitement that'd come over her the afternoon she downloaded the app.

Yes. She would do the unexpected. She would buy the couch.

The evening of his opening, William woke up from a nap feeling hollow. It wasn't a numbness, but a letting go. The space created when what he'd been working on had been extracted from inside himself and handed to the world, like a gift.

The smell of dinner wafted up as he made his way downstairs. In the living room, Jane and Lucy were sprawled out on the floor, heads bent over a puzzle. Restraint played across Jane's face; she knew where the piece they were searching for was hiding. As William leaned into the doorway, she glanced up at him. Already, her face was changing fast, so fast. He could see himself in her, and Sarah too. She smiled at him, a quick blond flare, then ducked back to the puzzle.

In the kitchen, Sarah moved in front of the stove, a faded floral apron tied around her waist and neck. She bent to open the oven door as he walked in, warm heat blowing her hair back, flushing her cheeks.

"I know, I know, you said you didn't need me to cook big dinners, but tonight's special." She pulled out the cast-iron skillet, filled with tender-crisp chicken thighs nestled in saffron rice, red skins of roasted peppers slick with oil. Fragrant spice unfurled immodestly from the pan.

"Hey, we haven't had this since New York." He recognized the dish as one they used to order at a Spanish restaurant down the street from their old apartment.

Sarah nodded. "I actually called them to ask about the recipe." She smiled at him, cheeks pink, then brushed the hair from her face with a hand still in its mitt. "There's that too." With her chin, she gestured at a package on the counter wrapped in butcher paper and twine.

"Can I open it?"

She nodded again and pivoted back to the stove. His thick fingers couldn't undo the knot; instead, he shimmied the twine up over the corners, then tore through the paper.

It was the photograph of them both, framed. He'd absentmindedly tucked it into their closet after bringing it in from the studio—she must have found it. She'd had it edged in maple, their happiness preserved behind thick glass. As he slid the photo out, a stiff rectangle of paper came sliding with it. He held one corner, reading the script across the front. It was a gift certificate for music lessons at a studio downtown. William glanced up just in time to catch Sarah watching him.

"Look in the pantry." She had an expression on her face that he'd only ever seen her use with the girls, on birthdays or holidays, when they were about to open a present she knew they wanted. He turned to the narrow pantry door and swung it open.

The light had already been flicked on, and there—perched on a stand, in front of shelves of soup cans and opened boxes of cereal—was a new guitar. It had a Sitka spruce top: pale and polished, inlaid with abalone and wrapped in gleaming rosewood. The type of instrument that would never be left out in a yard sale. William stepped into the pantry, was alone for a moment in the small room, warm and close with the faint smell of baking powder. He reached to touch the guitar strings, taut against his fingertips. Then he looked down at the photograph he was still holding in his other hand.

The image of him and Sarah smiling.

It'd been a warm enough day that Rose hadn't needed a jacket. She'd barely needed the thin blue cardigan she'd worn: summer was refusing to cede her crown of wilting blossoms, demanding a few more weeks still. But now that the sun was down, the air had chilled, and Rose was glad for the extra layer as she biked.

The gallery was near enough to her usual route, halfway between the shop and home. It'd be easy to say she was just passing by. Still, she decided to lock her bike a block away and walk there so that if she needed to leave quickly, she could just turn around and not have to deal with chains or keys. She avoided thinking too much about the why of it; like a sleight of hand trick, her mind let that card remain facedown.

Strolling the sidewalk, she was greeted on all sides by the bobbing heads of flowers: peeking over fences, edging the concrete, tumbling thickly from baskets the city had hitched to lampposts. Petunias and hollyhock, common yarrow and elegant pale roses that still held a bit of daylight in their petals. Rose thought of Alice's looking-glass garden and half-expected the flowers to begin chattering—the roses advising her to walk in the opposite direction if she wanted to get where she was going.

Where *was* she going? To William's opening. Uninvited. Wearing a dress she hadn't worn in years, with her hair, for once, down. After she'd closed the shop, she'd stood in front of the mirror in the small back bathroom and begun to retwist her bun. Then, inexplicably, she'd stopped. She'd looked at herself with her hair wild and tendriled past her breasts, and she'd left it that way—walked out of the shop with it swaying down her back, spiraling around her neck like a newfound familiar. Now as she turned the corner, her reflection confronted her in the darkened windows lining the street. Arms wrapped around her body as if she were cold or frightened, hair whipping out behind.

Up ahead the gallery emerged, silhouettes crisping into view as she approached. People on the sidewalk smoking, cigarettes glowing red on the inhale. Light from the show spilled out into the street, the brassy sounds of jazz and conversation, a woman laughing, all of it just audible over the pounding of her hummingbird heart. She neared a pair of smokers, deep in discussion—*and wasn't de Duve's stance on the avant garde perfection?*—both of them exhaling great gray gusts that unspooled lazily into the night air. Rose eased to the window and peeked in. The small gallery was crowded, but through the shifting bodies she could spy fragments of the paintings.

Suddenly, silence. No laughter, no jazz, not even the hum of blood in her ears.

The tree and the bird! She would recognize them anywhere. She'd known he was painting Giovanni's story, but seeing it made it real—brought back the afternoon they'd spent together looking at the images, standing side by side in the back room. The sharp, grassy smell of his cologne. Feather and wing, root and bough. She leaned in closer, caught the profile of a face on a canvas toward the back. Just glimpses through the window, through gaps in the crowd, but enough to see that he'd made something modern and stunning that still somehow spoke of late Renaissance technique. A swelling of pride bubbled in her chest as if she could claim some part in it.

And then there he was, laughing, dark eyes lighting up as he gestured carelessly with a cut-glass tumbler of whiskey in his hand. His face looked like it had in the desert portrait, like it had with her once, reckless and glinting. A chorus of his paintings backing him up. Rose noticed a woman beside him with her back to the window, blond hair coiled up tightly. Below them both, a young girl completed the composition.

With a start, Rose realized she'd never let herself imagine his
children before, not really. Now there the girl stood, real as blood
and bone, white-blond hair and a ruffled blue dress. She was holding a heavily frosted cupcake someone must have just given her.
Rose watched as the girl took her first bite: small teeth bared like a
kitten yawning, eyes shut tight. Between her grasping fingers, the
cake pillowed and crumbled. Her face reemerged with frosting
smeared on either edge of her mouth, a stiff dollop clinging tenaciously to the tip of her nose.

William had seen the bite too, was on his knees now, whiskey
set on the floor, using a cocktail napkin to wipe up the mess. As he
dabbed at her face, the child squirmed; he shook his head and
grinned down indulgently. At his elbow, another girl materialized.
Years older, she had darker hair and a serious expression—until
she noticed the frosting on her sister's nose and started giggling,
grasping William's arm, flopping her head onto his shoulder.

As Rose watched, a brief and unexpected memory surfaced.
She'd been very young; she remembered the shapes of both parents
towering over her, one on either side. Swatches of color and floating, faraway faces. Someone had been holding her hand. The warm
sensation of comfort without fear—how could she have known
that feeling would be so fleeting, so irretrievable? The world had
still been safe then, full of unfolding wonders designed for her delight alone. By their expressions, Rose could tell both children were
still swaddled in that same, tender cocoon.

Then the blond woman pivoted, was bending to kiss the crown
of the younger girl's head. When she straightened, a wedge of hair
swayed loose from its twist. Rose watched as William looked at his
wife, as he raised one hand tentatively, then tucked the wayward
strand behind her ear. The woman reached to catch his fingers in

her own, turned her face, pressed her mouth to the center of his open palm.

The very same act Rose had wanted to do herself.

He hadn't touched his wife that way in a long time. Rose could tell without being told—it was written plainly across both of their faces, in their hesitant, uncertain smiles. The two girls shifted in the space below, and for a brief moment she comprehended the family as a whole, a complete and connected system, set apart from the crowd. Bound together by invisible atoms, as perfect and breakable as the still surface of a lake. Then her eyes refocused and she was staring at her own reflection in the glass. Her corona of wild hair, her stricken expression, and it wasn't déjà vu so much as a sense of deep knowing: that she was always going to have ended up here, standing on the outside looking in.

That she was always going to have had to see it to understand.

In an instant, she spun away from herself and was off into the night—walking fast, fast, fast, back to her bike, past the wise white roses with their bobbing heads. When she finally got home, her face was streaked with mascara, though she didn't remember crying.

26

REMEMBERING THE TIME BEFORE SHE LEFT WAS LIKE trying to recall details from a fever dream. He'd stayed by her side in the hushed room with the sounds of the city jangling and bright below. Because the light hurt her eyes, they kept the drapes closed and the windows open. The heavy fabric of the curtains billowed sluggishly in the breeze, splintering sun across the floor. Together they passed through time in an ambient, marginless drift. He read to her, talked to her about inconsequential matters, drew for her until her eyes drooped, the calm of sleep falling like a curtain beneath her bruises. Then a memory would surface, threatening and unyielding, and she'd call out and shudder awake at the sound of her own voice.

In the first day after the attack, Veronica and Margherita would wander in every few hours to perch at her bedside—but Chiara didn't have the spirit to entertain them, and they kept their gazes fastened on the small thistles embroidered in the bed drapes, unable to look at her bandaged and discolored body. Like cats avoiding a sick member of the litter, they quickly reduced their visits to brief nightly inquiries, a head poked through a crack in the door. Meanwhile, Aurelio had arranged for sentries to be placed throughout the house: barrel-chested, blunt-featured men who stood guard like overgrown mastiffs. Gio avoided making eye contact, though they seemed to do the trick. No one had heard from the Crow.

One afternoon, nearly a week after the fire, Gio lay with Chiara in a drowsy lull. The half-drawn bed curtains swaddled them in a crimson tint. He was searing every part of her into his memory: the slender tips of her fingers, the pattern of blue veins on the insides of her wrists. The way she smelled now, without all her oils—musky and warm, slightly bitter, like the inside of a walnut shell.

"Tell me a story." Her voice was muffled by the sheet. At once, Gio thought of the story Torquato had recited, about the bird and the tree. He recalled it for her, trying to remember the exact phrases the poet had used.

"Draw it for me—draw it with us in it. I'll be the tree, and you'll be my bird." She smiled at the idea.

"Do you know, I'd planned to do just that . . ."

And so he had, sketching as she lay nestled beside him, supervising. She'd made suggestions as he went along: "Add more blossoms" or "Your shoulders are wider than that." Eventually she'd approved, and they both leaned back to survey the pictures with a sense of accomplishment, ignoring the drops of ink he'd spilled onto the sheets.

"And now we'll always be together."

"Always."

Later, as she meandered in and out of sleep, he whispered to her what Aurelio had planned. A safe future, one full of music, with Maddalena in Milan.

"And you'll come with me," she'd murmured into his shoulder, her breath feverish on his skin. He'd said more words then, vague phrases about setting his affairs in order, but the sounds carried no weight. He'd twisted a strand of her hair around his finger; without the constant tinting, her curls were already darkening, shade by shade.

On the seventh day, Aurelio announced the time had come.

They packed only what could be easily transported. Veronica swooped in, somber and severe, to direct the servants with brisk efficiency while Margherita followed in her wake, puffy-eyed and weepy. They dressed Chiara in men's clothing: plain black layers several sizes too large that made her seem even more fragile. Finally, all four found themselves sitting in the rose-colored room, silent except for Margherita, who from time to time stuffed a fist partway into her mouth to muffle her crying. Gio couldn't help but note that the scene seemed like a terrible mutation of his first visit: all of them together again in the same room—but this time they were anxious, tired, afraid. Chiara squeezed his hand in her lap, her fingers wrapped around his thumb.

As the light outside began to fade, the first cries of celebration could be heard.

Gradually, the shouting grew nearer; at the window, Gio leaned his head outside. The whole city seemed to be swarming toward the harbor, torches transforming the avenues and canals into ribbons of flame. They could hear laughter, songs, and chants floating up on the air like steam, all of Venice boiling over with excitement as confirmation of a victory spread from house to house.

Gio retreated from the window and strode to Chiara's side. He extended an elbow, as if he were escorting her to just another dance; rising with a quick wince of pain, she took hold of his forearm. Shoulder to shoulder, they exited the room, making their way toward the wide marble staircase while Veronica and Margherita trailed behind.

As they walked, images of his first visit ran through Gio's mind, time skipping and bending, tripping over itself. His reflection rippled across the polished floor—now he was following Cecilia that first afternoon, now he was escorting Chiara away. For once, she didn't need his help descending the stairs: her slippers were flat and silent. Still, she leaned into him, tucking her head under his shoulder. He looped an arm around her waist. Joined, they took the remaining steps together. An awful certainty—to know in the very act that his mind would surely circle back again and again to these minutes, the way a desperate creature returns to a place where there once had been water.

Outside on the canal, a large gondola waited, its cabin draped in black curtains. As the sky faded into star-dotted dusk overhead, the boat seemed to absorb all remaining light. The gondolier kept his face down, the end of his oar hidden beneath the water's surface. Other boats slid by, already-drunk celebrants leaning out, whooping, wearing masks as if it were Carnival again. White and gold and red faces streamed past, frozen smiles gliding through the dim. Gio glanced at Veronica and Margherita standing behind him, at their quivering chins, their clutching hands. The servants huddled in a cluster by the door. It all felt like a misstep someone would soon put right, a musician hitting a minor chord in a major key—only the conductor was missing, the minor chord kept playing. More servants emerged from the house, torches raised against the creeping night. In their flare, the boat itself seemed to flicker: trembling forward, retreating back into shadow.

Suddenly, Chiara was in front of him, rising up onto her toes to kiss him goodbye. He'd be able to remember that image of her precisely, months later. Wet-lashed violet eyes, a narrow cut bright on her cheek, torch glare wavering shadows across them both. Garish dark bruises that still couldn't undo the persistent symmetry of her face. One last time, she put her head to his chest.

How perfectly she fit against him.

Then she turned and ducked beneath the canopy of the boat. In the back of the cabin, her face became a pale moon, floating bodiless in the gloom. He took a step forward, to the edge of the water.

He didn't know what to say—what could he say? *It wasn't supposed to end like this.*

A quick elbow in his ribs. Before anyone could stop her, Cecilia had clambered into the boat, sending it rocking heavily side to side. Thin-lipped and determined, she sat down next to Chiara, hugging a large sack in her lap. Gio heard several of the servants behind him gasp audibly, but no one protested. With a dip and a thrust, the oarsman aimed the vessel out into the canal, straining against the current. The water swung the narrow boat around and carried it off, a wake of ripples echoing out from the stern.

Just like that, Gio watched her slip away from him, as though it were easy. The gondola lost itself in an ensemble of hulls out on the canal, steered into the dark vignette of his vision and then—

She was gone.

☙❧

Noise from the street ricocheted against the walls and shattered the quiet of his room. Corvino lay in bed, skin burning, spasms of shivers turning even his sweat frigid. His men set bowls of food outside his chamber door each day, but he couldn't trust them—their eyes shifted—and the meals went largely untouched. He let the fever rage through him.

"As the flesh burns, so is the Spirit purified."

Corvino whispered the words to himself through cracked and bleeding lips. The clamor from outside was shearing the skin from his flesh, every shout a new fracture in his skull. *Why so much noise?* He couldn't make out the words. Sliding to the edge of the bed, he placed one foot on the floor, then the other. Winced at the chill stone. The air itself seemed to vibrate in front of him, the way it sometimes did above a fire: wobbling apart, then back into place. His hair hung in strands stuck together with dried sweat.

With jerks and starts, Corvino neared the window. He'd lost weight; his hip bones grazed the linen of his tunic, rough against his skin. The fabric had gone yellow in spots. When he reached the stone ledge, he grasped it with both hands. Below, the city was flooded with torches, flaming streets and canals burning the stars overhead into submission. The streams of light were gathering at the harbor—if he squinted, Corvino could make out the mast of an unfamiliar vessel rocking on the waves with ghostly pale sails.

His attention was so focused on the ship he didn't notice the crow crouched beside him.

Corvino. The same, soundless voice.

Corvino startled, one hand slipping from the ledge. With a twitch of its head the crow beckoned him back. The dry rustle of feathers. Corvino should have been alarmed, should have tugged his shutters closed, but he didn't—he lacked all fear. Instead, a light-headed nothingness had come over him; his body weightless as a paper lantern.

You belong with us now, Corvino. Other crows came then, winging around buildings, shadows streaking. As before, the first crow began to swell and grow. Corvino watched, hypnotized.

You're one of us.

"I am?" Corvino's voice was a rasp, scratching up his throat.

You are. We have a gift for you, Corvino. The crow's gaping black pupils were welcoming now—invitations into an endless, restful night. Corvino straightened his back. He tried to swallow but his mouth was dry, filled with grit.

We have a gift.

A sudden sharp pain in his shoulder blades. Something gouging his skin—the sensation of tendons being stretched and pulled. A wave of nausea that buckled his knees; Corvino cried out, grasping the ledge to keep upright. He twisted his neck to look behind him.

Wings. Glossy, midnight wings extending upward, unfolding as he watched. Muscular wings. Strong wings. Wings so black they sheened purple, then indigo. Stiff feather and hollow bone. Corvino shifted his shoulder blades, felt the pinions adjust, responding

like limbs. They were part of him now: his glorious new append-
ages.

Fly with us, Corvino.

You belong, Corvino.

We are family, Corvino.

The crows repeated his name in a persistent incantation. Corvino's eyes glazed. Behind him, purple smoke came whispering in
under the door. It snaked around his ankles, unfurling upward. He
didn't feel himself breathe it in, didn't smell its faint acrid scent. He
saw only the wings. Heard only the crow's words.

You belong now, Corvino.

We are family now, Corvino.

Trembling, Corvino raised one foot to the stone ledge. Gripping
the window frame, he stepped up. The still-warm night air swept in
around him. It smelled of cinder and sage and ruffled his feathers,
breezing over his mantle. Below, the city stretched before him,
veined by rippling canals, a maze of shifting reflections. As Corvino
swayed on his sill, the murder of crows winged in great arcs, sweep-
ing into his room and back out again—tracing dark ovals in the sky.
They were playing.

Join us, Corvino. Their voices merged, a chorus.

You belong now, Corvino. Their shiny eyes, unblinking.

We are family now, Corvino. Their hard beaks open, grinning.

Corvino stepped out into the night.

He felt only the soaring then—only the sensation of wind passing over his powerful wings. How naturally, how effortlessly they
beat the air. He felt only the joy of flying alongside the others, heard
only their cries of kinship.

He did not feel the falling at all.

He did not feel the stone.

27

ONE MONTH AFTER WILLIAM'S SHOW, A NONDESCRIPT brown box arrived on Rose's doorstep, the familiar return address of the translation agency stamped in the corner. The box was heavier than she'd expected; she set it down on the coffee table and got a pair of scissors from the kitchen to slice open the cardboard flaps. Inside was another box, glossy white. She lifted the lid. A thick stack of pages lay underneath, bound with quarter-inch white plastic rings, an envelope resting on top. Rose tore it open and slid out the folded note inside: a personal letter from the lead translator at the agency, written on the type of heavyweight stock used by people who appreciate paper. The cursive was immaculate, marred only by a small ink drop on the bottom corner.

Never in my career as a translator have I seen my team so personally invested in a project . . . The note went on to thank Rose, to say the agency looked forward to working together again. Rose tucked the letter back into the envelope and tossed it on the table. Fumbling only slightly, she lifted the stack of pages and settled onto the new couch. That single purchase had launched a cavalcade of others—a dizzying buying spree in the wake of William's show, which had culminated in two burly deliverymen wrestling a new bed frame into the master bedroom and Joan helping to hang her clothes in the large wardrobe, spraying lavender-scented air freshener in every corner, telling her what a good change it was, how proud of herself she should be.

It *had* felt cathartic, the whirling burst of activity, not unlike a manic episode. The whole summer, in fact, was beginning to seem that way in retrospect: fuzzy and dislocated, like it'd all been a movie she'd watched, a series of scenes acted out by someone other than her. Or maybe that was the easiest way for her mind to grapple with the lingering uncertainty. It wasn't that she was still holding out hope for William—how could she be? It was just that she still wondered, she still wanted to know: had it mattered as much to him as it had to her?

Had it been real for him too?

She couldn't ask him, she'd never be able to ask him. And so, a new couch, a new ottoman, a new bed, a new rug, even a new coffee table. Now she felt like a stranger in her own home. She'd wanted change, she had, wanted the shock of the new like a dunk of the head in ice water. Something—anything—to jolt her back to her own life. She just hadn't counted on it being so disorienting; it still took her a few seconds to sort out where she was when she woke up, to remember which bedroom door to open when she stumbled back from the bathroom in the middle of the night.

It also made her realize—sitting alone in a rearranged living room, which, as Joan put it, was *truly hers* now—that new furniture wouldn't solve the sensation of having been emptied out but not filled back up again, as if there were a different version of herself she was supposed to be becoming if only someone would tell her *who* and *how*. Instead, it was only absence now, her days composed of negative space: no one to care for or think of, no treatise to repair. No new distraction to give her some sense of meaning—until now. Taking solace in the fact that her mind would surely be occupied for at least the next few hours, Rose folded her legs up beneath her and found a comfortable nook among the cushions.

She opened the first page. The book began with a sheet of instructions—how to download more copies, a reminder to sign up for the agency's newsletter—followed by the title page. Would she finally be able to finish the story? What if it ended abruptly or didn't answer all her questions? There'd been no clear indication of a conclusion, after all: the writing had simply stopped. Before beginning the first line, she made a quick pact with herself to read front to back. No skipping ahead.

She turned to the first paragraph of script:

> The year is 1571. I write this to record what I fear may be my final year of sight.

What followed was an autobiographical narrative, documenting Giovanni's training as an artist. The voice here was formal, as if written for an audience—so different from the excerpt she and William had pored over weeks ago. Undoubtedly, Giovanni had also read Vasari's *The Lives of the Artists;* she wondered if he was mimicking Vasari's structure, trying to insert his own chapter among those on Donatello, Raphael, Michelangelo. Still, she sensed an urgency in the language, as if he were trying to get it all down as quickly as he could. In broad strokes, he detailed his training in Milan, his development from early portraits of peasants to commissions for large-scale religious allegories. The only topic of the writing was his art: how he advanced his perspective, what subjects he sketched, the arrangements of his contracts.

The reading went quickly, and soon Rose found herself midway through the stack. Giovanni had just finished documenting his move to Venice and career in the city, and here the journal seemed to catch up with him in time. When she reached the moment of Venier's summons—the day Giovanni would have met the woman in the portrait—Rose noticed a shift in tone. Giovanni's frank candor on every subject, from El Greco's training to Veronese's commissions, suddenly turned guarded. Where he once recounted conversations in full, naming participants and locations as if for posterity, now he jotted down oblique phrases, more notes to himself than anything else. Yet between the notes and the sketches in the margins of the book, it wasn't hard to sort out what had happened:

He'd fallen in love.

Rose thought of the drawings Giovanni had made, how attentive he'd been to record even the smallest details of his muse. Her fingernails. The indents in her elbows. Her robe crumpled on the floor, the ribbons in her hair. If the woman were Venier's courtesan, it made sense that Giovanni would want to protect her. Rose recalled a passage from one of the library books, which had noted—in what had seemed to her a senselessly casual tone—that Renaissance men who'd believed themselves cuckolded would often arrange for the woman in question to be beaten and raped. It was clear Giovanni had grown only more concerned after war was declared and the mood of the city turned unstable. He detailed the public shaming of Anzola (*I believe they would have let her burn. This war has turned us to savages, all*), and again Rose remembered the woodcut print of an accused witch at the stake.

She shivered and began to quicken her pace.

As she scanned down the lines, she realized she'd reached the place where Giovanni was describing the origins of the illustrated story of the winged man and the woman-tree. He'd written with such clarity that she could picture the candlelit table, the narrow face of the poet leaning into the glow. She began to wonder how faithfully William had reproduced Giovanni's portraits in his paintings before chastising her mind, as she'd done every day since the gallery opening, the way a rider twitches the reins to keep a distracted horse on the path. *No, Rose. You know better.* She frowned and forced herself to focus on the sentences in front of her.

As the diary continued, the translation began to contain ellipses where Giovanni had written so quickly that entire words were rendered illegible. She started to skim the pages, impatient to know how it ended. A fire in the Ghetto; the text began to fragment further. *How could I not have known, how could she not have told me?* Rose's eyes flicked down the page. What had happened? What had the woman not told Giovanni?

Jewess.

Immediately, Rose thought of the images she'd seen in the archives: the yellow badges and hats, the crowded Ghetto. Appalling illustrations showing Jews as rodents and Christ killers. Giovanni was writing only a few decades before Shakespeare would have completed *The Merchant of Venice*. Rose thought of the shooting at a synagogue that'd been splayed across the front page of the paper not two weeks back. In late Renaissance Venice, anti-Semitism would have been considered not discrimination but a fact of life— part of the operating rules of society. A Jew engaging in an affair with the future doge? She would most certainly have been found guilty of provoking heresy. Had his muse been put on trial? Had she been burned? Rose sped down the next page.

No. The text here was calmer, more lucid. Giovanni's frankness returned, as if he no longer cared who might discover his writing. He even revealed the name of his muse—Chiara. *Bright.* Writing in retrospect, he put all the facts in order: the fire in the Ghetto, Chiara's lashing at the hands of Corvino. Giovanni glossed over the escape, but it was clear they'd somehow spirited Chiara away.

They'd been separated, after all.

At the bottom of the page, a single last line:

Daily, I revisit my memories of her. When I am sightless, sight of her will remain.

Rose stared out the window, at the eggshell sky deepening into twilight. Her lungs felt constricted. She could understand *why*, could imagine the limitations of his options. In his place, she might have done the same: slink away to go blind in private, not wanting to turn her lover into a nurse. She recalled William's question in the café: Was it worth them finding each other if they couldn't be together?

What would her answer be now?

A crow flew across the rectangle of sky bounded by the window frame with an effortless flap of black wing. Rose glanced back at the book, turning to the last page. In the end, Giovanni gave no explanation of why he'd scraped away the diary. No grand conclusion to sum it all up, no hint of a reunion. Instead, his thoughts seemed to have turned philosophical, as if he were questioning life itself. Rose read and reread the final paragraph:

As I face the fleeting nature of existence, I grow more convinced that the purest endeavor is that of creation. Certainly the physical body knows this, and strives as soon as it is able to perpetuate itself in the form of a child. Yet I believe the mind also seeks after eternity, desiring to preserve its perspective and thoughts. Increasingly, my attentions fix upon the idea of a treatise. I shall capture, to the best of my ability, my own knowledge and theories of painting. It will be my ultimate act of creation, an assurance that my life has perhaps been of value. I find comfort in imagining that long after I am gone to dust, I may yet remain connected to every man who reads what I have written.

Rose considered those words: creation, connection. They were what she wanted too. The fragments she'd seen of William's paintings sprang to mind, and she felt a sharp pinch in her chest. He'd created something from their experience, something tangible that other people could view and discuss, maybe even find inspiration in. He'd grown through it—he had whole canvases to show for it. She couldn't end up on the other side with only a house full of new furniture.

The idea of a survey on restoration fluttered to life again; that wild notion that'd been circling her mind for so long, looking for a soft spot to land. It'd take work, and lots of it. Research and planning, chasing down sources online, scheduling interviews. Rose thought of what that would mean: more nights in the back room, more hours hunched over a keyboard. More days spent alone.

She didn't want to do it alone.

The realization was unexpected, as surprising as waking up and discovering that one eye had changed color in the night. *She didn't want to do it alone.* Rose turned the idea over in her head, examining it from all sides, until a second realization arrived: she didn't have to.

❧

The reading room was quiet: the semester had reached a comfortable lull between the start of classes and fall midterms. As Rose descended the stairs, she watched Lucas's face light up, one hand waving at her before he leaned over the service desk, beaming.

"How are you? It's so good to see you again, I was wondering when you'd stop back in!" His words seemed to be racing one another to get out. She couldn't help but laugh.

"It's good to see you too." He was wearing a forest green cardigan she hadn't noticed before, a new purchase from his trip, maybe. "You're looking dapper." She watched color rise to his cheeks as he pulled on his cuffs and cocked his head self-consciously. Before he could respond, she rushed to continue: "I know we have a lot to catch up on, but I wanted to tell you: I have a new idea for a project and . . . well, I was hoping we could work on it together."

The expression on his face made it easy for her to imagine what he must have looked like as a young child on Christmas morning.

28

SEVEN MONTHS LATER, GIO SAT WATCHING THE SHADOWS of clouds. He'd stationed his chair several yards from the house, where he could feel the sun sink away behind the row of cypress trees. On his knees rested the finished treatise. He glanced at it, through the red latticework that now patterned his vision, his own blood vessels revealing themselves in a final composition. He slid a hand down the outer edges of the papers, measuring with his fingertips the unevenness where he'd added two pages: the illustration he'd done of Ippolito's story. He wanted her to have it—to remember the place where they were together, always.

The man would arrive soon. A friend of Aurelio's, en route to Milan, who'd agreed to bring a package along. Chiara would know what the book meant. He'd purposefully not scraped the vellum well so that she could see it'd been his journal. She'd find the sketches he'd done of her, be able to read the fragments in the margins. He knew she'd understand the message he was sending by scraping away the writing: that he was letting her go. Most of all, though, the book would prove that he'd finished his treatise. That he was a man who could keep at least one promise. When Aurelio had pressed the journal back into his hands, the day after she left, without doubt or reflection he'd known what he would do with it—just as surely as he knew that she'd see it was printed.

She'd help him live on.

From his robe, Gio retrieved the small vial—Aurelio's parting gift. He held it up to the fading sun, watching the liquid swim, viscous and heliotrope. Inside the house, he heard the sounds of Francesca and Lucio readying for dinner, the clatter of plates and bowls being set on the table. Soon, Lucio's voice called out to him in the gloaming. Time to come inside.

Chiara set her pen down. The last page of transcription was done: Giovanni's treatise, rewritten on fresh parchment, was ready to be sent to Venice, to the publisher Domenico had helped arrange. It'd taken far longer than she'd wanted it to, but life had been busier than anyone could have planned. She made a mental note that she'd need to rebind the sheets of the original diary somehow and find a safe place for it among their belongings. The journey back to Padua, to a sister she hadn't seen in a decade, would be long. Still, the thought of nieces and nephews beckoned, along with the promise of a fresh start. She'd arrive bearing a new story to share: no longer reticent courtesan, but widowed music tutor trained in Milan by Maddalena Casulana herself. For her part, Cecelia would stay on with Maddalena, assisting with tours—and finally getting her wish of travel.

Chiara picked up the pen again; there was something she'd forgotten. On the title page of the new treatise, she inked two additional words: *In Memoriam.*

"Mama! Mama!" Shouts from down the hall, followed by a pounding of heels on the wood floor. The arrival of a toddler at the door, breathless with excitement.

"Giovanni, come here." The boy launched his body toward her unsteadily, arms outstretched. She lifted him up and he wriggled onto her lap, a warm weight, familiar as any of her own limbs. "Do you want me to read you the story again?" He nodded, and Chiara sifted through the pages until she found it: the tale of the bird and the tree. After so long, she could recite it by heart.

She touched a finger to Giovanni's face, sketched next to her own. Her other hand rested on the boy's head, his nest of downy curls.

"Once upon a time . . ."

29

It was spring again, and Rose had missed the delivery driver. She'd been in the middle of pouring hot water into the French press when the bell rang. She'd set the kettle down, then made a dash for the door, arriving just in time to see the uniformed man—dark polo shirt, knee-length shorts—swing back into the FedEx truck. He'd left a brown box on the doorstep; she brought it in and set it on the kitchen counter. The return address was a children's book publisher she recognized. Was this something she'd ordered for Joan and forgotten? As if on cue, her cellphone started to vibrate on the table, Joan's number blazoned across the top.

"Hiiiiiiii." Joan's voice was ebullient. She was pregnant again, after months of trying, and nothing would shake her satisfied approval of the world at large.

"Hey, how are you feeling?" Rose held the phone up to her ear with one shoulder. Grabbing a pen from the bundle stashed in the kitchen drawer, she stabbed at the blue chevron tape that ran along the edges of the box.

"Oh, I'm wonderful! Still no sickness, this one's just nothing like Henry." Joan was convinced she was having a girl but refused to be told for certain; Rose was convinced she just wanted a reason to do the nursery up in pinks and bows. "Sooo, how's the survey coming?"

Rose glanced at the thick stack of papers sitting next to the French press. She and Lucas had put everything they had into the project—hours of research and interviews with experts. Just that week, they'd come up with a title: *From Papyrus to Palimpsest: The Art of Conservation.*

"Really well, actually, we only have a few chapters left. And Lucas has already spoken to a publisher who might be interested—"

"Oh, Rose, that's just fantastic!"

"And, we've been thinking, when it comes out, we can set up a gallery exhibit for the students so they can look at archive examples firsthand." Rose could hear the excitement in her own voice. She tugged hard at the flaps of the box.

"Well, that sounds perfect, sweetie; I'm just so proud of you!"

"Thanks . . ." The tape from the box had somehow managed to get stuck on the sleeve of her cashmere sweater. Rose plucked at it carefully, trying not to pull too many fibers.

"And when will you bring Lucas over for dinner next?" To no one's surprise except perhaps Rose's own, she and Lucas had become what Joan called "an item." It wasn't that one had formally asked the other out so much as they'd just begun spending all their free time together. At first it was for the book, but when the work went late—which it invariably did—they'd end up eating dinner. Occasionally Lucas would cook, as it quickly became clear that Rose's main culinary abilities consisted of opening canned soup and overboiling pasta. More often, they'd go out to restaurants, where Lucas always seemed to know at least one person on staff. When the Elizabethan club on campus opened their famous vault to display rare editions of Milton, Spenser, and Shakespeare, Lucas had made sure Rose got a front-row view. Then, over the holidays, he'd used the motivation of a well-placed sprig of mistletoe to kiss her, and she'd been genuinely shocked by the tingles that'd raced up her spine. She'd been doubly shocked when, three days later, he'd gone on vacation with his family and she'd missed him terribly. He'd fit so easily into her life that she hadn't grasped how much his presence meant until he'd gone. She'd shown up at the airport clutching a bouquet of paperwhite narcissus. Four months later, and half his clothes hung in the big wardrobe upstairs.

Now Rose peered into the box, saw it contained a slim hardcover book. "Oh, I'll have to check the calendar; he's always making plans."

"Well, you know, Mark is just dying to get his opinion on what he should put in that back planter. If this summer is as hot as last year's, then . . ." Joan's voice receded into the background as Rose slid the book out.

The Egg and the Tree.

It was Giovanni's story! Rewritten into a children's tale—and illustrated with William's artwork. On the cover, he'd painted himself in Giovanni's place: it was William now, beardless, with soaring white wings and broken eggshell shards at his feet. Staring up at Rose with those dark eyes.

She froze, then quickly flipped the book over, irrationally afraid for a second that Joan might see. The back was illustrated in a spiraling pattern of roots and leaves. "Joan, can I call you back?"

"Oh . . . okay. Sure?" Something in her tone must have warned Joan not to pry. Rose hung up the phone and set it down on the table. Steeling herself, she turned the book right-side up. She hadn't seen William's face since the night of his show. A dull ache whirlpooled in the center of her chest. She opened the cover and began to read, the forgotten coffee turning bitter in its glass beaker.

The art was unexpected. Minutely detailed yet still somehow

unstructured and spontaneous, it captured all the best elements of William's style. Wing and feather, root and bloom. Limb and mouth and sky. The woman's face was continuously hidden, obscured by leaves; mysterious, the way Giovanni had always kept her in his diary. William had added a new detail to this tree-woman, however: around her neck hung a strand of pearls with a dangling, brilliant sapphire.

"Wisdom and fidelity," Rose said out loud to no one.

After she read it through once, she turned to the back page, to the author's bio. *Lomazzo lives with his wife and two daughters in New York City.* He'd moved back, after all. Without thinking, she leafed to the front and began going through the story again, more slowly this time. On the third page, Rose paused. She blinked hard to clear her vision, then bent closer to the picture. There, on the neck of the woman . . . a birthmark.

Her birthmark.

One hand unconsciously flew up to touch her own neck. It was unmistakably hers. Rose spun back to the first page again, scrutinizing the images in order. The jawline, the curve of the mouth. The eyes that peered out through the limbs, sometimes gray-blue, sometimes green. Labradorite eyes.

So, he'd done it: he'd answered her question after all this time.

It had been real.

Hours later and the sun was nestling into the boughs of the neighbor's sycamore tree, turning the star-shaped leaves translucent. Rose found herself on the couch again, the book on the coffee table in front of her, its spine already cracked from use. She reached for her phone and dialed Joan's number.

"I was wondering when you were going to call." In the background, Rose could hear the animated soundtrack to Henry's favorite cartoon. From her own kitchen came the clatter of pans:

Lucas had arrived bearing a brown bag filled with sponge-like morels that smelled of fecund earth; now he was in the midst of making a risotto. Rose cupped one hand over the mouthpiece of the phone to lessen the noise.

"Sorry, I just got a book in the mail that I wasn't expecting."

"What kind of book?"

Rose stared at the glossy cover, hunting for the right words. William's gaze fixed her, framed by white feathers.

"A fairy tale," she answered. "It's a fairy tale."

Acknowledgments

My deepest thanks . . . .

To the memory of Giovanni Paolo Lomazzo, Sebastiano Venier, and all the others whose lives I took such creative license with. To my family—Ken, Sybil, and Vanessa—for the unceasing encouragement and kindness. Your love and support is my foundation. To agent extraordinaire, Alexandra Machinist, for seeing a spark of possibility in the earliest draft of this book, and for making dreams come true. Your presence in my life is nothing short of miraculous. To my editor, Shauna Summers, who transformed this story into what it always wanted to be: you are a midwife and a magician, and working with you is an honor. To Liz Dodd, for being on the frontlines—your honesty and your eye made all the difference. To Tamim Ansary, for believing in me before I had the courage to believe in myself, and to the SF writers workshop, for the much-needed community and feedback. To the women in my life who read and responded: Andrea Perdue, Meghan Arthur, Greta Perel, and Becca Anzalone, you each spurred me on when I needed it most. To my full moon companions, for the warmth of your friendship.

To Geraldo Sousa, for your generosity of spirit and infinite patience: without you I never would have met Giovanni (or earned my degree)! To Seth Thompson, thank you for your charming hospitality—and for the tea. To Maridette de Guzman, who always makes me feel I can do the impossible: I wish everyone had a cheerleader like you. To the entire Ballantine team, a million thank-yous.

Most of all to Caleb, best husband and father: thank you for being the calm center my whole world orbits around.

A Note to the Reader

In the summer of 2008, the world experienced an economic recession, and I—a struggling waitress at the time—was offered a generous scholarship to attend graduate school at the University of Kansas. So it was that I found myself as a young adult packing a book bag and hurrying off to class.

I decided to pursue a degree in rhetoric and composition. One of my favorite courses focused on literature from the 1500s, and for the semester's final paper I settled on studying examples of early color theory. The topic fit the assignment, and allowed me to pore over books filled with gorgeous reproductions of Renaissance paintings. I was happy for any excuse to linger in the library: it was winter by then, and bitter cold, and the stacks were much warmer than my apartment.

It was during one of those rambling afternoons that I first met Giovanni. His treatise, *Trattato dell' arte della pittura, scultura et architettura*, popped up in search results as an influential piece of art criticism—and when I got my hands on the book, I was instantly enthralled. Filled with intricate sketches and chapters titled after colors or emotions, it was a fascinating mix of the scientific and the mystic. A quick bit of research revealed that Giovanni, a Milanese painter, had turned to art criticism after losing his sight. This tragedy struck a deep chord in me: as an artist myself, I understood what such a loss might mean.

I felt driven to investigate further. What had his world been like? I discovered that just as Giovanni was losing his sight, Italy—as part of a league of European Catholic states—had gone to war against the Ottoman Empire in what became known as the Battle of Lepanto. My parents had recently moved to Istanbul and the city captivated me from the second I saw my first minaret. It wasn't hard to imagine an Ottoman fleet charging across the seas toward Venice. Though other classes soon stole my attention away, I still thought from time to time of that artist going blind while his country fought in one of the largest naval battles in history. It was too compelling an image to forget.

After graduating, however, life took on a frenetic pace, and Giovanni was relegated to the recesses of my mind. I moved to New York, then China, then San Francisco. It wasn't until I became a consultant to tech companies, however, that Gio's world resurfaced. By that time, I was boarding corporate buses that ferried their employees to work—deadly silent buses, where every head was bent over a laptop, every ear was plugged. I was learning about artificial intelligence. I was wearing all black. One day, while brainstorming how to make a machine sound more human, it struck me: somehow, I'd ended up in a life that seemed cold and calculating, devoid of passion.

I couldn't help but recall how alive I'd felt back in that warm library on those winter afternoons, paging through books on the Renaissance. In an effort to feel that way again, I picked up a blank journal and began to write. From the very first lines, characters and scenes came rushing forward as if they'd been there all along, just waiting. I knew I wanted to share my experience of getting lost in the stacks, discovering Giovanni—and in an instant Rose materialized, bestowed with my own introversion and enthusiasm for research. A hopeless romantic, of course I had to provide her with a love interest. I made William an artist out of my own desire to explore the nature of creativity; he also served as a logical way for Rose to encounter Giovanni's treatise.

While Rose and William are entirely fictional, the world they inhabit is anchored in reality. Knowing Rose would require top-tier academic facilities, I placed her imaginary bookshop near Yale's charming campus in New Haven, Connecticut. Eventually, I was able to pay a visit to the university myself. It was fall at the time, and the avenues were blanketed in brilliant leaves that gave a satisfying crunch underfoot. I spent hours exploring the Sterling Memorial Library as well as the Beinecke Rare Book and Manuscript Library, with its gleaming marble exterior. I could easily imagine Rose there, roaming the aisles, meeting Lucas in the hush of the reading room. I can only hope I was able to adequately capture the spirit of each institution.

Just as the modern day narrative contains both real and fictional elements, so too does Giovanni's tale combine the actual with the imagined. When I discovered that Gio's blindness coincided with the Battle of Lepanto, I knew I wanted to weave both stories together. I began by imagining Giovanni's famous treatise had been lost to history. I then transplanted Giovanni from Milan to Venice. Only in that port town could he encounter Sebastiano Venier, the real-life admiral of the Venetian fleet, who later became Doge. And what more dramatic way for the two men to meet than through an enchanting courtesan? During my research I'd come across a wonderful book, *Lives of the Courtesans: Portraits of the Renaissance*, by Lynne Lawner, which offers a fascinating glimpse into the world of Renaissance courtesans—including that of well-known Venetian Veronica Franco. (*The Honest Courtesan* by Margaret F. Rosenthal was another fabulous resource). A gifted poet, Veronica struggled mightily against the limitations set upon her gender. Using her as my inspiration, I developed the character of Chiara. Like Veronica, Chiara is beautiful, talented, and the star of Venetian salons. Unlike Veronica, Chiara is Jewish.

Initially, I had no thought of including a specifically Jewish character in my book. Then one Sunday, I chanced upon a *New York Times* article, written by David Laskin in honor of the 500th anniversary of one of the world's first ghettos—in Venice. Eagerly, I tore through the short piece. I learned that the very word *ghetto* is Venetian: the area used to house Jews in Venice was the site of a former foundry, or "geto" in Venetian dialect. Before I knew it, I was launched on a whole new round of research, exploring how Jews were expelled from much of Europe and how a vibrant—and very confined— ghetto was established in Venice.

My favorite books always include a twist, and I quickly realized that making Chiara Jewish would be a way to not only integrate the rich history of the Venetian ghetto, but to add an element to the story that might not be expected. During my reading, I'd also come across the real-life figure of Joseph Nassi, a Jew who fled religious persecution in Venice to become an influential figure in the Ottoman Empire and a key player during the Battle of Lepanto. The connection between Venice and Istanbul grew stronger.

To properly illustrate the precarious position Venetian Jews found themselves in, however, I needed a character to embody the religious fervor and intense anti-Semitism so present in Renaissance Europe. The outline of Corvino began to take shape. In my experience, bigotry is often born from personal pain and fear, so I made an effort to show how Corvino's character might have been influenced by trauma. I also took notes from the hunger for influence I'd encountered in Silicon Valley, and gave Corvino a position just outside the reach of power.

To provide all these narrative threads with an organizing structure, I relied upon the buildup to the battle. As soon as I began my investigations, I realized that entire books could be written about the battle—and they have been. The most helpful for me was Niccolò Capponi's excellent *Victory of the West: The Great Christian Muslim Clash at the Battle of Lepanto*, which provides a nuanced look into the political machinations that led to the conflict, and the complex maneuvers of the battle itself. One of the moments that struck me as truly remarkable was the way in which the new Venetian galleasses altered the battle formation, prompting the Holy League to arrange itself in a shape that many choose to see as a cross, while the Ottomans stuck to their traditional half-moon approach—a literal cross battling a crescent (a crescent being the image that is now on the Turkish flag). While I was forced to summarize or omit many details of the battle, of course I had to integrate this moment of real-life symbolism into the book. It may also interest readers to know that the characters of Ali Pasha and Mustafa Pasha are based on real people: Mustafa Pasha did indeed insist that Commander Bragadin be flayed alive, and Ali Pasha was killed in action.

Although so much of *The Lost Diary of Venice* was informed by research, I was genuinely surprised by how life conspired with me to fill in any gaps. For example, the afternoon I began to write about Corvino, a stately crow took up residence in the tree outside my living room window. When it seemed that Gio might need a friend, I went to a dinner party and met a modern-day alchemist. Myriad fragments of my own life began to fall into place within the book: the little tale of a bird and a tree that I'd drawn for my students when I was teaching children in the French Alps; the motivational signs my father—also a painter—had taped to his studio wall while I was growing up in Alaska. Even my favorite bookshop secured a role, complete with cozy nooks and companionable cat. It felt as if these experiences, initially so random, had carried a purpose all along that I was just now able to see. I found myself waking up to write while it was still dark, and sneaking art books into my work handbag.

I began to feel alive again.

Yet even though aspects of my personal life made their way onto the page, I never had the sensation that this book entirely belonged to me. I certainly derived a sense of purpose from the relevance of so many of the novel's themes—from women's rights to anti-Semitism and conflict between Christians and Muslims—but rather than feeling like a debut author, I instead felt more like a secretary taking a phone call that was just a bit muffled, doing her best to get the message down right. In the end, my deepest hope is that I've served the story well, so that it can reach all those it is meant for: to entertain, to inspire, and to maybe help them feel just a little bit more alive.

ABOUT THE AUTHOR

Margaux DeRoux was born in Juneau, Alaska. Before turning to fiction she was a waitress, a teacher, and a marketer. She now lives in California with her husband and daughter.